CLAIMED BY PASSION

"What do you want?" My heart, already knocking against my ribs, tumbled over itself.

"To make love to my wife," he said.

He stared down at me. I caught the gleam of his eyes.

"You're . . . drunk," I cried.

"I'm stone-cold sober," he said.

His eyes raked over me. I wanted to call out for help, but my tongue clove to the roof of my mouth. He lifted me in his arms. I beat at his chest, without effect. His arms were strong and he held me firmly against him. Then he set me down on the bed and a moment later I felt the weight of his body press down on mine.

I twisted and kicked, bit and cried, to no avail. His strength overpowered mine. His mouth stifled my cries. His hands roved over me, everywhere, weakening my resistance.

Suddenly my treacherous body began to revel in the sensations he aroused, and almost without my realizing it my arms entwined themselves around his neck. . . .

EXHILARATING ROMANCE
From Zebra Books

GOLDEN PARADISE (2007, $3.95)
by Constance O'Banyon
Desperate for money, the beautiful and innocent Valentina Barrett finds work as a veiled dancer, "Jordanna," at San Francisco's notorious Crystal Palace. There she falls in love with handsome, wealthy Marquis Vincente—a man she knew she could never trust as Valentina — but who Jordanna can't resist making her lover and reveling in love's GOLDEN PARADISE.

SAVAGE SPLENDOR (1855, $3.95)
by Constance O'Banyon
By day Mara questioned her decision to remain in her husband's world. But by night, when Tajarez crushed her in his strong, muscular arms, taking her to the peaks of rapture, she knew she could never live without him.

TEXAS TRIUMPH (2009, $3.95)
by Victoria Thompson
Nothing is more important to the determined Rachel McKinsey than the Circle M — and if it meant marrying her foreman to scare off rustlers, she would do it. Yet the gorgeous rancher feels a secret thrill that the towering Cole Elliot is to be her man — and despite her plan that they be business partners, all she truly desires is a glorious consummation of their vows.

KIMBERLY'S KISS (2184, $3.95)
by Kathleen Drymon
As a girl, Kimberly Davonwoods had spent her days racing her horse, perfecting her fencing, and roaming London's byways disguised as a boy. Then at nineteen the raven-haired beauty was forced to marry a complete stranger. Though the hot-tempered adventuress vowed to escape her new husband, she never dreamed that he would use the sweet chains of ecstasy to keep her from ever wanting to leave his side!

FOREVER FANCY (2185, $3.95)
by Jean Haught
After she killed a man in self-defense, alluring Fancy Broussard had no choice but to flee Clarence, Missouri. She sneaked aboard a private railcar, plotting to distract its owner with her womanly charms. Then the dashing Rafe Taggart strode into his compartment . . . and the frightened girl was swept up in a whirlwind of passion that flared into an undeniable, unstoppable prelude to ecstasy!

Available wherever paperbacks are sold, or order direct from the Publisher. Send cover price plus 50¢ per copy for mailing and handling to Zebra Books, Dept. 2690, 475 Park Avenue South, New York, N.Y. 10016. Residents of New York, New Jersey and Pennsylvania must include sales tax. DO NOT SEND CASH.

MIDNIGHT HEIRESS

BY KATE FREDERICK

ZEBRA BOOKS
KENSINGTON PUBLISHING CORP.

ZEBRA BOOKS

are published by

Kensington Publishing Corp.
475 Park Avenue South
New York, NY 10016

Second printing: June, 1989

Printed in the United States of America

Chapter One

Aunt Martha was dead. The funeral was over and we were assembled, my mother, my sister, and I, in the drawing room, awaiting the arrival of Mr. Parkes and the reading of the will.

My mother was fretting, anxious to know the size of her legacy, wanting to be gone. Beth was sitting beside her looking startlingly beautiful in the black that became her so well and me so ill. Bitterness I had thought forgotten rose up to choke me. I had not seen either of them in all of thirteen years, and I knew I should not have seen them now if they had not been lured by greed and the prospect of gain.

A flush of guilt stole to my cheek and I lowered my gaze quickly, for I also hoped to gain from my aunt's death. I had wished her dead. How many times had I wished her dead? How many times had she scolded me, derided me, torn my confidence to shreds?

Had there been any love lost between us? No, not really. Yet some bond of affection must have been forged over the years, for as I watched the last flicker of life leave her emaciated body, I had been sad. I mourned her.

I remembered the day I had first set eyes on Aunt Martha, a hot summer's day in 1818. I was ten years old, Beth was six. We had journeyed from London to the small Kentish village where she lived, with our mother and stepfather, Roger Fox, under strict orders, the two of us, to be "as good as gold" while we were there. When we reached our destination Roger Fox had added, "One word out of place and it will be the worse for you."

But he had looked straight at me as he said it, not at Beth, and I had cringed. Cringing even now at the memory, I put myself back into that time.

I hated my stepfather. He beat me. He maintained that fate had dealt him a rough hand and complained regularly. And as often as he complained, I was beaten.

Beth was never beaten. Unlike me, Beth was everybody's favorite. There were times when I hated her, too. She had charm and beauty. I lacked both. I should not have criticized Roger Fox for his grudge against fate, for I had one also.

I loved my mother dearly. She lavished all her care and affection on Beth and neglected me, but it made no difference, I still adored her. I did not blame her for preferring Beth. Beth was lovely. I was plain and unappealing. But I blamed Beth for her beauty and fought to gain my mother's interest. I fetched and carried for her, tried my hardest to please her, but the harder I tried, the less she seemed to care.

So I took refuge in dreams.

When I grew up I would marry a rich man, a nobleman, a prince. I would make my mother proud of me. I could give her everything her heart desired—clothes, jewels, furs; nothing would be too much. Then it would be me she would love, me she would want to sit beside her. Beth would be left out in the cold.

Childish dreams. A second's insight would have revealed to me that if either of us were to marry a rich man, a nobleman, a prince, it would be Beth, beautiful, adorable Beth, not plain, skinny me. I had not been put into the world to be pampered and petted. I was no ornament to be admired. I had been put into the world to be useful—and to be ignored.

As I grew older I came to accept it.

I had not known what to expect, but when I saw my aunt's house, Martha's Cottage, my breath caught in my throat. It was the most beautiful house I had ever seen. More. It was magical. It was long and low and rambling, with an overhanging thatched roof. There appeared to be more roof than wall and what wall there was seemed to be composed entirely of glass. I counted five arched windows rising from ground to roof and as many smaller ones peeping out of the thatch itself.

It put me in mind of a church, not only because of its Gothic windows, but also because of the peace and serenity that emanated from it. Perhaps that was why I was so drawn to it that first day. Peaceful serenity was sadly lacking in my life.

Aunt Martha received us with a sour expression and I viewed the thin-faced woman with misgiving. I had gleaned much about her from overheard conversations between my mother and Roger Fox—being unnoticeable had its advantages. I knew she was wealthy, had many, choicely described, character defects, and had deliberately misled us as to the extent of her wealth.

"Martha's Cottage!" I recalled my stepfather's astonished anger. "When old Blythe told me he had seen it while visiting the area and what it was like, I could not believe my ears. Martha's Cottage! What a name to give a bloody mansion."

"Martha always had odd ideas," said my mother. "But you surprise me. I did not think she was very well off."

"She did not wish you should. She wished to keep us in the dark as to the size of her estate. I never did like your sister, Mary."

"No, but perhaps we should not have cut ourselves off from her so completely. Perhaps we should have kept in touch."

"It is an omission that is easily repaired. We'll call on her. Take the children to soften her up. Shaw's started dunning me for the two hundred I owe him. I'll tap her for a loan."

We took tea in a large, airy room, its long arched windows thrown open to the sun. Landscaped gardens stretched away into the distance, beds and borders ablaze with summer flowers. Large, exotic birds, trailing their fanlike tails of gaudy blue and green and gold behind them, proudly strutted the close-cropped lawns. One, larger and bolder than the rest, ventured across the threshold and I held my breath in a magic moment of bliss, before my aunt shooed it away.

My stepfather brought up the subject he had come expressly to air.

"So," said my aunt, "we come at last to the purpose of your visit. A loan, you say? I am not in the business of giving loans to gamesters."

My mother said swiftly, "Why, of course not, Martha,

not in the usual way of things, but Roger *is* your brother-in-law."

"And you think that gives him a claim on me?"

"Why, yes. After all, I *am* your sister, these two dear little cherubs *are* your nieces. I think you have a duty toward us."

My aunt regarded her stonily. "Do you? Then I have a proposition to put to you. Let me have one of your children to bring up as my own. I will pay you well."

"How much?" Roger's demand was immediate.

"Enough to satisfy you, never fear," said my aunt contemptuously.

"Then I agree. Mighty sisterly of you, Martha."

My mother's voice wavered a little as she asked, "Which one?" though whichever one, she would bow to her husband's will.

Aunt Martha eyed the two of us, Beth and myself, and for the first time in my life I was glad I was thin, sticklike and plain. A joyous surge rose up in me. She would choose Beth.

"I'll take Barbara," she said.

I was stunned. Too stunned to move, too stunned to speak. "I will take Barbara," she had said, and my mother was smiling, nodding, agreeing.

They were going.

I sprang to life. "No. No. Don't leave me. I don't want to live with Aunt Martha. I want to live with you. Please . . . please . . . Mama . . ."

My mother frowned at me. "Control yourself, child," she said.

They were gone.

I could not believe that my mother would completely

desert me and for months believed she would come and visit me. But she never did, and as time went by, I knew she never would.

Aunt Martha was not a comfortable woman to live with. She was terse with me and put me down at every opportunity. She went off into long, strange silences that would sometimes last for days. I was left on my own with only the servants for company. But she saw that I was educated. I had private tutors for this and private tutors for that. I loved learning and saw no reason to quarrel with this. I was well fed, well housed, and well clothed. Nevertheless, I was no better off with Aunt Martha than I had been at home. I was still unloved. And worse—I loved my mother, I could not love Aunt Martha.

As I grew older and filled out, I thought I grew a little less plain, and with the help of my maid I experimented with new and flattering hair styles. My aunt roughly ordered them smoothed out again.

"You look foolish with all those curls. Ringlets do not become you. Accept the fact that God gave you a plain face and a quiet, retiring nature, not best served by elaborate hair styles and gewgaws."

I hated her. Mine was not a quiet, retiring nature, however it might appear to others. Beneath my passive exterior beat a heart that could hate with passionate intensity. Did I not hate Aunt Martha? Did I not hate Roger Fox? And if I could hate with such intensity, I knew I could also love with equal passion. And I dreamed oh, how I dreamed, about love. Romantic love. Passionate love. The love of a man for a woman.

I might not be, in reality, capable of inspiring passion in a man, but in my dreams it was altogether different. I ceased to be plain Miss Farrar and became beautiful, vivacious Miss Farrar with countless adoring swains beneath my spell. But there was only one who captured my heart, and he carried me away to some far distant land, far from Aunt Martha and the restricted life I led, to a world of fantastic adventures. And we loved. Oh, how we loved.

Inside my secret self I was far from quiet and retiring.

The years passed. The weight of maturity fell upon my shoulders. My dream withered and died. Roger Fox was killed during a drunken brawl. Still my mother did not come to visit me. But I had ceased to care. Only Martha's Cottage meant anything to me now.

I loved Martha's Cottage. The hold it had taken on my heart strengthened with the years. I walked its rooms in a kind of ecstasy. It became the lover I would never have, the child I would never bear. I gave it all the love no one else wanted.

Then Aunt Martha fell ill. I nursed her devotedly, crotchety though she was. Captive in her bed, she begged me to read to her. Soon, we were talking together, as we had never talked before. I listened to her and she listened to me. She must have gauged, from what I said, how much Martha's Cottage meant to me, for she said, "It will be yours after I am dead."

I stared at her. It had not crossed my mind that she might die. I had wished her dead often enough, as a child, but I had not really meant it. In any case, she had seemed indestructible to me.

"Don't say that, Aunt Martha," I begged, not wishing to see our newly sprung companionship come to an untimely end. "You're not going to die."

She waved my plea away with a weakening hand. "It must be faced, child. I shall not be sorry to go."

A maid announced the arrival of Mr. Parkes, my aunt's elderly solicitor, dragging me out of my reverie. He had brought someone with him. Clearing his throat, somewhat nervously, I thought, he introduced the stranger.

"Mr. Richard Goodall, from the West Indies."

"Goodall? The West Indies?" My mother's voice rose slightly, a sign she felt she was being threatened in some way. "I do not understand. Are you a distant relative I am unaware of?"

"Not so distant, ma'am," said the stranger coolly. "I am your nephew."

My mother was silenced for a moment, then, "Nonsense. I have no nephew—and certainly not one from the West Indies."

A tense little laugh underlined the absurdity of it.

"You are Martha Goodall's sister, are you not?" he asked.

"I am," she replied with a quelling look.

"Then you are my aunt. Martha Goodall was my mother."

Silenced again, my mother glared at him. Then she shrieked, "How dare you, sir. My sister was unmarried."

"That did not render her incapable of producing a child," came the retort.

My mother staggered a little and turned appealingly to Mr. Parkes. "This is a joke. Some sort of—joke."

"It is no joke," the stranger said. "I am Martha Goodall's son and I have papers to prove it."

My mother fell back onto the sofa. "I think I'm going

to . . . my smelling bottle. Quick."

I wafted her smelling bottle of vinegar and aromantic herbs beneath her nose wishing I, too, could take refuge in the vapors, for I was as stunned as she. But my stout constitution was not like hers and as I waited for her to recover I tried to weigh up this strange and unforeseen circumstance.

I stared at the man, elegantly garbed in coat and trousers of palest gray, standing so casually by. When he had first entered the room I had thought him the most handsome man I had ever seen. His nose might be a shade too Roman, his eyebrows too black and too heavy, overshadowing eyes of too piercing a blue, but the whole cast of his face was arresting, strong and confident, as I believed a man's should be. I looked at him now and hated him.

Aunt Martha's son! I could not believe it. As my mother had said, Aunt Martha had never married. She had hated men. How many times I had heard her say, "*Men! They're beasts. They'll fawn and flatter, but they have only one purpose in mind.*" She had not enlightened me as to what that purpose was, but I, who read every paper and book I could lay my hands on, had a shrewd idea of what she meant. "*Never let a man touch your heart,*" she would say. "*You'll only regret it.*" Then she would lapse into one of her many deep silences.

Was this, then, I wondered now, the reason behind all those silences I had never been able to understand? This—secret she had kept hidden from the world? An illegitimate son? Was this why she had hated all men so forcibly? Had she been seduced and abandoned by Richard's father?

My mother revived. "It's not true. I don't believe it. Be

so good as to turn this scoundrel out of the house, Mr. Parkes."

"I'm afraid I can't do that, ma'am," the elderly solicitor apologized sadly. "What Mr. Goodall has said is true. Miss Goodall gave birth to a male child on the fifteenth February in the year 1801. He was christened Richard. Mr. Goodall has furnished me with documents—copies of which I have in my possession—which prove his claim beyond any shadow of doubt."

"Perhaps my aunt would like to peruse the documents for herself," interposed Richard calmly.

My mother sprang up. "Indeed I would. And don't call me aunt. I refuse to accept I am your aunt."

Mr. Parkes took out the documents, saying somewhat testily, "There is no possible doubt as to their authenticity, ma'am, I do assure you. I can vouch for them with complete confidence. I should not have brought Mr. Goodall here if I could not."

He handed them over one by one. "Here is a document drawn up by Braden and Luce, your family solicitors during your parents' lifetime, and handed over to me when Miss Goodall kindly retained me to look after her affairs. You will see it is a signed statement by Miss Goodall in which she relinquishes her rights as a mother . . . and here is the agreement signed by both your late father, Mr. Arnold Goodall and a Mr. Joseph Pengarth of Cornwall, in which Pengarth declares he will bring up the said child as his own for the once only payment of . . ."

"One thousand pounds!" My mother took over in hushed, outraged tones. "She sold her son for one thousand pounds!"

Just as you sold your daughter. I sent my silent reproach winging toward her. "*Let me have one of your children . . . I will pay you well.*" Did she think of that now? I doubted it.

"No, Mrs. Fox." There was an edge of anger to the dry legal voice. "Miss Goodall did not sell her son. She would never have parted with him if she had had her way. But she was not consulted. The transaction was made, the bond signed while she was too weak to know what she was doing."

I wondered, for the first time, if Mr. Parkes knew of the transaction between my mother and my aunt regarding myself. Were there legal documents concerning me in his possession?

"There's no doubt these are genuine?"

"None whatsoever."

My mother swayed and let the papers fall from her grasp. I put out a hand to steady her, but she turned from me to Beth for comfort, as she had always done.

"I can see," began Mr. Parkes more gently, "it has come as something of a shock to you, Mrs. Fox. . . ."

My mother turned on him. "A shock! A shock! I have just heard my sister had a child born out of wedlock and you suggest it has come as something of a shock!" She turned to Richard, trembling with violent emotion. "How old are you?" she demanded and when he answered, "Thirty-one," mentally totted up the years, then went on, "Yes, I can see it all now. Martha went to Cornwall for a holiday in the summer of 1800. She did not return till the following spring. I always wondered why she stayed so long and was so changed on her return." Her face grew ugly and spite entered her voice. "The cunning creature! My so-puritanical sister! Butter wouldn't melt in her mouth! She was always so free with her advice. Always ready to call *me* to book, point out the foolhardiness of *my* ways. So quick with her criticism of Benjamin and Roger. So eager to pour poison into my father's ears. But I married my men, poor as they were, and cast off without a penny for my defiance, while she . . . she . . ." My mother rounded on us all in a blaze of fury. "She went whoring around. . . ."

Luckily, she choked on her fury. Whatever the rights or wrongs of the matter, I hated to hear her talk like this; but she flared up again.

"And now her sins have come home to roost. Her bastard has turned up."

I blushed deeply. Beth bit into her lower lip. Mr. Parkes looked extremely uncomfortable. Richard returned my mother's animosity impassively. No, not quite impassively. There was a small pulse throbbing away at his temple. My mother's thrust had hurt.

"And how convenient that he should turn up now, just when Martha's will is about to be read." Her voice was rising higher and higher. "Did you think to gain by it, sir? Is it pickings you're after? If so, you needn't have bothered to come. You'll find none. I have some knowledge of the law. Illegitimate sons have no rights. Is that not so, Mr. Parkes?"

Mr. Parkes cleared his throat. "As the law stands . . ."

"I did not come for 'pickings,'" Richard cut him short, "as you so quaintly term it, Aunt Mary. . . ."

My mother almost leapt at him. "Don't call me that. I shall never acknowledge you. Never. Martha is not here to suffer the outrage of society, but I am, I and my daughter—daughters. It is we who are left to bear the brunt of her wickedness. . . ."

"I had no idea my mother was dead," Richard's voice had the chill of winter in it, "till I reached England. In fact, I didn't even know of her existence up to a few months ago when I received a letter from her explaining the circumstances of my birth, telling me she was ill, begging me to come and see her. . . ."

"And of course you came at once."

"No, I did not. I had no intention of ever coming, but I considered it was my duty. . . ."

"Ah, yes, duty. A good word to hide behind. Bah! I don't believe a word of your story. You may have fooled Mr. Parkes, but . . ."

"If I may be allowed to interject," Mr. Parkes interrupted, "I was aware of the letter written by my client to her son, the letter Mr. Goodall has shown to me. It was sent by me, care of me. Her own address was unknown to Mr. Goodall. It was a safeguard I insisted upon in case the letter should fall into wrong hands. I was to receive him in my office. I was to bring him, once satisfied with his credentials, to see Miss Goodall."

The fight oozed out of my mother. She fell back onto the sofa again. "But why, after all these yesrs . . . ?" she whined.

"I will explain. When Mr. Pengarth agreed to bring up the child as his own son it was decided it would be best for all concerned if all connection between the two families was severed completely. Miss Goodall fought against it, pleading to be allowed to follow her son's progress, promising not to try to see him . . . her wishes were disregarded.

"Upon Mr. Arnold's death, as his heir, Miss Goodall saw no reason to honor an agreement entered into without her consent and immediately dismissed the solicitors who had played a part in the matter and transferred all her assets to Parkes, Parkes and Parkes, the firm of which, as you know, I am the, er, senior—partner."

The old man cleared his throat before continuing, "She then demanded to know the address of Mr. Joseph Pengarth and, against my advice, traveled to Cornwall in search of her son, there to learn the Pengarths had emigrated to America many years previously.

"Undaunted, she hired a detective, again against my advice, to find them. Over the course of the next two years he traced them to an island in the West Indies, Almada, where Mr. Pengarth had become a sugar planter. I was instructed to book passage for the two of us on the next available ship. I tried to dissuade her, but she was a strong-minded woman. A remarkable woman—in many ways. On the fourteenth day of May in the year 1817, we left the shores of England."

As I listened a feeling of compassion for my lonely old aunt swept through me. Perhaps there was an excuse for her crotchety ways, after all. "Poor Aunt Martha," I said and did not realize I had said it aloud till every eye turned toward me.

Mr. Parkes smiled kindly at me. "The detective was waiting for us when we landed in Seatown, the capital of Almada. He took us to a fashionable milliner's shop, where he indicated we should stand and wait. Eventually, a tall lad of about sixteen years came out, swinging a hat-box and escorting a plump little lady. He was saying, 'In this bonnet, my dear sweet Mama, you will cast them all in the shade.'

"Miss Goodall put out an arm to halt him. 'Richard,' she whispered. He swung away from her with a puzzled frown and passed on. I'll never forget the look on Miss Goodall's face. It was—ravaged. Ravaged. She watched them walk down the street, step into a carriage and drive off, the boy laughing and talking all the time, exceedingly attentive toward the lady he was with."

I glanced at Richard. Was he remembering any of this? Did he recall the lady who had tried to halt him in Almada?

His face was blank.

"Miss Goodall drew herself up, in the way she did whenever she reached a decision. 'He doesn't know me,' she said. 'So be it. He's happy, that is all that matters. I shall never try to contact him again.'"

"Then why," demanded my mother, "didn't she stick to her word?"

"During her illness the desire to see her son became an obsession with her. She became determined to see him at all costs, before it was too late. Too ill to write herself, she implored me to write under her dictation. I can't say I was happy about it, but the poor lady was desperate and—she was dying. I would have had to write, anyway, when . . ."

My mother reacted sharply. "Why? Is he mentioned in the will?"

Mr. Parkes looked her in the eye. "Yes, Mrs. Fox, he is."

The servants were sent for. Mr. Parkes began reading the last will and testament of Martha Amelia Goodall. Each servant had been remembered, down to the most menial.

"At this rate," my mother hissed in my ear, "there will be nothing left for us," adding, with a look of loathing at Richard, "if we get anything at all."

A bubble of fear welled up in me as I followed her gaze. I was afraid of Richard, of why he was here. Aunt Martha had sent for him. He was her own flesh and blood. And blood was thicker than water.

I was only her niece. But the blood of her forefathers flowed through me also, and I had lived with her for the past thirteen years. Surely that counted for something. It *must* count for something.

The minor bequests were concluded, the servants dismissed. Mr. Parkes continued reading the will.

"To my sister, Mary Belinda Farrar Fox, I bequeath the sum of ten thousand pounds. . . ."

"Ten thousand pounds!" My mother could not restrain herself. She beamed joyfully. "I never expected half, nay, a quarter as much. . . ."

Squinting reprovingly at her over the top of his rimless spectacles, Mr. Parkes went on in a firm voice, ". . . in the vain hope she will use it wisely."

"To my niece, Elizabeth Mary Farrar, the sum of five thousand pounds. . . ."

"Five!" My mother hugged Beth to her ecstatically.

". . . to be invested as I have directed."

"I wonder how much you will get, Babs," said my mother.

The house, I prayed, let me have the house, I don't care about anything else, only the house.

But with Richard sitting there, so at ease, I saw it slipping further and further out of my grasp.

"To my dear niece, Barbara Emily Farrar . . ."

My heart gave a great anxious leap. My mouth went dry.

". . . whom I have loved like a daughter . . ."

A spasm of pain shot through me. Loved me like a daughter! Why had she not shown it while she was alive? I could have loved her back.

". . . I bequeath Martha's Cottage and all its contents."

I had been holding my breath, now it escaped like a hiss of steam. Dear, dear Aunt Martha, she had not forgotten her promise to me.

Instinctively, my eyes sought Richard to triumph over him. I met his piercing blue gaze and my every nerve started to tingle at the expression I saw there. Anger? Resentment? While I puzzled over it, he smiled, and at once my cheeks flamed, my heart started to hammer. I must have misinterpreted that look. His eyes were alight with pure pleasure. He was pleased at my good fortune.

I felt ashamed of myself. I had been ready to crow over him and he had been pleased for me. A smile trembled on my lips, then I realized he was not smiling at me, but across me—at Beth. Beth was smiling back, bestowing all her charm on him. His face glowed with admiration.

I tore my gaze away from them both. It was as it had always been, smiles for Beth, black looks for me. My first impression had been the right one.

"Everything else I leave to my son," Mr. Parkes was continuing, "Richard Goodall, with the stipulation that he makes my niece, the aforementioned Barbara Emily Farrar, his wife. . . ."

"What?" My mother's shrill voice cut through the air.

". . . within the space of one month from the reading of this will, and that they live together in Martha's Cottage."

"I don't believe it. Are you sure you've got the name right? Are you sure it is not Elizabeth . . . ?"

"Failing this," Mr. Parkes paid no attention to my mother's interruption, "everything, including the proceeds from the sale of Martha's Cottage . . ."

"Sale?"

". . . for if there is no marriage between my son, Richard, and my niece, Barbara, the cottage becomes forfeit . . ."

"Forfeit?"

". . . and all monies accrued therefrom allocated among the following charitable institutions. . . ."

Numb with shock, I listened while he enumerated the various charities, watched him remove his spectacles from his nose and close up the parchment.

"That concludes the last will and testament of . . ."

My mother did not wait for him to finish. In a voice shaking with agitation, she demanded, "This last clause does not negate my legacy? Or Beth's?"

A grim line to his mouth, Mr. Parkes paid attention to her now. "No, Mrs. Fox, there are no strings attached to your legacies."

"Thank God for that," she said, sinking back with relief.

"It does not seem quite fair," Beth murmured.

"It is grossly unfair!" Richard declared angrily. "Ridiculous and impossible!"

I could utter no sound, though every fiber of my being repudiated every word that had issued out of the solicitor's mouth. I could only stare at Richard's face as it registered his repugnance to Aunt Martha's scheme, cold and silent as a stone, wishing I were a stone, without feelings, for I did not know how I should be able to support mine.

Chapter Two

"I can't believe it," my mother said for the umpteenth time. "I knew she had money—but so much! I never dreamed she had so much. Where did it all come from? She was the sole inheritor of Father's money—he never forgave me for marrying against his wishes—but I know for a fact he left numberless debts to be cleared up. She could not have been left with more than a few hundred; and she couldn't sell The Grange because it was entailed through the male line and passed to some distant cousin; so how to account for such a vast fortune?"

"She was an astute businesswoman," I said. Mr. Parkes had informed us of this. "She speculated wisely and invested well."

Nodding, Beth added to the echo of his words. "Everything she touched turned to gold."

"But so much!" My mother's frown deepened and her puzzlement gave way to resentment. "Roger was right, she could have given us more, much more. It's disgraceful the way she hoarded it all to herself, stored it away like a miser. It was downright dishonest of her to call this house Martha's Cottage, putting us off the scent. She did not want us to know she had money."

"You are being very unfair, Mama," I said sharply, hardly knowing why I was defending Aunt Martha—she had treated me wickedly in her will, humiliated and angered me. Perhaps that was why. I was angry and had to give vent to my feelings somehow, to alleviate the pain. "I very much doubt that that was the reasoning behind her naming of the house."

"And what can you know of it, miss, pray?"

"I know that after—after you left me with her she gave you and my stepfather a large sum of money plus a regular allowance and that she increased your allowance generously upon Stepfather's death. I can see no reason for you to complain."

"She could have given us more, much more, and never missed it."

"Why should she? You cared nothing for her. You never went near nor by her till you knew she had money."

My mother eyed me coldly. "I cannot understand why you are speaking up for her after the way she has treated you. And what about Richard? What a position for him to be in. He gets nothing unless he marries you, which he . . ."

"Won't," I finished for her, as she held her tongue too late, and moved quickly to the window to look through a sudden mist at early daffodils waving in the March breeze, at peacocks—the same ones that had so entranced me as a child—strutting about on the grass. But I had long grown accustomed to hearing such sentiments expressed regarding myself and had recovered by the time Beth's voice sounded.

"He said he would never agree to such a marriage."

"He'll change his mind," my mother forecast acidly. "No man in his right mind would throw away a fortune."

"He will," I said. "He doesn't need it. He is wealthy enough without it."

If only he had not been, I might have had a husband. But a husband I did not love, who did not love me, who had married me in order to gain a fortune . . . would I want that?

"No one can be too wealthy," was my mother's cynical comment.

"What a pity you are so plain, Babs. Now if it were me . . ."

My sister was not being deliberately unkind, merely underlining a truth. I was plain and uninteresting—born to be an old maid. Poor or rich, I was a most unattractive proposition for any man.

Why had she done it? Bitterness against Aunt Martha welled up in me again. She had given me Martha's Cottage with one hand and taken it away with the other. How could she have been so cruel? She must have known Richard would never agree to marry me. She should have left me out of the will altogether. It would have been kinder. She should have left everything to Richard, unconditionally. Yet the same condition that prevented me from owning Martha's Cottage prevented him from inheriting anything.

I could not understand it. Had it all been for vengeance's sake? Had she nursed a grudge against Richard's father all these years, nurtured a hate to be taken out on his son?

But Richard was her son, too. Mr. Parkes had said she had loved him and not wanted to part with him. She had written begging him to come and see her before she died. I could understand her wanting to hit out at the man who had seduced her, ruined her life—but through her son?

And what about me? Why should she seek revenge on me? What had I done to her that she should want to reach out from the grave and cause me such pain and humiliation? I had always obeyed her, done what she asked.

I could not puzzle it out. Aunt Martha was as much of an enigma to me as she had ever been.

What was to happen to me now? I glanced at my mother, small, dainty, elegantly clad, and Beth, my lovely sister, would I be welcome to live with them? As if she read my thoughts, Beth asked, "What will you do now, Babs?"

"I—I do not know. I . . ."

My mother rose quickly. "Well, you have a whole month in which to think about it. Come Beth, dear, it is time we were going."

They were gone. They would not give me another thought. I wandered round the house I loved and wept. I had thought, in my innocence, that while Aunt Martha had not exactly loved me, she had cared for me, about my welfare.

How wrong I had been. I could see now she had hated me. All that in the will about loving me as a daughter had been untrue. Why else devise this most diabolical torture for me? She had known how much I loved Martha's Cottage, what it meant to me, and promised me it would be mine—then laid down this impossible condition to make sure it never was.

Was she looking down on me now and laughing at my

misery? Had she worked toward this end from the very first day we had met? It was too much to believe. I drew away from it—yet kept returning to it. She had suffered. Had it twisted her so that she must make others suffer too?

Unable to sleep that night between tossing and weeping, I pondered my life, my future, and rose steeled to a new purpose.

I set out to see Mr. Parkes. The carriage sped along narrow lanes hardened by the drying winds of March. Hedges burgeoned into hazy green life. Primroses lifted young faces to the sun. I took a look at myself. I was a new me, thinking and acting for myself as I had never done; no one to care what I did, no one to stop me, no one to love me, no one to love. My mother did not love me. Beth was too careless, too much her mother's daughter, to think much beyond her own desires. My aunt's love had proved nonexistent, and no man would ever love me. There was no love for me anywhere. Therefore, any softness in me must be crushed or, at least, barricaded behind a wall of indifference. I could not inspire love; therefore, I would not offer it.

So I continued making myself over, not noticing the striking resemblance to my Aunt Martha.

"My dear young lady." Mr. Parkes drew out a chair. "Please sit down. You are not looking at all well, if I may say so."

"I'm perfectly well, thank you, Mr. Parkes." I summoned up a smile from somewhere. "I have come seeking your advice."

His kindly eyes searched my face. "I am at your service."

"I know I am allowed to remain at Martha's Cottage for

a month—but what about expenses?"

"They will be met," he said.

"Any expenses?"

"Any and all."

I drew in a deep breath. "Then I should like to travel to London, take lodgings there, and look for a job."

The old man's spectacles almost fell off his nose. "My dear young lady . . . !"

"I wish to acquire the post of governess or housekeeper to some family there."

"My dear young lady!" he said again.

"I have thought it over carefully and I have no time to waste if I am to be settled before the four weeks are up."

"My dear Miss Farrar, I beg you not to be hasty. Your aunt . . ."

"My aunt did not see fit to provide for me. I must do it for myself. Will you help me? Will you give me the name and address of someone who can put me in touch with the right people?"

"Miss Farrar, I beg you, wait. You have a whole month in front of you before you need come to a decision."

"A month will soon pass. I can't afford to waste time. If you won't help me, I must fend for myself."

He looked at me almost angrily, threw up his hands in a gesture of defeat, scribbled a note on a pad. "I will write you a letter of introduction to some friends of mine."

"Soon?"

"The letter will be with you in the morning."

"And the address of a decent hotel?"

"Surely, that will not be necessary. Your mother . . ."

"I do not wish to stay with my mother," I said firmly.

"Do you think that wise? You have led a very sheltered life. . . . A young lady alone in London . . ."

"I shall not be alone for long. I shall soon be installed as a governess or a housekeeper in someone's home."

I fled. I had taken the first step in reordering my life and it had cost me all my courage. More would have to be dredged up from somewhere before my journey to London on the morrow.

I sat in front of the fire and worried. How would I fare? I had never traveled anywhere alone. (Even the short journey into the nearby market town where Mr. Parkes had his office was the first I had taken by myself.) And once I reached London, what then? Would anybody employ me? Had I the courage necessary for such a venture? Had I acted too impulsively? Should I have waited a while, as Mr. Parkes had suggested?

I rang for tea to calm my nerves, not at all happy about what I had done. As I sipped the comforting brew, my cousin, Richard Goodall, was announced.

"Good morning, Barbara," he greeted me. "I hope I am not intruding."

My heart had jumped into my mouth. I forced it back to its rightful place. "No, sir," I replied. "Please sit down. Will you take some tea?"

He refused the tea, but sat down stretching his long legs out before him in his easy way. He regarded me steadily for a few moments while I sat not knowing what to say. Then, "I won't beat about the bush, Cousin Barbara," he said, "I have come to discuss the terms of the will with you."

"What is there to discuss?" I asked. "They were perfectly plain."

"They were despicable!" His vehemence shocked me. "How any woman could presume that, because she willed it, two people, strangers to each other, would marry—for money, escapes me. I would not, for one."

"I will never agree to such a thing." His words were burned deep in my memory. *"Let the money go to charity."* Yet I could not help thinking now that if I had not been as plain and uninteresting as I undoubtedly was, he might have reacted differently.

"I took it for granted you felt the same way?" His voice was questioning.

I nodded.

"Even though you would be left destitute, with nowhere to go?"

I caught my breath. How did he know that? Who could have told him? Mr. Parkes?

"I have somewhere to go," I cried, trying to salvage I knew not what. "I have a mother and sister who . . ."

"Should be here to support you now, but have chosen to return home." Richard suddenly clicked his tongue angrily. "She must have been deranged, that woman, to have conceived such a plan—to disinherit you in such a way. Why, your mother and sister come out of this better than you, whom she said she loved like a daughter. I can't understand it!"

Neither could I, but I said nothing.

"I feel I am to blame," he went on harshly. "I feel responsible for that woman's odd behavior."

"How can you be? Please don't concern yourself. . . ."

"But I am concerned—about you."

"You needn't be. I shall make out very well. I am already in the process of acquiring for myself the position of a governess, or a housekeeper."

"Governess! Housekeeper! You?"

"Why not?" I rose spiritedly to defend myself against his apparent disbelief in my capabilities. "I am well educated and have been my aunt's housekeeper for years."

"Unpaid," he snapped.

"I needed no pay. Aunt Martha provided me with all I could possibly want. . . ." My voice trailed away in the face of his cynicism. Then I continued defiantly. "I did not have to take on the duties of housekeeper. I did it because I wanted to. It was the least I could do."

"To repay her for her kindness?" His thick black brows joined together above his high-bridged nose. "She has been exceedingly kind to you, has she not, leaving you to make your own way in the world without a penny to your name?"

"I shall make out," I said again. "I am about to journey to London, where Mr. Parkes has friends who will help me find a suitable position. I'm sure I shall be comfortably settled very soon."

"And if you are not, what then? You can't be certain of success."

"I'll cross that bridge if and when I come to it," I declared loftily.

He took his leave and I sat pondering our conversation. My fine words, my confidence, were all sham. Behind them lay a terrible anxiety of what might be in store.

Richard called on me again the following day. He came straight to the point.

"I've thought about it all night long and I've come to the conclusion that you and I should marry."

"What?"

I did not think I could have heard aright, but he came to stand close to me, took my hands in his. "If you think about it," he continued, "you will see it is not such a bad idea. I think we would get along famously—and it would solve your problems."

His voice was gentle, persuasive, tempting, the blue of his eye beguiling. He was offering me marriage out of the kindness of his heart—out of pity. A loveless marriage held little attraction for me, but—why not? As he said, it would solve my problems. Yes, but it would raise others, and how should I deal with those? I gazed up into his handsome face and suddenly knew that the pain of living with him, knowing he had married me out of pity, would be more than I could bear. Such a marriage would be worse than no marriage at all.

"It's very kind of you," I said, "but . . ."

"Kind! It would take more than kindness to . . ." He broke off, sucking in his breath between strong white teeth. I should have paid more attention to those words and the way he said them. I might have done if he had not continued immediately with a smile that was my undoing. "Kindness doesn't come into it. I like you, Barbara and if you could like me, a little. . . ."

"I do like you." The words were out before I could stop them, but I was ready to like anyone who liked me, and his present kindness had knocked down all my defenses.

My heart went soaring. He liked me. I liked him. Might not love grow from that? But then Aunt Martha's chiding voice came to me. *"You are letting your romantic notions run away with you, child,"* and my heart spiraled downward again.

So love was out. Would liking be a sound enough basis for marriage? Yes, but would it be sufficient for me? It would lack the excitement and delight I had dreamed about, but it would have its compensations. I might—I might have a child.

"Then shall we take a chance?" Richard asked.

"Yes," I whispered.

He kissed me, and in my ignorance I did not know how much was withheld from me in that kiss. I only knew that my lips trembled beneath his, and that contact with his body set my pulses racing. I would have clung to him if he had not drawn away so quickly.

He became brisk and businesslike. "I must arrange passage for you on the *Indies Pride*. It sails in a few days; let's hope there is a cabin free. We can be married by the captain. But first, I will call on Mr. Parkes."

I listened to him making plans, unable to take my eyes off his strong, sunburned face, but I thought he had forgotten one important point.

"Aunt Martha's will stated we must live here," I reminded him timidly, "in Martha's Cottage."

He chuckled with sly triumph. "I've got that worked out. It only stipulated that we live here, not when or for how long. Therefore, it won't matter whether we live here this year or next year, for a month or a day. She was not so clever there as she thought."

What had I done? As I walked through the rooms of the house I loved, my heart was heavy. I had agreed to a marriage that would gain me a husband, but would deprive me of my lovely, beloved home. Mine. Mine. It belonged to me, in spite of Aunt Martha. Richard had beaten her at her own game. She could never have believed he would propose to me. But to leave it, perhaps never to see it again? To go with Richard far away, to the West Indies?

To be honest with myself, this last was not a prospect

that appalled me. It filled me with apprehension, but it was a thrilling apprehension, and when Richard called again the next morning, his smile, the touch of his lips on my cheek, dispelled all doubt. I had surely done the right thing. I should have lost Martha's Cottage anyway, if I had not agreed to marry him. And I could always come back to stay for a while. The house would always be here, waiting for me. This way I could have Richard *and* Martha's Cottage.

Mr. Parkes put a damper on my spirits for a while when he called on me later and asked in his fatherly way if I was sure I was doing the right thing.

"Oh, yes, I'm sure, Mr. Parkes," I said.

"Do you not think it would be wise to wait a while? You have not known each other long. Why not wait, at least till the end of your month's grace?"

"We can't. The *Indies Pride* sails next week."

"There are other ships, other dates of departure."

"But why delay, Mr. Parkes when there is no need for it? Do not be concerned for me, dear sir. I am happy. Please be happy for me."

"So you have quite made up your mind?"

"Yes."

For a moment he seemed on the verge of annoyance, then he smiled and patted my hand. "Very well, my dear. So be it. Now, what am I to do about Martha's Cottage? Mr. Goodall suggested I sell it when he came to see me yesterday. But it belongs to you, and I can do nothing without your authority."

"Sell it!" I was aghast. "Oh, no, don't sell it. Let it, that will do—in case we want to come back to it one day."

"Come back to it? Your aunt wished you to live here. Both of you. That was a condition in the will."

"I know. But Richard explained a way of getting round that. Did he not tell you . . . ?"

"Oh, yes." Mr. Parkes cast a jaundiced eye over me. "He was quick to point out the weakness of the wording there. Well, then, what shall I do about the servants, loyal to your aunt for years? She would not wish to see them . . ."

"They must be kept on, of course," I declared swiftly. "Those who wish to stay. Make it a condition of the let."

And so I dismissed airily the house I had adored for so many years.

As it happened I was denied the glamour of a shipboard wedding. My mother, informed of my forthcoming marriage came hotfoot to see I had "a proper wedding, in church, like any normal girl. I'm having no hole-in-the-corner wedding to give folk cause for comment."

"It's perfectly legal to be married aboard ship by the captain," I said. "Besides, there isn't time for the banns to be read."

She waived my protest aside. "There are ways of getting round that, my girl. If we are not careful, there'll be no stopping Martha's unsavory past coming to light. As it is, if Richard keeps quiet, no one need ever be any the wiser. As far as they are concerned, you will simply be marrying a distant cousin—once or twice removed. Father's solicitors, Braden and Luce, have long since died, and Mr. Parkes has kept quiet for so long it won't hurt him to continue his silence. A church wedding it must be, for respectability's sake."

So I was married in the tiny village church where I had worshipped Sunday by Sunday for the past thirteen years of my life, and, though the prospect of a wedding at sea had held the promise of romance, I was glad. It seemed fitting, and the ghost of Aunt Martha in her pew did not dim my happiness.

There was a little celebration after the ceremony. We drank champagne. Perhaps I drank too much—a glass of wine at dinner was all I had ever been used to—anyway, I could hear myself chattering and laughing out loud and could not believe it was I. Happiness bubbled inside me as I looked up at Richard, tall, slim, hard-muscled, standing by my side. Tomorrow we would embark on the first stage of our long journey to the sugar islands.

My heart clamored at the thought. A new life was beginning for me, not the life I had envisioned, of loneliness and servitude, but a life shared with this handsome man, Richard Goodall, my cousin. It was unbelievable that until a few days ago I had not even been aware of his existence, and now he was my husband—courtesy of Aunt Martha.

Suddenly I felt less than light-hearted. Aunt Martha had instigated our marriage. But for her, he would not be my husband. Then I looked up at his strong, firm jaw and thought, no, he had not married me because she had willed it, but because he was concerned about me, because he cared about what happened to me. If he had not wanted to marry me, nothing she or anyone else could have said would have made him.

He cared about me. That was sufficient to entitle him to all the affection I could give him in return. And I would give him affection, all I had to give, so much that he might even fall in love with me.

Encouraged by my befuddled brain, my heart began to dance and sing again. Indeed, as he smiled down at me, I believed he loved me already—a little, and I longed for the moment when we would be alone.

Mr. Parkes was the first of the guests to take his leave. He beckoned me to follow him, and when we were alone handed me a letter, saying, "I was to give you this if you and Richard married before the month was up." I thanked him and placed it on a side table—and forgot all about it.

My mother and sister were staying the night and seemed in no hurry to retire. At first I did not mind. Richard was an entertaining talker, and I was happy just to sit listening to him. But then a game of cards was suggested. It became two, then three, then four. The hour grew late and still we played cards. At last, when I had begun to think they would never leave us, they rose and went up to bed, and, contrarily, I wished they had not. I was suddenly afraid. The euphoric effect of the champagne had worn off.

I sat with my hands folded in my lap, not knowing what to say or do, waiting for Richard to make the first move. He remained seated at the table, his head bent over the cards, his long fingers shuffling and placing them into neat little stacks on the green baize. Then he rose and went to pour himself another drink. He had been drinking steadily all evening, I suddenly realized.

He brought it back to the table and started dealing the cards. "Another game?" he asked casually.

I felt hurt. I felt he should have gathered me up in his arms, carried me to our bedroom, and made love to me, as the lover of my dreams would have done.

But I was forgetting—Richard was not my lover. But we were married and I believed he would behave as a husband should.

I got up from my chair. "No," I said, "I think we ought to go up. It's getting late." Then, ashamed at being so bold, I added, "We have to leave early in the morning," as my reason, and walked quickly from the room.

I dismissed my maid after she had done her duty and helped me undress. I looked down at my nightgown. It was nothing special. None of my clothes were anything special. "*Plain and in keeping with your looks and nature,*" had been Aunt Martha's firm instruction. But at least it was white, not black. I had been married in black. My mother and sister had worn black. A somber group we must have looked, but anything else would have been unseemly so soon after my aunt's death. It was not how I had dreamed my wedding day would be, but then—I had never dreamed my wedding day would ever be anything but a dream.

I climbed into bed and pulled the covers up to my chin, trembling less from cold than from excitement and anticipation. Would he come? Surely he would. He was my husband.

My eyes fixed on the door, I waited for Richard's appearance, longing for, yet fearing the touch of his hands on my bare flesh, for the caresses that would lead to one inevitable end.

The minutes passed, lengthened into an hour. I counted the chimes of the grandfather clock in the hall. Midnight: I stopped trembling. I lay stiff as a board in the great double bed that had been Aunt Martha's. One o'clock. He would not come now.

I blew out the candle and buried my face in the pillow. I wished I could cry, but I had so disciplined myself never to give way and show my hurt, that even when I was alone the solace of tears was denied me.

Perhaps I dozed. I do not know. But suddenly I was wide awake and aware that someone was standing over me.

"Richard?" I murmured, my heart fluttering madly.

"Oh. You're awake."

Disappointment filled the tone of his voice, stilled the beat of my heart. His long stay downstairs had been deliberate, and I knew the reason why. He had hoped I would be asleep so that he would not be called upon to make love to me. I had smelled the reek of whisky on his breath. I closed my eyes and bit deeply into my lower lip as the tight ache that had knotted itself in my throat threatened to explode. He had had to dull his senses with strong liquor before he could bring himself to my bed, and the thought devastated me.

I felt the sheets raised, a draught of cold air, as he got in beside me. He lay stiff and straight as I, then, with a slowness that spoke of reluctant necessity—the necessity to do his duty no matter what it cost him—he turned and reached out for me. I felt his hand at my breast, his lips seeking mine. My flesh trembled beneath his touch, fire coursed through my veins as he drew me to him and as his thighs brushed mine, entwined themselves with mine. I thought my bones would melt. His body arched to cover mine. This was what I had been waiting for—what he had tried to avoid. The knowledge broke me. I grew rigid and unresponsive.

"Relax," he murmured.

"I can't," I cried.

"Why not?" he demanded.

"You don't love me," I moaned.

"What has that got to do with it?" he asked, brutally

frank. "I'm a man, you're a woman—all that is necessary for the sexual act."

The sexual act. That was all it was to him. And he was ready for it, wanted it now with a thrusting animal urgency. I pushed him away from me with a bitter cry, "No! No!"

He rolled off me, astonished at my rejection. "What's the matter?" he demanded angrily. "I thought you wanted me to make love to you."

I sprang out of bed distancing myself from him with the breadth of the room, glaring at him bitterly, miserably. "You thought! You didn't think at all! You just took it for granted that I wanted . . . would gladly submit to . . . no matter what . . . Aunt Martha was right. Men are beasts!"

He got out of bed and started coming toward me.

"Keep away!" I shrieked. "Don't come near me! Don't come near me!"

He hesitated. "All right, Barbara. Calm down. I shan't touch you again, if you don't want me to. Only, come back to bed. It's freezing and you're shivering. . . ."

"No! I don't care! I'll stay here."

I groped for the chair I knew stood by the wall and sank into it.

"Don't be foolish," he said tightly, anger rising in him again. "You can't stay there all night. Get back into bed. Or do you want me to carry you there?"

The threat in his voice was enough to make me obey him. I scrambled back into bed and lay as near to the edge as possible. The bed sagged a little beneath his weight and I held my breath, afraid he might draw me to the warmth in the middle—but he kept his word and did not touch me.

In the morning I was dressed and out of the room before he was awake. Gray and hollow-eyed, I was afraid my mother and sister might notice and ask what was amiss, but, as usual, they noticed nothing.

Richard put in an appearance just before they were about to leave. I could have wept when I saw how completely unaffected he was by the previous night's developments. While I had lain awake wide-eyed and numb with misery, he had slept well and woken clear-eyed and handsome as ever.

Good-byes were said. My mother's cheek touched mine in its usual careless manner. I made an impulsive effort to embrace her, but, with her usual expertise, she managed to evade me. Even now, when it was doubtful I should ever see her again, she could not offer me one crumb of her love. I was doubly grateful, therefore, for Beth's embrace, which she offered spontaneously, but when she turned to Richard and raised her lovely face to his, luscious lips parted invitingly, I could cheerfully have strangled her. There was nothing sisterly in her glance, nor brotherly in his.

I turned away. Why should I care after last night's fiasco?

A last wave and I was alone with Richard. He followed me indoors.

"Barbara."

I leapt like a startled rabbit at the touch of his hand.

"About last night . . ."

"I don't wish to talk about it," I said.

"But we must. I've thought it over and realize you felt hurt, insulted by my behavior. I wish to apologize and . . ."

"There's no need." I turned to look levelly at him,

coolly confident that he would never guess from my demeanor how much it cost me to appear so unconcerned. Never again would he feel I expected him to do his duty in bed. "Let's not pretend, Richard. We're not in love with each other. We married because it suited us to do so. You wanted money. I wanted Martha's Cottage. So long as we keep up a face for the world, we can be honest with ourselves. We'll manage tolerably well together, I dare say, with a little planning and common sense."

Richard gaped at me, his piercing blue gaze striving to strip away my pretense. But I had become too practiced at hiding my feelings to allow any chink in my armor.

"I would stay on at Martha's Cottage, only it might give rise to talk, and we don't want that, do we? Therefore, I suggest I accompany you to Almada—I would enjoy the experience of a sea voyage—say, for about a year. Of course," I could not keep the sarcasm out of my voice, "if you'd rather I stayed here, then I will bow to your wishes, as a dutiful wife should."

He was angry now. I had made him so. His mouth was tight set. His eyes hard and steely. It was a cold anger I had evoked, and I did not care. I had turned the tables on him. Aunt Martha would have been proud of me.

"I wouldn't dream of placing you in such an intolerable situation," he responded stiffly. "Of course you must come to Almada, for as long as you wish."

"With no strings attached," I added, with seeming carelessness.

"No strings. A marriage of convenience. In name only."

"In name only," I echoed, and only just made it.

Chapter Three

I had longed all my life for romance, excitement and adventure. For a time it had seemed as if all three were about to be realized. But my romance had been short-lived. Excitement had died. Only adventure remained—and that lost its appeal during a voyage bedeviled by storms that kept me to my cabin with a sickness that made me wish for death.

Richard and I had separate cabins on board ship. Luckily, for it saved a lot of embarrassment, all the double cabins had been taken when Richard had booked passage for me.

He had no difficulty in finding his sea-legs, being a good sailor, and sympathized with me in my agony, visiting me regularly, achieving the appearance of an attentive, caring husband, playing his part well.

When at last the winds abated and the sea grew calm, and I ventured up on deck in my high-buttoned mourning black, Richard was standing by the rail in conversation with a group of people. I hesitated a short distance away, and a young woman in green drew

Richard's attention to me.

He turned with a slightly startled expression and came toward me. "Barbara, you're better."

"Yes." I tried to form a smile, but my lips seemed numb.

He gave me a peck on the cheek. It was for the benefit of the others, but it quickened my heartbeat.

"Have you eaten?" he asked solicitously.

"A little."

"Good. You'll be fine from now on, even if the weather deteriorates again."

I groaned. "Oh, Richard," the memory of my seasickness fresh in my mind, "there won't be more storms? I don't think I could bear it."

"There's always the possibility. Don't worry, you won't be sick again. You've had your initiation. Come, let me introduce you to some of our fellow travelers."

I was introduced first to a married couple returning to their home in the Virgin Islands, Mr. and Mrs. Thomas Green. He was fat, florid, and bellicose. She was little and thin and cowed. "Glad you're up and about at last, Mrs. Pengarth," he said.

I looked at him sharply, then at Richard, then remembered; he had married me as Richard Goodall Pengarth. I had wondered whether it was legal at the time and had been assured that it was.

Next I was introduced to Dr. Philip Rose and his wife, the young woman in green, Sarah. Without knowing why, I liked them at once.

"Your husband has just been telling me that doctors are badly needed in the West Indies," Dr. Rose declared, after greeting me. "All manner of diseases are rife among the people there."

"I said they are rampant among the poorer classes," Richard corrected him, with some acerbity. "You will not find your fortune among them, I fancy."

"I am not out to make a fortune—not for myself. Naturally, I wish to secure sufficient income to provide a reasonable standard of living for my wife—and family, if we are lucky enough to have one, but I hope to make enough out of treating the sick who are wealthy to enable me to set up a hospital for the poor, where they can receive care and medicine whether they can afford to pay for it or not."

"A charity hospital," Thomas Green spat contemptuously.

"And what is wrong with that?"

Before Mr. Green could reply, Richard spoke. "Nothing. It is a very laudable enterprise, but you could have done that in your own country. I do not think England so well endowed that she could not do with another charitable institution."

"Maybe not, but there are many willing and able to do such work there. I wanted . . . something . . ."

"More challenging?"

"Something where the need was greater, and I believe it is, in the West Indies."

"You will have your work cut out," Richard scoffed. "The people are not used to getting something for nothing. They will eye you with suspicion."

"Then I will have to change their way of thinking," Philip returned, calmly.

"You will have to change their whole attitude."

"Then I shall do so."

I listened to Philip Rose with rapt attention. I had never met anyone like him before. There was something almost sublime about him. An aura of humility, otherworldliness. Yet it was mixed with a down-to-earth confidence in his own abilities. The light that shone out of his eyes reflected his belief in himself, and in the goodness of God. I almost believed I was looking at a saint.

"You're a misguided fool." Thomas Green denigrated him.

"Is it misguided to want to alleviate the sufferings of others?" Philip Rose asked. "I do not think so."

"Neither do I," I cried impulsively. "I wish you well in your endeavors, sir."

"Thank you, Mrs. Pengarth. I know it will be difficult, requiring hard work and a great deal of money, but I am not afraid of hard work and I hope to persuade some of the prosperous men on the island of Almada to dip into their pockets. . . ."

"So that's your game." Thomas Green's face increased its redness. "You want financing in this dream of yours. Well, I can tell you now, it won't work. The poor are poor because they are too lazy to do an honest day's work. They are a ragbag of race and color. Vermin. If you expect men who have worked hard all their lives for the prosperity they now enjoy to fork out for such a crew, I can tell you, you'll get short shrift."

"The prosperity *they* have worked so hard to enjoy?" Philip's voice was scathing. "Their prosperity results from the labors of thousands of slaves, black men, transported miles from their homeland by greedy whites who . . ."

"Watch your words, Rose." Richard's voice cut like a razor. "Abuse is no way to achieve your aims."

"I'm sorry, but I feel strongly about it. I will not paper over the truth."

"A nigger-lover. He's a nigger-lover," Mr. Green exploded, his eyes popping over the fat red folds of his cheeks. "One of Wilberforce's disciples, no doubt."

"I believe in Wilberforce's aims, that all men should be free."

"Go back home, young man. Don't land in Almada. We don't want the likes of you stirring up trouble in the islands. We've had more than our fair share of it since the Abolition of the Slave Trade bill went through. Why can't he be satisfied with what he has achieved? It ought to be enough for him, but no, now he wants emancipation for all slaves. And what does he think the result of that will be? The man's a menace. You're a menace, and everyone like you. Thank God there are still some men in the Palace of Westminster with enough sound common sense to stop *that* bill going through."

"I believe the bill will go through," argued Philip Rose.

"Then heaven help the sugar industry if it does. It will be ruined . . . and God knows what will happen to his precious slaves. . . ."

"They will be free," Philip's wife, Sarah, said with quiet assurance.

"Just so. And how do you think they will fare, madam?"

"Like anybody else." She returned his angry glare calmly. "They will work. . . ."

"You're a fool!" he cut her short bluntly, so that she colored, and her husband demanded an apology from him.

He disregarded the demand. "I'll tell you what will happen if they get their freedom. They'll carve us up, that's what they'll do. They'll drink themselves into bloody insensibility and carve us up. They'll work, you say. Work? Ha! You make me laugh. They won't work. They're too bloody lazy. Too bloody arrogant. They have to be made to work. They have to be . . ."

"Beaten and humiliated." Philip was now as angry as he.

"It's all they know. They're animals. . . ."

"They're human beings." Richard's voice sliced through the argument.

"What? Are you on their side?" Thomas Green turned to him. "I thought you said you owned a plantation in Almada?"

"I did. I do."

"Then what are you talking about? You can't agree with this Emancipation Act. Do you want to see your plantation ruined?"

"No, of course not, but . . ."

"Then stop talking like an idiot. Be a man and stand up for what you believe. Wilberforce and his ilk will have everyone believe our slaves aren't fed and clothed. . . ."

"They are clothed in rags and fed on filth," Philip said. "I have heard . . ."

"You have heard . . . you have heard . . . you don't know anything," shouted Mr. Green.

"If they had been treated like men instead of . . ."

"Men! They're bloody savages, straight from the jungle."

"The act will be passed. The people will demand it," Philip said, his face white and stretched across his fine cheekbones.

"Oh, will they? And what do they think will happen to their sugar supply? What about the sweet cakes and pies they have come to take for granted, when there is no one to work the cane fields?"

"The freed slaves will work. Free Negroes, working for a fair day's pay . . ."

Thomas Green threw up his arms in frustration. "May God preserve me from such fools as you," he cried and swung away from us. His silent, cowed little wife followed in his wake.

"What a terrible man," I said.

"I'd heard about men like that, but I truly did not believe they existed!" Philip exclaimed.

"You'd better believe it," Richard said. "There are many more like him."

"They have had their day. A fresh wind is blowing. . . ."

"You are an idealist, Rose," Richard said abruptly. "Take my advice and return to England on the first ship out of Almada. Don't stop for anything, not even to look around. The Indies is no place for an idealist like you."

What had been said worried me. I had come across references to William Wilberforce and the slave trade in my reading, but, like Dr. Rose, I had not been able to credit that all the things that were said of the planters were true. After all, they were Christian men and women, weren't they? They would not do such things. As for slavery itself—that was wrong, of course, and must be abolished, and I believed, with Philip, that the English Parliament would abolish it, but the cruelties reported—they must be exaggerated, they were just too unbelievable.

I looked at Richard. Too unbelievable.

We formed a friendship, Richard and I, with Sarah and

Philip during the long hot days at sea, though it was not always an easy friendship. Philip's burning zeal for reform provoked many an argument. Sarah was a well-educated young woman who came from a very enlightened family. Her father was a member of Parliament and an ardent supporter of Wilberforce. During our hours of conversation together I learned a great deal from her.

But our days were not all spent in a serious vein. We enjoyed much fun and laughter also. Richard treated me with kindness, tenderness. His behavior toward me was every bit as considerate as Philip's toward Sarah. He epitomized the kind and loving husband. No one would have guessed it was all an act. It almost fooled me. Only at night, alone in my bunk, was the truth borne in upon me in all its agonizing clarity.

I think I surprised him, for there were not many topics on which I could not converse with him. "You have lived such a quiet life," he said, "yet you have such a wide knowledge."

"It all comes out of books," I said. "I've always read a great deal . . . anything that came to hand . . . but I've had no real experience."

"Yet you've managed to form your own opinions from what you've read. You do not just spout the arguments of others."

"It's all Aunt Martha's doing. She taught me to think for myself. 'Never follow one line of argument,' she used to say to me. 'There are always two, often more, sides to any argument. Discover them all and find your own conclusion.' Aunt Martha may have had her faults, but . . ." I broke off.

Richard's face had tightened. The pulse that denoted anger was throbbing at his temple. By some unspoken agreement we had both drawn back from any discussion regarding my aunt, and now I had broken it. Our friendly footing faltered. A wiser woman might have known how to retrieve it. I did not.

We were not many days away from Almada. During the crossing the temperature had increased, and at times it became unbearable. I had never known such heat. My mourning gowns were completely unsuitable for such a climate, and I felt increasingly fatigued and, at times, positively faint.

The day came when I swooned at Richard's feet.

"My dear Barbara," he chastised me afterward, "it is a long time now since that woman" (he always referred to Aunt Martha as "that woman") "died. How much longer do you intend mourning her? I should like you to cease at once. In fact, as your husband, I order it. In future you will wear dresses that are cool and pretty."

Cool and pretty. I eyed my garments. Not one of them could be called pretty. Aunt Martha's stern supervision had seen to it that all my clothes were plain and simple. *"No sense in decking yourself out like a lady of fashion. It's not your style."*

So what was my style? Plain and ordinary. Richard would have to accept it, as I had had to accept it.

My maid had packed for me before she left my employment. I had pleaded with her to accompany me to Almada, but she told me she was hoping to marry Jacob Holt, a young farmer, and did not want to distance herself from him. I had said I understood and wished her well.

We had embraced. She was only a year older than I and had been my maid ever since I had become my aunt's ward. We would miss each other.

There had not been time to fine a replacement maid,

but Richard had said it did not matter, I should have as many maids as I wished once we reached High Place.

High Place. Richard's plantation, and his home. Soon to be my home, too. I blinked back a tear as I raked through the clothes Aggie had packed for me.

I chose a summer cotton in pale mauve. It had short sleeves and a low neckline, but not so low that it had offended Aunt Martha's rigorous sense of fitness. It was dull and plain. I had nothing with which to offset its plainness, no necklace, no earrings. I had never possessed any jewelry till the plain gold band had been placed on the third finger of my left hand by Richard at our wedding. I had not come into any on my aunt's death; there had been none for her to leave. She did not believe in the wearing of jewelry.

I heaved a sigh and placed a black lacy shawl round my shoulders. I felt my aunt willed it. I would be too exposed without it.

I went up on deck. I met Richard's eyes. They were unimpressed.

"Is that the best you can do?" he asked.

We docked in Seatown, Almada's capital. It was late afternoon and the hot sun shone high in a cloudless sky, burning the skin, hurting the eye. I was grateful for the shade of my parasol.

I stood at the ship's side with Richard and Philip and Sarah and gazed in wonder at the scene on the quayside. There was so much color, so much noise, so many faces—some black as coal—turned upward, so many raised voices. There was a singsong quality about the voices. I thought it was a foreign language at first, then I realized it was English. A strange kind of English, but English.

There was color everywhere, the soft color of peeling paint on warehouse walls, the harsher, vibrant color of Negro women's skirts and the cloths they had bound round their heads. There was a bustle and a clamor and an excitement such as I had never encountered, but as my eye roamed over the whole, a tremor of unease passed through me. This was a strange, new world I was entering. A world far removed from the gentle, peaceful fields of England. What would it hold for me?

I thought of High Place, imagined my life there, and longed to be back in Martha's Cottage.

A swift, sharp sound cut through the brilliance of the day. A sound I had never heard before, but was to hear many times during my stay in Almada, and which I hope never to hear again. The sound of a whip flashing through the air to descend upon the back of some poor, unfortunate slave.

"God! It's true!"

I heard Philip's shocked tones as our eyes became transfixed on a column of black men, their heads like black wool, their bodies glistening with sweat, bent double under heavy loads. No sound came from the men, though the whip licked their skin. No one took any notice of them. They seemed set apart from the vibrant, noisy scene. A man was walking with them, a white man, for all his mahogany tan, dressed in white trousers and jacket and floppy straw hat. He was wielding the whip, letting it fall with careless indiscrimination.

Till one man stumbled and fell. His bale slipped to the ground. Then the whip landed viciously, purposefully, across his bare back. I saw the gleam of blood as he screamed. Then he was silent again. He humped the bale onto his scarred back and took his place in the column again.

It was an eerie silence that hung about that column of black men—slaves, as I guessed them to be. It dried my throat with fear. I could almost feel the hate rising from them, and in spite of the heat, I started to shiver.

Richard placed an arm round me. "Don't worry," he said. "You'll see none of this at High Place."

Philip spoke again. "It shouldn't be seen anywhere. It's barbaric. They're being treated like animals—worse. If this can be true," he turned to Sarah, white-faced beneath her parasol, "what else may be?"

"I tried to warn you," Richard said. "Try to persuade your husband to return to England, Mrs. Rose. You and he will never fit in here. I can see nothing but misery ahead for both of you, if you stay."

"We did not come expecting to find it easy," Philip said.

"I shall stand by Philip and be guided by him," Sarah declared.

Richard seemed to want to say something more, but they looked at him unflinchingly, immovably, and he gave up.

"Massa Adam. Massa Adam."

A voice rising above the general clamor drew our attention. It belonged to a plump, round-faced black man standing beside a carriage of shiny indigo blue with dashing yellow-spoked wheels. He was dressed in some kind of uniform and was frantically waving a tricorn-shaped hat above his grizzled gray head to attact someone's notice.

"Over here, Massa Adam," he called, and his white

teeth gleamed in a wide smile as Richard waved back and took my arm.

"That's Daniel. He's come to take us to High Place."

"But . . . he's calling for Adam."

"Yes. That's my name—my second name—the name I am known by in Almada."

"But . . . why did you never tell me?"

He shrugged. "I don't know. It did not seem important, I suppose, at the time—but from now on I shall expect you to call me Adam."

"I don't know if I can," I said snappily, irritated by his offhand manner. "I don't think I shall be able to get used to it."

"Oh, I think you will," he returned carelessly.

"We will meet again," Philip smiled confidently as we took our leave of him and his wife.

With a brief nod, Richard hurried me away.

"Perhaps we can invite them to High Place, Richard—Adam." I hurriedly corrected myself at the look of anger that swept across his face.

"It's doubtful we shall ever see them again," he forecast, frowning. "I give them a month, maybe two, and they will be off back to England."

"I think they will stay," I contradicted him. "You said yourself that Philip was an idealist, and idealists are notoriously single-minded, following their goal right through to the end."

"We shall see," he said.

He handed me into the carriage, the door of which was held open for me by a small, grinning boy. His face was not coal black, like Daniel's, but a rich, dark chocolate brown. When Richard was settled beside me, the boy shut the carriage door with a flourish before jumping up to sit next to Daniel and survey the world around him in a very superior fashion. He was obviously extremely proud of his position as groom's boy.

Richard—Adam—ordered Daniel to "move on," but before Daniel could spur the horses, a carriage the color of port wine drew to a halt at our side.

A vision of white taffeta and lace, a frilly parasol, a pink and white complexion, ringlets like spun gold tumbling from under a beribboned bonnet, eyes of aquamarine blue, red lips parted in a dazzling smile, presented itself to my entranced gaze.

A voice, sweet as any cooing dove, issued through the parted lips. "Adam, you're back. How wonderful. I've missed you so much."

"Minty!" Richard's mouth widened in an answering smile. He bent his dark head to kiss the mittened hand presented to him. "You look ravishing."

"Thank you, kind sir." The aquamarine eyes sparkled with pleasure. The pink cheeks dimpled.

"I never expected such a treat, the Governor's daughter waiting to greet me on the quay." Richard's voice—Adam's voice, I must remember—was affectionately teasing.

"I was not waiting to greet you, you naughty man." The red lips pouted prettily. "How could I be when I was not informed as to the date of your return?"

"I wrote a letter home. News gets about fast. I took it for granted you would have heard."

"It is of no consequence." She tossed her golden ringlets. "I am waiting for my father. He is discussing business with Mr. Ridley. I have been shopping." Her mittened hand indicated the pile of parcels and boxes that cramped the brown-faced girl sitting opposite her, nursing yet more parcels. "I finished sooner than I had anticipated, otherwise I should not have seen you. Oh, Adam," she could keep up her careless pretense no longer, "I am so glad you have returned. Life has been so dismal without you."

"Minty." My presence was remembered. "Allow me to introduce you to my wife, Barbara. Barbara, Araminta Belmont."

I tried to smile at the golden-haired beauty, whose glance now rested on me, but my lips were stiff and refused to move. I need not have worried, there was no smile on her face, either. Her aquamarine eyes had iced over, chilling me to the bone with their cold stare, and I knew she had not been unaware of my presence. I also knew, beyond the shadow of a doubt, that she was in love with my husband.

Was he in love with her? What if he were? What difference would it make to me? Why torture myself asking such questions? I had no hold on him. I was no true wife to him. He did not wish for me to be a true wife to him. He would go his own way, now he was back in Almada, doing as he pleased, as he had done before we met.

His next words convinced me of this—if I had needed any convincing.

"Araminta is a very dear friend of mine. A close neighbor. I hope you will make her your friend, too. You will be seeing a lot of each other."

Araminta's aquamarine eyes changed. Their smug expression told me quite plainly: I might be his wife, but I posed no threat. They returned to their prime object of interest. Adam. She was in love with Adam and saw no reason to hide the fact from me.

Was Adam in love with her? She was so beautiful, he

must be. "*Men set great store by physical beauty.*" Was it my mother or Aunt Martha who had said that? What did it matter? The point was, with a girl like Araminta Belmont waiting for him, why had he married me? Concern for a cousin he had only just met could not be sufficient reason, surely.

So perhaps he was not in love with her. I did not believe this—one look at his face was enough to crush that hope. No, he had married me to save me from a life of penury and loneliness, and that was as much as I had any right to expect of him. He now expected me to allow him to continue his life in his own way, with no interruptions from me. Would he make Araminta his mistress? Would she be willing? If not, what then? A divorce? I had not thought of that. Had he? If Araminta would not become his mistress . . . if she held out for marriage . . . what chance had I of holding him? I saw myself back in Martha's Cottage much sooner than I had expected.

I watched Araminta's lips moving, hearing no word, as she addressed herself exclusively to Adam—funny how quickly I had come to think of him as Adam. How lovely she was, lovelier, even, than my sister, Beth. But I detected a hard, steely quality about her that was missing in my little sister. Beth was soft and pliable, easily molded to another's will. Nothing, I felt, would bend this woman's will.

". . . we must have a celebration. A party." Her voice came through to me. "I must arrange a party for you. Meanwhile, you must come to dinner. Tonight."

I took the invitation, voiced so dictatorially, to include me, though she never once glanced in my direction. Adam did not glance at me, either, as he refused the invitation.

"It's sweet of you, Minty, but we've had a long journey. My wife finds the heat taxing and is very tired. So am I. When we reach High Place the only thing either of us will want is a good night's rest."

"Very well." She lowered her white parasol and gave her black driver a poke in the back, her indication that she was ready to move off. "But the party is on. I shall start planning it at once."

We waited till the smart vehicle with its attractive occupant had drawn away, come to a halt further along at the entrance to a pink-painted warehouse, and the lady had stepped down, turned and waved, dazzling us again, and disappeared into the darkened interior.

Only then did Adam reiterate his order to move on.

Chapter Four

I hardly noticed the drive through the town I had so much looked forward to seeing. My eyes were turned inward, dwelling on Araminta Belmont's beauty and the place I believed she held in my husband's heart.

My husband. I must stop thinking of him as that. He was not my husband, not really, not truly. I should look upon him as a brother. I *would* look upon him as a brother. It would save me a lot of heartache when the time came for me to return to England, and I should not be so desolate at leaving him, to face life on my own again.

So I reasoned with myself, foolishly, perhaps, but I believed it the best thing I could do. The only thing I could do. I had long ago developed the art of self-deception. It had been the only way for a loveless child to get by. It stood me in good stead now.

As the drive progressed, the sheer beauty of the island forced its way through my introspection, drawing me into a magic, scented world. Flowers of flame and yellow, white and purple delighted my eye, strangers to me, with strange-sounding names. Hibiscus and oleander, Adam called them. Trees, long and thin, with tufts of feathery leaves swaying in some breeze which did not seem to reach us, fascinated me. I was even more fascinated when I saw those same leaves, lopped and at ground level—they were enormous. Birds, brighter than the flowers, darted and swooped and soared. The sea sparkled and glistened, burnished gold by the unremitting sun. It was magic.

Until we reached the cane fields. Then the magic drained away. Among the tall growing canes, taller than a man, half-naked Negroes worked methodically, silently. A man on horseback watching over them, regulation whip in hand.

I shuddered and turned away as I heard the whistle and crack of the whip through the air. I do not know if it fell across anyone's back, I heard no cry of pain; but I remembered the sullen silence of the column of men on the quay, and knew it could have.

I felt sick and faint. I wanted to go home. I did not want to live in a place where men treated men in such a savage fashion.

Richard—Adam—said, with a swift glance at me as if he knew what I was thinking, "A whip is a necessary accoutrement for an overseer—even if it is not used."

We reached High Place, startlingly white against a background of vivid blue sky, and so large it took my breath away. Martha's Cottage would have been dwarfed beside it.

A veranda ran all the way round it at ground level and another at first-floor level, to afford relief from the relentless sun. Huge wooden latticed shutters rested at either side of each window, many which did double duty as doors. I learned later that these shutters were closed during the middle heat of the day to keep the house as cool as possible while we, the white masters, rested indoors lest the slightest movement caused the sweat to drip from us like a waterfall.

There was no respite for the slaves, however. Their work continued till the hours of darkness, when they would return from the fields exhausted to their dark, cramped cabins and fall on the hard, rough ground. They would sleep; then they would rise and eat the food their women had prepared for them, though even some women, I was to learn later, labored in the fields. Then there would be a period of singing around their cooking fires, after which they would lie with their wives and fall asleep again, only to be awakened by the first rays of light for another hard day's labor in the cane fields.

I was surprised they should sing when their lives were lived under such terrible conditions. They were not unhappy, I was told. They were glad to be at High Place.

So much for the slaves who labored in the fields. But there were other slaves, house slaves, whose lives were as different again, not far removed from the lives of English servants. They were well dressed, they ate well, they slept indoors in quarters at the back of the house. The only difference between them and the servants back home was their bondage, as far as I could see.

But I knew none of this as I gazed at the beautiful house from my seat in the carriage as it rolled up the drive, which widened into a courtyard flanked by stables and surrounded by gardens of great, lush beauty.

There was a sudden eruption of men, women, and children, all shouting, "Massa Adam. Massa Adam. Yo's back." Dogs of all shapes and sizes ran about, barking frenziedly, getting underfoot. When they saw me they drew back and were silent, even the dogs. There was not a white face to be seen.

The little brown groom's boy jumped down and opened the carriage door, almost before the carriage had stopped. Adam descended and held out his hand for me. But I could see he looked anxious, and as soon as I was down he turned to the gray-mopped Negro, dressed in livery, waiting at the bottom of the wide white marble steps.

"What is it? What's the matter," he demanded, suspicion in his voice. "Where's my mother? Mr. Harding?"

"Mistress in her room, massa. Massa Harding, he go down Ransom place. Der's been trouble, massa. Bad trouble."

"What kind of trouble?"

"Slave trouble, massa. Billy Joe, he done run away again. Dey foun' 'im down by Long Field stream. Blood all over."

"Blood?" Adam cried quickly. "Shot?"

"No shot, massa. He bleed from de head and de stomach and de legs, but he not shot. He been beat, Massa Adam, beat bad. He 'most dead."

"And Mr. Harding's taken him back, you say?"

"Sho, massa." The gray head shook sadly. "Billy Joe, he want stay. He beg . . . but Massa Harding, he say no, Billy Joe must go back. Billy Joe, he try fight. Massa Harding, he tie up Billy Joe. Billy Joe say he won't stay Ransom slave. He run 'way again. All time. Till he die."

I listened. I heard it all. I could not take it in, not all of it, but enough to make me stare with incredulity at Adam, drawing his eyes toward me. Our eyes held in a silent moment, then he drew in a deep breath, caught my arm, and hurried me indoors, calling back to the old Negro. "Ask Mr. Harding to come and see me immediately he returns."

Once inside the cool interior I turned to him.

"Don't say anything," he said in a harsh, tight voice. "You don't understand."

"I understand a man has been beaten almost to death and he came here for help and it was denied him," I declared hotly.

"He had to go back. He's a slave," he said with a fierce anger I was not sure was directed at me.

"He's a human being. He was injured. He should have been taken in and his wounds tended."

"His wounds would have been tended, but he had to go back. He couldn't stay here . . . not even Billy Joe. . . ."

"You sound as if he were someone special. Was he?"

"He belonged to me once. I had to sell him."

"Sell him!"

I had read about slaves being bought and sold, but it had not had the impact on me this simple statement from Adam had. It had not seemed real when I had read about it. Intellectually, I had understood and known it to be wrong, but I hardly conceived what it really meant.

But this was real. This was close. I had seen slaves for myself. I had seen them as men and women. I had heard their cries of pain, even while they were silent. I began to appreciate more fully all that Mr. Wilberforce had written and said about the slaves of the West Indies and what he was trying to achieve.

"I had to. I needed the money." Adam's voice was a rasp. I gazed at him open-mouthed. "Slaves are commodities here. Possessions. You had better learn to accept it."

A number of black people had gathered nearby, clean, smart, dressed like any parlormaid or footman back home. At first I did not think of them as slaves, but, of course, that was what they were. I did not know how much they had heard—they stood silently servile and their expressions gave nothing away.

One of them came forward—the housekeeper, it transpired. She was dignified and quite beautiful. Her hair was as black as any of the others', but her skin was paler, like milky coffee. She was tall and moved with an easy grace.

Adam introduced me as his wife and the woman's eyes flashed with surprise and a certain displeasure, which she quickly concealed.

"Prepare the White Room for my wife, Bella," Adam said.

"The White Room!" she echoed. "Surely you mean . . ."

"The White Room, Bella—for the present."

"Of course." She bowed and backed away at the peremptory tone of his voice. "It shall be done, master."

She issued instructions to the others. They scurried to do her bidding. She turned to us again.

"Food and drink will be brought at once to refresh you, master—mistress."

She departed with the grace I envied.

"What a beautiful woman," I exclaimed as Adam led me to a table on the shady veranda at the back of the house, which overlooked a paved courtyard where beds of gaudy flowers provided breathtaking splashes of color; bushes grew out of huge pots spilling blooms the size of a man's hand, vines twined themselves around pillars and trellises with strong, fleshy tendrils. "She's paler than the others."

"She's a mulatta," Adam said, and went on to explain at my querying look, "She's of mixed blood. Her father was an English officer."

"So she's not a slave," I said.

"Yes she is. Her mother was a slave; that makes her a slave."

"But surely, if her father . . ."

He heaved a sigh of exasperation. "My dear, you must understand that life in the West Indies differs greatly from life in the United Kingdom. Men, white men, often father children by their female slaves. It's an accepted thing. But such offspring are not recognized as their own. The women have merely been a means of gratifying a fleeting passion. If they conceive, it is not the white man's responsibility. Mostly, the children of such a union are sold to work on other plantations as soon as they are old enough, usually when they are six or seven. If the mother is sold before the child is that old, the child usually goes with her."

"I think that's—deplorable."

"Maybe," he agreed, "but that's the way it is. Slaves are owned. They have no rights. They belong body and soul to their master. Bella was one of the lucky ones. She was sold along with her mother while she was still a baby. My father bought them. Bella's mother became my mother's devoted servant and her baby was brought up inside the house. She received an education alongside me. In fact, as time went on, my father began educating all his house slaves—not with me, and not up to the standard of Bella, but sufficiently—enough for their needs.

"People said he was making a mistake, setting up

trouble for himself. Slaves should be kept in ignorance, they said. So long as they knew how to work hard and long, that was all that should be required of them. Give them a smattering of education and . . . but my father did not listen to them. He never took anyone's advice."

"Was Billy Joe educated?" I asked.

"Yes. He was very bright. Uncannily good at figures. He helped me in my office with the books."

"Yet you sold him—like an animal."

"He was a slave. I owned him. I could do what I liked with him."

I stared at him. He sounded so callous. What had happened to the reasonable man I had crossed the seas with? He had changed his name and, it seemed, his nature with it.

"He was a man!" I cried. "Slave or not, he was a human being. *Is* a human being. Why are we talking about him in the past tense, as if he were dead?"

"He may well be—now."

It took a moment for the significance of this remark to sink into my brain, and when it did, my heart grew cold within me.

"It is more than high time slavery was abolished," I whispered, hardly daring to contemplate what his words had conjured up in my imagination.

"Maybe," Adam whipped back, "but it has not been abolished yet. Only the slave trade bill has been passed—and that doesn't work. Accept things as they are, Barbara, if you are to be happy here at all."

Bella came to escort me to my room. "This is Meta," she said, without a smile and with barely concealed dislike in her beautiful eyes. "She will look after you."

She left me in the care of a diminutive curly-haired,

black-eyed creature, who regarded me with wary speculation. I smiled at her, and at my glance her eyes fell. I looked at her consideringly. She seemed very young, hardly more than fourteen. Young enough, maybe, not to have developed a hatred for her white masters. Perhaps I could establish a friendly relationship with her.

But at my smile she darted from the room.

It was a large, airy room, aptly named the White Room, for it was predominantly white. The windows were festooned with crisp white lace, as was the canopy above the elegant four poster bed. The bed cover was white satin embroidered in white silk. The richly gleaming mahogany floorboards were strewn with white woven rugs patterned with flowers in pastel shades of pink, blue, and green. Besides the usual bedroom furniture, made out of white-painted wood and picked out in gold, there was a gilt-legged day bed upholstered in pink and white striped cloth, and a spindly-legged dressing table chair, the seat of which was covered with the same.

It was an extremely elegant and feminine room, and I was so taken by it that the bitterness left my heart, albeit momentarily, and I found myself smiling with pleasure.

Meta returned, followed by a hulking black fellow whose eyes rested shiftily on me before dropping as he carefully carried an elegantly shaped tub of steaming hot water into the middle of the room. A middle-aged woman carrying two large jugs of cold water was close behind him. She set the jugs beside the tub.

The man and woman left as silently as they had come. Meta set out soap, sponges, towels; cooled the hot water in the tub with cold water from the jugs; then turned her attention to me.

I felt embarrassed being undressed by her. Her black

hands, remarkably small and neat, with pink palms and fingernails, were nimble, and my buttons were quickly undone. I slipped into the bathtub, with her help, but waved her away when she would have soaped my skin.

"I can manage," I said, covering my breasts with my hands as if I were in the presence of some alien being—as indeed I was. I had never seen a Negro in the flesh before coming to the West Indies, and I could not, in spite of myself, look upon Meta in quite the way I would have looked upon a girl whose skin was the same color as my own. I knew it was a fault in me, but I could not help it.

She turned away at once and began heaving my trunks and boxes about. I watched her while I bathed, unearthing chemisettes, pantalettes, petticoats, stockings, shoes, gowns. Gown after gown was cast aside with varying comments. "Not good. Too heavy. Too dark."

I felt obliged to explain, "I have been in mourning for my aunt."

At last she came up with one that seemed to satisfy her, a white one with tiny puffed sleeves that Aunt Martha had liked. *"Virginal. Right for you."*

It had been right for me then. It was right for me now. The White Virgin of the White Room, I said to myself, fighting down a hysterical urge to laugh.

With a bounce of black curls Meta came toward me with a thick white towel, which she held out wide for me to step into. She began patting me dry. I shrugged her off.

"I'll dry myself," I said brusquely.

She stood back immediately and waited, head bowed. Hurt by my brusqueness? Afraid? Looking at her black face, eyes downcast, I bit into my lip. She was a slave, my slave. I could do anything I liked with her, as Adam had with Billy Joe, say anything to her, no matter how hurtful, and she would accept it—have to accept it.

I drew in a deep, shuddering breath. It was wrong. All so wrong. She was black, but she was a human being. A young girl. She had feelings, just as I had. I must remember that. I must not be drawn into believing she had no rights, that she was a thing, a possession, that happened to have two arms and two legs and was capable of doing countless tasks without a moment's resistance.

I remembered the servants at home—in Martha's Cottage, Aggie, my personal maid, Mrs. Perkins, the cook, Wilkins, the butler, and all the others. They had been a happy band, giving total—and loving, I realized now—allegiance to my aunt. And to me. They had all, apart from Aggie, who was to be married, been prepared to remain at Martha's Cottage working for people they did not know till I returned, as I had promised I would.

But they could have left me, gone somewhere else, and I would not have been able to stop them. That was the difference in being a slave and being a free man, even if a poor one.

I said, "Will you help me dress?" and was rewarded by a brilliant flash of sparkling white teeth.

I allowed her to do my hair. I was very proud of my hair—it was so long I could sit on it. It was mousy in color, but there were golden strands running through it that shone brightly in sunlight or candlelight. It was not much to cheer, but it was my only claim to beauty—and Aunt Martha never knew of my weakness. If she had, my hair would have been cut without so much as a moment's pause.

Meta let my hair fall down over her hands in amazement. I felt sure she was wishing she had long hair—hers was so short, like a boy's, though I had to admit it suited her. Then she cheerfully wielded my silver-backed hair-brush down the length of my hair, handling the heavy tresses with great dexterity.

She began piling it on top of my head.

I gazed through the mirror, bemused. Very cleverly she plaited and looped it till it looked like a glistening crown, and then she coaxed ringlets—ringlets! Aunt Martha would have been horrified—out of it, and they fell around my ears and danced and dangled as I moved my head.

I looked at myself half in anguish, half in joy. I looked at someone I did not recognize, someone who was not pretty, but someone who made an impact stronger than mere prettiness, someone who frightened me.

"Take it down," I ordered, "and dress it as it was before."

"But, mistress, it look nice. It make you look good."

Yes, I thought so, too. But it was impossible for me to go downstairs like that. The style made me look different, interesting. Adam might think I had done it deliberately to attract him. I did not want him to think that. It would be too humiliating. He had made it plain enough I held no attraction for him. We were man and wife in name only. I must not put myself in such a position that he need remind me of it again. In any case, there was Araminta Belmont. Whatever I did, however I altered myself, I could not compete with her.

"Take it down," I said again. "At once."

Meta sighed heavily, but she obeyed me. She emitted many more sighs in the course of undoing all those plaits, but I took no notice, and soon my hair was smoothly combed into flatness and pinned into a tight knot at the nape of my neck.

Now I sighed. I was recognizable again. Barbara Emily Farrar. Plain, ordinary, uninteresting. It was on the tip of my tongue to tell Meta to do it up again, when there came the loud clamoring of a gong.

"Dinner gong, mistress," Meta said in her singsong voice, which I found pleasant. "I show you dining room."

With an anxious, palpitating heart, I followed her down the wide curving staircase. I was going to eat my first dinner at High Place. I was going to meet Adam's father and mother. I had to accept them as such, for Aunt Martha, "that woman" as Adam called her, had, I knew, no place here.

A door was open and as we reached the bottom of the polished flight of stairs I saw Adam standing in the middle of what seemed to be the drawing room. He was talking to someone I could not see. He caught sight of me, excused himself, and came to meet me. With a little bob, Meta darted away. I felt strangely bereft.

Adam held out his hand. I placed mine in his. He must have felt me tremble.

"Don't be afraid," he said in the kindly way he had had on board the *Indies Pride*. "There is no need, I do assure you." He placed my arm through his, retaining his hold on my hand. I found it very comforting. "Everything is bound to seem strange to you at first, but you will soon get used to it. Before long you will feel you have never lived anywhere else."

"I'm not afraid," I said. "It's just that everything is so new to me."

He nodded understandingly and steered me toward the drawing room. "And now there is someone you must meet. My brother."

"Your brother?" I squeaked, amazed. "I didn't know you had a brother." Then, as my brain worked, I added, "You can't have a brother."

"So I've been trying to make myself believe these past months," he grated, suddenly harsh. "Nevertheless, he is my brother—as much as any man alive is."

We entered the drawing room. "Robert," Adam said, and the gentleness in his voice surprised me, "Here is my wife, Barbara."

Adam had not told me about Robert, and now, as Robert shambled toward me, I thought I knew why. But it could be no reflection on him that Robert's legs were not of an even size, or that his oversized head lolled as if it did not belong to him. He was no real relation.

Robert held out a large, very soft hand. "Hello," he said.

A shudder of unease ran through me as I placed my hand in his. He was a frightening sight and it required all my courage to touch him.

"I'm glad you've come. I've always wanted a sister."

I murmured something, I did not know what, I was far too conscious of the fact that for all the softness of his hand there was a great strength in its grip.

"You look kind," he went on, peering into my face.

"Thank you," I said, swallowing anxiously. He still held on to my hand, but apart from that there was something about him that bothered me—more than his looks, and I did not know what it was. Perhaps I was afraid of him.

But then he smiled. I looked into his eyes, large, light blue and candid as a child's. My fear ebbed. Sympathy flowed between us, as if we had always known each other. I smiled back at him.

He continued, "I like you. May I sit beside you at dinner?"

"Why, yes—if you wish to," I replied hesitantly, a little surprised by the ingenuousness of the question.

"You will sit in your usual place, Robert. Barbara, as mistress of High Place, will sit opposite me. Run along and tell Mother we are on our way."

Adam's hand had come to rest on my shoulder with detaining zeal. I stared up at him, puzzled by what he had said and the autocratic way in which he had said it.

Robert, however, made no demur. He scuttled out of the room rather like a crab, and with more speed than might have been expected of him.

"Thank you," Adam said.

"For what?"

"For not rebuffing Robert. It would have been understandable if you had ignored him; it's what most people do. They are frightened by his appearance and either try to pretend he is not there or make fun of him."

"I couldn't do that," I cried, knowing only too well the suffering being made fun of could create.

"No. You have too tender a heart." His eyes locked on mine.

My too tender heart, my stupid, easily coerced heart, began jumping and bounding, knocking itself against my ribs in wild abandon beneath his appreciative gaze.

He was continuing, "I thought at first you were going to be just like all the rest."

"I was taken by surprise. You should have told me about him, warned me what to expect," I said.

"I didn't know how to. What could I say? I have a brother whose head is too big for his body, who has one leg shorter than the other, and the sight of him will frighten you out of your wits? I kept putting it off and putting it off, till it got too late."

"I wish you had prepared me. I admit I was shocked when I saw him, but then he was so friendly and . . ."

"But he isn't normal, you realize that?"

I had been aware of something about him, something I could not put a name to, and I realized what it was.

"I thought he seemed a little—childish."

"Exactly. That's what he is, a child. He has the years and shape of a man, but his brain did not grow with him. He can comprehend nothing beyond a seven-year-old's grasp. That, added to his strange appearance, antagonizes people . . . makes them feel afraid."

"But he's not dangerous, is he?"

"No, but he's different, and that is enough to make people fear him."

I had feared him in those first few moments of meeting him. But I had soon discovered there was nothing to fear. Others must discover it also. I asked Adam if this was not so.

"Yes, and that is when they start to make fun of him."

"How cruel! They should treat him, respond to him on his own terms. Does he realize people make fun of him?"

"I'm not sure. I don't think so."

"Is he aware that anything is wrong with him?"

"No. I believe he is quite happy."

"Then, surely, that is all that matters. So long as he is happy and unaware of his misfortune, we . . . I mean . . . you and . . ." I was beginning to falter under the calculating light that appeared in his eyes, ". . . and others . . . must do the suffering for him. If you see what I mean."

"You are a remarkable woman," Adam said softly.

Then his hand was under my elbow and he was escorting me in to dinner.

I said, remembering something he had mentioned earlier, "You said that I was now mistress of High Place and should sit opposite you at table, but, surely, your mother and father . . ."

"I am master of High Place." He cut me short. "My father is dead. He died before I left for England."

I swallowed this piece of information in further bewilderment. Why had he not told me his father was dead? During all those talks we had had on the *Indies Pride* he had not mentioned the fact. That he fully intended to continue to look upon his adoptive parents as his mother and father and to call them that, I had soon discovered. That he hated the thought and very mention of his real mother, Aunt Martha, had been made equally plain. Yet not once had he mentioned that his father was dead. Just as he had never mentioned Robert—or Araminta. Even if he had withheld Robert's afflictions from me, he could at least have mentioned him.

How strange, I thought now, and shivered. It betokened a secretiveness about my husband's nature I had not suspected. It alarmed me.

Then I thought: Robert! Robert was Joseph Pengarth's son. He, Robert, was master of High Place, not Adam. I would have confronted Adam with this if we had not reached the dining room and three pairs of eyes had not fixed themselves on me, filling me with anxiety.

Chapter Five

I knew Morvah Pengarth could not have been more than two or three years older than my aunt—and she had been forty-nine when she had died; yet Morvah Pengarth looked ancient. I stared in astonishment at her brown, dried, shriveled face, almost as dark as those of the slaves around us.

It must all be due to the sun, I guessed, and made a mental vow never to venture outside without a parasol to protect me. I did not wish to end up with a skin like hers.

She averted her eyes as she greeted me, almost as if she were afraid of me. I decided it was because she felt shy at meeting me, as I felt shy at meeting her. I tried to conquer my own shyness and smiled warmly at her. If I had thought, I would have realized that it should have been she, a lady twice my age, in her own home, at far greater advantage than I, who should have been trying to set me at ease, instead of the other way round.

Jem Harding, Adam's right-hand man, was big and strong. He was not handsome in the arresting way that Adam was, but his brown weathered face was not unpleasing. "You're a damn lucky fellow, Adam," he said. "You've captured an English rose."

He was only being polite. There was nothing of the English rose about me. But it was kindly meant and very pleasant to my ears. I smiled gratefully at him.

Robert smiled at me, but remained silent. In fact, he remained silent throughout the entire meal, though I noticed he listened intently to all that was said, his eyes swiveling from one to the other, and when, on occasion, they fell on me, I was surprised at the shrewdness in their depths. I found myself wondering if his intelligence was as limited as the others believed.

"How strange and how fortunate that you and your cousin should fall in love so soon after meeting," Jem Harding observed, I did not know whether to me or to Adam, but I saw Robert's eyes swing back and forth from one end of the table to the other with the rapidity of a bird in flight. "I suppose it was love at first sight?"

"You could say that," Adam returned without a blink, while I blushed and lowered my gaze to my plate and kept it there.

How strange and how fortunate. What strange words Jem had used. What, exactly, had he meant by them? I was looking for an underlying, mysterious reason. I did not know why. I only felt there was one. Was he aware of the circumstances behind our marriage? He could not be. No one in Almada knew. Unless Adam had told them—and I did not think he had, or would.

"You must have been surprised to find you had an unknown cousin so far away on the other side of the world." Jem definitely addressed himself to me.

I raised my head, nodded, and lowered it again. I wished he would change the subject. It was setting off all sorts of upsetting emotions in me.

"As surprised as we were to hear he had brought a wife back from England with him. He had written to tell us he was bringing back a fortune, but never a word about a wife. However, we forgive him, do we not, Mrs. Pengarth, for it is a very pleasant surprise."

Morvah Pengarth's eyes, small in their deep sockets, flashed across the table at him. I did not attempt to interpret their message.

"Perhaps he had not found one when he wrote the letter," I said sharply, and returned Adam's frowning glance with a steady eye.

If he understood the reason for my sharpness I was glad. He would know I was no fool. I was starkly aware that he must have written to them before he even proposed to me, sure of what my answer would be, and I was angry. Angry.

Jem laughed, believing I had made a joke. "Adam's always been one for springing surprises on us, eh, Adam?"

He grinned at Adam, jocular himself, yet beneath his easy manner I fancied I detected censure. Perhaps he did not care for Adam's surprises. My eyes rested on him, wholly in sympathy with him.

The meal over, Morvah and I left the men to their port and cigars. At the foot of the stairs Morvah excused herself and left me to enter the drawing room alone. I noted the fact that it was a beautiful room, with many paintings adorning the walls. In pride of place above the mantel hung a portrait of a pretty young woman seated in a wicker chair, the white pillars and verandas of High Place with their twining vines as a background. A small boy played at her feet. Adam. There could not be two pairs of eyes of so piercing a blue. So the pretty lady must be Morvah Pengarth.

I let my gaze rest on her again. How she had changed. The delicate porcelain complexion beneath the shady hat gave no hint of the brown decay that was to come.

I wondered why Robert was not in the picture. Had he been too young? Then I realized she would not have wanted him in the picture. She would not have wanted his likeness captured for posterity.

I swung round as the door opened. Adam entered. He walked up to me, looked at the portrait. "My mother," he said, with no reservations.

And why should there have been? Morvah Pengarth had more right to the title than Aunt Martha.

We both gazed in silence at the portrait. Then I asked, "Is there a portrait of Mr. Pengarth?"

He looked at me angrily. "My father, you mean? No. He was a very active man. His nature would not allow him to sit still long enough for a portrait to be made."

"What a pity," I said. "I should have liked to see what he looked like."

His anger left his face. He visibly relaxed. "He was very good looking. Tall and dark. He always used to say he was taller than the average Cornishman. He seemed proud of it. He was very clever, too. Not only did he help to build High Place, he designed it. He laid out the gardens. You will see he had an artist's eye. I may have been sold to a poor man. I was not sold to an ignorant one."

I thought he had every right to the bitterness that crept into his voice toward the end.

"How old were you when you first came to Almada?" I asked.

"About a year and a half, I believe. I don't remember it."

"No, of course not," I murmured, my heart beginning to hammer.

When he smiled at me like that, with his eyes as well as his lips, my heart always began to hammer, threatening to topple my carefully built barricade.

"I'll show you round tomorrow. My land is extensive and incorporates some of the island's most beautiful scenery."

"I shall look forward to it," I said shyly.

The old comradeship was developing between us again. At least, it would if I gave it a chance. I vowed I would. Friendship with Adam was better than nothing and would be needed if my life were to be tolerable while I remained in Almada.

The beautiful Bella glided in bearing coffee on a silver tray. She set it down upon a highly polished table and began to pour. I watched her, surprised. The pouring of coffee should surely have devolved on me.

"Cream, Mistress Barbara?" Opaque eyes that gave nothing away flickered briefly over me.

"Please," I said, experiencing an odd twinge of fear as I saw her long chocolate fingers curl around the cream jug.

"Sugar?"

I nodded, with a swallow.

I watched her add sticky brown sugar and bring the cup to me. Then she poured a cup for Adam. She did not need to ask if he took cream and sugar. She knew, and added the appropriate amount. She handed it to him, looking boldly into his face, then she inclined her head in the merest of bows and departed.

I was glad to see her go.

Adam stretched his long legs out in front of him in the manner so characteristic of him, and sipped his coffee.

After a few moments, I asked, "Is no one else joining us?"

He shook his head. "My mother has retired for the night. Robert has gone swimming. . . ."

"Swimming? In the dark?"

"He enjoys swimming in the dark. Jem has gone into town."

"Is Jem a relation?" I asked, curious about his status in the household.

"No, though he might well be, having lived with us for the past twenty-odd years. My father took him in as a foundling of about nine or ten, educated him, and when he was old enough, gave him the job of steward, which he still holds."

"Does he know the story of your true parentage?"

"No." Adam turned from me abruptly.

"Oh. Does anyone know—apart from us? I feel I ought to know in case . . ." He spun round to face me again.

"I understand," he said swiftly. "My mother knows, of course."

"And Robert?"

"No, not Robert. It is beyond his understanding."

"I wonder."

"And what does that cryptic remark mean?"

"Well, it struck me more than once this evening that he may be more aware of what goes on than you seem to think."

"I see," he said coldly. "On the strength of one hour's acquaintance with my brother, you consider yourself more capable of assessing the depths of his understanding than we who have known him all his life."

"No . . . I wouldn't presume . . . but I know how easy it is for children to hear things . . . things not meant for their ears." I was remembering how easy I had found it to overhear adult conversations simply by keeping very quiet so that they forgot I was there. "Supposing he has heard something? He's not deaf. Supposing, not understanding the implications, he is indiscreet, and . . ."

"If he were, no one would take any notice of him," Adam broke in. "No one listens to him. As I told you, they like to pretend he doesn't exist."

"Yes, and I think it's cruel. It must hurt him very much."

"I don't think so. He lives very much in a world of his own. Nothing outside bothers him."

"How can you be sure?"

"I'm sure." Adam frowned at me. "Don't go imagining he is less of a simpleton than he is. If you try to treat him in any way other than as a child, you will find yourself up against something. . . ." He broke off.

He rose abruptly and crossed to the open window, which led out onto the veranda. I rose, too, following him, thinking he was going out. I had the feeling he had broken off because he was saying too much, and I wanted to know what it was he had left unsaid.

"What will I find myself up against, Adam?" I asked.

"He can't cope with the adult world," he replied, staring out into the darkness. "He thinks as a child, reasons as a child. It is utterly impossible for him to understand the things we understand. They are beyond his grasp."

"I think he understands more than you give him credit for. Have you ever tried . . . ?"

My tongue ceased at the face he turned on me, dark with anger. "Haven't you listened to a word I've said?"

My mouth was half open, but my tongue remained silent. We were losing our pleasant camaraderie.

"Take note of what I say, Barbara. Do not meddle with things that do not concern you."

Humiliated by that "Do not meddle with things that do not concern you," I could only stare at him miserably.

"Robert's mind is not like other peoples. He's—not always as he was this evening."

A prickle of apprehension ran about the back of my neck.

"Are you warning me against him? I thought you said he was not dangerous."

"I am simply trying to get through to you that he has the mind of a seven-year-old and that to force him beyond his limited understanding makes him ill. Kindly see to it that you do not give me cause to . . ."

"To what?" I asked provokingly. "To beat me?"

"To caution you again," he said with disdain.

His quiet, superior manner galled me. I cried out wildly, "You beat your slaves."

"I do not beat my slaves," he returned in the same quiet manner, but with a flash of anger in his eyes.

"You do. You told me you do."

"Then you were not listening properly. It seems to be a failing of yours. No slave has ever been beaten at High Place in my lifetime."

"I don't believe you."

I could not stop myself. I hardly knew what had got into me. From defense of Robert I had slid into accusation of Adam. I saw his mouth tighten, his eyes fill with bitterness.

"Then it is useless for me to say any more."

Meta was laying out my nightgown, turning down the bedclothes. Did she wonder where Adam's nightshirt was? I sat down disconsolately at my dressing table. Immediately, she was by my side, taking out the pins from my hair, her gleaming white teeth showing in a huge, friendly grin.

"You got lovely hair, Missie Barbry." This was the first time she had used this mode of address. Soon all the slaves were using it. "It shine like gold."

"Nonsense," I said roughly. "It's plain mousy."

She caressed the long tresses with her plump little hands, then let them fall in a soft cloud about my shoulders. "See? Like gold."

"Hidden gold," I groused. "Seen only when the light is right."

I rose irritably. Meta helped me undress. I still felt strange as I watched her black hands unfastening my buttons, removing my clothing. As time went on I got used to it. In fact, as time went on, I got so used to Meta I did not see her as black at all. But, at present, I was extremely conscious of the difference between us.

"Too thick, Missie Barbry. Too thick," Meta crooned, holding up my cambric nightgown.

It, and the others I owned, had not been too thick for England, but here—here anything would be too thick. She slipped it over my head. I blew air out of my mouth and breathed, "Oh, it *is* hot, Meta."

Meta lifted up my nightgown. "You take off. You not need it when Massa Adam come, anyway." A sly, secret smile accompanied her words.

Cheeks scorching, I ordered her sharply to leave me. With her usual swift obedience, she departed, the secret smile still playing about her lips.

I stood where she left me, beside my bed, staring at the door as it closed behind her. *You not need it when Massa Adam come.* Massa Adam would not come. Massa Adam would never come—to me.

With a strangled moan I swung round, and through the window opposite me caught sight of the moon resting on the rim of the sea, busily erecting a silvery ladder across the waves. A myriad stars, silver pinpoints of light, winked knowingly out of a soft, velvety sky. Palm fronds stirred gently in an unfelt breeze. A romantic setting. A romantic island. Made for love and for lovers. In bitter imagination I saw two lovers walking by the water's edge. I saw them turn to each other, merge into one. I saw them sink slowly to the soft sand. Adam and Araminta.

I collapsed into a heap on my bed and wept and wept, and dried my tears, and wept again.

It was hot. My emotional thrashings had so heated me that my body ran with sweat. I plucked at my nightgown sticking to my skin. Take it off, Meta had said. Why not? I was alone. There was no one to care what I did. I threw it off.

I lay on my back and reminisced over the past unusual months of my life. Months that had seen me seesawing between the heights and the depths. Few heights, mostly depths. My first meeting with Adam—Richard, as he had been then. His proposal. The timorous hopes it had evoked. Our marriage. The joyful, delightful—fearful, anticipation of our wedding night. The awful, grinding bitterness of the reality.

I thought about Mr. Parkes, how he had begged me to wait, to allow myself time to become more acquainted with Richard. I thought of how I had laughed scornfully. I was happy, happy, happy, I had cried. That was enough. That was all I needed to know. I wished now I had listened to him.

I remembered the letter he had handed to me on my wedding day. I had put it on one side and forgotten all about it. Where was it now? Had it been packed in my trunk with the rest of my things? It must have been. Aggie would not have left it out. And if it had been packed, it must have been unpacked.

I went to search through the drawers of the little writing desk by the wall and found it tucked among a pile of letters of condolence received at the time of my aunt's death.

I stared down at Aunt Martha's handwriting. Not the usual small, pinched hand I remembered, yet unmistakably hers, though spidery and meandering, as if the hand that held the pen had been too weak to guide it. *Mr. and Mrs. Richard Goodall.*

A strange feeling ran through me as I read the words she had penned. I felt as if she were in the room with me, eyeing me with a cold, disapproving stare.

"Barbara, girl, what are you doing standing about like that? Put some clothes on at once. You ought to be ashamed of yourself."

It sounded so plain. I looked up quickly, expecting to see her there, and encountered my own reflection in the mirror.

I blushed to see my nakedness.

Yet why should I feel ashamed? I was alone. There was

no one to see me. Aunt Martha was *dead.*

A tap came at my door. I swung to face it. "Just a m . . ."

Adam walked in.

There was a frozen moment of time while we stared at each other. Then I started to shiver uncontrollably. I reached frantically for my nightgown still lying on the floor beside the bed where it had landed when I threw it off and clutched it to me, pulling it close to hide from him what he had already so plainly seen.

Why had he come? What did he want? What did any man want who came to a woman's room late at night? To make love to her. Had Adam come to make love to me? It was a foolish hope, but I prayed it was so. It would be different from our wedding night. This time he had come because he wanted to, not because he felt he had to. I thought he made a slight movement toward me and my whole body tingled with desire. Had he been roused by the sight of my naked body? Did he wish to thrust aside my nightgown as I wished him to do? Could he see how I was longing for his caresses? Oh, Adam, Adam, take me in your arms and love me!

It was a silent cry, but I felt he must have heard it, and in sudden shyness I stared down at my feet, waiting, glorying in my unashamed desire.

Then I heard the door close. When I looked up, Adam had gone.

I slept late and woke with a headache. Meta brought me grapefruit drenched in golden sugar and cinnamon, coffee, and foamy scrambled egg. I thought I would not be able to eat any of it. I ate the lot and felt better for it—able to cope with the task ahead of me.

I made my way to Adam's office, knocked, and entered.

"Good morning, Adam." (How steady my voice was.) "Can you spare me a few minutes of your time, please?"

He rose at once and drew out a chair for me. "Certainly. What is it?"

I held out Aunt Martha's letter. "It's this. Mr. Parkes gave it to me—on our wedding day. It's addressed to both of us."

Adam frowned, puzzled. "Both of us?"

"I should have mentioned it sooner, only—I forgot all about it."

"Forgot!"

I prepared myself for the sarcastic comment I expected to follow, but all he said was, with a little incredulous shake of his head, "What does it say?"

"I don't know. I haven't opened it yet. As it's addressed to both of us, I thought we should read it together."

"Who is it from?"

"Aunt Martha."

His face darkened. "I have no wish to read any letter penned by her," he ground out angrily.

"But you must—we must—it may be important."

"A letter from a dead woman?" The sneer curling his lip marred his handsome looks. "I hardly think so."

My eyes fell. I looked at the letter between my hands. What should I do? He hated Aunt Martha so much, perhaps it would be better if I took the letter away and read it by myself. Though if the truth were known, I was no more eager to learn the contents than he. But it had to be read. Duty demanded it.

About to rise and excuse myself, I heard him say, "Oh, very well. Read it, if you must—out loud. I'll listen."

I tore the letter open and began to read.

"'My dears, if you are reading this letter, it means only one thing, that you are married. Why did you marry? For love? I wonder. I have no doubt, Barbara, that with your romantic notions, you did. But what about you, Richard? Did you fall in love with my mousy little niece, or with my money?

"'I suspect it was the latter. Barbara's face is not her fortune. A sterling character, a loving and steadfast heart count for nothing beside a pretty face—that, and riches. So was it the riches, Richard?

"'Yes, it must have been. You would not be reading this letter if you had not married in haste, thereby proving the mercenary motive behind it. I spit on you, Richard—my son—I had hoped better of you."

My voice was shaking. My hands were shaking. *I* was shaking. I looked at Adam. He stared back at me out of hard, unreadable eyes.

"'My poor Barbara. So trusting. So foolish. Did you learn nothing from me? I tried so hard to warn you. Why did you not wait, give yourself time to get to know Richard, for Richard to get to know you? I gave you the chance you would never have in the normal way of things. You and Richard, I thought, the two beings I love most in the world, given time, might come together in love. But time was needed, and time had to be made to keep Richard in England long enough for him to see your true worth.

"'Mr. Parkes has instructions to give you this letter only if you marry before the month's grace I set is up. If you have listened to him, this letter will be destroyed. If, however, you are reading this letter, you will have disregarded his advice and will not have been told that which I will tell you now.

"'The condition laid down in my will is valid for one month only. If that condition is not met, a codicil will come into effect. In it everything I die possessed of, after earlier bequests are granted, is to be shared between you both, excepting Martha's Cottage, which is yours alone, Barbara.

"I hope you never read this letter, but if you do, I beg you, Richard, to take care of my little Barbara, give her affection if you cannot give her love. She will repay it ten thousandfold. Unfortunately, remembering your father, I fear . . .'"

"That's enough. I don't want to hear any more."

I raised my eyes to Adam's face. It was livid.

"She said all the money would go to charity. She gave no hint of anything else," he said.

"She did," I ventured, with the knowledge of hindsight. "A slight one, if we had but listened more carefully to the wording of the will. She gave us a month's grace in which to make up our minds. Why do that for no reason? And Mr. Parkes hinted. He tried to persuade me to wait. . . ."

Adam was hardly listening. "My God!" he bit out, "I've been tricked. We needn't have married."

I was suddenly suffused with anger. He thought of nothing but himself, how it affected him. He was cold, selfish, calculating. If I had waited the month, I might have seen it. Oh, Aunt Martha was wise, and I was so foolish.

"At least you were only tricked once," I lashed out at

him. "I was tricked twice."

"What do you mean?" he demanded.

"I was tricked into believing you cared about me."

"I did. I . . ."

I turned away from him. "Oh, don't pretend anymore, Adam, please. Grant me some intelligence. You wanted Aunt Martha's money and intended to have it, even if it meant taking me with it. You never cared for me. I knew it, deep inside me, but your words were fair, and you seemed kind—you said you liked me, cared about me. . . . You should have been honest with me. I would have married you . . . only you had to wrap it all up in lies and now—there's nothing. . . ."

"I didn't lie to you, Barbara," Adam protested.

"No," I had to admit, "not exactly. You just led me on to believe what I wanted to believe, and left me to find out the truth the hard way."

"Barbara, listen to me. I must tell you something. . . ."

He began to walk round the desk toward me. I stopped him with a sneer.

"Listen? To you? Have I not listened enough already to a man to whom money and possessions mean more than human beings? Why, even Robert . . ."

"Robert? What has Robert to do with this?" His eyes narrowed suspiciously.

"He is master of High Place," I flung at him gladly. "Joseph Pengarth was his father, not yours."

"I am master of High Place." Adam's narrowed eyes glittered dangerously. "I am the oldest son. . . ."

"No, you're not. You may have thought so once, but since Aunt Martha's revelations . . ."

"Whatever that woman has said or done alters not one whit the situation here. Our marriage was contrived, but you are my wife, whether you like it or not, and as such, will say and do nothing that might jeopardize my position here. Give me your word on it."

I stared belligerently into his hard, cold eyes, longing to defy him, but to my shame, before that penetrating blue gaze, my eyes fell and I gave him my word.

Chapter Six

I was Adam's wife, but he never came to my room. I was his wife in name only. He had said once, oh, it seemed so long ago, that we would get on famously together, and for a while it had seemed, in spite of everything, that we could. A kind of companionship had sprung up between us—an uneasy companionship, it was true, but companionship, nevertheless. Now that was gone, destroyed by Aunt Martha's letter.

I was alone and friendless in an alien world. Why had I come? Had I thought things would be any different for me here? They were not. I had thought marriage would make things different—me, different. It had not. I had thought I would find romance, excitement, adventure, given the chance. Well, I had been given the chance, and things were just the same.

I had entered into a marriage of convenience where no love existed, and I was paying the price. I had allowed myself to hope, to dream, that where liking was love could grow. I knew better now. The truth had been revealed to me on my wedding night. I should not have forgotten it.

I hated Aunt Martha. Why could she not have left well enough alone? Why could she not have left Martha's Cottage to me and her money to Richard without conditions? Why had I accepted Richard's proposal of marriage? What a fool I had been. I should have refused him and we could have gone our separate ways. But he had been so persuasive, had overcome my doubts. He had not said he loved me, but he had said he liked me and asked if I could like him, too. His blue eyes had looked straight into mine. He had seemed sincere. He had fooled me into believing love would grow.

No! I had fooled myself. I had continued to fool myself. Even after my awful wedding night I had kept on hoping and dreaming, praying that in the fullness of time all would come right. And then Richard became Adam and I found out he was in love with Araminta. . . .

Oh, why had I not listened to Aunt Martha's cautionary tales? She had warned me not to expect more from life than my share of looks warranted. She had told me I should never be able to attract a man. "Become reconciled," she had said, "to your spinsterhood."

I hated Aunt Martha.

I hated Adam.

I hated myself.

My days dragged. Adam, when he was not cooped up in his office, was always out. If our paths crossed it was a stiff bow and a curtsey, and relief when we had passed. I wandered about the house, lonely and bored. If only I could have the running of the house like I did at Aunt Martha's. Why not? I was mistress of High Place, I should have some say in the running of it.

I approached Morvah Pengarth.

"I have nothing to do," I said, "and feel I may be of some use to you in running the house—if you do not object."

"Why should I object?" she said. "You are mistress here now. But speak to Bella about it. She is the housekeeper."

I spoke to Bella.

She said, "You are the master's lady. Master's lady's business is to tend her husband's wishes, make herself beautiful for him, be there when he wants her, not concern herself with house business."

I glanced at her sharply. She must know, the whole household must know, that Adam and I did not share the same room. The master bedroom, overlooking the front of the house with its vistas of lawns and gardens, sea and mountain, was still occupied by Morvah Pengarth—and she showed as few signs of wishing to vacate it as Adam did of wishing to occupy it.

"I wish to make myself useful," I said, attempting to assert my authority and not be cowed by this beautiful, self-possessed woman, who appeared to have been given a great deal of license, considering she was a slave.

Taken aback by the trend of my thoughts, I hesitated, but, as she stared back at me out of insolent black eyes, I continued imperiously, "I will start on the menus. Report to me every morning at—nine o'clock. . . ."

"There is not need, Mistress Barbara, to concern yourself with such matters," Bella stressed again. "Master Adam is satisfied with my services, as was Master Joseph before him. The mistress—Mistress Morvah—never interferes. Is there anything else?"

I was speechless. She had effectively told me I had no status in this household, no say in the running of it. I was to be what I had never thought to be, an ornament—a useless ornament, of no service to anyone, least of all to Adam, who rejected me. And what, exactly, were her services to him?

Bella dipped her head and took herself off, a veiled, secret smile playing about her eyes.

Robert Pengarth, after his initial friendly overtures, became strangely remote with me. I cannot say I was not glad of this. Being so full of my own troubles, I felt I could not cope with a fully grown man who was yet a child.

I used to come upon him lolling in a chair, turning the pages of a book or scribbling with charcoal upon paper. He would look up, his grotesquely overgrown head on one side, and survey me out of round blue eyes, then without comment return to whatever his occupation was, for all the world as if I had not put in an appearance. Or I would meet him in a room or corridor, veranda or garden, and he would sheer away from me as if I constituted a threat of some kind.

Of course, I spoke to him. I wished him good morning and asked him how he was, but never a word did I receive from him in return, which, considering how friendly he had been when we had first met, seemed strange, to say the least. It was as if he took his cue from Adam, who hardly ever spoke to me these days, even at mealtimes. I knew Robert watched and listened. His eyes darted restlessly from one face to another. He made me feel uncomfortable. I could not get used to it.

I was thankful for Jem Harding's presence in the house. I did not see a great deal of him, but when we did meet he was affable. I was grateful for his attendance at the dinner table. Without his constant stream of chatter mealtimes would have been burdensome indeed. He must have noticed that relations between Adam and myself were very strained, since almost every word we spoke to each other rang with hurt or censure, but he gave no sign that he did.

I settled into a routine. I breakfasted in bed listening lazily to Meta's chatter while she prepared my bath. It was a beautiful bath, shaped like a shell and painted the palest pink, with a geometric pattern running all the way round the thick rim picked out in gold leaf. The inside gleamed like mother-of-pearl.

Slaves would cart huge jugs of water, some steaming hot, some cold, up the stairs and wait outside my bedroom door till Meta allowed them to enter and deposit their burdens on the floor beside the bath. Then they would leave and Meta would fill the bath. I was amazed that so diminutive a creature should lift such huge vessels, but when I made a demur she cried cheerfully, "My job, Missie Barbry, my job."

So then I would bathe. In the beginning I tried to send Meta out of the room, for I still felt shy about undressing in her presence, but she sang, "I not look, missie," obviously aware of how I felt and not blaming me for it. "I make bed, tidy room, bring you big towel when you ready."

Meta was my slave, but she ruled me.

Afterwards I would go downstairs. Adam was always out by this time—or in his office. Morvah Pengarth and her son, Robert, avoided me with consummate ease. Robert's avoidance of me I did not question overmuch. He was—strange; but Morvah . . . she had taken an aversion to me from the start, and nothing I did or said enabled me to breach her reserve.

The house-slaves would be about their varied tasks, dusting, sweeping, polishing, singing while they worked. I found it hard to remember they were slaves, they seemed so cheerful and happy, and I would think about the poor, wretched souls, the black column of men, I had seen on the quayside in Seatown, remember the man's cry of pain as the whip lashed his back, the eerie silence afterwards. There had been no happiness there, only hatred and sullen resentment.

My thoughts would carry me on to Sarah and Philip Rose. They had become my friends, the only friends I had ever had of my own age. I wondered if I would ever see them again. Surely it should be possible. I could invite them to dinner at High Place. Would Adam agree? I should have to ask him. I would ask him—sometime.

The interior of the house was kept as cool as possible by doors and windows that were always open to capture any breeze there might be, and gleaming white blinds that were drawn against the scorching noonday sun. There were flies and insects everywhere and I was bitten frequently at first, but must have developed a quick immunity, for they soon ceased to bother me, and I could relax on the veranda fearlessly.

I was always drawn outside in the mornings. In the afternoons it got much too hot. There was nothing to do then, but rest. The slightest movement caused discomfort and the sweat poured off one like a stream. But early in the morning it was different, like a hot summer's day back in England—only you knew it was not England when you saw the palms reaching up into the dazzling blue sky and the brown-skinned men and women padding about.

The gardens blazed with a brilliance unseen outside

the tropics. I was fascinated by the rich colors and shapes of the strange flowers, the glaucous leaves, and the birds, which vied with the plants for color. In their vivid blues and greens, reds and yellows, pinks and purples, they cavorted through the trees pecking at insects, which, in their turn, were as vividly and ornately attired. It was a fantasy world I entered each time I descended the white marble steps leading from the house.

Then there was the music room, with its blue-silk-covered walls and furniture, soothing and restful. The big, shiny black pianoforte drew me like a magnet. It was a fine instrument, perfectly tuned. It afforded me much delight and solace. I spent a great deal of my time there shut away from everybody.

On the first occasion that I opened the piano and slid my fingers over the keys Robert stuck his head through the door, only to veer away with his quick shuffling gait the moment I looked up and smiled. Moments later Morvah hovered in the doorway. I stopped playing. My heart started to flutter. Would she come in? Would she speak? Did she like music? She made a vague gesture with her hand, which could have meant continue or desist, and departed.

She left the door open. With a sigh I went to close it. I sat down to play again. I had played about half a dozen bars when the door was flung open and Adam entered.

"Oh, it's you, Barbara," he said. "I heard the music. I couldn't think who it was. No one but my father ever—I didn't know you played."

"Oh, yes," I said, my hands, lying on my lap, clasping and unclasping themselves nervously as I tried to control my fast-beating heart. "Aunt Martha insisted I have music lessons. I objected to spending so much time practicing, but she said, 'Practice makes perfect,' and turned a deaf ear to my pleas to be excused."

I had mentioned Aunt Martha. I saw the muscles of his face tighten. I did not care. I waited for him to go. He just gazed at me. I wondered if he expected me to resume my playing.

"I hope you do not mind my playing the piano," I said.

"Mind?" he whipped back. "Why should I mind?"

"I should not wish to disturb anybody."

"Who is there to disturb?"

"So you don't object . . . ?"

"Why should I object?"

"I don't know. It's just that . . ." If only he would give me a plain yes or no and not answer my questions with questions of his own.

"This is your home, Barbara," he said. "You must do as you like in it."

"I don't feel it is my home," I blurted out unintentionally, goaded by anxiety.

"I'm sorry. I can't help that."

"No, and you don't care," I cried defiantly.

He frowned. His lips tightened. I rushed on, guided by stupidity.

"You don't want me here, I know that. You've made it very plain."

"If I didn't want you here, why do you think I brought you?" he asked.

"I thought it was because you felt sorry for me . . . I know better now."

He heaved a great sigh. "We might have got on tolerably well together if that woman had not spoiled everything."

I played my heart out when he left.

The music room became my haven. I was left alone—though I often had the feeling someone was listening outside the door. Then one day Adam came in again.

"Don't stop," he said, as I immediately raised my hands from the keys. "Bach, isn't it? A delightful piece."

Though disconcerted by his gaze, my fingers did not falter. I had been taught by a master who brooked no nonsense, allowed no nerves. The notes filled the air, pure, sparkling, crystal clear. They were still there, lighting up the room, when I had finished.

Adam and I looked at each other, probably for no more than a few seconds, yet an age seemed to pass before he said, "That was beautiful, Barbara. Thank you."

Then I lowered my eyes, disturbed by the intensity of his gaze. I was glad he was here, yet, paradoxically, I wished he would go.

"Barbara." Adam's voice was tense.

I raised my eyes questioningly.

"We can't go on like this. We were getting on so well together before that woman . . . her letter . . . couldn't we try again? This is no way for an intelligent couple to behave, hardly speaking to each other. Let's try to be friends."

Friends! My heart reacted painfully. Friends! Not husband and wife. But friends was better than nothing. Fighting to keep my voice cool, I said, "Yes, let's be friends."

At once the grim visage I had grown accustomed to seeing disappeared and I looked once more upon the man with whom I had shared many happy hours on board the *Indies Pride* on our voyage over the seas from England. If friendship could bring such a change in him, then with friendship I would be content and not expect anything more.

I felt much lighter myself and ran my fingers up and down the piano keys in a joyful little coda.

Adam and I sat on the veranda drinking cool lemonade. We were getting on so well together I felt I could speak to him about Philip and Sarah Rose.

"Adam . . ."

"Yes?" He turned a smiling face to me.

"I have been thinking about the Roses." Adam stopped smiling. "It's—it's been a long time since we saw them. Do you think we might invite them over to High Place sometime? I should so love to see them again. Sarah and I became great friends on the voyage over."

Adam did not reply at once. I went on, "Do you happen to know where they are living? Have you heard anything about them?" I imagined he must have done, he was out such a lot. He went into Seatown often. Perhaps he had already seen them, had had converse with them. If he had and had not told me about it, it was not to be wondered at—we had hardly been on speaking terms till recently.

"I—have seen Philip," he said hesitantly.

"I thought you might have," I said crisply, meriting a sharp glance from his penetrating eyes, but I smiled placatingly. "How is he . . . and Sarah?"

"They are both well," he said.

I thought he looked uncomfortable and had the feeling he would rather not be discussing them. But I was eager for news of them.

"And the hospital, have they done anything about it yet?"

Again Adam hesitated. "They—have run up against trouble."

"What sort of trouble?" I asked quickly, alarmed.

"The sort of trouble I told him to expect if he attempted to put his ideas into practice."

"You mean the planters are against him?"

He did not reply, but I had my answer. He looked extremely angry—whether with the planters or the Roses, or me, I could not decide.

A slight noise and movement caught our attention. Half hidden by one of the pillars flanking the steps up to the house Robert was watching us. I just had time to glimpse his face, set, frowning, angry-eyed, before he disappeared from view.

"Robert, what are you doing there?" Adam called, as if addressing a naughty schoolboy. "What do you want?"

Robert's face appeared again, his eyes with their usual vacancy, his grin wide and meaningless. "Minty, Minty," he began chanting, shuffling his feet backwards and forwards in a strange lolloping kind of dance. "Minty. Minty."

Adam rose. "Minty?"

I noticed the eager tone in his voice.

"Good morning."

Araminta's voice reached us as she came into view riding a gleaming chestnut mare, astride—like a man. I watched, astonished, as she jumped down unaided and ran up the steps toward us. She was dressed like a man in a white silk shirt, open at the neck, showing off her slender throat, and fawn trousers and shining boots. Yet she did not look mannish. On the contrary, she looked more feminine than ever. Her golden tresses were hidden by a scarf tied over a floppy hat that protected her complexion from the sun.

"I'm angry with you," she purred, placing her hands in Adam's as he moved toward her, arms outstretched in greeting. She was tall, taller than I had expected, yet she had to stand on tiptoe to kiss his cheek. "It is three weeks now since your return and you have not called on me."

This bit of news, so contrary to what I had imagined to be the case, delighted me.

"I've had a lot of work to catch up on," Adam said.

"Nonsense. I'm sure Jem has kept things running smoothly. And work never stopped you before from coming to see me."

I rose. She caught sight of me.

"But of course," she cooed, "you are married now. I suppose we must expect there to be changes. But you must not keep him to yourself all the time, Mrs. Pengarth." She stood by Adam's side, her arm through his. "You must allow his friends to see something of him. After all, the honeymoon's over. . . ." Her tinkling laugh echoed round the veranda. "Isn't it?"

I felt the color in my cheeks deepen and I turned slightly aside. I heard her light voice addressing Adam.

"I have arranged a dinner party. I told you I would. Just a few old friends all anxious to meet your new wife . . . And to see you, of course. You have been greatly missed."

I wondered if anyone else noticed the slight change of tone, the meaning behind those last few words. Of course, Adam must have.

"Now I will not take no for an answer, Adam. It is all

arranged for next week." Minty's voice grew light again.

"Well, thank you, Minty. It will be good to meet all my friends again. I have neglected them . . . what do you say, Barbara?" He remembered just in time to consult my wishes. "Shall we accept Minty's kind invitation?"

It was all for show. He would go anyway, whether I agreed or not. But why should I not agree? It would be fun to go out and meet new people.

"Thank you, Araminta," I said. "We should love to come."

It gave me a peculiar thrill to include Adam in my acceptance.

"Good. That's settled." Araminta's full attention was on Adam again. My purpose had been served. "Now you can escort me back to Government House."

"I'm sorry, Minty, I can't." Her face fell a mile. I was certain she had not expected such a rebuff. "But I'm sure Jem will be happy to ride back with you."

The two men, Adam and Jem, went with Araminta. I stared after them unhappily, unwanted. Then I heard a deep-throated, knowing laugh. Robert, forgotten by us all, was lolloping about, his large head bouncing up and down as the laughter rolled out of his mouth.

"A party. A party. Minty's giving a party."

He started chanting again in time to his weird dance routine.

"It's only a small dinner party," I said, hardly knowing why I should feel the need to clarify this fact. "Just a few friends."

I wondered if Robert would be going.

"A party. A party."

Robert's mood changed. He came to stand before me, suddenly conspiratorial.

"Minty's a naughty girl. A naughty, naughty girl. She does naughty things. I've seen her. I've seen him. Both of them. Naughty."

I tried to make sense of his words. "What . . . ?" "Who . . . ?"

But I had already reached a conclusion and it made me gasp.

"I've seen them together. They didn't know. But I know."

Robert's eyes looked into mine and they sent a shudder down my spine. They were not vacant now, but full of knowledge. Knowledge of what?

He danced away again. "I've seen them. I've seen them."

Who? Adam and Araminta? How? They were in love, had they . . . ? I tried to stop myself thinking it. They wouldn't. They couldn't. Adam was a gentleman. Araminta was a lady. They wouldn't. . . .

Robert was grinning at me—mischievously. He was a mischievous child, making up stories to alarm the adults. He had, after all, the mind of a child. I must not forget that. I watched him lollop away into the house. The mind of a child. But an evil child? To believe he was deliberately sowing seeds of mistrust was tantamount to branding him as evil.

Oh, *I* was evil for thinking such things! Robert might be nearly six feet tall, but I must remember he was a child at heart, and children were not evil.

But what was it Robert had seen? And *had* he seen it? I could not stop myself going over his words and trying to find meaning in them. At last, I decided to put them out of my mind. Even if Robert's words were true I would not dwell on them. And they were not. They could not be.

Robert had not known what he had been saying. He was a child, making up stories.

Why is it, that when we reason out a course of action for ourselves, we are so reluctant to follow our own advice? Of course, I continued to dress up Robert's words. Of course, I continued to visualize Araminta in Adam's arms. Of course, I rent myself in two over it. And, of course, it put our renewed friendship in jeopardy.

"Why are you so prickly with me?" Adam confronted me at last.

"Prickly? Me? I'm not prickly."

"Indeed you are. I hardly have to say a word to you and you rear and kick like a stung mule. What's happened? I thought we were friends. We were getting along so nicely."

"That was before . . ." I broke off quickly.

"Before what?" His angry scowl disturbed me.

"Oh, nothing."

"I know things are not quite as you would like them to be . . . they are not as I would like them to be, either, but you could at least try to make the best of it—as I do."

"What is the matter with you two?" Morvah Pengarth entered the room. "You can be heard all the way down the hall."

Looking from one to the other of us, she waited for an explanation. Adam glared at her, then at me, then he swung away. "Nothing," he muttered, and slammed the door behind him.

Morvah turned on me.

"Why did you marry him, if you didn't love him?"

"I . . . I . . ." Her attack left me bereft of speech.

"I thought at first it was just shyness with you, that

standoffish air, but I can close my eyes no longer to the truth. You are a cold fish, Barbara, and you are making my son's life a misery."

"No . . ."

"You haven't given him a moment's happiness since you came here. Not only are you frigid, you have a tongue like a whiplash." She turned from me with a look of distaste. "He deserved better."

I went out into the garden and walked down to the sea. I was mortified that Morvah Pengarth should blame me for something that was not my fault. It appeared Adam had not thought to enlighten her as to the true nature of our marriage, and from what she observed of our relationship Morvah had concluded it was I who was in the wrong. She knew, the whole household knew Adam and I did not sleep together. But they did not know why. Did everyone lay the blame at my door?

The lacy waves lapped the shore. The hot sand burned through the soles of my fine kid slippers. Without my parasol to shade me, the full power of the blazing sun hit my head and shoulders. For a while I hardly noticed, bitterly reviewing my situation, but inevitably the moment came when I could ignore the heat no longer.

I headed for the shelter of the palms fringing the sand and sat down, resting my back against the twisted trunk of a tree that nature had caused to grow in an arc curving toward the sea, so that its great fronds trailed in the sand and almost into the water. I gazed across the golden sand to the turquoise sea. A ship, sails gleaming white, appeared motionless on the purple horizon. But it was going somewhere. Where? Was it bound for England?

England. If only I were back in England, in Martha's

Cottage, pale skies, pale flowers, lovely gentle rolling hills, little brown birds—sparrows . . . I fell asleep.

I awoke with a start.

The sun was obscured by great black clouds. A wild wind was tearing at the palm fronds, whipping white horses from the sea. Sitting in the curve of the tree I had been sheltered from the wind—now I jumped up and the wind almost lifted me off my feet. I had to grab hold of the trunk to remain on terra firma.

It started to rain, not gently, gradually, as it would have done in England, but in a sudden solid sheet, almost as strong as the wind itself in its power to knock one off one's feet. Terrified, I heard the thunder rumble and groan all around me, saw the lightning cut like silver knives through the darkening sky, showing everything as bright as day.

And I saw a man, on top of a high rock, dressed all in gray in the Spanish style, with a flat-topped broad-brimmed hat and tight-fitting jacket and trousers, astride a massive gray.

I waited for the next lightning flash, eager to attract his attention, his help. That massive gray would carry the two of us with ease to safety . . . but when the flash came, the man and his horse had gone.

Blinking the rain from my eyes, I stared up into the darkness. More lightning flashes lit the scene. No, he was not there. He had disappeared completely. Had I seen him? Or had I only imagined him? There had been only the briefest space between flashes, yet he had disappeared as completely as if he had never been. Had he been? Or had it been a trick of the light?

I would have remained transfixed waiting for him to reappear had the wind not lifted me off my feet, my hands having relaxed their hold on the tree trunk, and dropped me wet and sprawling yards away, pushing and shoving me into the thick clammy foliage, like some evil demon.

With difficulty I scrambled to my feet, thankful I was not being pushed in the other direction, into the sea, and clung onto some thick-rooted plant growing higher than my waist. I had to get back to High Place. But how? Which way? How far was it? How far had I walked? It could be miles.

Panic rose to my mouth. What would I do if I could not find my way back? With the wind rising as it was, if I were not drowned in the downpour, or struck by lightning, I would be crushed by its mighty power against some rock.

I was scrambling through undergrowth. Some sixth sense told me to make my way back to the beach. If I kept to the beach I stood a chance of finding my way back to High Place. If I continued slopping through this jungle, there was no knowing where I would end up.

Unfortunately, along the beach the wind met no resistance, and I was fair game, to be lifted up and flown for yards, dropped, picked up and transported again. Buffeted forward and sideways, any way the wind's fancy took it, I found myself back among the tangled jungle growth, submerged and on my knees. I was slapped about the face and body by huge wet leaves, yet I remained in place, protected from the wind by tenacious plantlife.

Deciding it was better to stay under their protection, I started battling my way forward, miserable, aching, but determined to reach High Place. I knew I was heading in the right direction, for on my walk the sea had been on my right, and now it was on my left. I would be all right so long as I skirted the beach and did not wander off inland.

I stumbled on, aware that I was weakening, afraid I would not be able to go much longer. The man in gray swept into my mind. If only he had noticed me, rescued me. . . .

But he had been a mirage.

My hair, loosened by the wind, whipped my face, clung in clammy strands round my neck, covered my eyes. I tried to pluck it away, and fell. Sand scratched my face and entered my mouth. The wind screamed with wild laughter in my ears. I had strayed from my path and would pay the penalty. I would die out here on this lonely West Indies beach, or drown in the turbulent ocean, trampled by raging white horses. I had come all the way from England, across the world, to die out here, alone, exhausted, finished.

I was on my knees, my head sunk in my chest, waiting for the wind to summon sufficient strength to raise me from my position and send me flying, willy-nilly, where it would. Let it do its worst. I was resigned.

"Barbara. Barbara."

I raised my head. Someone calling my name? Was this what it was like, then, to die, with someone calling your name?

Well, if I was being called, I must answer.

"Here I am. Here I am!"

But the wind blew the words back in my face.

Chapter Seven

I had reached heaven. I knew it was heaven because it was warm and light. I knew it was light because a rosy glow played on my closed eyelids, making them flicker.

"She's coming round."

I heard a voice I recognized and opened my eyes. I was not dead. I was in my own room and Adam was holding my hands above the sheets on my bed.

His face was dark with anxiety. "Thank God!" he breathed. We thought . . . we were afraid. . . ." A shudder ran through him, transmitting itself to me through his hands. "Why did you . . . ?"

"That's enough, Adam." Morvah was standing by his side. "Questions can wait. She needs rest and sleep now."

"Yes. Yes." He rose quickly. "You must get some sleep. I'll see you in the morning."

Meta brought me a soothing drink. It must have been laced with laudanum, for I slept the whole night through, in spite of my bruised and aching body.

Adam came to see me as promised. His brow, clouded

with concern, cleared as soon as he saw me sitting up and eating breakfast. "You are looking much better," he smiled.

"I am better," I smiled in return. "A few aches and bruises still, but they will soon go away. I shall get up soon."

"No. Not yet. Not until Atkinson has been in to see you."

"Atkinson?"

"Dr. Atkinson. I've sent for him. He shouldn't be long now. Oh, Barbara, whatever made you go out alone, and so far?"

"I don't know," I hedged. "I . . . I got caught in a storm."

"A hurricane, you mean. A minor one, but it could have developed. We might have lost you."

"Who found me?"

"I did. When we discovered you were missing . . ."

"How did you know where I was?"

"I didn't. It was sheer chance that took me to that part of the beach. What were you doing so near to Jutting Rock? So far from home?"

"Jutting Rock?" I said quickly. "Is that the rock that rises above the others and appears to lean out toward the sea?"

"Yes. It is an ancient burial ground—or so people believe. It is riddled with caves, which, I must admit, appear to have been manmade—though they are more likely to have been nature's work."

"I saw a man up there," I said. "A man in gray. He looked like a Spaniard. I thought I must have imagined him, but—now I'm not so sure."

I stared into his face. He liked gray. He wore a lot of

gray. He was dark, like a Spaniard. I shook myself. What fancies were going through my head?

"When was this and what was he doing?" Adam asked.

"Yesterday, while I was out. He was riding a big horse."

"You must have been mistaken. No one would ride atop of Jutting Rock with a hurricane on the way, and in any case, it's considered bad luck to go anywhere near it."

"Why?"

"I don't know. It's just one of those legends that grow." But what were you doing there? You were almost at its foot when I found you."

"I couldn't have been," I cried. "I thought I'd left it far behind."

Our eyes held. A little frown appeared between his. Then he smiled and bent to kiss my forehead with a feather-light touch. "You must have been going round in circles," he said.

I slept heavily again that night. Had they dosed me again with laudanum? But toward morning I woke with a start. I sat up and glanced round the room. What had woken me? Something had. It was dark, but I could see. Nothing appeared untoward. There was no sound—only the dull thud, thud, thud of my heartbeat in my ears.

Perhaps someone had knocked on my door. If they had, they would knock again, or go away. I sank back against my pillows and waited. No sound. Nothing. I slid further down. I must have been dreaming. I closed my eyes, seeking sleep again.

I heard a sound; a shuffling, a dragging. My head jerked up. It seemed to be coming from outside my door. What was it? It sounded as if something—someone . . .

my breath stopped. I heard voices, low-pitched, indistinct. Was someone in distress? Should I go and investigate? One half of me wanted to, the other half did not. But I was mistress of High Place. It was my duty to investigate. I should be ready to give my help.

Still I hesitated. There was more than one person outside. I could hear more than one voice. Therefore, was it necessary for me to go out there? The whispering faded away and the dragging sound with it.

I should have settled down then, but some perversity drew me out of bed and to the door. With my hand on the knob, I listened. I could hear nothing. Whatever, whoever, had been out there was not there now. I opened the door quietly and crossed the passageway—and froze. I saw Adam's retreating figure rounding a corner.

I went back to bed, my mind a tangle of questions. What was Adam doing up, fully dressed, in the middle of the night? Where had he been? Where was he going? Had there been some damage to the property during the storm and had he been summoned to deal with it? Wouldn't that have been Jem's job? What about the dragging sound? Had he had something to do with that? And what had it been? I lay on my pillow with staring eyes, unable to answer myself.

"Is you awake, Missie Barbry?"

A singsong voice penetrated my stupor. I opened my eyes and closed them again quickly as the sunlight streaming across my bed stung them.

"Is you awake, Missie Barbry?"

"Yes, Meta." I struggled up, shading my eyes with my hand. "I'm awake. What time is it?"

"Eleven 'clock, missie. That Bella, she tell me wake you. I say I let you sleep on, you still not well, but she say . . ."

"That's all right, Meta. I am better. I should be getting up."

"If you say so, missie," she said, looking unconvinced. Then she grinned. "I bring you breakfast. Bella, she say, you not want much to eat, but I bring you plenty." She placed the tray before me. "I your maid," she said with firm assurance, "not Bella. Bella housekeeper. She look after High Place. I look after my Missie Barbry."

I ate and bathed and dressed. I sat before my mirror and Meta dressed my hair in the simple style I insisted upon, much to her annoyance.

"Meta," I said.

"Yes, Missie?" Black eyes met mine.

"Was there . . . did you . . . hear some sort of disturbance last night?"

Her eyes flashed and fell. "Disturbance, missie?"

"Yes. I heard a noise in the corridor outside my room . . . in the early hours . . . it wakened me."

"I not hear anything, missie." The black head was bent low over her task, avoiding my eyes in the mirror.

"Are you sure?" I asked sternly.

"I sure, missie."

"Has anyone else mentioned a disturbance? Mrs. Pengarth? Anybody?"

"No, missie." She concentrated very hard on my hair.

"But someone must have heard it." I willed her to look at me, but her eyes remained lowered.

"No, missie. P'raps you dream, missie."

"I was not dreaming," I said tersely. "I was wide awake. I went to the door to look outside."

Black eyes fluttered to meet mine, then away again. She looked—shifty.

"Are you sure you heard nothing?" I demanded, pressing it.

"I hear nothing, Missie Barbry. Nothing."

I did not believe her, but I could not force her to tell me the truth if she did not wish to. To learn what was going on in this house I must seek elsewhere. My conversation with Meta, so innocently begun, had taken a mysterious turn that puzzled me.

So, to whom should I turn for enlightenment? Adam himself? No, that would take too much courage. Morvah? No, she was unapproachable. Jem? Yes, Jem. He would tell me what I wanted to know.

I descended the stairs determined to waylay him the minute I saw him. Bella, crossing the marble-floored hall, looked up at me. "Good morning, Mistress Barbara," she said with the slight inclination of her head that passed for submission with her. If other slaves did not bow low, she was quick to reprimand them, but she got away with much less. It annoyed me. I was against slavery, the animallike submission expected of them, and yet Bella's assumption of airs and graces irked me. I wished to put her in her place.

I made my way to the music room, hating myself. What *was* Bella's place, anyway? I was not sure. She was a slave, but her attitude was that of a freeborn woman. She had been brought up at High Place, been educated, given special privileges. . . . That might account for her supercilious attitude toward the other slaves—but toward me? She was much more deferential to other members of the family than she was toward me. Was it because she knew I was not—not *really*—Adam's wife?

She disliked me, I knew. But, then, I disliked her. Furthermore, I distrusted her.

I sat down at the piano. As usual it soothed me, and my mind leapt as I played, from the troubled present to the past, the days of my childhood, when I had kicked against the lessons Aunt Martha insisted I take. I blessed her for it now. If she had not insisted I would not have had this solace, this balm to my heart.

I remembered Aunt Martha and all she had done for me. I had thought I hated her. I did not. She had rescued me from a life of servitude—I should have been an unpaid servant to my mother if I had remained with her. My mother did not love me; she never had. Aunt Martha had known this and had chosen me, the plain one, to live with her, in preference to my beautiful sister.

I had hated her that day. I had gone on hating her. She had scolded me. I had rebelled. She had scolded me the more. *"You may not like it, but it's for your own good. You'll thank me for it one day."*

I tasted bitterness. That day had not come yet. I did not thank her one little bit for all the scoldings, the deriding comments. I admitted to being grateful to her for providing me with an education, a music master, a dancing master. She, herself, had taught me to think for *my*self. I thanked her for that. She had tried to teach me the quality of acceptance. In this she had failed. I did not accept, would not accept, that things could not be changed if one had the will to change them. One need look no further than William Wilberforce for an example of this. If he, and other like-minded men, had sat back and accepted things as they were, there would have been no antislavery movement. And there were hundreds of similar examples.

But still Aunt Martha reached out from the grave to mold my mind to her way of thinking. The purpose behind her extraordinary will had been to make me see the folly of indulging in romantic dreams. Had she succeeded at last? Yes, I thought she had—though I did not understand her use of such a strange strategy.

My thoughts were interrupted by a loud commotion from outside. I went to see the cause of it and was convulsed with anger. Tommyboy, the elderly slave who had greeted Adam with the unhappy news of Billy Joe's defection and recapture the day I first saw High Place, was facing up to a heavily built man whose back was toward me. As I watched, a hefty blow from a hamlike fist sent Tommyboy sprawling.

The man moved forward to climb the steps into the house and I caught the glimpse of heavy jowls, thick lips, a bulbous nose.

Tommyboy tried to rise, reaching out with an unsteady hand to deter the man from his purpose. "You not go in. Massa, he not here. Massa, he say you not . . ."

The man's back was to me again as his riding crop fell with sudden swiftness across Tommyboy's cheek with a savagery that appalled me, then he kicked the man aside as if he were a sack of potatoes. Tommyboy writhed and shrieked in agony on the hard ground. Blood oozed through the fingers of the hand he held to his cheek, ran down his arm, stained the white ruffles at the neck and wrists of his green livery.

A bevy of black men and women stood around watching it all, making no movement, sullenly silent. Their silence was frightening, but the man appeared unconcerned. He ran up the steps shouting to someone inside the house.

"You. Tell your mistress I want to see her."

But I was racing along the verandah to confront him. "How dare you, sir?" I screamed, almost choking on my rage. "How dare you attack Tommyboy in that brutal manner?"

He halted and turned, astonishment written all over his destestable face. "What the . . . ? Who the devil . . . ?"

I rushed past him. I was half aware of Bella wringing her hands in the doorway, for once seeming unsure of herself. I ran down the steps. The bevy of black-skinned men and women, once all so alike to me, but becoming recognizable now as individual human beings, had imperceptibly closed ranks round Tommyboy, as if to guard him against further attack. They parted to let me through.

I was sickened to my soul by the sight that met my eyes. Tommyboy's right eye appeared to have been gouged clean out of its socket. The whole area was awash with blood.

I felt myself sway. I thought, I'm going to faint. Then I knew I must not. They were all looking to me to deal with the situation. I dragged myself back from the brink of oblivion and gave orders for Tommyboy to be taken indoors, then I told somebody to tell Daniel to go for a doctor.

Nobody moved. I repeated my orders. Bella appeared at my side. "No doctor come for slave," she said. "Do not worry. I will deal with this."

She then ordered two men to lift Tommyboy and carry him into the house. They obeyed at once. I felt snubbed, inadequate. I watched in silence and did nothing, till a loud roar came from behind. "Good God! I don't believe this! A slave ordering a white woman around."

It stung me into action again. "No. I will deal with it. Get Tommyboy to bed. I will send for a doctor I know will come."

Bella drew herself up. She must have been all of six feet tall and towered above me. She pinched her lips at me. Her eyes flashed. I received the impression of a wild creature preparing to attack and felt chilled. Then she turned and followed the two men, bearing the frail old man between them, into the house.

Relief surged through me and I rounded on the stranger. "As for you, leave my house at once."

"Don't talk so daft," he said and pushed on up the stairs.

Flabbergasted, I called after him, "I am Mrs. Pengarth. I order you to leave my house."

The man stopped. Time seemed never ending before he turned to face me. "Well, well, well." His eyes raked me up and down. "So you're Adam's wife. They told me you were no beauty; though I might say anger gives you a certain—spark."

"I demand that you leave," I said, and swallowed nervously as his piggy eyes, almost lost beneath fatty lids, suddenly widened in a most alarming manner.

"I came to see Adam," he said. "I'll not leave till I have."

His eyes disappeared beneath their folds of fat again. He turned his back on me and went into the house.

"Adam's out," I cried.

"Then I'll wait till he comes back. Boy! Fetch me a brandy."

"No!" I stopped the footman from carrying out this order. "You are not welcome to take refreshment here. I do not know who you are, sir, but you forced your way into my house, attacked one of my servants. . . ."

"Your house? Your servants?" He leered sarcastically. "Since when did High Place change hands?"

"I am mistress here. . . ."

"With Morvah Pengarth still alive? She'll not hand the keys of High Place over to anyone. She'll have to be carried out in a box first." His piggy eyes surveyed me with venom. "Listen to me, little woman. I've been coming to this house as and when I pleased since it was first built. I shall continue to do so."

"No, Jack Ransom, you will not."

My heart quailed on hearing Morvah Pengarth pronounce the man's name. I should not have been surprised. I should have known it was he. His savagery toward Tommyboy should have told me.

"Those days are over," Morvah continued. "My daughter-in-law was right to refuse you admittance. I should have done so myself had I seen you first."

"Fine talk, Morvah," Jack Ransom said, recovering from his initial surprise, "with little Miss Moneybags beside you. It would have been a different tale had Adam not returned with a rich wife."

"That's enough," Morvah rapped out.

"Is it?" he asked with a certain menace. "Does she know why she's here?" He looked at me, hatred scorching every word he directed at me. "If it weren't for you, High Place would have been mine now."

"I—I don't understand," I whispered, my mouth drying.

"No?" he snarled; then the dawning of truth softened his face. "No, I can see you don't. Adam never thought to enlighten you."

"Say no more, Jack Ransom," Morvah said, a touch of

fear entering her voice.

"No more? No more? I've been done out of High Place by this little lady." His voice was soft and menacing again. "I intend to make sure she knows how and why. Why should I be the only one to suffer?"

He smiled at me, a thick, brutish smile, showing stained and yellowing teeth, visible evidence of the rank breath that wafted over me as he spoke. Folds of flesh beneath his eyes rose to meet the fleshy lids above, leaving only slits for his piggy eyes to peer through. I wanted to run from him. I wanted to run far and fast and not listen to what he had to say. But I was rooted to the spot.

"You were brought here to pay a gambler's debts."

I moaned faintly. It seemed to delight him.

He chuckled. "Oh, yes. Adam Pengarth needed your money in order to pay off his father's gambling debts." His eyes roamed my face, delighting in my discomfiture. "You surely know he would never have married you if your moneybags had not weighed so heavily? With Araminta Belmont waiting for him?"

"Jack! Don't." Morvah gave a beseeching cry.

I stared at Morvah. She had had the gall to chastize me for making Adam unhappy, when all the time she had known why he had married me, known he did not love me.

"Have you not heard the talk?" He took no notice of Morvah's cry. "Poor little Mrs. Pengarth, they say. She's so plain Adam keeps her cooped up at High Place, afraid to show her off. . . ."

"Jack! That's enough." Morvah had Jack's attention now, and mine. We were both startled by the force in her voice. "You've been paid back every penny owed to you.

With any ordinary man that would have been the end of the matter, but not for you—not for you. You had to come and cause heartache and misery, as you always did. As you always do."

"You'd never have been able to raise the money by the time it fell due . . . If you hadn't got the governor to back you in the court over your application for an extension period. Whose idea was it to send Adam seeking an heiress in England, yours or Joe's? Yours, I think. Joe wouldn't have had the nouse."

"It was no one's. Adam did not go seeking an heiress. He went to visit an aunt—who was dying. I'm surprised you did not know about it. There's not much that escapes your attention."

"I did know about it. I didn't believe it."

"It's true," I said. "Aunt Martha sent for him."

He looked taken aback.

Morvah cried triumphantly. "And she left Adam her fortune. So you see, you were wrong in everything you said."

"Everything?" he sneered, his piggy eyes swiveling toward me again.

"I advise you to leave now," Morvah said, "before Adam gets wind of this day's work."

Jack Ransom's insolent manner never faltered. "I'll go when I get what I came for," he said.

"What did you come for, Ransom?"

None of us had heard Adam ride up and mount the steps. At the sound of his harsh voice we spun round.

Ransom said, a cruel curl to his lip, "Billy Joe."

Morvah and I gasped. Neither of us had thought to ask Jack Ransom's reason for coming here, his behavior not meriting it. Adam raised an eyebrow, queryingly.

"He disappeared this morning. Ran off again."

"Do you expect me to be surprised?"

"I want him back. No damned nigger's going to get the better of me. And when I've got him, I'll make him wish he'd never been born. I'll give him a taste of medicine he'll never forget. I've been too lenient with him so far."

"Lenient!" Adam exploded. I was glad to see it. I felt he had been treating the whole matter with far too much restraint. I forgot he did not know as much as we knew.

"Lenient!" Adam cried again. "You don't know the meaning of the word. If I'd realized how you would treat Billy Joe, I'd never have sold him to you in the first place."

"Oh, no?" Ransom's lips drew back in a sneer. "When it was the only way you could buy time to . . ."

"Billy Joe was a house slave, yet you put him to work in the fields and expected him to work as well as men used to being out in the fields all day, and when . . . I heard . . . I know you treat your own slaves badly, but I thought, one of mine, who'd never known the touch of a whip. . . ."

"A touch of the whip is necessary. It's the only way to let them know who's master," said Jack Ransom as Adam's voice faded out.

There was no softness in Jack Ransom's eyes. He was utterly callous. Did he really believe men worked better if they were ill treated, or, as I suspected, did he enjoy inflicting pain and suffering on those unable to defend themselves?

"We've never used the whip at High Place," Adam said.

I stared at him angrily. Why was he bothering with this man? Why did he not just order him from the house, as I had done? As his mother had done? Ransom had taken no notice of either of us, but he could not flout a command given by Adam, the six-foot owner of High Place.

Ransom sneered. "More fool you. If you had, you might not have found yourself pushed into the position of marrying Miss Moneybags here."

I gasped and fell back. Morvah's arms went round me. I did not even wonder at it. Adam, too, sucked in his breath. He moved a step toward the bull-like man, his fists clenched into tight balls. I thought he would hit Ransom and was ready to applaud.

He said, "I think you'd better leave."

I experienced a sharp feeling of disappointment.

"Not without Billy Joe."

"He's not here."

"I don't believe you."

"It's true."

Oh, don't argue with him, insist that he leave. Why offer a man like him a minute more of your time? If only I were a man, I would not be afraid . . . I halted my thoughts. They were leading me on to believe Adam was a coward. I was also surprised that I, with my gentle upbringing, could so long for one man to use violence upon another—but in this instance, I felt it would be excusable.

"I demand to search the grounds for him." Ransom said.

"Demand?" Adam's brow lowered. Now, I thought, he will knock Ransom down. I knew I would be happy to see it. Then Adam relaxed, turned aside with a gesture of invitation. "Do as you please. You won't find him on my land."

Ransom started to go. I caught hold of Adam's arm.

"No," I cried. "Not alone. Don't let him search alone."

"Why not?" Adam looked down at me a trifle impatiently. "He won't find Billy Joe." He sounded very confident.

"Maybe not, but he's a cruel man. I'm afraid of what he might do to the other slaves."

"He won't harm any of mine," he said, still confident.

"But he will. He has."

That caught him. "Has? What do you mean?"

"He hit Tommyboy with his riding crop. He . . ."

Adam turned to Ransom, who had stopped to listen, "Is this true?"

I felt a wrench of pain. Why couldn't he believe me? Why did he turn to Ransom for confirmation?

"Take no notice of her." Ransom's voice sounded a little shaky. "She doesn't understand. They don't feel pain like we do. . . ."

"They do. They do. There's something wrong with you if you can think otherwise. Adam!" I turned in petition to him. "Tommyboy's eye was gouged out. He was in agony. He was covered in blood."

Adam's lips had disappeared. His face blazed with a frightening anger.

Ransom backed away, though Adam made no move against him.

"It was an accident, Pengarth," he said quickly.

"Nothing you do is by accident, Ransom."

Adam's voice was coldly controlled, strangely at odds with the fire in his eyes.

"I—I was angry over Billy Joe's disappearance." Ransom's voice was urgent, conciliatory. "Your boy was obstructing me."

Adam moved. Ransom backed away, stumbling down

the steps.

"He wouldn't let me in. He said you weren't in. He . . ."

He had reached ground level, looking up at Adam, his piggy eyes registering fear. I was not surprised. And Adam as angry as this was enough to inspire fear in anyone. I waited for the outcome. I did not wish for "an eye for an eye." I would settle for a punch on the jaw. I felt ignoble chagrin when Adam came to a halt on the second step, and said:

"I've changed my mind. Get off my land, Jack Ransom. I withdraw permission for you to search High Place."

"But . . ."

"Get off and stay off. You are no longer welcome here."

"Pengarth . . ."

So many words. So much talk. It seemed that Adam, for all his anger, for all his strength, was not a man of action.

Then he said, "If you so much as set toe here again, I'll set the dogs on you. And if you're not out of my sight within the space of a few seconds, I shall . . ." he descended to the lowest step, "break your neck."

Ransom did not wait for his neck to be broken. He could see Adam meant it. He ran to his horse, mounted, and rode off with speed.

"That's the best day's work you've ever done," Morvah said, with grim satisfaction. "The man's a monster." She hesitated fractionally, and added, "I've never liked him."

A glance, perhaps of significance, passed between the two of them, but I did not pay any special attention to it.

I said to Adam, "You should have punched him on

the jaw."

A smile touched his lips. "Why, Barbara, you surprise me. I thought you were against violence."

"I am, but . . ." I grew flustered beneath his gaze.

His smile widened. "I understand." Then, seriously, he asked, "Where's Tommyboy now?"

"Bella's taken him through to the slave quarters. I wanted to send for a doctor, but she said no doctor would come to see a slave. Surely, that can't be. . . ."

I trotted to keep up with Adam as he marched through the hall and down the passage that led to the rooms allocated to the few privileged slaves allowed to live in the house, Bella, Meta, Tommyboy, the cook, various maids and footmen.

When he saw Tommyboy inert on a trestle bed, his face grew livid. "God!" he muttered. "Ransom—the bastard!"

"Has he fainted?" Morvah inquired breathily.

"Yes, mistress." Bella was staunching the blood with cloths that became soaked in seconds. A basin of red water bore testimony to how many times the cloth had been rinsed. "I can't stop the bleeding."

Her manner was calm, but great concern underlined her words.

"We must get a doctor to him," I cried, turning my head away from the sight of all that blood.

"We doctor our own slaves," Morvah said. "Adam will . . ."

"Adam's not a doctor!" I stared at her in horror. "He can't deal with this. Tommyboy needs a real doctor." I turned to Adam. "You must send for Philip Rose."

"Would he come?" Adam asked ruminatively.

"Yes. Remember what he said? 'Rich man, poor man,

or slave, if he is sick, I will tend him.'"

"You're right." Adam gave swift instructions for Daniel to ride into town, then changed his mind. "No, have a fresh horse saddled for me. I'll go myself."

He turned to look at me again. "You're as white as a sheet," he said. "And you're trembling." He took my arm. "Come. There's nothing for you to do. Bella is quite capable."

We went downstairs. Adam handed me a drink. The smell rose to my nostrils. It reminded me of my wedding night when Adam had had to sodden his brain with drink before he could come to my bed.

"Drink it," he ordered, as I hesitated.

I raised my eyes to his. Did he see my unhappiness mirrored there? A shadow flickered across his face. Was he remembering, too? He did not wish to be reminded.

"Do as you're told, Barbara," he said angrily, and swung away.

"Don't be harsh with her, Adam." Morvah looked kindly at me for the first time since I had known her. "She's been through a very nasty experience."

"All the more reason why she should get it down her. But as usual, she prefers to thwart my wishes."

It was unfair. I stared at him reproachfully. His blue eyes glittered an irate response. "Drink it," he said.

I obeyed. The golden liquid rushed down my throat, burning it, making me cough, making me shudder, but then a warm, comforting glow began to spread to every part of me. I relaxed against the soft cushions at my back.

"That's better." He tossed off his own brandy. "The color's coming back into your cheeks."

A messenger came to report that Adam's horse was ready.

"How long do you think you'll be?" I asked, going with Adam to the door.

"That depends on how soon I can trace him. If I find him quickly, we'll be back within a couple of hours."

"But I thought you knew where he lived?"

He gave me a long, silent glance as he sat his horse. "He may not be at home," he said from the saddle, and rode away.

"It was foolish of me to say that," I said uncomfortably to Morvah, as she came to stand beside me.

"No," she said. "It was your anxiety speaking."

She led me back indoors. She sat with me. She took refreshment with me, a thing she had never done on her own before. She seemed concerned about me. She appeared to want to be friendly, to wipe out past differences. In a strange way, Jack Ransom seemed to have brought us closer together.

It was nearer three hours than two when Adam finally returned, bringing Philip with him. I was overjoyed to see Philip again, but had no time for converse with him. Adam took him straight to Tommyboy's room after greetings had been exchanged.

"Can Philip save Tommyboy's eye?" I asked Adam when he rejoined us a few moments later.

Adam went to pour himself a drink. "I shouldn't bank on it," he said, the rough edge to his voice betraying an anxiety to match my own.

I turned on them with a suddenness that surprised both them and me. "I don't know how you could receive a man like Jack Ransom in your home, knowing the way he treats his slaves."

"I am not happy about the way he treats his slaves," said Adam, "but there is nothing I can do about it. A man's slaves are his own, his property. No one has the right to interfere."

"The right? You must have the right to interfere when you see cruelty and aggression. Mr. Wilberforce says . . ."

"Wilberforce is a dreamer. Well meaning, but short-sighted. We've been into all this before. I thought you understood. . . ."

"Mr. Wilberforce is a great man," I interrupted spiritedly. "A reformer. A true humanitarian."

"He's a liability. He should leave us to manage our own affairs."

"Then nothing would get done."

"He's stirred up a hornet's nest with his antislavery bill."

"Who cares, if it needed stirring up?"

"I care." Adam exploded with rage. "We all care. Every white man and woman in these islands care. As you should care. You are one of us now. Your fate lies with ours. What do you think has been happening since the antislavery bill was passed? Do you imagine it has stopped the traders bringing in their pitiful cargoes? I can tell you, it has not. It has driven them underground, that's all. Trading still goes on, cloaked by darkness and secrecy, with more bloodiness, more unholy anguish than ever before.

"You saw those men on the quay. You saw their sullen resentment, the hate in their eyes. How long have they been in Almada, do you think? What do you think would happen if they suddenly found themselves freed? What do you think would happen if all that bitterness and anger were allowed to spill over, unchecked? All hell would be let loose. No white man, woman, or child would be safe. And you might say it will be no more than we deserve. And you may well be right."

I was taken aback by his ferocity. His passionate anger opened questions in my mind. Yet I faced him defiantly.

"Are you asking me to believe every slave will rise up in vengeance to . . . ?"

"Murder, rape, pillage? Yes. I'm asking you to believe that."

"I can't. I won't. These people aren't savages. They're gentle. I've been here long enough to find that out. You have only to look at Meta . . . Daniel. . . ."

"Meta? Daniel? Oh, my poor Barbara, you don't know what you are talking about. You have been led away by idealists who know nothing of the realities of the situation. Meta and Daniel were born here. They serve us, their white masters, cheerfully, content with their lot. Meta and Daniel would be as vulnerable as the rest of us."

"He's right, my dear." Morvah spoke now. "You do not understand. You cannot understand. Almada is not England. Our ways are different. Whether we like it or not, a pattern of life was established here long before we came. We had to accustom ourselves to it. So must you. The sooner you do, the happier you will be."

"I shall never become accustomed to slavery," I said.

"Slavery will die out of its own accord," Adam said, more gently. "As each new generation is born . . ."

"You don't believe that," I said. "You can't believe it. Not while there are men like Jack Ransom about. They will not let it die out."

Adam was silent.

"You don't believe it is right for one man to own

another," I said with quiet contempt, "yet you will do nothing to change it. Somehow, I find that worse."

His blue gaze chilled me. "As you will. I've tried to be patient with you and explain things. You refuse to take my word on the seriousness of the situation. I can't reason with you. Your obstinacy prevents it. So now I tell you, order you, to hold your tongue. I wish to hear no more such talk from you. It's dangerous and—it's unwomanly."

Unwomanly! That one word danced before my eyes. Unwomanly!

I met his hard, bright gaze. I held it unflinchingly.

"So I am a woman when it suits you to remember it," I said. "Not a reasonable woman, but a poor miserable creature who must be told what to do, what to think. Whose brain must cease to function at your command. Well, it will not. You can't shut me up because I'm a woman. I'm not like other women. I have no feminine allure, but I have a mind and I use it. I thought you respected me for it. Now I see I was wrong. But you were wrong about me. I was never a coward and I will not remain quiet about the things I feel strongly about, simply because you require it."

"Be careful, Barbara." Adam moved a step closer to me.

I would have stepped back from him, just as Jack Ransom had stepped back from him earlier, but I was prevented from doing so by the sofa jutting into my legs. So I stood up to him, my heart beating frantically, but not from fear. Anger. Anger consumed me. Anger at Adam. Anger at my uncomeliness. Anger at life. Anger that spilled out of me.

"Nay, my lord and master, I will not be careful. I have

been careful all my life. Careful not to say the wrong thing—or maybe the right thing—for fear of offending people. All my life I have tried to please others, afraid of losing what little affection I might manage to inspire in them . . . and lost myself in the process.

"But no more. That's finished. You have opened my eyes to my foolish ways. All Aunt Martha's teaching did not achieve what you have just achieved. In future I shall please myself."

"Barbara, I didn't mean . . ."

"I know, as my husband, you are entitled to obedience from your wife. But I am not your wife. I am only the woman you married."

Adam's face grew blurred. I could not, at first, understand why, then I realized . . . I was looking at him through a haze of tears.

"Barbara . . ." Adam placed his hands on my arms.

I wrenched myself away. "Leave me alone. Don't touch me. I never want you to touch me. Ever. You have no right."

My outburst should have made me feel better. It did not. For another moment Adam stood there, then he turned and left the room. A sob caught in my throat.

"Oh, Barbara." A soft voice murmured my name. Morvah. I had forgotten she was there. "Why don't you listen to what he says? He was only telling you to keep quiet for your own good. No other reason. It doesn't do to air liberal views on this island, or any of the islands. He was only trying to protect you."

But I did not believe her.

Chapter Eight

"Philip!"

I had seen him through the open drawing room door as he passed on his way downstairs, Adam with him, speaking in low tones. I had heard the clatter of their boots on the hall's marble floor and been appalled as the sound retreated and I realized they were on their way out.

"Philip!" I rushed from the room, forgetting to excuse myself from Morvah in my haste. "You're not going? Won't you stay and take tea? There's so much I want to ask you."

"He can't stay." Adam answered for him, a shade too quickly. "He's in a hurry."

"Yes," said Philip. "I'm sorry, Barbara. I'll be back tomorrow. I'll take tea with you then, if I may."

"Yes, of course," I mumbled, disappointed.

I followed them outside. Philip's horse waited patiently for him in the shade of a large tree. It raised its head at our approach and whinnied a greeting. It had been given a rubdown, been fed and watered. It looked sleek, glossy and content. Philip swung himself up into the saddle.

"How is Tommyboy?" I asked.

"He'll survive."

"And his eye?"

"We'll have to wait and see."

He spurred his animal round, nodded, and was gone.

I felt vaguely disturbed. There had been something about his manner that had seemed not quite right. I was not quite sure what. An awkwardness? A—drawing back? It might be that he was worried over Tommyboy? Yes, that was probably it. What else could it have been?

"Cheer up," said Adam, seeing my troubled face. "Tommyboy will be fine. He has a good nurse in Bella, and Philip—he's a marvel."

"Yes, I know," I said, "but it wasn't Tommyboy I was thinking about just then, it was Philip. I mean, he seemed different, didn't you think so? Not at all like he was aboard the *Indies Pride*.

Adam made no comment and I went on, needing him to agree with me, "Perhaps he was just worried about Tommyboy, his eye."

Adam remained silent.

We mounted the steps. "I don't suppose you thought to ask him to dine with us?" I said.

He threw me a sharp look. "Did you expect me to? under the circumstances?"

"No . . . of course not. Do you think I could see Tommyboy?"

"Certainly, if you wish," said Adam. "I'll escort you to his room."

Bella was sitting beside the bed. She rose as we entered and bowed her head meekly. Adam's benefit, not mine. Tommyboy lay quietly, half his face covered in a white bandage. I noticed with relief the stench of blood had gone, as had the basin of red water, the bloody cloths.

"He's very still," I whispered.

"Philip dosed him with laudanum to dull the pain. He'll sleep till morning."

We parted then. Adam went—wherever he went. I went to my room to sort through my clothes and decide what to wear for Araminta's party, which I had just remembered, was to take place that evening.

There came a light tap at my door. I went to open it and cried out in surprise.

"Mrs. Pengarth!"

"May I speak with you?"

"Why, yes, of course. Come in." I stood to one side, closed the door. "Please sit down."

"I feel I owe you an explanation," she said, making a great display of spreading her skirts around her. "About Joe—and Jack."

"There's no need," I said, sensing distress and embarrassment.

"Jack made it appear that Adam had married you for your money. You are entitled to an explanation. I want you to know what lay behind his cruel words. I saw the effect they had on you.

"Jack Ransom is an evil man. The devil lives in his pocket. Joe . . . my Joe . . . liked to gamble, but he always kept within strict limits. At least, he did, until . . . Jack tricked him into believing . . ."

She stopped. She had traveled back in time. Her eyes were glazed. Then she gave a shudder and she was back in my room again.

"Joe started drinking—heavily. He gambled more and more, laying bigger and bigger stakes. He lost more than he won. In the end there was nothing left to gamble with . . . only High Place.

"Jack began buying up all Joe's debts. Joe thought . . . Oh, my poor Joe thought . . ." Her voice broke on a dry sob.

"Please, Mrs. Pengarth. You don't have to tell me any more. I can see it's painful for you. And as it happens, I am indebted to Jack Ransom. I understand now why Adam married me. I never could . . . quite . . . before. I always thought him a wealthy man . . . now it's all perfectly clear."

"It was all part of his plan to get his hands on High Place." She had not been listening. "He always said he would ruin us. And now he could do it, legitimately. He challenged Joe to gamble High Place on the turn of a card. He could not lose either way. If he won, High Place went to him and Joe's debts would be wiped out. If Joe won, we kept High Place, but we still owed an exorbitant amount of money to Jack Ransom, money we could never hope to raise by the date he set for repayment in full. So we were ruined, whatever the outcome of the wager.

"Then Martha's letter came. It was like an angel from heaven. She was rich. She had money. She was dying. She wanted to see her son. We took it for granted it was because she intended leaving him her fortune. We had to tell Adam—everything. He was devastated. He refused point blank to go to England. But then, Joe died. We don't know why. He . . . just . . . collapsed. Our future, the future of High Place was now Adam's responsibility. He knew he had to go to England, and, if she did not die, coerce her into giving us the financial help we needed so desperately."

"I see," I said, able to feel sorry for Adam now, and

feel a certain sympathy for him. "Yes, I can see he had to marry me, although the whole idea was utterly repugnant to him."

Morvah looked puzzled, tilting her head to one side like a little dog trying to interpret her master's words.

"He hasn't told you about the condition in Aunt Martha's will, has he?" I went on, ready to share confidences.

"Condition? What do you mean?"

"I thought not. He needn't have married me, you know. If he had waited for just one month, he would have found all his money troubles resolved. He need not have cheated me."

"Adam never cheated anybody in his life."

"He cheated me. Oh, I knew from the start he didn't love me, but I thought he cared—he said he cared—about what became of me."

"He does care about you. . . ."

"No, he does not! It did not take me long to find that out he cared nothing for me."

"But, Barbara . . ."

"We don't sleep together, you know that. The whole household knows it. Adam is at no pains to hide the fact. He deliberately installed me in the White Room rather than the master bedroom, not because you already occupied it and he did not like to ask you to vacate it, but because he never had any intention that we should sleep there."

"If Adam doesn't sleep with you, it's your fault, not his," Morvah said sharply.

I shook my head. "Ours is no true marriage. Adam never meant it to be. He married me because he was forced to."

"Adam would not have married you if he had not wanted to. No one could ever force Adam to do anything."

"No *one*, maybe. But High Place . . ."

"But if the money was to be his, anyway. . . ."

"He didn't know that then. Neither of us did," I said.

We looked at each other, the little, wrinkled, brown-skinned lady who looked so much older than she was, and I, younger than she, but feeling every bit as old as she looked, and sympathy flowed between us.

"Oh, my dear child," she murmured. "I had no idea. I thought it was you . . . I blamed you. . . ."

I smiled wryly. "It doesn't matter. I'm resigned to it."

I held my breath. I recognized Aunt Martha's words.

I dressed in my finest black for Araminta's party. Meta was most unhappy about it.

"You not look good in black," she said, stating her opinion boldly.

Perhaps I indulged her more than I ought, but I did not think she took advantage of my softness. She seemed only to have my best interests at heart—and, I thought now, her approach was vastly different from Aunt Martha's.

"I not look good in any color," I sighed.

"Tha's not true, missie. You striking woman. You not treat yourself right."

Meta sulked as she arranged the deep flounce of lace that fell in heavy folds about my shoulders. She sulked while she brushed and combed my hair. I looked at myself in the mirror. Little and dark, I was, like a black crow. Beside Araminta's bird of paradise . . . a tap came at the door.

Meta went to answer it. There was a lot of whispering and a sudden exclamation of delight.

"What is it, Meta? What's all the whispering about?"

She came to me, grinning broadly, displaying an open case. Diamonds, resting upon black satin, spat fire at me.

"They're beautiful," I breathed. "But . . . who . . . where . . . ?"

"For you, Missie Barbry. Missie Pengarth send them."

"For me? But . . . I can't wear those."

"You wear them," Meta said firmly, placing the necklace round my neck, adding for good measure, "Missie Pengarth say so."

The effect they had on my skin astonished me into silent acquiescence. They brought out a translucence I had never seen before. The candlelight caught the gleam of gold in my hair. Suddenly, I was a crow no longer.

Meta set about dressing my hair. I watched entranced while she plaited it and pinned it high on my head, looping it into a crown. In a moment I would tell her to take it down again, but for now. . . .

I watched with a growing excitement, till it was not I, but a stranger, who stared back at me from the mirror. Someone who, while not exactly beautiful, was . . . arresting. Her eyes sparkled. Her skin glowed. She commanded attention.

Another tap came at the door. Through the mirror I saw it open and Adam, handsome beyond words in his splendid evening dress, halt on the threshold. He gazed at me silently for a moment. I held my breath. Would he see the vision I saw? Would he smile in wonderment and pleasure? Would he find attraction there?—Would I ever stop thinking this way?

He said: "Aren't you ready yet, Barbara? It's time we were going."

The sparkle disappeared from the eyes of the woman in the mirror. The diamonds lost their brilliance, dulling the skin. The hair grew mousy and limp. I was looking at myself again.

We descended the staircase side by side, my limbs strangely heavy, and it was with the greatest difficulty that I placed one foot before the other.

The others were waiting for us in the hall. Morvah Pengarth, small and thin, smiled at me. She wore brown silk. Her hair was tucked underneath a matching head-dress. The color matched her skin exactly. Inevitably, I thought of the hazel trees in the grounds surrounding Martha's Cottage.

I conquered a sudden urge to cry and looked at Robert. I had not expected him to be going. He was grinning in his usual fatuous manner, but I thought I saw something in his eyes, something I could not read. It disturbed me.

I looked at Jem. He was a big man. An outdoors man. Evening dress did not sit well on him. He gave the impression he would much rather be casually dressed, and sitting a horse.

My heart somersalted. He was looking up at me with naked admiration in his eyes. I had never been on the receiving end of such a look before. It was a heady experience.

"You're looking very beautiful tonight, Barbara," he greeted me as we reached the bottom step.

I could see he meant it, and I smiled at him with all the warmth I could muster, and something else sprang to his eyes: the light of desire. I felt near to fainting at the unbelievability of it. Had the woman in the mirror come down after all? Had Barbara Pengarth changed places with her? Was I still in my room upstairs? I could not resist looking at Adam to see if he had noticed the effect I had had on Jem.

Adam looked back at me, unmoved.

Daniel and the chocolate-faced groom's boy appeared to say the carriage was waiting. We all turned to go.

The five miles to the Governor's Mansion ran along dirt tracks between sugar cane fields, meandered through lush vegetation, edged the sea, wound through bustling Seatown, and rose thereafter through landscaped gardens to reach the big house, standing in lone splendor high above the capital of Almada.

Every window in the house was alive with glowing, welcoming light. All the doors were thrown wide open. A slave in maroon livery directed our carriage away. More slaves stood at intervals around a vast hall filled with laughing, chattering guests. Small black pages scuttled about with trays of drinks, nuts, and sweetmeats.

I started to shake. "I thought it was to be a small dinner party," I whispered, viewing the grand affair.

"Araminta's parties are never small," Adam said. "Only by degree. This, by her standards, is small."

People waved and called out greetings as we passed through the throng to be announced. Araminta was standing beside her father, the governor, a vision of white satin and silver gauze. I was presented to her father and curtsied before a tall figure in a dark blue uniform, adorned with gold buttons and epaulettes. As I rose I looked into an aging face surrounded by pure white hair and whiskers. He spoke kindly to me for a few moments, then I was whisked away and soon enveloped in the midst of an eager, questioning crowd.

There was nothing reticent about these people. I was overawed by them. And I was alone. Adam had left my side.

"How do you like our island, Mrs. Pengarth?" I was asked.

"It's very beautiful," I said.

"Have you seen Coral Beach?" asked a young woman.

"And have you visited Shark's Fin Bay?" asked another.

"No," I said. "I'm afraid I haven't been very far from High Place as yet."

"Adam's been keeping you pretty closely guarded," a young man in scarlet uniform said. "And it's not difficult to see why."

"Are you still in mourning, my dear?" An elderly lady was eyeing my black with surprised brown eyes.

I said nothing. How could I tell her I was mourning a husband I had never had?

She was nodding sagely. "Your aunt, I believe?"

"Yes," I said.

"The one who left Adam his immense fortune?"

I must keep up the pretense that Aunt Martha was his aunt, too. I nodded.

"Is it true you did not know of Adam's existence before he arrived in England?" breathed a young woman at my elbow.

"Quite true."

"Was it love at first sight?" she gushed, and, thankfully, did not wait for an answer, but went straight on to proclaim, "How romantic! I wish something like that would happen to me!"

She turned to giggle with her friend, who, equally silly, piped up, "We were never so surprised at anything. We all expected Adam to marry . . ."

"You would have been quite alone in the world, would you not, Barbara, if Adam had not married you?"

I turned in surprise to see Araminta behind me. I replied with a fast-beating heart, "No. Not quite alone. I do have a mother and a sister."

"Oh." Her brows knit together in an angry silence.

So Adam had not told her. I was glad. It did my heart good to see her at a loss, something, I was certain, that did not happen often.

"They were sorry to see you go, I expect?"

"Will they come and visit you?"

The questioners pushed forward, firing questions, not giving me time to answer them. I was twisting this way and that. It was hot. My head was swimming and I felt myself sway. If only someone would come and rescue me. Morvah. Jem.

"You didn't know you had two cousins in Almada?" Araminta had found her voice again.

I turned to her innocently. "Two?"

"Adam and Robert."

"Oh, but Robert is not . . . I mean . . ."

"I think that's enough questions for one evening, my friends." Adam's voice sounded above my head. How long had he been behind me? "You can't expect to get to know everything about my wife on first acquaintance."

His voice was light, but I thought I detected an edge of annoyance there. He swept me away from the crowd and led me out onto the veranda, a necessary appendage to any house built on Almada, and I knew I was right. The annoyance flared into anger as soon as we were alone.

"What did you think you were up to?" he demanded fiercely.

"I . . . I don't understand."

"If I hadn't stopped you in time, you'd have told everybody that Robert isn't your cousin. Then we'd have been in a mess."

"I wouldn't. I remembered just in time."

"You'd better stay by my side for the rest of the evening, and keep your mouth shut."

"I can't do that." I was growing angry now. "I must speak."

He frowned blackly at me. "Yes," he said regretfully. "I suppose you must. But from now on refrain from saying anything about yourself, Aunt Martha or the will."

"Why should I mention the will? And how can I not tell them about myself, if they ask me?"

"Fend them off. You're good at that sort of thing."

I hardly knew what he meant by that. I said, "It will seem very strange. They're bound to think . . ."

"I don't give a damn what they think." He turned from me and gazed out into the velvety darkness, his hands gripping the edge of the balustrade as if he wished to tear it apart. He was like a dog straining at its leash, anxious to be rid of its trammels. Then, with a deep sigh, he turned back to me. "Very well. Of course you must answer their questions. But evade anything that concerns me and—that woman. Surely, that should not be too difficult."

"Why are you so afraid I may give something away about your birth and parentage?" I cried. "Why don't you trust me?"

"You've given me precious little reason to so far," he threw at me bitterly.

I reproached him as bitterly. "Adam!"

"Listen," he said, "As far as anyone, other than you and I and my mother, is concerned, Martha Goodall was my aunt. I was her heir. She left everything to me. That is all they know. All they need to know. Understand?"

"Yes," I said huffily. "I understand it would be disagreeable for you if the true nature of your parentage became known."

He came to stand closer to me. "And I shall know who to blame should they ever discover it," he said with menace.

He took my arm and guided me back indoors, remaining by my side until dinner was served, when we were forced to part.

Araminta had arranged the seating so that Adam sat on the right of her at one end of the table and I on the right of her father at the other.

I have no recollection of the food we ate, only the sound of Araminta's tinkling laughter and Adam's deep-throated responses. I tried to pay attention to what Sir George was saying to me, but he might have been speaking in a foreign tongue for all the sense I made of it. My ears were tuned, my head was pulled, as if by a string, to the other end of the table where Araminta's hand rested repeatedly on Adam's, and her gaze was adoring. Once her glance caught mine and she smiled a slow, secret smile. Others must have noticed and must have pitied me.

The ladies rose from the table, to my great relief, leaving the men to their port and cigars. Morvah came quickly to my side.

"Take no notice of Minty Belmont," she whispered fiercely. "She likes to think she has every man under her spell."

"It doesn't matter," I said quietly. "It is of no consequence."

"It was disgraceful, her behavior at table," Morvah continued. "Disgraceful! But you're not the first young wife she's been out to separate from her husband, and you won't be the last. It's up to you to see she does not succeed this time."

"Mrs. Pengarth, did you not understand what I said to you the other day?" I cried desperately.

"Of course, I understood." She had led me to a crimson-silk-covered sofa. "Sit down and listen to me. You are his wife, no matter how it came about. You must fight for him."

"I can't. I won't. He's shown quite plainly . . ."

"Tut, tut. Such pride. There's no room for pride. You must . . ."

"Morvah!" A formidable lady was bearing down on us in full burgundy sail, a red-haired young lady at her side.

"You'll lose him if you don't do something about it, and quick," Morvah hissed in my ear. Then she greeted the lady. "Hello, Mollie. It's good to see you. Have you come for the dancing?"

"Aye, we have. We may ha' missed the grand sit-down, but ye canna keep a Macpherson away frae a jig." A great roll of laughter issued from her mouth. "We're a wee bit early, so I said we'd join the ladies for coffee. Sam's outside. He's quite happy. He has a wee dram in his hand." She looked at me. "And this is your wee daughter-in-law, Morvah?"

Morvah introduced me formerly to Mollie and her daughter, Agnes, then she asked, "How is Sam?"

"Och, d'ye ha' tae ask?" And another jolly roll of

laughter left her mouth as she deposited herself in a wide armchair. Agnes remained standing beside her.

A little black boy, splendidly attired in blue velvet, with a froth of white lace at his neck, white satin stockings and silver-buckled shoes, brought a spindly straight-backed chair for Agnes. Another served us with coffee.

"And how is the rest of the Macpherson clan?" asked Morvah.

"Fine and bonnie. Fine and bonnie. D'ye ken I'm a grannie ten times o'er?" She flashed large, strong teeth at me. "I am. Six lads, four lassies. Five bonnie bairns o' my ain, I had. A' lassies. And each proving as fecund as mysel'."

She slapped her ample thigh and peeled off into laughter again.

"Tut, Mollie." Morvah tried to hide a smile. "You're bringing a blush to my daughter-in-law's cheeks."

"Och, away wi' ye. She'll be a mother hersel' before long. She smiled at me. "Ye'll be finding life here on Almada a wee bit different frae England, I'm thinking."

"A bit," I smiled, warming to her. She was overwhelming in her person and manner, but there was something immeasurably kindly and friendly about her.

"Ye'll get used tae it. Ye'll have tae, will ye no?" She seemed to find this funny and went into gales of laughter again. Then she sobered. "High Place, 'tis a fine wee hoose."

I smiled broadly. Wee? "Yes, it's beautiful," I said.

"I dinna mind tellin' ye I had it in mind for my wee girl, Agnes." She cocked her head in Agnes' direction. "She's the only one left on the shelf. Ah, weel, 'twas not tae be." She sighed with exaggerated sadness, then her laughter rang out again. "But we've got our eyes on a certain young captain, ha' we not Agnes?"

Agnes blushed and hung her head. "Oh, Mother!"

"Well now." Mollie Macpherson turned to Morvah, serious now. "'Tis good tae see you about again, Morvah Pengarth. "We've missed seein' your smilin' face about Seatown."

Morvah's eyes clouded over. "Well, Mollie, since Joe passed on . . ." Her voice trailed away.

"Aye, I ken." Mollie's voice was full of sympathy; then she slapped her thigh again and boomed, "But life must go on Morvah. Life must go on."

"What tale is Mollie spinning now?" a dark-haired lady from across the room called out.

"Whatever, 'tis nothing too do wi' ye, Enid Carstairs," Mollie called back rudely, but with a broad grin.

Enid took no offense. No one, I was to learn, took any offense at anything Mollie Macpherson said. She had no malice in her and everything she said was tinged with humor.

"Don't believe a word she says, Mrs. Adam Pengarth. Our Mollie's an incorrigible embroiderer of the truth. If you believe half of what she says, it will be too much."

A titter of laughter arose from the interested assembly.

"I'm sure Barbara is far too astute to be taken in by any of Mollie's stories."

Araminta's lazy observation held an underlying sharpness. Toward Mollie—or me? Her eyes gave no clue.

Mollie said, with mock chagrin, "I wasna about to tell any stories, but I'll tell one now. I'll tell it tae ye all." Her glance ranged the room, silently, slyly, and an eerie air of expectancy descended on the company. Then, with slow, dramatic persuasion, she went on, "The Gray Phantom is abroad again."

There came a sound like rushing water as everyone's breath was sucked in in uniformity. I felt a prickling sensation at the back of my neck and I swallowed nervously, remembering the man on the rock, dressed in gray, astride a big gray horse.

"Nonsense, Mollie." Morvah's sudden exclamation made me jump. "You know very well the Gray Phantom doesn't exist."

"Of course not." Though Araminta's voice trembled, it was spirited. "If he did, my father would have had him caught and hung by now."

"How d'ye catch and hang a phantom? He's no made o' flesh. . . ."

"Stop it Mollie, you're frightening my daughter-in-law. There is no phantom. It's a tale put about by some prankster."

Mollie smiled ghoulishly at me. "Whenever he's seen, disaster strikes."

I could see she was relishing her tale. Her eyes were twinkling wickedly. How would she feel, I wondered, if I told her I had seen the Gray Phantom myself, staring down at me from a rock, stiff and silent as a statue? How would they all feel?

"You see what I mean, Mrs. Pengarth?" Enid Carstairs said lightly. "She's full of such tales."

Mollie's loud laugh rang out then, and with an audible sigh of relief filling the room, everyone else joined in.

"Tell me, Mrs. Pengarth, how do you like it here in Almada? What do you find most different from life in England?"

"Just about everything," I answered Enid Carstairs. "Mostly the . . ." I stopped myself just in time from saying "the slavery situation," and substituted, "the heat, the brilliant flowers, the luxuriant foliage."

"What about the clothes?" Araminta chipped in. "You must surely find a difference there. We are way behind the fashion here. You must tell us about the latest London fashions."

"I'm afraid I can't. I have never been to London . . . not since I lived there as a small child."

"Oh, yes, you went to live with your aunt in Kent, I believe?"

"Yes. I lived with her for thirteen years. I—we never traveled."

"Till you came here," Araminta's voice was quiet. I did not see the trap she was setting for me.

"It's strange that Adam said nothing about having a cousin in England before he left to visit his aunt."

"He did not know."

"How very odd."

She eyed me shrewdly. At last I was alerted.

"He knew *of* me, of course." I tried to extricate myself from her snare. "What I mean is, he didn't *know* me. He knew he had relatives in England besides Aunt Martha, but . . ."

I was lost. I looked at Morvah for support. She did not fail me. "We never kept in close touch," she said swiftly.

"Martha was your sister, Mrs. Pengarth?" Araminta's expression was one of complete innocence.

"No." Morvah was put off her guard. "She wasn't any . . ." Then she saw the net. "She wasn't mine," she finished lamely.

"That's strange," Araminta mused. "I mean, she couldn't have been Mr. Pengarth's sister. Adam told me her name was Goodall, *Miss* Goodall. You must admit it *is* strange, isn't it?"

As luck would have it, the gentlemen chose that moment to join us. I sent a mute appeal to Adam, who came quickly to my side. "What is it?" He bent toward me. "Something wrong?"

"Your mother and I were being forced into a corner," I began and was interrupted by Araminta.

"We were talking about your Aunt Martha, Adam. I'm certain you told me her name was Martha *Goodall,* yet Mrs. Pengarth tells us she was not her sister. That's strange, isn't it? For if she was Mr. Pengarth's sister, her name would have been Miss Pengarth, would it not?"

"There's nothing strange about it at all," Adam returned casually. "Aunt Martha was really my great aunt—on the distaff side."

"Oh." She frowned as she tried to work this out, while I thought how neatly he had turned the tables, albeit with a lie.

"You and Mrs. Pengarth met at the funeral, did you not?"

The young woman who had gushed at me earlier now gushed at Adam.

"No. We met at the reading of the will."

"And you fell in love at first sight. How romantic! Isn't it romantic, Jane?" She turned to her friend and they giggled together as before.

"Were you a beneficiary, Barbara?" Araminta seemed unwilling to let the matter drop.

"Yes . . . no . . ."

"Yes. No." Araminta's laugh rang high. "You do not seem very sure. I must say, it would seem churlish, to say the least, if she did not leave you something after all those years you lived with her. Thirteen, you said?"

"I can't see that it's any business of yours, Minty."

Adam's voice was calm, polite, even amused. "But to satisfy that inquisitive nature of yours, let me explain what my wife means. Aunt Martha left her fortune to me, but her house in Kent to Barbara."

Araminta did not appear to be satisfied with this and would have pursued the matter further if Adam had not said:

"Now let us leave the subject. It is painful to my wife. She was very close to her aunt and has not fully recovered from the shock of her demise."

There were murmurs of sympathy from all around, then their interest waned. But I pondered Araminta's questioning. It suggested she was suspicious. But of what? She could not possibly guess at the truth about Adam's relationship to my aunt. No one knew of it apart from Adam and myself and Mrs. Pengarth—and the two or three people back home, who would never speak of it to anyone. So what was she after? What was she trying to prove? Perhaps she was just chasing shadows, hoping to win Adam back to herself, though it seemed to me she had never lost him—not really.

I abandoned conjecture as other guests began to arrive. Dancing commenced and other worries presented themselves to me.

Aunt Martha had provided me with a dancing master. "*For grace and deportment. You will not be invited to many balls, I fancy.*"

I could count the balls I had been invited to on one hand. Three. I had attended only one, given by Mr. Parkes to mark his fortieth wedding anniversary, and had stayed only a short time, dancing once—with Mr. Parkes—before my aunt decided she had had enough and called for the carriage to take us home. So now, with this *small* dinner party having expanded into a full-fledged ball, I sat trembling with anxiety.

Would Adam ask me to dance? Would anyone ask me to dance? Or would I sit on the sidelines with the matrons looking on whilst the prettier girls twirled with their partners.

When the governor asked me to dance—I was, after all, the guest of honour—I thought, this is much as I can expect. But then I was whirled away in a succession of dances, and not always by old men. Handsome young officers made a beeline for me, begging to book dances. Was it my new hair style? The diamonds enhancing my skin? Or because I was Adam's wife and they were determined to find out what it was that had made him marry me, that compensated for my lack of looks?

I did not care what the reason was. I loved dancing. I loved the music, and once over my initial shyness found I could amuse my partners, make them laugh. They seemed to like me. Perhaps plainness did not matter as much as my aunt had made out. My dance card was almost full.

I danced with Samuel Macpherson, Mollie's husband. He was a big, bluff, red-headed Scot, who had retained his native accent, just as his wife had done, in spite of having lived in Almada for over twenty years. He told me he was a merchantman who had traveled the world as a young man and had found no place to rival the beauties of Almada. Apart from Scotland, he had added with a grin. "I've never regretted settling here," he said, "though I dinna like the slave system. I only employ free men mysel'."

I danced with Dr. Atkinson. I danced with young officers. I danced with plantation owners and with a ship's captain. Yet among all the people present at Araminta's party there was not a sign of Philip and Sarah Rose. Nor, thankfully, of Jack Ransom.

Morvah and Mollie were deep in conversation, leaving me free to gaze around the assembled company. Then I held my breath. Adam was coming toward me. Was he coming to claim me for a dance? It was not his turn yet. So far I had seen him dance only once—with Araminta. Then he had disappeared and I had not seen him again till now. However, before he reached my side, Robert presented himself to me.

I did not remember writing his name on my card, but when I looked at it, there it was. Robert.

I had seen Robert dancing, partnering his mother. He danced well, remarkably well, and was very light on his feet, but he looked grotesque, and I had been unable to suppress the twinge of revulsion that rose in me.

Ashamed, I had chastised myself. I was like all the others. I had noticed how they ignored him, turned their backs on him as he approached, giggled behind their fans. I had despised them for it, though Robert, as Adam had said, did not seem to notice or care. Yet the feelings that motivated their actions, I discovered, had a place in me as well.

I was disgusted with myself. So now I went with him, smiling, onto the dance floor. I was surprised at the gentle way he guided me there, and when we danced, if I did not look at him, I could almost believe he was the same as other men.

"Do you like dancing?" I asked at one point. "You dance very well."

"I like dancing with you," he said, and his eyes rolled with sudden intelligence.

I swallowed nervously.

"I like you," he said, a moment later.

I tried to smile. It was difficult. I was glad when the dance ended.

He escorted me to a chair and sat down beside me, his sloppy grin very much in evidence. Everyone avoided us. I intercepted many pitying glances.

"May I bring you something to eat or drink?" he asked me, as any other man might have done.

Before I could frame an answer, Jem Harding appeared in front of us. "My dance, I think, Barbara," he said, holding out his hand. Without thinking, I rose and took it.

"You looked as if you needed rescuing," he whispered into my ear as we joined the dancers already in position.

"Not really," I began, then gave a slightly embarrassed laugh as a knowledgeable gleam appeared in his eye. "Well, perhaps I was finding it a bit of a strain. It's difficult to know how to treat Robert. Sometimes he seems just like anybody else, and then . . . I try to understand, but . . ."

"I know. He sends shivers down your spine."

"Yes," I sighed and nodded unhappily, because it was true and I did not want it to be.

"This is not your dance, you know," I said then, aware of black looks being directed our way from the young man I should have been dancing with.

Jem laughed carelessly and twirled me around.

When the dance was over he returned me to where Morvah was sitting chatting with her friends. I thanked him and sat down to wait—in trepidation. The next dance was Adam's, a duty dance, I knew, but the prospect of being held in his arms filled me with—what? I hardly dared to try to sort out the emotions the prospect engendered.

Jem sat down next to me. "What do you think of Minty Belmont?" he asked suddenly.

My heart jumped. "Minty? She's—very pretty."

"Yes. And very clever. Watch out for her, Barbara, she—she's . . ." He broke off, but I knew what he had been going to say. He had been going to say, "She's out to steal Adam from you."

Morvah leaned forward and attracted his attention by patting his knee with her fan. "Have you seen Adam, Jem?"

"No, Mrs. Pengarth. Not for some time."

"Will you go and look for him? I have a headache and wish to go home. Besides which, I fear we are in for another storm. The wind is rising, they tell me."

He rose at once. "You might try the garden, by the fountain," she added acidly, and I guessed she had known all the time where he was and with whom. Araminta. She turned to me. "I hope you don't mind, my dear?"

"Of course not," I said, tasting the familiar gall of letdown. I knew she was doing it for my sake, to drag Adam away from Araminta, but oh, if only she could have waited till after my dance with Adam.

We waited, and in due course Adam presented himself.

"Jem tells me you wish to leave, Mother."

"Yes. Where's Robert?"

"Isn't he with you?"

"I haven't seen him since he danced with Barbara."

Adam turned a questioning glance toward me.

"Neither have I," I said.

Jem said, "I'll go and look for him."

Adam stopped him. "No. I'll go. You see to the carriage."

Morvah and I went to collect our wraps, then sat down on damask-covered chairs in the spacious hall to await our menfolk. We waited a long time. Morvah grew restless, and with a click of her tongue, she muttered, "What's keeping them?"

At last Adam returned with Robert. They both looked disheveled—as if they had been fighting. Had Adam had trouble in persuading Robert to accompany him?

"Where's Jem?" Adam demanded. "Is the carriage ready?"

"I don't know," Morvah snapped. "He hasn't called us yet."

"I'd better go and see what's holding him up," Adam said irritably. "Robert, stay with Mother."

Robert kicked at the ground and looked mutinous.

I had never known everyone to be so irritable all at once. It must have had something to do with the approaching storm. I knew storms had such an adverse effect on some people.

It started to rain. More people decided to leave and said their good-byes. We continued to wait for Jem and Adam. Sir George grew most concerned about us.

"I can't understand what's happening." He shook his head sympathetically. "I'll send one of my men to see what the trouble is. Carrington!"

"Sir!" A young officer in scarlet leapt to attention.

"Go and see what's keeping . . . confound it! What's going on out there?" He swung round to see what was causing the disturbance that arose outside the door. Then, in horror, "Good God!"

Women screamed. Men shouted, crowding forward, all speaking at once. "Who is it?" "What's happened?" "He's been set upon."

"Give him air. Give him air," cried Adam, as he and Jem half carried, half dragged a young soldier into the house between them. "Where's Atkinson? The man needs attention."

They laid him on a settee. His face was streaked with blood and dirt, his hair was matted, his uniform muddied. He could not have been much more than eighteen years of age.

Atkinson pushed forward, loosened the soldier's clothing, and sent a slave running to fetch water and cloths, another to bring his bag from his carriage, which he always carried with him in case of emergency.

"He looks as though he's been bludgeond," the doctor said after inspecting the boy's head. Then he called for some brandy.

Brandy was put into his hand almost immediately. He held the glass to the soldier's lips. The soldier coughed and spluttered. He opened his eyes. They were a very light blue—full of terror. He cringed as Sir George bent over him and began trembling violently.

"Who did this to you?" Sir George demanded. "What happened?"

"Give him time, sir," Adam pleaded. "The man's terrified out of his wits."

"But we must know who did it. We must get after the brute."

"Do you think . . . some animal . . . ?"

Dr. Atkinson turned to the matron who spoke. "No animal did this." He started to staunch the head wound with the water and cloths that had arrived. "This was man-inflicted."

"Can't you tell us, man?" Sir George's voice was less harsh, though his anxiety to know was still as strong. "Tell us who it was so we can get after him."

The man—the boy—shivered and shook, but the brandy was beginning to have its enlivening effect. He opened his mouth. For a while nothing came out of it. Then, "The Gray . . . the Gray . . ."

It was all he could manage. He fainted away.

"The Gray Phantom!" The cry was taken up all round. "The Gray Phantom!"

Ladies started screaming again. Morvah clutched at me convulsively, surprising me, for I had thought she did not believe in the Gray Phantom. Then Mollie Macpherson declared in a loud whisper, "So he does exist, after all."

The governor swung round, his face red and angry. "Colonel, get your men together. If the blackguard's out there, find him. Gun him down, like the dog he is."

Chapter Nine

We were off. Adam and Jem had been lent clean, dry clothes, and both were dressed as officers. Jem looked ill at ease in his, but Adam . . . I thought Adam looked superb.

It still rained. It thundered. It lightninged. There was sound all around the carriage, but inside, no one spoke. I was thinking, I suspect we were all thinking, about the injured soldier, and the Gray Phantom.

The Gray Phantom. Was he the man I had seen up on the rock? He must have been. Was he a man—or insubstantial? He had looked solid enough during the brief moment I had spied him. But he had disappeared so swiftly. Adam had been confident I could not have seen anyone up there, yet . . .

"I think I've seen the Gray Phantom," I heard myself say.

"What?" they all cried. All except Adam, whom I felt stiffen beside me.

I told them about the man on the rock.

"Jutting Rock? Impossible. No man can ride up there.

No horse could get up there." Morvah sounded very certain.

"That's what Adam said," I began, and was interrupted by Jem.

"You knew, Adam?"

"Barbara told me of it, but I paid no special attention to it. I did not see the need."

I turned to him eagerly. "I knew you said I must have imagined it, but how could I have? I knew nothing about the Gray Phantom then. But it must have been he I saw, or how could I describe him? He was all in gray and riding a gray horse. And . . . *is* he a phantom? He looked very real to me. And that young soldier said he had been attacked by the Gray Phantom."

"He was attacked . . . by someone. His injuries were very real."

"But that's what I mean. The Gray Phantom is a real man, not a ghost."

"Oh, Barbara, stop it," Morvah snapped at me angrily. "You're letting your imagination run away with you. You're worse than Mollie Macpherson. "Now let's change the subject, for goodness' sake. I'm sick to death of the whole business."

"But Barbara has a point, Mrs. Pengarth," Jem said quietly. "If, as she says, she has seen him . . ."

"I have," I intervened assertively.

"Just so. Then perhaps we should start thinking along the lines that he does exist and that he is real, and that we should seriously set about running him to earth."

"And how do you suggest we do that?" asked Adam. "The army have had no success."

"They haven't been taking the matter seriously."

"Well, perhaps now that that young soldier . . ."

"Oh, please, please, boys." Morvah sounded near to tears.

"I'm sorry, Mother," Adam said. "But it is a matter we should discuss. However, this is not the time."

We all lapsed into silence, then, suddenly, Robert said, "I like gray. I shall have a gray outfit made for me. Do you think it would suit me, Mother?"

Morvah did not reply.

"Mother?" Robert required an answer.

"I . . . Why . . . I don't know, dear, I . . ."

Morvah sounded distressed. There was fear in her voice. Why? Did she think . . . did she suspect . . . ? I looked at Robert, vaguely visible in the dark interior of the carriage. He was big and very substantial, but he lurched and his head was overlarge. He could not have been the man on the rock. The man I had seen had been upright and had held his head high. Morvah could not think Robert was the Gray Phantom. It was laughable. But she was afraid. Was it because he had said he liked gray and wished to have a gray suit made? Had that put the idea into her mind? But he often said things like that, out of the blue, picking out a word from our conversations that appealed to him and making use of it. She must know that.

Then was her fear for Adam? Adam, who often wore gray? A little shiver of fear ran through me as I sat beside him. He placed an arm around me. "Are you cold, my dear?"

I could not relax against him. Was he the Gray Phantom? He must have noticed my stiffness. He removed his arm.

* * *

Tommyboy's eye had not been gouged from its socket. It had been hidden behind the sea of blood that had emanated from the deep cut across his face. Philip stitched it and it was healing. I visited the old man every day and I think he looked forward to my visits. He gazed at me with the adoring eyes of a spaniel, trusting and wholly dependent. As I had said to Adam, these people were not vicious. They would not rise in their hordes to murder us if—when—they received their freedom.

Philip's visits were a joy to me, I was so much alone and enjoyed a chat with him. I inquired after Sarah. He said, "She's well and asks after you. She remembers your friendship with affection." But I thought he looked unhappy.

I said, "I'm looking forward to renewing our friendship when you come to dinner."

"To dinner?"

"Yes. When can you come?"

He did not reply at once, and now I thought he looked *very* unhappy.

"Is anything wrong?" I asked.

"No." But he sounded reserved. As he had been on his first visit to High Place.

"Are you sure?"

"Yes." He tried to look cheerful, but I was not convinced.

"I'd like you to come and spend a day with us, if you can." If he did not wish to tell me what was wrong I could not force him. "Sarah and I will have so much to talk about."

"Does Adam wish it?"

"That you and Sarah come for a whole day? Of course. Why should he not? He knows how I am looking forward to seeing Sarah again, and we all got on so well on board the *Indies Pride*. I was hoping you could come on Friday. Do you think you could manage that?"

"Well . . . yes . . . I should think so."

"You don't sound too enthusiastic."

He summoned a smile. "I am, of course. It will do Sarah good to get away for a while."

I was so delighted with his acceptance that I did not consider the oddness of those words till he had gone.

I had always begged him to stay and take tea with me after he had seen Tommyboy, but he was ever in a hurry and always refused, till the day he pronounced Tommyboy fit enough to start work again.

"But don't let him do anything too strenuous. He's an old man."

I promised I would not. "He could sit back and do nothing. It is by his own wish he performs such duties he deems himself capable of. He will not take orders from the man placed in his position a long time ago. And Adam shuts his eyes to it and allows him to go his own way."

Philip nodded. "Adam's a compassionate master. Reasonable and enlightened. Unlike some I could name. Pity he can't go all the way and join those of us who . . ."

"Adam wishes to see the end of slavery." I sprang instinctively to Adam's defense.

"But his way is too slow. With every day that passes things get worse. The bill against slavery was passed a long time ago, but trading still goes on—and worse than before. You saw those men on the quay the day we arrived in Almada. That was nothing. If I were to tell you . . ." He broke off, his eyes darkening with some remembered horror he could not impart to me.

I tried to turn his mind away from it. "When can I

come and see your hospital?" I asked as I poured him another cup of tea.

"I think, perhaps . . ." He avoided my eyes. "It's better that you don't."

"Why?"

He paused, looking down into his tea, then he said, "There are such dreadful things . . . terrible sights . . . not fit for a lady's eyes."

"Sarah sees them. She's a lady."

"Sarah's different. A doctor's wife gets used to . . . Sarah's grown used to . . ."

"I am not a milksop," I declared with the vehemence of unsureness. "I am not unaware of the dreadful things that happen here. I have seen evidence of it on my own doorstep."

"So you have, Barbara, so you have. But . . ."

"What?"

"There's worse. Much worse. You have no idea, cocooned here at High Place, of the terrible things . . . the slaves here are happy, as happy as they can be in bondage, but I've seen places where . . ."

He broke off. I thought at first it was because he was afraid to tell me more, but then I realized he was listening to something that had not reached my ears.

"What is it?" I asked, with a prick of fear.

"I thought I heard something . . . someone at the door . . . Listen."

We were silent.

"There. Did you hear it?"

I heard it. An odd scraping sound. A sound I had heard before. A sound I recognized.

"I think it's Robert."

"Robert?" Philip strode to the door and wrenched it

open. He glanced around outside and came back to me. "No one. Perhaps it wasn't anybody, only our imagination."

"No, it was Robert," I said, with certainty now. "I often hear him, but do not see him. And he moves so quickly, in spite of his lameness." I gazed at Philip anxiously. "I sometimes wonder . . ."

"What?"

"Oh, nothing. It's just that . . . well, you've seen him. He has a strange effect on one."

"He's an unfortunate man. A victim of a cruel fate."

"Yes." My eyes fell before Philip's compassionate gaze. "I try to keep that at the front of my mind—but I am not always successful."

"You fear him." He made the statement with a quick, searching glance.

"No, no, of course not."

I rejected the absurd idea quickly. But it was true. I did fear him. I often came across him loitering outside doors and windows. Listening? Secretly? Sometimes he saw me, sometimes not. When he did, he grinned, and sidled away. Sometimes I thought he was not so innocent and childlike as everybody seemed to think.

I went with Philip to the door. Our footsteps echoed on the marble floor of the hall. I stood at the foot of the white marble steps and waved him good-bye. As I watched him ride away, a slight figure in dark coat and trousers, a wide-brimmed hat shading his head from the sun, I smiled and thought back over the many happy hours the four of us had shared on the voyage over from England. How I looked forward to meeting Sarah again. I could hardly wait for Friday to arrive.

He was out of sight. I turned to go in. I was standing in

the hot sun without a parasol and I did not want to end up with a skin like Morvah Pengarth's.

As I turned, I noticed Jem Harding standing a little way off, tall, broad, arms and face like mahogany. His face was set in serious lines. For a moment he did not seem aware that I had noticed him, then he smiled and waved.

"Good morning, Barbara," he called out. "Was that Philip Rose I saw riding away?"

"Yes. It's his last visit to Tommyboy. He says Tommyboy is fully recovered."

Jem nodded and went on about his business. I stared after him and saw Robert come out of the bushes and shamble along behind him. I half raised my arm to wave to him, but he took no notice of me, did not even seem to see me. He was intent on following Jem. His whole concentration was to that purpose.

"You've acquired a willing slave," Adam observed, smiling as we sat sipping lemonade on the veranda.

Tommyboy, since his recovery, had taken to following me about adoringly, anticipating my every wish, presenting me with posies of flowers. This was the only duty he recognized now—waiting on me.

"And one, I am sure, who would gladly die for you."

"I don't want . . . I have no wish for . . ."

"Whether you like it or not," Adam's voice was crisply dry, "you are a slave owner now."

"If I were," I returned as crisply, "I would free him."

"Tommyboy? But he's free already."

"What?"

"A number of my slaves are free," he said, smiling at my astonishment.

"What . . . ? But . . . then . . . why don't they go?"

"Because they don't want to."

I was speechless for a moment. There were times when I did not understand him at all. Then I fired at him, "If you can free some, why not all?"

"Because that, my sweet, idiotic Barbara, would set a torch to a fuse. Wholesale freedom of slaves is a thing to be worked for slowly. It cannot be achieved without the cooperation of all slave owners—and I can assure you that is not forthcoming at present."

"Philip thinks . . ."

An angry shadow crossed his face. "Philip thinks too much," he said, and placing his empty glass on the table, rose and took his leave.

My mind was an ants' nest of activity. Adam was a veritable contradiction to me. One minute we could be talking amicably together, the next he would grow cold and distant. He could be hard, almost cruel, but he did not beat his slaves and had already freed some of them. I had thought him against slave reform from the way he argued against the words and deeds of men like Wilberforce and Clarkson, yet he had ideas of his own on how to achieve this aim, which were clear and seemed sound. He treated me in an offhand, careless manner and left me to my own devices, not seeming to realize I needed and wanted his company. He told me to mind my own business, had even pronounced me unwomanly, yet he appreciated my questing mind, applauded my desire to form my own opinions and not blindly follow another's dictates. And he could treat me gently, consider my feelings. And just now he had used an endearment to me. He had called me his sweet, idiotic Barbara. That was an endearment, was it not? Did it mean that he . . . ?

No, it did not. I stopped my thoughts from running away with me. It did not mean anything. It just proved how inconsistent he was. The only thing he was consistent about, I told myself angrily, was Araminta Belmont.

Araminta—I could not bring myself to call her Minty, like everyone else—called almost every day, always on horseback, I believed deliberately. She knew I could not ride, so could not join them. She would greet me briefly, then whisk my not-reluctant husband away for a gallop along the golden sands by the edge of the violet sea and up into the hills.

How did I know where they went? Because I saw them from my bedroom window where I raced after they had left. There I would unashamedly watch their progress, till they disappeared among the waving palms. My imagination supplied the rest, powered by longing and despair, and the ache inside me would grow. Sometimes I seemed to be one great ache, from top to toe. Araminta was where I, Adam's wife should be, and I could do nothing but accept it.

I decided to go out. It was still early, and the sun had not yet reached its height. Nevertheless, I was already feeling hot and sticky. It was my fault. I had taken to wearing black all the time since Araminta's party, in an odd form of defiance, secretly hoping Adam would take exception to it, as he had done aboard the *Indies Pride.* But he had not seemed to notice, and out of a mixture of stubbornness and annoyance I continued to wear it, though I knew I was cutting off my nose to spite my face—black seemed to draw the heat more than any other color.

Meta was busy in my room putting clean linen into

drawers and cupboards. Passing a hand across my sticky brow and blowing an upward breath from between my lips, I requested my parasol. Her response was immediate. "Miss Barbry, you not go out in that. You too hot."

"I'm perfectly all right," I retorted, holding out my hand for the parasol.

"You one crazy lady," she said with a sigh.

"That's enough, Meta," I cried angrily. "Hand me my parasol at once, or I'll . . ." I bit back the words hovering on the end of my tongue. I had almost said I would have her beaten.

I gave her a great deal of license, and she may have gotten into the habit of thinking she could say anything she liked to me without fear of correction. Did she know what my hastily bitten-back words were to have been? I fear she did. She handed me my parasol with downcast eyes and a submissive stance.

I left her, hating myself. That I should even think of saying such a thing astonished me. Was I growing callous? Was the worst aspect of West Indian life brushing off onto me? No. No. I would not believe it. I had spoken harshly to her from out of a deep well of unhappiness. But that was no excuse, and I knew it. I have never spoken harshly to a servant in my life. I was only too well aware of the hurt a harshly spoken word could cause. Yet I had spoken harshly to one who could not, *dared* not, answer me back—for fear.

Miserable on more counts than one, I hurried out into the solace of the gardens. They were beautiful. The lawns were carpets of emerald green. Bushes as tall as trees were laden with flowers—red, yellow, white, purple—perfuming the air. I made my way to a favorite resting place, a shady seat looking out across sloping lawns to sand and sea.

I sighed deeply. What was I doing here? Why had I not remained in England? I would have been much happier there growing into an old maid than here in Almada as Adam's wife. Adam's wife! What a laugh! I was as much of a spinster as I had ever been. He did not want me for a wife. He had had to get drunk before he could come to me on our wedding night. And how quick he had been to accept my rejection of him then—with what relief! If only I had not denied him. If only I had accepted his advances, drunken stupor and all. There might have been a child. Someone to love, who loved me.

Tears stung my eyes as longing for that might-have-been child overcame me. I let them fall. They dried on my cheeks.

At last, I rose and turned to go back to the house, when something made me stop and turn my head. A movement? A sound? I could not be sure. I could see no one, and yet I felt instinctively I was being watched. Then I heard a rustling in the bushes. Common sense told me it was probably only some small animal or a bird—there were plenty of them about, but I did not believe it, and my heart started hammering painfully. It could have been one of the gardeners. I tried to believe it.

I forced myself to go on, straining my ears for any unusual sound, my eyes darting hither and thither. My mouth had grown uncomfortably dry. I knew someone was there, somewhere behind me, following me. Not closely, not obviously, but following me.

If only I had not walked so far from the house. But surely I could not be in danger in the gardens of High Place. Surely no one would dare molest me here. I was, after all, Adam's wife, the mistress of High Place. But in spite of all, I was afraid.

I had come to a full stop, stock still with fear and trembling. I was certain I was about to be attacked . . . murdered . . . at the very least, maimed, yet I could not move.

Then a twig cracked. The sound relieved me and I turned in the direction of it. At first I could see no one, then a brown face was peering out at me from behind a leafy bush. It disappeared on the instant, but not before I had seen the fear bright in its eyes, then, a streak of brown, and a man sped away, down toward the seashore.

It took me a little time to realize he had been as frightened as I, so thankful was I that it had not been the Phantom hiding there, waiting to pounce. I wondered who he was. I had not recognized him as one of our slaves, but then, I did not know all the Pengarth slaves. Indeed, many of them I had not even seen. But why should he have been so afraid? A Pengarth slave had nothing to fear. I knew this for a fact now. So it could only mean that he had been a slave from some other plantation. But whose? And why? What was he doing lurking in the bushes? There could only be one answer. He was a runaway slave.

Thoughtfully, I returned to the house. Its white pillars, entwined with vines, the white marble steps, the white starkness of the whole building stood out against the vivid blue sky. Inside it was richly furnished, kept clean and fresh by a happy band of singing men and women, slaves; but how many of them were free to go if they wished, I wondered. And at how many other plantations would I have been able to ask that?

With a little thrill of pride, both in Adam and in High Place, I ran up the white marble steps. This was my home. And yet, not my home. There were still times when I felt like an outsider. Not that I was not made welcome. Morvah, though she still kept very much to herself, appeared glad to have me to talk to; and Jem made me welcome; Robert—was friendly, after his own fashion. But there was something . . . I could not put a finger on it . . . odd little undercurrents that set up an anxiety within me.

I was crossing the veranda when my attention was caught by Robert appearing from around a corner. I halted. Had it been he stalking me in the garden? Of course not, what was the matter with me? It had been a brown face I had seen. A slave's face.

I hailed him as he lolloped toward me. "Hello, Robert."

He stopped before me. "I know something you don't know," he grinned slyly.

"Oh? What?"

"Can't tell you. Adam says you're not to know."

"Oh," I said tightly. "Then in that case you had better not." I turned to go in, then stopped again as he continued.

"Jem thinks you ought to know. Jem likes you. I like you. Do you like me?"

I forced myself to smile at him. His voice was so plaintive, so childlike, so innocent.

"Yes, of course I like you," I said.

He grinned hugely and I felt myself warm toward him.

"Jem says . . ." he began.

"What?"

"Mustn't say."

He lolloped away. I stood and watched him go. At the far end of the veranda he turned, grinned, and waved.

Once more I was struck by a strange familiarity about him, as if I knew him, as if I had met him before somewhere. But, of course, this could not be.

I entered the cool hall and Tommyboy appeared at my side as if by magic. The scar on the side of his face jolted me. It would probably always be there. It had been a vicious blow Jack Ransom had given him. I smiled. "Hello Tommy."

He smiled a toothless smile. "Missie Barbry like lemonade?"

"That would be most acceptable," I said. "My throat feels parched."

He bowed me along through the morning room. It gave out onto the veranda at the east side of the house and was cooler than anywhere else—if anywhere at all could be said to be cool. Its great windows were thrown open and on the wicker table outside I could see a tall glass jug, clouding over. He must have been watching for my arrival and brought it straight from the cold room below the kitchens, so that it should be ice cold for me to drink. Lemon slices floated on the top and I waited eagerly for the glass he poured me.

"There, Missie Barbry. Cool, cool drink. I make myself."

"Thank you Tommy." I took a mouthful. "It's delicious."

Beaming with joy at my praise, he backed away, leaving me to finish my drink. It was good. I reached out to pour myself another glass, but Tommyboy was there before my fingers could curl round the jug's handle.

"I'm not an invalid, Tommy," I protested.

He just beamed. "No, missie." He filled my glass with more lemonade and disappeared again—but I knew he would not have gone far.

If only he had been near me in the gardens when I needed someone. But Tommyboy never left the house now since Ransom's attack on him.

I sighed and closed my eyes, lying back against the cushions. Who was it that had stared at me out of the bushes with such wide, terrified eyes? Who had run with such speed from me, as if he expected some terrible calamity to befall him? A runaway slave? If caught, what would happen to him? Would his punishment be the lash? I heard again in memory the whine of the whip through the air, the horrifying crack as it landed. Or would he be hanged? I knew there were such examples made.

Why had he run away, knowing the kind of punishment that lay in store for him if he were caught? His life must have been unbearable to risk it.

My heart bled for him. Besides his troubles my own seemed puny indeed. I, at least, had the right to decide my own fate. I need not have left the comfort and safety of Martha's Cottage. I could have spared myself a lot of unhappiness if I had made the right choice. He had no choice.

Thoughts of Martha's Cottage filled my mind now. The gardens there. The bright-eyed peacocks strutting the lawns, showing off. The great cathedrallike windows. The peace. The serenity.

A dark shadow crossed my inward gaze and my eyes flew open. Adam was standing before me, looking down at me with pensive gaze.

"I'm sorry," he said. "I didn't mean to wake you."

"I wasn't asleep," I said, and watched him pour himself a glass of lemonade. My own glass was still full.

"You appeared to be," he said, sitting and stretching

his legs.

"I was dreaming," I said, with a reminiscent smile. "About Martha's Cottage."

I noticed a stiffening in him, but I did not care. There was a growing defiance in me. I was going to do and say what I had a mind for. I had told him so.

"You miss Martha's Cottage," he said, after a moment's hesitation.

"Yes. Yes, I do."

"It can't hold a candle to High Place."

He was not boasting, just stating a fact. He gulped down his lemonade.

"Not in size, I agree, but there was peace there, and serenity."

"And there isn't here."

"I didn't say that."

"No, but you implied it. Well, you're right. This place is anything but peaceful—now."

He chose to misunderstand me. Well, I was used to it. We sat in silence for a minute or so. To explain might involve too much.

I said, "I think I saw a runaway slave in the gardens a short time ago."

"What?" His black brows knitted together above his nose.

"I think," I had a sudden inspiration, "it might have been Billy Joe."

"Billy Joe?" If his brows could have knitted further, they would have. "Don't talk nonsense."

"Do you know if he's been found yet?" I refused to be cowed.

"No, I—don't believe he has."

"Then it could have been he. He was very frightened.

He ran away as soon as he caught me looking at him."

"Where was this?"

"At the farthest part of the house near the palms that edge the sand. There's a seat there. . . ."

"What were you doing down there?"

"I often go there. I take a book with me and . . ."

"You were alone?"

"Of course, I was alone," I retorted briskly. This was the second time he had interrupted me. "I'm always alone," I added accusingly. Let him take that as he might.

He drew in his breath and seemed about to say something else, but desisted.

"If it was Billy Joe . . ."

"It wasn't Billy Joe."

"How do you know? How can you be sure?"

"Because Billy Joe is still incapacitated, and . . ."

He broke off as I gave a muffled exclamation and threw back his head with gesture of irritation at himself. Then he sat forward and leaned toward me.

"He's still in this house, Barbara," he said quietly. "He never left it the second time he escaped."

"He's been here all the time? Even while Jack Ransom . . . ?"

"All the time. He arrived around midnight the night before Ransom called round. Everyone but Jem and I had retired. . . . God knows how he managed to reach us. He was nearer to death than I care to remember. You thought Tommyboy badly treated—you should have seen Billy Joe. What they must have done to him!"

"You took him in? You harbored him? Another man's slave?"

"Would you expect me to do anything else?"

"No, but . . ."

He gave a knowing smile.

My eyes fell before his. "I'm sorry," I mumbled, a little ashamed of myself. I had been surprised at his show of Christian spirit.

"Jem and I got him up to the attic between us."

"So that was the noise I heard. I knew I hadn't imagined it." He raised a questioning eyebrow and I went on quickly. "Does anyone else know Billy Joe is in the house? Meta does, doesn't she?" When I spoke to her about it the following morning she was most evasive. It made me think she knew more than she was telling."

"Yes, Meta knows," he said, "and Bella. They are nursing him. Tommyboy knows, too. He's Billy Joe's father."

"Oh." I digested this piece of surprising information, then asked. "Does your mother know?"

"No. And I don't want her to. It will distress her, for more reasons than one. Besides, the fewer people who know, the better. I've told you because of your strange encounter in the garden."

"So you think it might have been Billy Joe?"

"No." He picked up the jug. "Another glass?"

I shook my head. He poured one for himself.

"Robert knows," I said.

"No, he doesn't." Adam returned confidently. "He was in bed, fast asleep. I know. I looked in on him as I passed his door."

"Well, he knows. He told me so. Not in so many words, but he said he knew something I didn't and when I asked him what it was he told me you had told him not to tell me. So unless there is something else you have told him not to tell me . . ."

"But how could he know?" Adam frowned furiously.

"I never told him. Unless . . . he may not have been asleep. He may have been pretending. He . . . can be sly at times."

"But why should he say you had told him not to tell me? He said you would be angry if he did."

Adam shook his head. "Who knows why Robert says any of the things he does?"

I said, after a moment's pause. "You won't send him back, will you, Adam? Billy Joe, I mean."

"No. Never."

"I wonder who it was I saw skulking in the bushes." I said.

"You said yourself, a runaway slave. It's happening all the time."

"He looked so scared."

"He would not want to be caught. He would be afraid of the punishment."

"But you don't punish . . ."

"He would not know that. He would only think . . . oh, Barbara!" He gave a huge sigh and rose to take hold of the veranda rail and gaze into the distance. "If you only knew how sick and tired I am of . . ."

"Of what?"

"Oh . . . nothing." Then he swung to face me and cried fiercely, "Everything." I gazed up at him, anxious and a little afraid, certainly puzzled by his ferocity. "I sometimes wish . . . oh, Barbara, what have I brought you to?"

Then he gave a light laugh. Perhaps he had noticed my anxiety and was sorry he had occasioned it. He sat down again, and leaning forward, took my hands in his. "Barbara," he said, "why do you insist on wearing black?"

His eyes were teasing, yet soft. I was so surprised by his sudden change of manner that I could not think what to say. I was extremely aware of the warm, satisfying grip of his hands on mine. His eyes probed deep into mine. For a moment it was as if we were one; almost as if he made love to me.

Chapter Ten

"Oh, there you are!"

Morvah's voice wrenched us apart. But she had seen us holding hands and sent me a quick, secret smile. Though she still kept very much to herself, her attitude toward me had changed and had become almost motherly.

Adam sprang up. "Sit here, Mother. I'll pour you some lemonade."

"Thank you, Adam." She sat down and looked at me, and a slight warning entered her smile. "I saw you walking down toward the sea, Barbara. Do you think it wise to stray so far from the house alone, after what happened the last time?"

"I stayed within the confines of the garden. There was no danger there," I said reassuringly, catching Adam's eye. Neither of us was sure of how much she knew and had no wish to alarm her unnecessarily.

"Of course not," said Adam. "What harm could come to her in our own gardens?"

"None at all, of course, only . . ."

"There is nothing to fear, Mother." Adam handed her

the glass of lemonade. "I have great faith in Barbara's common sense. She will not venture too far afield in future, alone."

His eyes and tone held a warning I could not ignore. He was laying down the law to me.

We sipped our drinks in silence for a while in the shade of the veranda. The hum of insects had a soporific effect, and I felt my eyelids drooping in spite of the two small black slaves laboriously waving palm leaves about in an effort to create a breeze for us. I wondered if they would be sent out to work in the fields when they grew older, or if they would be put to work inside the house. Or would slavery have been abolished by then?

"If I remember correctly," Morvah said, "you promised to teach Barbara to ride, Adam, quite some time ago."

"Yes, you're perfectly right, Mother."

"Yet you don't appear to have done anything about it."

"No. I haven't."

"Why not?"

"Because . . ."

"Because he'd forgotten all about it," I interrupted tartly.

"No," he returned quietly, "I hadn't forgotten. I thought . . . You showed no further interest."

"How could I? You never raised the subject again."

Morvah must have noticed the note of asperity in my voice. She cut in quickly. "We have full stabling once more, have we not, Adam? Surely a suitable horse can be found for Barbara to learn on. Something not too frisky."

"I will look one out for her," Adam replied.

"And I think you should escort her about more. She

must get very bored staying around the house all day. No wonder she goes wandering off. There is a great deal of beauty and interest on the island. I'm sure you would like to be taken to see it, would you not, my dear?"

I swallowed. "Yes," I murmured faintly, not daring to look at Adam. Her plan to throw us together was so blatantly obvious.

"You must arrange something," Morvah continued. "A picnic, maybe. Just for the two of you."

"I'll arrange something," he said, but he did not sound at all enthusiastic.

Adam had gone riding with Araminta. If he had not forgotten his promise to teach me to ride, he had no intention of carrying it out quickly. I had not indulged my usual habit of racing up to my room to watch them out of sight, but instead had gone into the music room, where I had proceeded to play all the most demanding music I knew in an effort to override my anguish. I was trying, I was trying very hard, to accept things as they were. But now I had played myself out and sat looking into space, my hands idle in my lap.

Adam found me so. I must have been playing for hours.

He came in with an eager step. "I've been looking everywhere for you," he said, with a smile.

"Everywhere? Tommyboy knew I was in here," I returned coldly.

"I know that now, I've just asked him." My cool reception had erased his smile momentarily, but it was soon back. "On my return I didn't think twice, I went straight along to your secret resting place in the garden. I know you spend most of your mornings in the garden. Have you got a riding habit?"

"A riding habit?"

"Yes, a riding habit." He smiled, but teasingly at me.

I wanted to return his smile, but I could not.

"No," I said through stiff lips.

"Then we must get you one. I'll have some sent down from Seatown—if they have any, if not, rolls of cloth so you can have one made. Meta is clever with her needle, she . . ."

"Why must they be sent?" I checked his flow of words. "Why cannot I go into Seatown myself and choose?"

Taken by surprise, Adam said, "Well, you can, of course. I didn't think . . ."

"It is a fine, bustling town with many shops. I should like to visit Seatown." And I added, with sudden daring, "Why can't you take me?"

A slow smile spread across his face. "Very well, if that is your wish."

"It is."

His smile broadened and his eyes lit up. "Good! I would have suggested it myself, only I thought . . . I didn't think you'd . . . we could make a long day of it."

I began to respond to his enthusiasm and I smiled happily. "Yes, that would be lovely."

"We could take Mother. I'm sure she would love to accompany us."

My smile froze on my face as a chill attacked my body. I knew why he wished his mother to accompany us. Though I was sure she would have rejected his invitation, happy to see us go off alone together, I reacted sharply. "I'm sure she would. And it would suit your purpose."

His smile faded. "I don't understand."

"You would not have to be alone with me," I obliged.

"I didn't mean it that way," he protested, his face setting into grim lines.

"I think you did. While we're about it, let us take Robert with us as well, and Jem, and Tom and Dick and Harry."

"You're being childish," Adam said.

"I feel childish," I returned, on the verge of tears.

"I'll speak to you later," he said, turning to go. "When you've regained your senses."

I was angry with myself. Far from accepting the fact that mine was a loveless marriage, I resisted at every turn. That I, who had learned to control my emotions so well under my aunt's instruction, should behave with such crass stupidity as to allow my feelings to run away with me was beyond belief. It seemed without Aunt Martha's restraining influence I was unable to sustain my dignity.

But no, this was not true. I would not allow it to be true. What had happened to all the plans I had formulated since Araminta's party when my self-esteem had received such a lift? I had received a lot of attention. People had talked to me and listened to what I had to say with interest. Young men had been eager to dance with me. I did not think it was all merely because I was Adam Pengarth's wife, though that might have had something to do with it.

My plans had depended on a determination not to wait on Adam's good will, which was not outstandingly evident, but to work out my own destiny, as Aunt Martha had done.

No. Not as Aunt Martha had done. I would not retire into a hermitlike existence as she had. I would go out and meet the world.

Where had they gone then, those plans? I had made no use of them.

Meta dressed me for dinner in a gown of gray silk. I did not recognize it as my own. Meta's magic fingers had transformed it. The top had been cut off, leaving it so low back and front that it made me gasp. The ballooning sleeves, narrowing at the elbows to cling tightly from there to the wrists, had disappeared. In their stead were puffy sleeves standing up high at the tops of my arms, oversewn with stiff white lace, which also edged the bodice.

"What a difference you've made to this dress," I praised her. "You've wrought such a change. It's beautiful."

She beamed. "I change them all, in time. But you need new gowns, missie. Many new gowns."

"Yes," I said, watching her set to work looping my long hair and piling it into high standing wedges in the fashion of the moment. "I do, don't I? I shall have to do something about it."

We smiled at each other in the mirror.

"Where did you get that?" I asked, as she began to thread a pearl-encrusted band of velvet through my hair. I knew it had not come from among my belongings.

"The velvet I take from store cupboard. Pearls come

from old gown belonging Missie Pengarth. She not want anymore."

We smiled at each other again. I was blessed with Meta for a personal maid.

I went downstairs knowing I looked my best. I was no longer afraid of appearing in my new guise. Adam frowned when he saw me, but he made no comment. A footman came forward with a tray of drinks. I took one and heard Morvah's voice come from deep within her favorite armchair.

"Are you feeling better, my dear?"

"Better, Mrs. Pengarth?"

"Adam told me you were not feeling well. He seemed to think you might not feel up to coming down to dinner."

I cast a cool glance in Adam's direction. "Oh. Did he? I wonder why."

"That's not quite true, Mother," Adam said. "I merely said I thought it would be better if she did not."

I drew in an angry breath. "Surely, you must know, Adam, nothing would keep me from greeting my friends here tonight. Nothing."

Sarah and Philip Rose were coming to dinner. They had not, after all, been able to manage a full day. The Macphersons were also coming, as was Agnes, to make up an even number at table. But as yet no one had arrived. I went to the open window and gazed out across the blackened gardens to where an unseen sea washed an unseen shore. For some reason, I shivered.

"Cold, Barbara?" Adam had moved to stand beside me. "Shall I get you a shawl?"

"No." I moved a step or two away from him and saw his eyes snap. "It was just a gray goose walking over my grave."

"I see. Do you get many of those?" There was a quizzical gleam in his eyes now.

I backed further away. His body was far too close to mine.

"No, not many."

Jem entered the room just then and I moved quickly up to him. "Hello, Jem." I do not know what else I said, but we were soon engaged in conversation, while Adam stared gloomily at us from across the room.

Then Robert made his entrance and lolloped across to us, collecting a drink on the way. It always surprised me that he was allowed to drink. Though he had the years and appearance of a man, he was still a child. However, he never drank to excess. I never saw him anything other than sober. He gave me a little bow and said, "You look nice tonight, sister."

It pleased him to refer to me as sister, which he did quite often.

"Thank you," I smiled.

"Barbara always looks nice," Jem said, and I saw Adam's eyes narrow and an angry expression cross his face. I could not understand why. Why would it matter to him if others gave me compliments? I got few enough from him.

The Macphersons arrived, Mollie as effusive as ever, Agnes as quiet, Sam as friendly. Hard on their heels came Philip and Sarah.

I greeted Sarah affectionately. "How pretty you look," I exclaimed as the removal of her wrap revealed a gown of rich blue hue that added depth to her light blue eyes. Then I noticed the wary expression lurking in her eyes, the dark smudges beneath, and I sensed in her what I had sensed in her husband on my first renewal of acquaintance with him—a kind of drawing back, almost of fear.

Utter nonsense, of course. What had she to fear from me? I kissed her cheek warmly and was rewarded with a smile in her old charming manner. However, I noticed the wariness return at intervals throughout dinner. Only with Robert did she appear completely relaxed. Because she considered him of no account? Or was her compassion for him greater than her distrust?

Distrust? What put that word into my head?

"Is anything wrong?" I asked her as soon as I had a chance. Bella had poured coffee and gone. The men were at their port and cigars. Morvah—I did not know where Morvah was, but she had taken Mollie and Agnes with her. Perhaps it had been deliberately planned in order to give me a few minutes alone with my friend. Sarah did not reply to my question immediately.

"You look strained. Is it perhaps that the climate does not agree with you?"

Still she did not reply.

"What is wrong, Sarah? Something is, I'm sure. You were not like this on the *Indies Pride.* Neither was Philip. Then you were both full of vigor. There was none of this—tenseness I observe in you both now. There were no shadows under your eyes. Can't you unburden yourself to me? I am your friend."

"I am grateful for your friendship." She spoke at last. "You can have no idea how much your invitation to visit you meant to me."

"Friendship does not seek gratitude," I observed gently, a little sad that she should think mine required it.

"Forgive me, Barbara," she cried at once. "I did not mean to sound offensive, only—I have not experienced any unselfish conduct lately. I am afraid I am growing cynical."

"I think perhaps you may have been working too hard. You have become too wrapped up in your new hospital and . . ."

"We have not had the success we had hoped for in that direction," she cut in on me.

"Oh. Adam did tell me once things were not working out quite as you and Philip had hoped, but . . ."

"It has not worked out at all as we had hoped. At first the planters and rich businessmen were all in favor of a hospital, but as soon as it was made clear to them that it would be a charity hospital, they withdrew their support. They told Philip to get out of Almada, they didn't want his kind here—just as Adam had warned us they would."

"Oh, Sarah!" I said in sympathy. "But do not despair. They will come round. They will see. . . ."

"They will not. They will never see. Their eyes are turned inward. And they distrust us now more than ever. We have opened our hospital in spite of them, but to our great cost." She gave me a long sad look, then went on. "We are ostracized by white society in Almada."

"Sarah!"

"We receive no invitations and ours are not accepted—nor even acknowledged. Philip's medical knowledge is not sought, and we are not spoken to in the streets. We are treated like lepers, and I do not know how long I shall be able to withstand it."

Her eyes suddenly swam with tears. I sprang from my seat and dropped to my knees before her, catching hold of her hands.

"Do not cry. Sarah. Please do not cry. We will fight these men. Adam and I will help you fight them." I used

Adam's name without a second's thought. "Everything will come right, you will see."

Sarah tried to smile through her tears. "Dear Barbara." She bent to kiss me. "I know it would be a hard life we were coming to. Philip told me we should come up against prejudice and anger . . . but I was totally unprepared for such fierce antagonism, such threatening opposition."

"Threatening?"

"They have threatened us with . . ."

She broke off as Morvah returned with Mollie and Agnes. I rose from my crouching position and returned to my seat. Not one of them said anything, but they all looked a little oddly at me. The conversation became innocuous.

When the menfolk joined us a few minutes later it was quite obvious they had been discussing the same thing that had occupied Sarah's attention and mine.

"The best thing you can do is give up and return to England," Jem was saying.

"Let them drive me away? I can't. I won't. I have much work to do here."

Adam said, "It sounds as if you have made up your mind. I wish you luck—but I'm very much afraid you will need more than that."

"I will. I'll need the help of the Lord, which I believe I have. I shall also need the help of right-thinking men, such as yourself, Adam, and you, Sam Macpherson. You can't stand on the sidelines forever."

Philip had put them both uncomfortably on the spot. I waited in silence to see what their responses would be. But before either of them could say anything Morvah intervened.

"Adam is a planter. He must remain loyal to the others."

"Even when they are wrong?" I cried out passionately.

"Who are you to say what is right or wrong here?" She eyed me with a coldness I had not seen in her for a long time. "You do not know this country. It is by strength we survive, and only by strength. The planters must always stand together. It would be disastrous if we did not."

"You speak like one afraid, Mrs. Pengarth," said Philip. "I do not think . . ."

But before he could say anything else, Morvah snapped, "Yes, Dr. Rose, I am afraid. As you should be. I have lived through a Negro uprising, and I can assure you it is not something to look forward to. When my husband and I first came to Almada, there was unrest among the slaves. A number of them took to the hills, armed themselves, I know not how. They did dreadful things, appalling things, to white men and women, but it was nothing to what the whites did to the insurrectionists when the rebellion was squashed. I never wish to live through anything like that again. There is too much suffering by both black and white. Better to leave things as they are."

"I do not think you need fear an uprising when the bill goes through. You have always treated your slaves well at High Place. They will not attack you," said Philip reasonably.

"If you think my mother, or any of us, would be safe once the slaves received their freedom, you are more blinkered than any of us." Adam's voice was laced with contempt. "Our own slaves might not turn against us, but there would be no holding back the black tide of revenge seekers. They will not differentiate between the good and the bad masters. And there *are* some good masters in these islands. Not all are vicious. Freedom will come. I only wish it could have been allowed to emerge gradually."

"We believe things should have been left to take their own course," Sam Macpherson said.

"Yes." Mollie emphatically agreed with him.

"Then nothing would have been done," Philip declared. Whether you like it or not, the emancipation bill will go through, and the slave owners will be forced to free their slaves, as they have been forced to cease trading in slaves."

"Look around you, Rose," Adam exploded. "See if the trade has stopped. You know it has not. Trading still goes on. They're crying out for slaves in America. There's a lot of money in slave trading. A bit of paper signed in England won't put a stop to it."

"That's because there are not enough men prepared to speak out against the abuse of the act. But slavery will be abolished. The slaves will be freed. And quickly."

"Then pray you are not here when it happens, for I promise you, not all your virtuous phrases, your humanitarian beliefs, will save you from the horrors that will be let loose."

"And you, with your misplaced idealism, will be as much to blame for it as the others of your ilk in Parliament," Jem added with an ugly look, and Sam nodded vigorously.

"You will never see my point of view," Philip said a trifle pompously, "so we must agree to differ. But I had thought that in this house I should meet with a more enlightened outlook."

"That's unfair, Philip," I objected sharply. This *was* an enlightened household. I had come to appreciate that.

"What else can you expect from a prating, single-minded Quaker?" Jem sneered. "They are more ruthless than any of us."

I saw the color rise in Philip's cheeks and feared he might lunge at Jem, but Adam stepped casually between them. "Change will come, Philip, we all know that. We only wish it could have come more gradually, more slowly. . . ."

"Or never." Philip's tone was scathing. "You know very well, left to . . ."

"I think we have had enough of this conversation." Morvah's voice was controlled, but full of anger. "Such arguments are best pursued elsewhere, not in my drawing room. This was to have been a friendly gathering in which my daughter-in-law could renew old acquaintances. It is more like a conclave of enemies."

The men were immediately apologetic, and from then on the conversation was innocuous, but, "a conclave of enemies" suddenly rumbled from the throat of Robert who, till now, had been silently sipping coffee, which he had poured for himself, seemingly uninterested in anything that was going on around him, and I could not help the tingle of fear that touched my spine.

Those two conversations worried me. It was difficult to credit Sarah's story, but it must be true, and I felt angry on her behalf. Why should the people of Almada behave so cruelly toward the Roses when they were only doing what they believed to be right? Then I thought of Sam and Mollie. If what Sarah had said was true, they would have have been distant with her, refused to speak to either her or Philip, though that would have been insupportably impolite, seeing they were all guests of mine. But there had been no antagonism—and in any case, I remembered now, the Macphersons had known the Roses were coming.

Without for a moment doubting Sarah's honor, I wondered if she might not have been exaggerating a little—out of unhappiness. For one thing was perfectly clear, she was unhappy, constantly on the defensive, and anxious. So was Philip, I felt, but he had the armor of his powerful vision to sustain him. Sarah's vision was not so great. She had followed where Philip had led.

I was, nevertheless, sorely troubled about them both.

I admired Philip. I admired his aims. The rich were able to take care of themselves. The poor needed men like him to look out for them. He had the strength of mind to persist against all opposition. Very laudable—but what was it doing to Sarah?

I wandered about the gardens, pondering, and all the while my eyes roved restlessly, searching the bushes for a frightened brown face and more than half afraid I might see one. However, nothing untoward disturbed my perambulations this day.

The sun was rising higher. I took my thoughts into the house. I went to my favorite room, the music room, but, instead of sitting down to the pianoforte to play, I chose to relax on a long, low sofa with my feet up.

I had hardly settled when Tommyboy was by my side with the inevitable tray of jug and glasses and this time with the added extra of a little bowl of golden sugar.

"Grapefruit juice, missie?" he grinned toothlessly, pouring before I nodded. "Sugar?"

This time he waited for my nod, then stirred in a spoonful for me, before slipping away, bowing happily—to sit just outside the door within call. Not that I ever needed to call him. He seemed to know what I wanted before I knew myself.

I sipped the juice gratefully and closed my eyes. The shutters had not been closed yet and I listened to the sound of a myriad insects, secure in the knowledge that they could not penetrate the closely woven hanging at the open windows.

"All alone?"

I must have been dropping off into a doze, for I jumped at the sound of Jem Harding's voice. I opened my eyes to see him standing above me. He was smiling. He was always smiling at me, always kind and polite. I had grown to like him very much. But as I looked up at him, the thought flashed across my mind—I should not like to get on the wrong side of him. And I remembered the ugly look he had directed at Philip and his uncompromising words.

"Am I not always alone?" I asked, trying to keep my voice light.

"You need not be," he said, and I looked away from him quickly, for a light had appeared in his eyes that set my heart thumping.

"Adam tells me he's going to teach you to ride," he said after a moment's pause.

"If he can ever find the time," I said bitterly, then bit my lip. I should not have said that. It would embarrass Jem.

But why should I care. I had decided to finish with pretense. Everyone knew how things stood between me and Adam.

Jem dropped to one knee and took my hand. "I would spend time with you, if you would allow me."

His voice was husky. His meaning unmistakable. I attempted to withdraw my hand, but he held it fast.

I tugged at it. "Please Jem . . ." I was not sure how to deal with this situation, never having had any experience with such things.

"I hate to see you unhappy, Barbara. It tears at my soul. If I were in Adam's place . . ."

An explosion of demoniacal laughter caused him to release his hold on me and spring to his feet with an angry snarl. "Robert!"

How long had Robert been there, standing with the net curtains parted by his hands? Neither of us had heard him come up. Not that that was anything unusual. Nobody ever heard Robert come up if he did not wish them to.

"What do you mean by creeping up on me?" Jem shouted harshly.

Robert just smiled and crooned, "I heard. I heard."

"You heard nothing, you miserable oaf. Nothing, do you hear?"

Jem's face was suffused with fury and Robert started backing away.

"Don't speak to him like that, Jem," I said. "He's done nothing wrong."

"He's an eavesdropper." Jem did not bother to look at me. "He's always listening in on other people's conversations. It ought to be stopped. He needs to be taught a lesson."

Jem made a sudden movement forward. I jumped up from my couch and caught him by the sleeve. "No, Jem."

Robert threw me a swift, frightened glance and

shuffled away as fast as he could. We heard his dragging footsteps fade.

Jem turned to me with a shamefaced air. "I'm sorry. I shouldn't have gone for him like that. But *he* shouldn't come up on people like that . . . silently . . . and laughing in that imbecilic way. . . . It startled me. I spoke without thinking."

"I understand, but . . . you've hurt him."

"He'll soon forget. Nothing stays with him for long."

I was not so sure of this. "I think you ought to go and apologize to him."

"Apologize to him?" He looked amazed.

I was surprised by his attitude. He was not an outsider, after all. He had lived under the same roof as Robert for years, was like a second brother to him. Till now I had never seen him use anything but kindness toward Robert.

"He's very fond of you," I said. "He looks up to you, follows you about like a . . ."

"Dog." Jem supplied the word I had bitten back, unhesitatingly. Then he smiled sweetly. "Very well, I'll go after him. But, Barbara"—he was serious again—"I meant what I said. I should be very happy to be of service to you."

Now I had something else to tax my mind. I had no yardstick to go by, but every instinct told me that Jem found me attractive, more than as a friend.

Oh, but this was ridiculous. I was deluding myself. I was still plain Barbara Farrar, the girl who was undesirable to men, for all that I had changed my name to Pengarth, the girl whom Aunt Martha had said no man would offer for, not having the attraction of physical beauty—and that was all a man looked for in a woman. *Unless he wanted her money.*

A stab of pain racked me at Aunt Martha's remembered words. Adam had wanted my money. At least, the money he could not have had without me. Then, slowly, I began to realize that I was not that girl any longer. Almada had worked a change in me. Adam might not find me attractive, but others did. I did possess beauty—a kind of beauty—I had observed it in the mirror, though there were still times when I thought that rare creature was not myself. And people liked me. I had never had the opportunity of finding this out before.

I thought of all the good friends I had made since leaving England. Sarah, Philip, Morvah . . . Jem. I thought of all the young men who had danced with me at Araminta's party, and had seemed glad to. Still . . . to think men could find me attractive! Had I changed that much? At one time I would not have entertained such a thought. No, only the woman in the mirror who sometimes changed places with me would dare to think that.

Barbara Farrar, or Goodall, or Pengarth, or whatever your name is," I asked myself, suddenly pounding the piano, "who are you? What are you?"

I posed the question and could not find any answers. But I knew I was undergoing a metamorphosis, and I was more than half afraid.

My fingers moved into a Mozart air, and as usual my music brought me comfort. As I played, Morvah came in.

"Please don't stop, dear," she said. "I'll sit here quietly and listen."

She did not sit listening quietly for long. "I saw Adam go out riding with that Belmont girl again this morning," she said, heart-stoppingly, and with a swift, shrewd glance continued, "are things no different between you and him?"

My hands fell to my lap. "You must know they are not," I whispered hoarsely.

"Don't you think it's about time you did something about it?" she asked impatiently. "Didn't I make it plain you would lose him if . . ."

"What can I do?" I said. "He has no desire for me."

"Nonsense. Any woman can make a man desire her."

"I can't. I don't know how. Perhaps if I were beautiful and alluring . . ."

Why was I bothering to argue? No matter what I was like Adam would not want me. I was not Araminta.

"Beautiful? Alluring?" Morvah spat the words back at me. "What are they? Words. There are many kinds of beauty, not all obvious. And allure . . . what is allure, but persuasion? You have adequate means of persuasion at your disposal. You have a great deal of charm—use it. Don't leave all the running to Minty Belmont. She'll take him from you, if she can." Then she surprised me with a sudden change of topic. "Do you sing?"

"Yes. Aunt Martha provided tuition for me in that as in many things."

"Will you sing for me?"

I did not feel at all like singing, but, trained as I was in obedience, I sang. The song I sang was a sad song. It suited my despondent mood.

When it was over Morvah, eyeing me intently, said, "There you are. There's a kind of beauty you possess, a beautiful singing voice."

I sighed. "I know you're trying to be kind, Mrs. Pengarth, but I know what I am. I know what my shortcomings are."

Morvah gave a click of her tongue. "You set too much store on physical charms. They count, of course, but are by no means all. Take Araminta's looks away from her and what has she got? Nothing. Not enough to hold a man like Adam, anyway. But she's clever. With men she's all sweetness and light. That, more than her beauty, is what attracts so many men to her."

I did not believe her, though I appreciated her reason for belittling Araminta's charms to me. Beauty was what attracted a man to a woman. Aunt Martha had said so, and I knew it to be true.

"Get with child, Barbara," Morvah exhorted me. "Then you will be safe."

On a catch of breath, I said, "It is impossible. Adam is no true husband to me. We have not shared the same bedroom since the day we were married."

"Get with child," Morvah said, as if she had not heard a word. "Now, sing for me again."

I stared in amazement at the lady whose skin was like wrinkled brown silk. "I don't think I can," I said.

"Nonsense," she returned, and settled back.

My fingers strayed over the keys while I tried to compose myself. Her words had hit at the very core of my being, undoing all the good work I had put into thinking of Adam as no more than a friend. My friend he was willing to be. It had been, still was, difficult for me to accustom myself to expect nothing more from him. Now it would become more difficult than ever. I should keep remembering Morvah's words—and wondering.

I began to sing, softly, hesitantly, but with mounting confidence, till, emotionally spent, I let my hands rest silently on the keys.

"Thank you, my dear," Morvah said. "A sad song, but

very beautifully sung. Was it not, Adam?"

I looked up quickly. I had not heard Adam enter, and my heart started beating faster.

"Indeed it was." He walked up to me. "I did not know you could sing."

"There's a lot you don't know about your wife, my boy," Morvah said crisply. She went out, leaving us alone together.

"Is my mother right, do you think?" Adam asked softly.

"Who am I to say?" I made a foolish attempt at coquetry and slanted my eyes upward to him. Then, as he leaned his elbows on the gleaming black top of the pianoforte and set his face in his hands, bringing it closer to mine, I panicked. "Please don't think you must stay here and keep me company. I—was just about to go for a walk, anyway."

"There are times," he said, not moving, "when I could cheerfully strangle you."

"It could be a way of getting rid of me, would it not, but one which, unfortunately, is unlawful. No, you must find other means. In fact, I have been thinking . . ."

He removed his elbows from the pianoforte top and stood upright. "You think too much," he cut in. "I've never in my life come across such a woman for thinking."

"It's not a crime for a woman to think," I said.

"No," he agreed, "it's not. Did you say you were going for a walk?"

"Yes."

"May I accompany you?"

I stared at him in astonishment. "You have never wished to before."

"Correction. You have never given me the slightest

indication that you wished for my company, always seeming to prefer to stroll through the gardens on your own."

I was astonished at his words and wondered briefly if Jem had been talking to him, telling him of my complaints of loneliness. Or was it that he really had wished to accompany me before?

"I was not aware I gave that impression," I said.

"No, perhaps not." A heavy black eyebrow raised itself quizzically and I thought a smile lurked behind the brilliant blue of his eyes. "But it is a fact that besides being the most thinking woman I have ever come across, you are also the most prickly."

"I . . ." I started to protest, but he would not let me finish.

"At every turn you raise your spikes at me. You're a veritable porcupine."

"I . . ."

"Shall we go?"

Speechless, I went with him, unable to believe he was by my side—and at his request.

Chapter Eleven

If I had expected anything to result from that unexpected occurrence, I was disappointed. When I walked in to dinner that night, attired in a gown of dark blue cloth altered and furbished with lace and ribbons by Meta's expert hand, Adam gave me scarcely a glance.

Meta had dressed my hair in a way that changed my face completely. Before my eyes the mirror-lady emerged—ringleted, eager, fascinating. I had no qualms about going downstairs as her. Indeed, I was growing quite used to her.

Adam and Morvah were the only ones present in the drawing room as I entered for my evening sherry. Immediately, Morvah exclaimed: "How exceedingly attractive you look, Barbara. Does she not, Adam?"

Adam's glance was cursory and dismissive. "Indeed," he said, and drained his glass.

I watched Morvah's face and could see she pitied me. "Get with child. Make Adam desire you," she had said. Was she satisfied now that that could never be? I had played a charade, tried to change places with a mirror image. How foolish. How idiotic. How pitiable. As Adam handed me my drink, I rebelled.

There had not been many times in my life when I had rebelled and always, till now, my rebellions had been timorous and easily crushed, but now I was a strange new being, imbued with the spirit of the woman in the mirror. *She* would not sit back and let people pity her. *She* would get up and do something about it. *I* would do something about it. My metamorphosis was complete.

The following day I bade Meta arrange for Daniel to bring the carriage round to the door. "We are going into Seatown," I said, "to do some shopping."

"Do you think you should," Morvah asked when I informed her of my plans, "without Adam's permission?"

"Yes," I said without clarification, and, full of excitement, Meta and I set off.

"Oh, missie! Oh, missie!" Meta kept exclaiming. "Dis de mos' tremendous day in my whole life!"

"Have you never been into town before?" I asked her.

"No, missie. Oh, missie! Oh, missie!"

We called at all the grandest shops and came away laden with boxes and packages, which soon piled up on the seat opposite me, threatening to squeeze Meta out. I told her to come and sit beside me, but she demurred. Black slaves did not sit beside their owners in their carriages. I pooh-poohed such nonsense and insisted she sit next to me. What did I care for the cold, curious glances directed at me from all sides?

I bought gowns and shoes, bonnets, ribbons, yards and yards of brightly colored materials, and charged them all to Adam. I was quite lightheaded. I had never tasted such freedom before. In a way, I thought, I had been just as much a slave as Meta sitting beside me. Then I blushed with shame. There was no comparison.

When I had bought what must surely have been almost half the entire stock of the Almada shops, I thought of Sarah and Philip Rose and decided to call on them, I made inquiries of a portly gentleman about to enter his carriage to sit beside an equally portly lady. I thought they looked familiar. Perhaps I had met them at Araminta's party. But I could not be sure.

"Could you direct me to the home of Dr. Philip Rose?" I asked, and received a cold and haughty stare, a grudging reply.

I directed Daniel to the address I had been given, but when we reached there it was to be told that the Roses had moved. But when I directed Daniel to their new address, he appeared greatly distressed.

"What is the matter?" I asked him.

"You not go there, Missie Barbry," he said anxiously. "It bad place."

"Nonsense. How can it be, if Dr. Rose lives there?"

Daniel insisted. "Bad place, missie. Massa Adam, he angry if I take you such place."

I drew in a sharp breath and raised my voice authoritatively. "You will do as I say, Daniel. Drive me there at once."

He bowed to my wishes. He could do nothing else. But I could see he was not at all happy about it.

It was not long before I began to appreciate his reluctance. As we left the fashionable streets of Almada behind and came to a sleazy part of the town where down-and-outs sat by the roadside and begged for alms, I could not help wishing we would soon be out of it. I saw men and women in rags and children with pot bellies and no clothes at all. I saw one man beating another and a group of women crouched by a wall, one of them lying flat in an advanced stage of pregnancy.

Daniel reined in the horses. "We's here, Missie Barbry," he said, turning mournful eyes on me.

"What? Here?"

I gazed with incredulity at a dilapidated building. Building? It was hardly that—only planks of wood nailed roughly together, with a sheet of some kind of material for a roof—which did not quite fit. There were no windows, only a door.

"This can't be the place," I began, stopping as Sarah appeared in the doorway. She gazed at me in astonishment.

"Barbara! What are you doing here?"

"What are *you* doing here, Sarah?" I responded in equal astonishment.

"I live here."

"What?"

"I told you we were ostracized by society . . . if you don't leave at once, you will be, too."

"Nonsense," I cried. "No one will dare ostracize Adam Pengarth's wife, he's far too important a man on the island . . . oh!" I broke off and blushed with shame as Sarah winced. "I'm sorry, Sarah, I didn't mean . . . but you can't live here. It's obscene. What can Philip be thinking of allowing you to come to such a place. What . . . ? Why . . . ? Can't you go and live in your new hospital?"

"This is our hospital. Our home is attached, just behind. Philip is tending a young Negro. I was helping him, but when we heard the carriage wheels I came out to see . . . come in. Come in and see to what reduced circumstances we are put by your Almadian friends, then you can go back to your beautiful, well-cared-for house and . . ."

"Sarah!" I cried out at her bitterness. "What are you saying? How can you say such things to me? You surely don't believe that I came here to . . . oh, Sarah, you didn't . . ."

Her eyes fell before mine. "I'm sorry," she said. "Forgive me."

I bade Daniel help me down and I took her in my arms, then went with her into the dark, smelly interior of the hospital.

The only light came in through the open doorway and through a hole in the roof where a piece of the material had been drawn aside. Flies were everywhere. A row of makeshift beds lined one of the walls, bearing the bodies of sick men and women—some had running sores upon which the flies fed. Others lay on the floor or propped up against walls. I recoiled in horror when one of them suddenly vomited all over the floor. Sarah got down on her knees and started to clean the mess up.

I felt sick myself and turned blindly for the door. My stomach heaved, and, unable to stop myself, I, too, vomited, adding to the mess on the floor.

"I'm sorry," I murmured ashamedly into the sleeve of someone who helped me outside. When I looked, it was Philip, in a bloodstained gown, his fair hair lank and sticking to his forehead. "Forgive me," I said, clutching him. "I couldn't help myself. It's all so—horrible."

"You shouldn't have come," he said kindly and handed me over to Daniel. "Take your mistress home at once. She's not feeling well."

"Yes, massa. Straightway, massa. You come, Missie

Barbry. Meta, she look after you. Massa Adam, he very angry when he know. You white as sheet, missie."

I was handed into the carriage, and as the horses leapt away at Daniel's command I turned back to look at Philip. Sarah had joined him and they were both looking after me anxiously. "I'll return." I called. "I'll return with Adam. He'll do something." The horses sped away.

I was filled with sorrow and greatly worried about my friends, and as soon as we reached High Place I went in search of Adam, confident he would agree to return with me at once and rescue them from the miserable place Sarah had called their hospital and their home.

I found him in his office attending to his books. I launched immediately into my desperate tale. "Oh, Adam, you must come at once. Sarah and Philip . . ."

Adam rose from his desk and came round to take me by the shoulders and sit me down.

"Calm yourself," he said. "I don't know what has been happening, but you look dreadful."

"But Adam . . ."

"Not another word. Drink this first."

He gave me brandy. I drank—and coughed. I set it down.

"All of it," he said.

I drank it all. "Adam . . ." I was immediately off again, and this time he sat in silence and heard me out.

"Let me get this straight," Adam said. I had not noticed his face grow cold, his eyes turn into twin blue stones, but now his grim visage became most apparent. "Am I to understand you have been into town on your own?"

"I had Meta and Daniel with me," I said defensively.

"You did not think to seek my permission or to ask me to escort you?"

"I did not think it necessary."

His eyes flashed angrily. I began to feel shaky. "You did not think it necessary! You went out of your way to call on the Roses . . . You even asked the way. . . ."

"Why shouldn't I?" I returned, determined not to be cowed.

But Adam's growing anger exploded. "You fool!" he thundered.

"Adam!" I protested, but feebly.

"If you had come to me I could have told you how things were. I could have dissuaded you from going there."

"You mean—you knew the straits they were in?"

"Well, perhaps now you've seen things for yourself you'll be satisfied."

"Is that all you can say, Adam? What kind of a man are you? You must do something about it. We can't leave Philip and Sarah—sweet Sarah, to live in such conditions."

"They choose to live in such conditions."

"They don't *choose*," I reacted scornfully.

"They could leave Almada."

"You know they won't."

"That's their folly," he shrugged. "Don't go there again."

"So you will do nothing to help them?"

"I can't. My hands are tied."

I flounced from him, choked by his careless attitude.

"Barbara!" His angry voice halted me, my hand on the doorknob. "I warn you, don't try to interfere."

"How can I not?" I wrenched the door open. "They are my friends."

* * *

I defied Adam and went to see Sarah and Philip again. I did not see what I could do to help them, but at least they would see I had not turned against them, that my friendship was true. They chastised me and begged me not to come again, but I continued my visits.

Gradually I overcame my nausea on entering the hospital and became a help and not a hindrance. I learned to do everything. I helped with the nursing. I washed the patients, my initial temerity at seeing and making contact with their black bodies never completely overcome, but pushed firmly back out of sight. I boiled surgical instruments for Philip, but I did not help with the operations—that was completely beyond my power. My willingness to help with other things, however, gave Sarah more time to help her husband in this respect.

In the beginning I scrubbed floors and washed the stained linen that continually found its way into the bucket provided for that purpose, mostly with closed eyes, half fainting at the stench, till Meta, who always accompanied me, seeing me at the task, relieved me of it. It was Meta who pressed Daniel into service, and he was soon fetching, carrying, helping with the removal of corpses.

Philip could not afford to pay for help and previously had had to rely on the occasional services proffered by the local community, so, with the three of us providing continual help, things became more organized. Philip and Sarah could not express their gratitude. In any case, I waved such expressions away. It was the least we could do.

I worked hard, but no harder than anyone else, and less hard than Philip and Sarah, who were never off duty. At first I spent only the mornings there, arriving home dog tired, with red, sore hands. Meta would lather them with a thick, soothing cream while I soaked in a tub of hot water. Then I would rest on my bed and try to erase some of the terrible sights I had seen from my mind. But as time went on, I left home earlier and stayed at the hospital longer. I felt, for the first time in my life, that I was doing something worthwhile. I felt needed.

The day inevitably came when Morvah said, in front of the others, "What are you doing with yourself these days? I hardly see anything of you now. And you seem to have given up your playing."

All eyes swung to me.

"I . . . I . . . have been keeping to my room." It was the only thing I could think of on the spur of the moment, and I knew how inadequate it sounded.

"Why? Have you not been feeling well?" asked Morvah, immediately concerned.

"I'm perfectly well," I averred.

"Are you sure?" Adam frowned at me. "I've noticed myself how very quiet you have become of late, and disturbing shadows have appeared beneath your eyes."

"Perhaps she's sickening for something," Jem said. "It might be wise to get Atkinson to take a look at her, Adam."

"Yes," Adam agreed.

"No," I cried out vehemently. They all stared in astonishment at me, "I mean, there's no need. I'm not sickening for anything. If you must know, I haven't been sleeping very well . . . because of the heat. . . ."

"I thought you had become accustomed to the heat," Jem said. "We all agreed you had acclimatized well."

"That is so, but . . ."

I had run out of arguments and was glad when Adam

came in with, "I'll keep an eye on you. If you don't improve, you will see Atkinson."

And that put an effective end to the conversation.

I stayed away from the hospital for a week after that, careful to be seen strolling through the gardens and heard playing the pianoforte, both of which occupations I had not realized I had missed so much. But, as my looks improved and Adam relaxed his watch on me, I started my visits again, though less frequently than before.

I explained the situation to my friends, not wishing them to think I was less enthusiastic than I had been.

"You mean Adam has no knowledge of your work here?" Philip looked aghast.

"No. And I do not wish him to. He—would not approve."

"Then I can't allow you to come here again," said Philip, "if Adam is against it."

"Adam has no control over me." I lifted my chin aggressively.

They both regarded me oddly, but said no more. Perhaps the sudden entry of a man in a near state of collapse had more to do with it than a desire not to argue further.

So I continued with my work and was happy.

Of course, it could not last.

I discovered that Philip, as Adam had told me, was indeed stirring up trouble for himself—and everybody else, too.

"He is becoming far too political in his outlook," Sarah confessed to me. "The whole issue of slavery has become—an obsession with him. It's no longer enough for him to minister to the sick. His hospital—his dream—is fast becoming just that, a dream. I'm so afraid for him, Barbara. He's out almost every night making speeches. I don't know how much longer he can get away with it. I know something dreadful will happen to him soon."

I tried to dispel her worries. "Nothing will happen to Philip. He is in no danger from the slaves. He is their champion."

"It's not the slaves I'm worried about," she said.

"Then who? Who would harm Philip?"

"The planters. The other white men on the island."

"Oh, Sarah, that's nonsense. Philip's a free-born man. Of good family and background. Your father's a member of Parliament."

"That didn't stop them from ostracizing us. Oh, Barbara, you've been here long enough to know what it's like in Almada. The island is run by the plantation owners. They do what they like. Live by their own rules. They care nothing for Parliament. It's too far away."

"But the governor . . ."

"The governor sides with the planters. Till the act is passed he will do nothing to keep them in check. He closes his eyes to much that happens here."

"I can't believe it," I said. "Sir George seemed so . . ."

But Sarah had ceased wringing her hands and had started to weep.

"Oh, Sarah, don't despair. I'm sure everything will be all right. You need not fear for Philip's safety."

"Barbara." It was wrenched from the depths of her soul. "He has come home bleeding more than once . . . attacked by men with masks over their faces . . . and they were white men. Philip was sure of that. And last night . . . last night . . . he was brought home unconscious. He had been kicked and beaten and a placard was pinned to his coat . . . Get out, dirty nigger lover, while you can still walk."

Stupefied, I mumbled, "Who . . . ? Who . . . ? Does he know who . . . ?"

"He was attacked from behind, but he heard their voices before he was knocked completely unconscious. One said, 'Why not finish him now? Why wait? We've given him enough chances.' Another said. 'No, leave him. We'll do it the way we planned.' Philip swears the first voice belonged to a planter named Ransom, Jack Ransom."

"Ransom!" I drew in a horrified gasp. "And—the other?"

She shifted her gaze from mine so swiftly, so nervously, my heart leapt.

"It wasn't—Adam?" I held my breath while awaiting her reply.

"No."

I breathed again. Of course not. How could it have been? What had I been thinking of?

"Then who? Did Philip recognize the voice?" I asked.

"Yes. At least . . . he wasn't completely sure."

"Who did he think it was?"

"I think . . . perhaps . . . I'd better not say. I've said too much already. Please don't mention any of this to Philip, Barbara. Promise me."

She looked so alarmed at the prospect that I might talk of it that I immediately gave her my promise.

When we reached High Place later that afternoon Meta carried my purchases indoors for me. I always did a little shopping as an excuse for my outings. I criticized myself for my deception, but I had no alternative. If Adam knew my real purpose for going into town, he would stop me. For all my brave talk, I knew he had the power.

"Hello, shopping again?" Jem Harding crossed the hall as I was about to follow Meta up the stairs. "I declare, you'll empty all the shelves in Almada at this rate. What is it this time? More gowns? More pretty hats?"

"I can't see that it's any business of yours," I replied icily—afraid. If he had noticed sufficiently to remark upon the amount of shopping I had been doing, might not Adam? And wonder? And put two and two together?

Jem's face fell. "I'm sorry. I didn't mean to appear critical. I was trying, clumsily as it turns out, to be jocular."

I was immediately contrite and evoked a smile of sorts. "No, Jem, *I* should apologize. I was rude. Please forgive me. I've had such a busy shopping day and feel so hot and tired. And I've got a headache," I added as good measure to my excuse.

Jem's face cleared. "No apologies necessary. Come and drink lemonade with me."

"I should love to, Jem, but later, please, after I have changed and rid myself of Seatown's dust."

"I'll be waiting on the veranda," he said.

I joined him there about half an hour later. "Still waiting?" I smiled.

"I'd wait forever for you, fair lady," he replied in the same vein, but I lowered my eyes, for I was afraid of what I might see in his. He held out a chair for me and I sat. "I'll pour you a glass of lemonade," he said into my ear.

"I can see Tommyboy hovering," I murmured, moving my head away slightly. "He'll be most upset if you don't let him pour. He considers it his right."

"He has no rights. He's a slave. I'll pour."

"He's not a slave," I said, angry at his words. "Adam freed him years ago."

Jem's lip curled in disbelief. "Did he?"

He handed me my lemonade and sat down opposite me. I made no answer. He did not require one. It was obvious he did not believe Adam had freed Tommy—and now I did not know whether I believed it, either. I could ask Tommy, of course . . . but no . . . I could not ask Tommy. And why should I feel the need to? Why should I doubt Adam's word? I hadn't—till now.

Jem said, "Is Adam teaching you to ride yet?"

"You know very well he is not," I said pertly.

Jem grinned. "I'll teach you, if you like."

"Would you?"

"I did offer some time ago, if you cast your mind back."

"You offered me your services, I seem to remember."

"Well . . . as Adam does not seem to be able to find the time . . ." I looked at him sharply, but there appeared to be no underlying motive to his words—though he must know about Araminta, ". . . what about taking advantage of my services? The sooner you learn to ride, the better it will be for you. You will not be dependent upon the carriage—and Daniel."

Again I looked at him sharply. Had I detected a note of warning? Did he know where Daniel drove me on our expeditions into town?

Jem's face was a picture of innocence as he waited for my reply. I must have imagined the warning. The whole underhanded nature of my involvement with the hospital was playing on my nerves. How I wished I could be open about it. How I wished Adam thought as I did.

I wished lots of things where Adam was concerned.

"Thank you, Jem." I accepted his offer. "I should be most grateful if you would teach me to ride."

Robert came shuffling along the veranda toward us.

"Hello, Robert," I smiled. "Would you like a drink of lemonade?"

He shook his head. "Did you bring me anything?"

I always brought him back a small gift—a handkerchief, a picture book, a sketch pad—for I had learned he liked to draw, though I had seen none of his work. But I did not think I had missed anything. Today I had a little figurine wrapped up for him—a little black horse, a tiny replica of the one he rode.

He came with me to my room to receive it, but instead of ripping off the paper, as was his usual practice as soon as he had the gift in his hands, he clutched it to him and made no attempt to open it. He stood before me and stared at me. There was no grin on his face, only a strange working of his mouth, as if he were searching for words. His eyes, usually so elusive, were still and fixed on mine in mute appeal.

I thought he wanted to thank me. I smiled at him. I wanted no thanks. "I hope you like it, Robert."

"Barbara!" he blurted out my name suddenly. "Don't . . ."

His eyes shifted to the door as footsteps were heard coming up the stairs, then they came back to me. "Don't . . ."

Jem's appearance in the open doorway interrupted him once more.

"Don't what?" I asked. But already his face had changed. His sloppy grin came into play again. I felt a chill take hold of me. How swiftly he could change.

"Forgive me Barbara," said Jem. "Robert and I had

arranged to ride over to the Macphersons. There is a matter I have to discuss with Sam, and Robert said he would like to accompany me. If we don't leave soon it will be too late to go today."

I felt anxious, and as soon as they had departed I sat down and sought the cause and could discover none—other than Robert's strangeness. But he was always a little strange, and I had got used to it by now. Nevertheless, I felt anxious.

As luck would have it, Adam asked me that night at dinner, "Have you got yourself a riding habit yet, Barbara?"

"Yes, I have," I replied, suddenly tense.

"Then we'll begin your riding lessons tomorrow."

"I thought you'd lost interest in them," I said.

"No, no." He smiled. "I admit a fair time has elapsed since we last discussed them . . . I became rather tied up in . . . things. However, I am completely at your disposal now. Shall we make an early start in the morning, about seven, before it gets too hot?"

"I'm sorry, Adam," I said, not without a little smugness. "I've already agreed with Jem that he . . ." Adam's eyes snapped. "He offered to teach me. I saw no reason to reject his offer," I finished with my chin up.

"Indeed no. Why should you?" Adam's voice had the calm control about it I disliked. It meant he was angry with me. Yet he could not blame me for making an earlier commitment. It was his own fault for being so tardy with his offer.

"I suggest Frenchie for Barbara, Jem," Adam was saying. "She's a quiet, reliable mare and won't pose any problems."

"I agree and should do as you say, only I withdraw my

offer. I have no wish to be the cause of friction between you and . . ."

"You are not the cause," snapped Adam. "Teach Barbara to ride, by all means. In fact, I insist that you do."

"And so do I," I said. I had been quietly simmering while the two men debated who should teach me to ride. I had my own views on the matter. "I accepted your offer Jem. You can't withdraw it now."

From her seat, Morvah sent me a stern look of disapproval. Adam stared at me, stony-eyed. Jem looked most uncomfortable. Robert's eyes darted backward and forward. I felt I had committed an unforgivable sin.

I can't understand you, Barbara," Morvah declared as we drank coffee together.

I raised puzzled eyes above the rim of my cup.

"You go out of your way to antagonize Adam," she elucidated.

I protested feebly, "I do not."

"Well, you gave a very good imitation of it tonight."

"Because I stuck to my word and refused to reject Jem's kind offer? Because Adam had decided he could spare some of his precious time for me? I did not see that as sufficient reason to change my mind."

"He was very annoyed."

"I know."

"He *is* your husband."

"For what it's worth."

"He deserves your consideration."

"If he spent less time with Araminta Belmont and more with me, I might agree with you."

"He spends very little time with Araminta these days."

"She still rides over every day seeking his companionship."

"Maybe, but she does not get it. It is Jem who squires her around now. She seems to be casting her net wider."

"Only in order to make Adam jealous."

I terminated the conversation by wishing Morvah good night.

Morvah would never understand the relationship between Adam and me. There were times when I hardly understood it myself . . . when I understood Adam not at all.

I ran into him on my way downstairs the following morning. I was dressed in my new green habit. I thought the color suited me, I knew my cheeks were flushed with excitement, and Meta had tilted my hat to an angle, so that it gave me a roguish air. "Very fetching," he said as we drew level. "I envy Jem this morning."

Now what could he have meant by that?

I did not allow myself time to cogitate upon it. I hurried out to my first riding lesson, which I proceeded to enjoy enormously. I was abjectly sorry when it was all over.

Jem laughed at my disappointment. "Easy does it at first," he said. "I can see you are a natural horsewoman; nevertheless, you are as prone to saddle-soreness and aches and pains as the rest of us, and must take it slowly. But it will not be long before you are up and away."

The rest of the day passed slowly. I missed going to the hospital and decided I should go tomorrow. There would be plenty of time after my lesson. I wondered how Sarah was coping; what Philip was doing—but, of course, he would be busy operating or dispensing medicines. It was only at night that he went out speechmaking. I thought I should like to hear some of Philip's speeches. I was sure they would be well worth listening to. But, of course, there would be no chance. . . .

At dinner that night when we were all together and I was asked if I had enjoyed my first lesson, I was full of enthusiasm. Adam seemed to have come to terms with the fact that Jem was my teacher and discussed my progress with good humor, saying finally, "It is a pity you were kept so long from indulging what is obviously going to be a great source of pleasure for you."

Morvah retired soon after finishing her coffee. Jem and Robert had gone for their usual nighttime swim. I believed Adam had gone with them; he had left at the same time. I went to sit at the pianoforte, first blowing out all the candles, for it was bright moonlight outside, and I was in the mood for moonlight.

It slanted across the keys as I played *Fur Elise*. I did not need the moonlight. I knew the piece by heart and could have played it in the dark. A delightful piece, it could sound gay or sad, according to the player's mood.

I left my fingers to find the notes and let my thoughts run loose round one central theme: Had Morvah been right when she had said Adam did not go riding any more with Araminta? And if not, why not? Or had she got it all wrong—which was more likely? What had Adam meant when he had said he envied Jem? Had he meant it? Probably not.

The final notes faded and I sighed deeply—a loud hiss in that quiet room.

"That was a deep sigh, Barbara."

I jumped as Adam's voice came out of the shadowed darkness. I could not see him and thought for a moment I had imagined it, but then he came into view, silhouetted in the moonlight, rising from a chaise longue. He started to walk toward me, and I found myself thinking how white the stock at his throat looked.

"Why did you play so sadly tonight? It was almost heartbreaking. Did it reflect your mood, perhaps?"

"Yes . . . no . . ." I could not take my eyes off his stock and floundered. "It's a sad piece of music."

"Nonsense," he said firmly. "I've heard you play it often, and never the same twice—though never as heart-rendingly as now." He leaned toward me. I kept my eyes glued to his stock. "Why are you so sad, Barbara?" His voice held a note I had never heard before.

"I'm not . . . I . . ." Floundering again, I rose from my stool and went out onto the veranda.

He followed me. I moved further along, kept on walking, found myself descending the marble steps, translucent in the moonlight. He remained with me.

"How long had you been listening?" I asked in a rush. "I didn't know you were there."

"I often go in there at night," he said. "I find it—peaceful."

Why? I asked myself, when he knew it was my favorite room in the house and I often played there alone at night. Had I been alone all those times in the past? Or had he been there, hidden from me by the back of a chair or sofa? I did not always blow all the candles out.

I walked quickly, hardly knowing what I was doing or where I was going. I was only aware of him, of Adam, close beside me. And he was close, very close, almost touching me.

"It is very pleasant out here in the garden, is it not, with this cool breeze blowing?" he said.

"Yes," I replied.

He was silent for a while, then he said, "Are you growing used to Almada now, to life here at High Place? Are you happier than you were when first you came here?"

I did not know how to answer that. I hardly knew the correct answer myself. But there was one thing I was sure about. "I don't think I shall ever grow used to living here," I said, meaning Almada and thinking about the slave situation.

We walked on in silence. I felt him withdraw from me and knew he had misunderstood me again. I wondered how I could put it right, but the silence became somehow overpowering, and I remained quiet. We came to the avenue of oleander bushes, which Adam had once told me his father had planted many years ago, and turned into it, coming to a halt in the little white-trellised gazebo at the end.

I sat down on the seat that ran all the way round inside the circular edifice. Adam sat down beside me. My heart hammered.

"What have you done to yourself?" he asked. "Why have you changed your appearance?"

"I didn't think you'd noticed," I said.

"I'm not blind," he replied. "Nor am I insensitive." He hesitated a moment then added, "I preferred you the way you were."

"I like myself this way," I said.

"And don't think I do not know why," he returned

swiftly, "but remember, you are *my* wife."

"I am glad you remembered, Adam. I have often wondered. . . ."

I could hardly believe my boldness, but there was something in the air tonight that released my inhibitions, and I felt I could say what I liked.

His face was blurred. I could not see his bright blue gaze, but I could feel it, burning into me with that intensity that suggested he could see deep into my soul. Therefore I was surprised to hear him say:

"I wish I knew you, Barbara. Sometimes I think I do; then I am not so sure."

"I think you do not know me at all," I said.

"Oh, I think I know something," he contradicted himself and me. "I know, for instance, that you bring Robert little presents home from your shopping expeditions. Not many people would take the trouble. . . ."

"It's no trouble," I murmured.

"Most people . . ."

"I'm not most people," I raised my voice somewhat, "I'm me, Barbara Farrar Pengarth. I know you don't think much of me, but . . ."

"That's not true," he said softly. "I think a lot about you. I always have."

My heart somersaulted. "You've never shown it. You've never said."

"Haven't I?" His voice was a caress melting my bones. "Well, let me say it now. I think you have a fine mind, a courageous heart, a gentle nature. I remember when you first met my brother . . . you were shocked, I saw that, but you did not let him see it, you greeted him as if he were perfectly normal. And your concern for Tommy-boy . . . the way you stood up to Jack Ransom . . . your feelings of sympathy for the slaves . . . knowing all this, I wonder why I am never on the receiving end of your sweetness."

I jumped up. He was too close for comfort. His words were scattering my wits. "How delightful it is here," I cried, twirling round on the mosaic floor upon which animals and birds of every description sported and urns holding displays of brilliant flowers stood at intervals beside the trellis. "I've always liked . . ."

My words dried in my throat. He had risen with me, and I had come round to face him. He was looking at me in a way that left me breathless. "Barbara," he whispered, and I felt his arms go round me, his warm breath on my cheek. I saw his lips part, the gleam of his teeth . . . and then I was drowning, drowning in a sea of honeyed sweetness.

His hands roamed where they would. I was powerless to stop them. I did not want to stop them. I wanted only one thing, needed only one thing, to be one with Adam.

And it might have come to pass, there in the sweetly scented gazebo, if the laughing voices of Robert and Jem returning from their swim had not broken the spell and forced us apart.

Chapter Twelve

I did not understand Adam. Did he or did he not find me attractive now? I could have sworn the night before that he did. I had waited for him to come to my room, feeling sure he would, but as the hands of the clock moved round relentlessly to one o'clock, two o'clock, I knew he would not.

So had I been mistaken in thinking he would have made love to me in the gazebo? In the critical light of day I deemed it so. Whatever had led Adam to behave as he had, it certainly had not been love, nor even desire. If it had been either of these things he would have made his way to my room. It had surely been plain I would not have resisted. But he had not, so had he simply been proving to himself, and to me, that he could master me, if he so wished?

Well, he had proved it, and shown he wished to take it no further.

I was no worse off than I had been before, I told myself, leaving an uneaten breakfast tray behind me as I made my way downstairs to join Jem for my second riding lesson, smiling away my hurt. It had been foolish of me to think I might rival Araminta in Adam's affections.

I saw nothing of Adam that day. Nobody knew where he had gone, only that he had said he would be back late. And so I went to bed early, glad of the extra hours in which to come to terms with myself again before we met. When we did meet I could not help being distant with him, and he responded in the same way.

I took to equestrian life with remarkable ease, and it was not long before I graduated from a "safe" mount to a slightly more spirited one. As my riding prowess increased, Jem and I went farther afield, and we got to know each other very well. Jem admired me greatly and was not slow to show it. It did me a power of good to know that if I were not already married, I would have a suitor in him. Not that he ever overstepped the mark of respect, but he let me see, nevertheless, how deeply he cared for me.

Robert accompanied us sometimes. Robert was a magnificent horseman. He rode a superb black stallion, aptly named Black Satin. No one else could handle him, but Robert had no difficulty at all in controlling him. On horseback Robert was a different person. His head still lolled, but it did not seem to matter, it did not seem so grotesque, and from the back he looked like any other normal human being. When we rode together it was hard to believe he had the mental age of seven or eight.

Sometimes we rode along the beach. Occasionally we took a picnic with us. Jem and I would sit on the soft sand and talk while Robert wandered off, scuffing his feet in the sand, to disappear among the lush vegetation and reappear holding some flower or fantastically shaped leaf, which he would present to me almost shyly.

Sometimes we ran into Adam. He would join us, briefly, then continue about his business.

The time came when it was deemed safe for me to go out riding on my own. Cautioned not to go too far from home, I set off, confident and excited, came to no harm, and increased my distances day by day, till at last I rode all the way into Seatown.

I had not been to the hospital for quite a while, having been completely taken up with my riding, but now I was ready to resume my duties. Sarah and Philip were glad to see me, and I was soon back in the swim of things. I thought they both looked worn out.

"You ought to take some time off," I said to Sarah one day.

"How can we?" she replied.

"I could take over your duties for a while."

Sarah smiled. "You do more than your fair share already, and what about Philip's work? You could not take over that."

I agreed I could not, but I still felt she should have a rest. However, I could not prevail upon her to shed her burden of work on me.

I was worried about them both. Sarah's delicate English complexion had toughened to a leathery tan. She had no time to spare for the niceties of parasols and wide-brimmed hats whenever she ventured out of doors. Philip's skin, too, had darkened to a shade not many times removed from the brown-skinned men he tended, though his hair had lightened, almost to the color of silver. They both appeared cheerful on the surface, but I soon detected that all was not as well as they would have me believe.

"Has Philip received any more warnings?" I asked

Sarah during a rare moment of respite.

She was silent for a moment, then she said. "A firebrand was thrown into the hospital a few days ago."

"What?"

"It terrified the patients, and we—Philip—managed to get hold of it and fling it into a bucket of water. It went out. We've had nothing like it since, but I can't help wondering what they will do next. I thought they'd given up . . . things had been quiet for so long . . . but they won't. They'll never give up till we've left, or . . . till we're dead."

"You went to the authorities, of course?"

"No. It does no good. They listen, say they'll investigate our complaints—and that's the last we hear of it."

"It's deplorable. Philip must apply to see the governor."

"He can't get anywhere near him. Not that it would do any good if he did . . . there's a conspiracy against us and he's in on it."

"I can't believe that, Sarah."

"It is hard to believe, isn't it? But it's true. Oh, Barbara, I want to go home! I thought I could hold on, fight back . . . Philip says it's only a question of time . . . but I can't. I can't. I'm so afraid."

She was trembling visibly. I put my arms round her. "Then you must go, Sarah. Philip must abandon his hospital. It will be a great pity, but you, your health, must take precedence over all else."

"Philip won't give up his hospital. I thought he was beginning to lose interest in it . . . I told you, remember? But he isn't, he still works as hard as he ever did tending the sick and wounded. He wants me to go home. He even booked passage for me, but I refused to take it. I won't leave without him. I'd never know a moment's peace wondering what was happening to him, whether I should ever see him again."

"You'll never know a moment's peace if you stay," I said. Then I was struck by a splendid idea. "Sarah! Why not come and stay at High Place?"

Her face lit up, then darkened. "It's sweet of you to think of it, but I can't."

"Why not? Philip can come, too."

"We can't leave the hospital," she cried.

I started to argue. She silenced me.

"No, we must go on, with trust in the Lord. Philip believes strongly that all will be well. If only I . . ."

She straightened her shoulders and smoothed her stained apron. "All is for the best," she said and went back to work.

Philip, who had gone outside for a breath of air, returned. He passed me with a ghost of a smile. He spoke to Sarah, who without a word, went to help him lift an inert child onto the operating table. I averted my gaze and continued with my work of tending the patients who were getting better. It always amazed me that any did, considering the appalling condition of the hospital and the scarcity of medicines.

The day grew hotter. It was soporific inside the ramshackle building. The silence was broken only by the intermittent groans of patients, the buzz of flies, and the click of insects. Suddenly there was an explosion.

It seemed like an explosion. Adam crashed his way in. "Barbara! What are you doing here! How dare you disobey me?"

Adam's eyes were blazing. He carried a whip in his hand. I felt it would not take much for him to use it—

on me.

Frightened by his anger, I started to stammer, "I . . . I . . . I . . ."

"Come home at once."

"No." He grabbed my arm angrily. I pulled away from him.

"Goddamnit, woman, do you dare to defy me? You will do as I say. I have given you too much leeway, allowing you to come and go as you please, but I never expected you to disobey my express order not to come here."

"I . . ."

"You've gone too far now. You will not leave High Place again without my permission."

"I'll do as I please."

His grip tightened. "You will do as I say. You are my wife and I will have obedience from you. Is that clear?"

"Let me go, you're hurting me."

Philip put a restraining hand on Adam's arm. "Yes, let her go. If you wish to blame anybody it must be me. It's my fault Barbara's here. I should have stopped her coming long ago, only we needed her help."

Adam glared at Philip, and though his grip on my arm did not lessen, I felt that at any moment it would and he would send his fist crashing into Philip's worried face. Then, slowly, his anger fled away, his grip on my arm slackened. He let me go and I sank back into Sarah's waiting arms.

"You should have had more sense, Rose," Adam said tightly. "You know what could happen if . . . I told you . . . how many more are aware that she comes here? My informant is trustworthy, but . . ."

"No one else, I'm sure," Philip said. "But you're right, I've been foolish, putting everything at risk." He turned to me. "Go home, Barbara, with Adam—and don't come back."

"But Philip . . ."

"Don't argue," Adam frowned at me. "Just do as you're told for once."

"Please do not think I'm not grateful for all you've done," said Philip, "I am. You've done all and more than I had any right to expect of you."

"I did it willingly," I cried.

"I know, but it's over." He drew away from me, his face closed against me. "You are not to come here again. You will not be welcome."

I stared at him in dismay, then beseechingly at Sarah. She moved from me to stand by Philip's side in unsmiling agreement with him. "But I'm needed here," I almost sobbed.

"Not anymore, Barbara," Sarah said. "Go home."

Adam took my arm again, gently now, but still forcefully, and led me out of the overcrowded, smelly place where I had worked with such fervor for so long—and yet not so long. I allowed him to remove my stained overgown, stunned by the strange behavior of my friends. I could not believe they had turned against me. Adam helped me mount Lady, my chestnut mare, and I rode beside him away from the slummy quarter of Almada, through the respectable streets where the wealthy lived, and out of the town, too dazed to adjust to the unexpected turn of events.

But after a while my senses returned and I glared across at Adam. "How dare you make a fool of me before my friends?"

"I'm glad to hear you admit it." He slanted a hard look back at me. "For indeed that is what you are. A stupid . . . idiotic . . . courageous fool."

I had opened my mouth in outrage at the start of his speech. I had closed it again by the end, any protest I had been about to make banished by the softened tone of his voice.

"Who told you where I was?" I asked sulkily.

"Does it matter?" he asked.

"I suppose it was Daniel," I grumbled.

We rode in silence for a while, but now that Adam knew, I felt a great need to talk to him about it. I talked and talked, and he listened without comment. I told him all I had done, all that had happened; how sickened I had been by the sights I had witnessed; how I had conquered my distaste and discovered the joy in caring for others. I told him about the attacks on Philip, how he and Sarah were being terrified out of their lives. I wondered aloud who they could be . . . what kind of people could do such things.

Adam ignored my questions and said tightly, "So all the time I thought you were out shopping, you were going to the hospital."

"Yes."

"And later, when you could ride, Jem escorted you there."

I gaped at him in astonishment. "No, he did not."

"No?" He eyed me obliquely.

"No."

"I wish I could believe you."

"You can. Since learning to ride I have always gone alone."

"You have deceived me in other things, why not in this?"

"I have not deceived you," I said. "Defied, yes, and I

would have continued to defy you if Philip had not made it plain he did not wish me to go to the hospital again."

"That I can well believe," he said. "So it's just as well he showed a little sense at last."

"Sense!" I exploded. "There is no sense in this—any of it. Philip and Sarah are good, kind people who have been hounded out of society . . . attacked . . . and all because they wish to alleviate the sufferings of . . ."

"If only that were all," Adam interrupted, "but it is not, I fear. He has become politically involved."

"That is no excuse. . . ."

"I tried to talk to him . . . he wouldn't listen."

"He believes all men should be free. He only . . ."

"Barbara, Barbara, listen to me. Philip has been making speeches calculated to incite riot. He has got the white population of Almada worried—more, afraid. You might not agree with their way of life, but it is all most of them have ever known. It is asking too much of them to give up without a struggle all they, and their fathers before them, have worked for. . . ."

"They haven't worked for their prosperity, the slaves have. They have grown rich on the subjugation of . . ."

"You have listened to Philip's words—good, honest, heartfelt though they may be from one viewpoint, and you have taken them at face value—which surprises me. What has happened to your much vaunted talent for looking at all sides of a question, listening to all arguments and reaching your own conclusion?"

"I have done so," I said, "and am in complete agreement with Philip."

Adam sighed deeply. I burst out, "Adam, I do wish you would try to understand."

"I understand the situation better than you, or Philip,

I think," he said tersely, and then, a few moments later, "I am a planter. In common with certain other planters, I wish to see an end to slavery and will work toward that end, but not Philip's way. That way lies bloodshed. Things are very bad. We have to tread carefully if we are to contain the situation. There's unrest among the slaves and it's growing daily."

"You can't blame Philip for that. It was happening before he came here."

"No, but he's not helping any by going about, telling the slaves their freedom is on the way, that men in the English Parliament are fighting on their behalf. He says he is not trying to effect an uprising, but that is exactly what he is doing. He doesn't understand these people, their naiveté . . . The end result of his meddling will be to bring the whole black community about our ears."

We had reached High Place and handed our horses over to Daniel and Charlie, his deputy. I followed Adam into the house. He made straight for his office. I went with him. He did not seem surprised.

"Why can't he leave politics alone?" he cried as he shut the door and went to pour himself a drink. He raised the decanter toward me in a silent question. I shook my head. As he poured his own, he went on, "Let him run his hospital, by all means, but he should *leave politics alone.* He doesn't know what he is about. He should leave it to those of us who—know the pitfalls."

"And like he said, nothing would get done," I sneered.

He shrugged and tossed off his drink. His carelessness made me angry.

"I believe you're like all the rest," I cried. "You don't want things to change."

"Believe what you like, Barbara," he said harshly,

"but don't defy me again. Keep away from Philip and Sarah Rose."

I stared at him. He was a hard, rushless man with no real tenderness. Any I thought I might have seen was purely illusory. Nevertheless, I had to beseech his help, for my friends' sake.

I said, "They will kill Philip one day, if something is not done soon. He has been to the police, he's been to the governor. No one will help him. He's your friend, Adam, or you say he is, can't you do something? You have influence. . . ."

"You don't know what you ask," Adam burst out. "If I'm seen to take sides with him. . . ."

I drew in a harsh, bitter breath. "You're a coward," I cried. "You desert your friends when they most need you. Philip and Sarah could have given in to pressure and abandoned their efforts to help the poor and oppressed—and that would have pleased you, wouldn't it? But they fought against their opponents and were driven out of their home and forced to live in a shack. A shack, Adam! Have you seen it? It would grieve your heart, if you had."

I stared into his stern, unyielding face. His mouth had tightened into a thin line. His eyes were like twin points of blue ice. I flung away from him and wrenched the door open.

"They need friends," I choked. "It seems I am the only one they have."

I heard his voice call after me, "Barbara!" I took no notice and went out onto the veranda, urgently seeking fresh air. Tommy was there at once, pulling out a chair for me, ordering the boy, nodding, and with the great palm leaf idle in his hand, to stir himself.

"Missie like lemonade?" he grinned toothlessly.

"Tommyboy fetch."

"No thank you," I said. "I don't want anything."

He went to sit on his chair, out of my sight, but I was certain I was not out of his.

I closed my eyes. My heart was beating furiously after my encounter with Adam. If only he thought and felt as I did, I thought hopelessly, how much simpler life would be. As it was, we were constantly at war with each other.

The sound of horses' hooves, a tinkling laugh, disturbed me. I knew the owner of that laugh and wished I could escape, but Araminta had seen me.

"Hello, Barbara. How nice to see you again after such a long time."

She dismounted and came to join me on the veranda. Jem was at her side. She was dressed as usual in a white silk shirt, trousered and booted, with a broad-brimmed hat shading her face from the sun. She looked cool and lovely. I felt hotter than ever looking at her and very much aware of my travel-stained appearance.

"Whenever I come here," she continued, "you always seem to be elsewhere. I was almost on the verge of believing you had taken ship for England."

"Oh, no," I said, sweetly dissembling. I knew her pleasant manner held as deep a dislike of me as mine did for her. "I have no plans for that."

"I should hope not indeed," laughed Jem, snapping his fingers for a slave's attention.

"Then you must have other interesting pursuits that take up your time," she responded calmly.

My heart jumped. What did she mean? Did she know how I spent my time? But no, how could she? She never went anywhere near the slum quarter of Seatown, and I was always careful not to be seen making my way there, having discovered a very secluded route.

"You certainly seem to have settled down in Almada," Araminta went on. "It surprises me somewhat, for I had been led to believe you wished ardently to return to your native shores."

I said nothing. I knew who had been responsible for giving her that piece of information. Adam.

"You know, I still haven't been able to work out the exact relationship between you and Adam—apart from being man and wife, I mean—or why your aunt should leave Adam her fortune, whom she had never seen, and not you who had lived with her for years as her ward."

"My aunt was an eccentric," I said, wondering why she was so set on seeking the truth. What good would it do her if she knew? I would still be married to Adam, the main cause of her hatred for me. Was it that she wished to discredit me in the eyes of everybody in Almada? If she only knew—it would not be I who would be discredited, but Adam. How would she feel if, as the result of her probings, the man she loved was held up to shame?

"But that is not enough," she went on, her luminous eyes sliding from me to Jem, "do you not agree, to explain . . . ?"

I rose abruptly. "I must beg you to excuse me. I . . ." I indicated my travel-stained habit, ". . . must go and change."

Her high, tinkling laugh followed me. She said something to Jem that I did not catch, but his reply, deep and carrying, reached me as I climbed the stairs, "There may be something in what you say, Minty."

Did Jem suspect the truth? If only Adam were not so determined to keep the true nature of his birth a secret—after all, what difference would it make if the truth were known? None to me. Aunt Martha was dead, so it could not matter to her. Morvah could come in for no criticism. And people would soon forget. It would be a nine-day wonder; then it would be over. People would find something else to talk about. Meanwhile, this life of pretense on all levels did not agree with me at all.

"Adam!" Araminta's exclamation of delight reached my ears. He had joined them on the veranda. I could not see him, but I heard his deep response, full of warmth, "I thought I heard your voice, Minty."

And you could not wait to get to her side quickly enough, I seethed, slamming my bedroom door behind me in frustration.

Araminta. Araminta. I hated the name. I hated her. I hated her with all my soul. Yet what right had I to hate her for holding a place in my husband's heart I could not fill? I should not blame her because he preferred her to me. But I was in no mood for reason. I hated him, too. He was ruthless and uncaring. I hated him . . . I hated him . . . No . . . I loved him . . . that was the truth of it.

I faced it at last. I was in love with Adam, and now, all of a sudden, I realized I had always been in love with him; right from the moment when he had smiled at me—or I thought he had smiled at me—and my cheeks had flamed and my heart had soared. It had been sent tumbling back to earth so quickly I had not grasped what had happened to me. Now I knew. Now I knew why I needed Adam so. Now I could admit it.

Meta came and helped me out of my riding habit, placed my wrap around my shoulders, and departed. Within the hour she was back with my habit sponged and pressed. She gave me a wide white smile as she hung it away.

"What you wan' wear for tea, Missie Barbry?"

I was still standing where she had left me, numbed by my shattering discovery. Her question jolted me to respond. "Is Miss Belmont still here?"

"Yes, missie. She stay to tea."

"Then I will not go down. Bring mine up to me."

I threw myself on my bed when she had gone with an overwhelming desire to cry rising in me. I bunched a fist into my mouth. I would not cry. I would not. Then I heard footsteps running up the stairs. I raised my head. They were not Meta's. Her tread was softer than a cat's. Then my door was flung open and Adam entered.

"Meta said you will not come down to tea? Why? Are you ill?"

"No, I am not ill."

"Then why will you not come down?"

"Because I have no wish to."

"We have a guest."

"I know. Araminta."

"Then put some clothes on and come and do your duty as mistress of High Place."

"No."

He glared at me. "You must. What excuse can I give?"

I shrugged carelessly. It seemed to enrage him.

"Get up and come down at once," he rasped.

I did not move.

"You're my wife, dammit. A wife should obey her husband."

"That's the second time you have said that to me today." I was stung to retaliation. "But I'm not your wife. Not truly. I am married to you, but ours is not a true marriage. It is a marriage in name only. A marriage of convenience, allowing you to go your way and I mine.

But it appears, judging by your attitude of late, that you are changing the rules. If what I do does not meet with your agreement, I must not do it. Well, I refuse to bow to your wishes. I have every right to decide for myself what I shall do. If I choose not to come and take tea with you and Araminta, you must accept it. I should think," I added on a note of spite, "you would welcome it."

He drew in a long breath. "And what do you mean by that, pray?"

"I know how you feel about her," I charged.

That hit home. His eyes blazed. "Get up and come down to tea," he ordered again, and I thought for a moment he would come and haul me from my bed by force. Against all reason I wished he would, imagining his anger evaporating as he lifted me up in his arms. If I had been Araminta it would have happened that way. Adam would not have remained in the doorway, dark-browed and cold. He would have reached out for me and kissed me till my head reeled.

But I was not Araminta. I licked my lips and said with some difficulty, "Adam . . . do you not think . . . should we not be . . . divorced?"

"Divorced?" His frown deepened and a sudden stillness took hold of him.

"We should never have married," I rushed on. "Our marriage was a mistake. It was clear from the first it would never work. You don't love me. You never wanted to marry me. You wouldn't have done it if you'd known . . . there was no need."

Adam stood as still as a rock staring at me.

"Let me go, Adam," I begged, "back home to England . . . back to Martha's Cottage."

"Martha's Cottage!" He ground out the name between

his teeth. "That's all you care about, isn't it? That's the reason you married me—to keep Martha's Cottage."

"Yes," I whispered, not understanding why it made him so angry. I had expected him to agree at once to a divorce.

"Nothing else means anything to you, does it?"

"No."

"Then go and be damned," he grated. "But there'll be no divorce. I'll not have you bringing shame on the Pengarth name."

He went, slamming the door behind him.

I did not go down to dinner that evening. Meta brought me some food on a tray, but I could not eat a thing and she took it away again, mumbling under her breath something about nothing being worth starving for.

Morvah came to see me later. "Everyone's worried about you," she said.

I told her I just felt tired and wished to rest. "I shall be all right in the morning," I added, "if I am left alone."

"Very well, my dear." She took the hint. "I will ask the others not to disturb you. Good night."

"Goodnight, Mrs. Pengarth."

She gazed at me silently for a few moments, a sad little frown on her face, then with a gentle shake of her head she left me to myself. I thought her sadness was because she knew of Araminta's visit and understood how I felt.

I lay on my bed and tried to sleep. It was hopeless. My mind was a whirl of activity. I got up and went to stand by the open window. It was a bright starry night, with the moon, more than half full, weaving, as ever, its ladder upon the dark waves. A slight breeze wafted its way through my flimsy night garment, cooling me, so that I stayed there for a long time. But, at last, with a sigh, I turned back to my bed. It was eleven o'clock. I must try to get some sleep.

A light tap came at my door and Meta entered. "You all right, missie? I worry. I hear you moving about."

"I'm fine, Meta. Go to bed," I said.

"You sure, Missie Barbry?"

"Yes, Meta."

She went, her round face still full of concern.

I drew the sheet over me and lay back, closed my eyes and begged for sleep to come. Then my eyelids flew open. Someone had entered my room.

"Who is it?" I cried. "Meta, is that you?"

A figure moved toward my bed. "It is I, Adam."

"Oh." My heart, already knocking against my ribs, tumbled over itself. "What do you want?"

"To make love to my wife," he said.

He stared down at me. I caught the gleam of his eyes.

"You're . . . drunk," I cried. My wedding night flashed before my eyes.

"I'm stone-cold sober," he said.

Then, swiftly, he leaned forward and pulled the sheet from my clutching hands and threw it away.

"Adam," I whispered fearfully, making an ineffective effort to retrieve it.

Then his hands were at my nightgown and the tear sounded like an explosion as it ripped apart.

I screamed and tried to cover myself with my hands. "Adam! What are you doing? Have you gone mad?"

"On the contrary. I have come to my senses." He brushed my hands aside. "No, you will not hide anything from me any more. You are my wife and I intend you shall know it. It is high time."

I cowered away from him, drew my knees up to my chin. My teeth were chattering. I felt cold, cold in the warmth of the room. He started to remove his clothing, calmly, unhurriedly. I stared at him in anguished silence, unable to believe this was really happening. Adam was preparing to make me his wife in fact as well as name. It was what I had longed for, but not like this. Not like this.

I watched his clothes fall to the floor, garment by garment, till he was as naked as I, unable to move or say a word. Then he bent toward me and caught hold of my hands, removed them from my knees, and I screamed, "Adam, no! Not like this!"

"How then?" His voice was hard, cruel. "On the floor of the little summer house? You were begging for it there."

It was as if he had kicked me in the stomach. "Oh, Adam," I whispered brokenly. "Don't . . . please . . . don't. . . ."

He forced my arms outward till my back was against my pillow and my breasts were fully exposed to his gaze. His head swooped down. He kissed my breasts. With one hand, he pushed my knees down. "You're my wife," he said thickly. "I have rights. You have duties." And my whole body clamored for him; but not like this. Not like this.

I pushed at him with my freed hand, shrieking, "No, Adam! No!"

With a laugh that pierced my soul, he breathed, "Oh, yes, Barbara, yes."

A voice came from the doorway. "You call, missie . . . oh!"

Adam leapt up. "Get out, damn you. Get out and stay out."

He was at the other side of the room locking the door. I

rolled off the bed and grabbed my robe. What good did I think it would do? He tore it from my grasp, sneering, "You won't be needing that."

His eyes raked my vulnerable naked body with insolent avidity, and an uncontrollable trembling took hold of me. I wanted to call out for help, but my tongue clove to the roof of my mouth. He lifted me up in his arms. I beat at his chest, without effect. His arms were strong and he held my naked flesh firmly against his own. Then he set me down on the bed, and a moment later I felt the weight of his body press down on mine.

I held my breath. This was the moment I had waited for, prayed for, when he would make me truly his wife, and now it had come I hated it. I hated it because it was not happening because of love, but because his masculine ego demanded it.

I twisted and kicked, bit and cried, to no avail. His strength overpowered mine. His mouth stifled my cries. His hands roved over my breasts, my hips, my thighs, weakening my resistance. My treacherous body began to revel in the sensations he aroused, and almost without my realizing it, my arms entwined themselves about his neck. I sensed a sudden change in him. His kisses became deeper, more passionate, and I responded, glorying in the feel of his body against mine. In a blaze of desire, I curled my legs around his, moved in unison with him, oblivious of everything but the moment, the hard forceful penetration. Then an exquisite, agonizing pain made me cry out. Then all was still. Adam's body was at rest on mine—and I was weeping silently. Now that the madness was over I felt ashamed of myself, of the wanton way in which my treacherous body had responded beneath his touch. Ashamed to admit I had enjoyed it.

Adam shifted his weight, drawing me round to face him with arms that held me close and whispered in my ear, "You are my wife now. Completely mine, at last." Then he noticed the tears on my cheeks and cried, "Barbara, what is it? Did I hurt you? Oh, my dear, forgive me. I should have been more careful."

A sob forced its way from my throat and I whispered fiercely, "I hate you. I shall never forgive you for forcing yourself on me."

His embrace slackened slightly. "But you responded. I thought you wanted . . ."

"I hate you." I hurled my hate in his face again, hate of him, of myself, of the situation. "I wish I never had to see you again."

He recoiled from me and slipped out of bed. He started to dress in silence, then he spoke again. "Please try to forgive me, Barbara. I never intended . . . but I thought . . . I was living in a fool's paradise. I should have known . . . you have every right to hate me. I behaved like a beast. I did not intend to . . . I merely wished to frighten you, teach you a lesson. I was driven by . . . but there's no excuse for what I have done. I should have left you alone."

And that's what he did. He went and left me alone.

Chapter Thirteen

I had to get away. I could not remain at High Place. I had no illusions as to why Adam had come to my room. He did not love me. He loved Araminta. But I had defied him once too often and he had determined to bring me to heel. So he had to place his mark on me . . . to prove his power over me.

I buried my face in my pillow and raged against him. "I hate you, Adam Pengarth. I hate you. I hate you."

But it was myself I hated for loving him in spite of it all. It was myself I hated for behaving so shamelessly, abandoning myself to passion. I had behaved like a wanton. I had forfeited all claim to respect.

I had tried to disregard the words Adam had proclaimed while he dressed. I did not want to admit any saving grace for him, but they thrust themselves to the forefront of my brain and made me look at them. He had not meant to force himself on me, only to frighten me, he had said. That would have been wickedness enough, but forgivable—the unforgivable had been brought about by my own desires. My own wayward passions, so long controlled and repressed, had been to blame.

I had to get away. Adam would despise me now, but he would not let me go, that realization became clearer the more I thought about it. He might not want me, but he had married me; I was his wife, his possession—and he kept what he owned. There will be no divorce, he had stated categorically.

So I would have to deceive him and make my own secret arrangements to leave him. But how? How could such a thing be kept secret from Adam? If I so much as attempted to purchase a passage to England, the intelligence would be transmitted to him. And I would not make a stowaway—I had not the courage.

I thought of Philip. If he could book passage for me . . . passage for two . . . that would provoke no questions; everyone would simply assume he and Sarah had decided to leave Almada. And if he left it till the last minute, there would be less time for speculation. He could escort me aboard—I would be suitably bonneted to hide my face; Sarah and I were not so different in height that I could not pass for her, and if it were a night sailing so much the better. Then he could slip ashore unnoticed, and with any luck I should be well away on the high seas long before Adam was even aware I had gone.

So I planned, carried away by my scheming, believing all that was necessary for my plans to come to fruition was my ability to persuade Philip to help me; and I was predisposed to see no problem there.

Meta found me in the morning rolled up into a ball in the middle of the bed. She beamed as she set my breakfast tray on a side table. Her knowledgeable eyes took in my nakedness, the torn nightgown on the floor, the sheet nearby.

"Massa Adam," she said, "he some man!"

I frowned at her. Unabashed, she went to get a light robe for me to put on.

"He gone now. Riding out to see dat Ransom fella."

I could not help asking, "Why?"

"Some big trouble there," she said, rolling her round eyes.

"What kind of trouble?"

"Slave trouble." She shrugged, as if to say, what else?

I ate my breakfast, surprised I could do so, but the truth was that after twenty-four hours without food I was starving. I bathed and dressed in a dilatory fashion, delaying the moment when I might risk running into Adam. The morning had already been far advanced when Meta had woken me with my breakfast, therefore determining beforehand that my visit to Philip Rose must be put off till the following morning when I would make a point of rising early and leaving before most people were up. However, I could not avoid meeting Adam sooner or later, so, gathering my courage together, I resolutely descended the stairs prepared to meet him stonily, but politely, in the full knowledge it would not be for long; Philip would soon arrange passage for me to England.

I headed for the garden nodding to Tommyboy, who appeared from nowhere to greet me. Morvah, already seated on the veranda, attracted my attention.

"Good morning, my dear. Won't you come and join me?"

I did, but with some reluctance. I would much rather have been out strolling through the gardens, as was my usual practice in the mornings. But perhaps it was better this way. I should only have dwelt on my unfortunate situation.

I thought Morvah looked worried. "Is anything

wrong?" I asked.

"Not really," she replied, but I thought her airiness unconvincing.

"Are you sure?"

"Well—it's just that . . . Robert has not returned home. He left with Adam to call on Jack Ransom early this morning, then he rode off saying he was going to see Jem, who is overseeing some clearance work up beyond Welbeck's Way."

"Well, then, if he's with Jem . . ."

"But he isn't. He never reached there. When Adam came home about an hour ago he said he had been to the clearance site and Jem told him he hadn't seen Robert."

I said gently, for I could see she was worried, "He probably changed his mind and went for a gallop over the hills. He'll call on Jem later, no doubt. He's a fine horseman. . . ." I broke off while I tried to catch and identify a wisp of a thought that strayed into my mind, but it fled as swiftly as it had arrived. "You can't suspect an accident," I concluded.

"No. You must be right, of course." But she sighed as she said it, and the worried frown did not lift from her face.

We took luncheon together. I was afraid at first that Adam would join us, but Morvah explained at my inquiry that he had ridden out again soon after his return. I stayed with her throughout the rest of the afternoon, chattering nonstop to try to take her mind off her concern over Robert, with very little success. At her request we took tea on the veranda, and all the time her eyes were on the drive looking for Robert's return.

I found it difficult to understand why she was so worried. Robert had gone off on his own many times before, and though he might have the mind of a child, he had the body of a man. He was strong, well able to take care of himself, if attacked. But who would attack him? The inhabitants of Almada might look upon him as an oddity, laugh at him behind his back, but they knew he was not dangerous. Besides, he was a Pengarth, and the Pengarths were a very respected family. So, if he had not been attacked, was it possible he could have had an accident? It was possible, I supposed, but difficult to believe of so fine a horseman. He could not possibly have been unseated. He knew the countryside well and would not get lost. Yet, in spite of all this, the fact still remained: He had the limited intelligence of a child. He thought and behaved like a child, trusted like a child. Supposing somebody . . . I began at last to appreciate Morvah's fretfulness.

I reached out to touch her arm. "Please don't worry, Mrs. Pengarth. I'm sure Robert is . . ."

I withdrew my hand in astonishment as she turned on me. "Mrs. Pengarth again. Is it so difficult for you to call me Mother? Is it too much to ask? I have waited and waited . . . I am Adam's mother, even though . . . you are my daughter-in-law, whether you like it or not, couldn't you . . . please . . . ?"

Her voice broke. Her face crumpled. It was suddenly brought home to me how much I must have hurt her by refusing to call her Mother. I had been unable to bring myself to call her that because I knew the title belonged to my Aunt Martha by rights, and in a way I suppose I resented the fact that she had been prevented from claiming it; perhaps I even apportioned some of the blame to Morvah herself. But now I saw with the utmost clarity that Morvah had more right to the title than Aunt Martha ever had. It was Morvah who had given Adam a mother's love, Morvah who had worried over and nursed him through his childish ailments. And she could not have been prouder of him if she really were his mother. Why, she *was* his mother, more than Aunt Martha had ever been. Almost from the first moment he had drawn breath she had taken him to her heart and loved him, and I, who had married him, had refused to grant her the courtesy of recognizing this.

I dropped to my knees and clasped both her hands in mine.

"Forgive me, Mother."

Morvah smiled at me through tear-filled eyes. Tears streamed down my face. She kissed my forehead. No more needed to be said.

It grew dark. We remained on the veranda. Morvah would not go in to change for dinner, so neither did I.

"Where is everybody?" she moaned. "What is happening? Why aren't they back?"

I could not answer her and stared into the darkness with her, longing for someone, anyone, to return. Out of the corner of my eye I noticed a movement from behind one of the curtained windows along the veranda. I slewed round. A tall figure drew back—but she was not quick enough.

"What do you want, Bella?" I called out sharply.

After a moment's hesitation, Bella came forward. In the pale light that shone out onto the veranda her face was shadowed, yet I fancied I saw truculence there. Had she been spying on us? Was she annoyed at being found out? Or was it simply that I was her mistress and she had to obey me, and hated me for it? She always showed antagonism toward me, tried to avoid receiving orders from me. At first I had tried to overcome her aversion to me, but as I appeared to reap no success I had ceased to bother. She held great sway in the house and ruled the other slaves with a rod of iron. Morvah never tried to interfere, and after my initial efforts to take the reins of the household management into my own hands had failed, I did not either—and it must be admitted that she ran the house with superlative competence.

"I was wondering about dinner," she said smoothly. "You have not changed. Neither has," she glanced pointedly toward Morvah, "the mistress."

I ground my teeth together to control my aggravation. She had never accepted my status as mistress of High Place. I believed she never would.

"No, we—may not do so," I said curtly.

"And the master? Will he be in?"

"Of course."

"And . . ."

"We will all be in." I cut her short. "Please see that it is ready to serve when I call for it."

She backed away with the slightest inclination of her head. There was a half-smile on her face, as if she knew that something was going on—something I did not know about. But that was foolish. I shook myself. What could she know, apart from the fact that Robert had been out all day and that Morvah was worried about him? What was secret about that?

"Oh, here comes someone."

Morvah jumped up and I turned with her to stare into the darkness of the driveway. As the rider came into the light we saw that it was Adam. It may have been my imagination, but I thought he stiffened when he saw me. However, when he dismounted and came toward us he greeted me normally.

Morvah asked quickly, "Isn't Robert with you?"

His eyes swung to her, suddenly anxious. "No. Isn't he back? I thought he would be back by now."

"Oh, Adam," Morvah clutched at him. "What can have happened to him?"

"Nothing," he snapped, which showed he was worried, for he was never short with his mother. "Is Jem back?"

"No."

"That's strange." Adam's eyes seemed to look inward. Searching for what? An answer? "I've just come from Welbeck Way," he said then, "Johnson was in charge of the working party. He informed me Jem left the site soon after I had called to see him this morning."

"Perhaps he went looking for Robert," I suggested.

"Perhaps," said Adam.

"In which case," I turned comfortingly to Morvah, "you have no further case for worry. Jem will find him."

Adam's eyes glinted at me blackly in the diffused candlelight. "You have great faith in Jem, have you not?" he said caustically.

We went to change for dinner, hoping, expecting, Robert and Jem to turn up in the meanwhile. But they had not arrived by the time we regathered downstairs. Morvah's distress was grievous.

"Oh, Adam!" Her voice wavered, her hands flew to her mouth in a prayerful attitude, and I thought she was going to cry. "What if . . . do you think . . . ?"

"No, I do not," Adam said firmly.

"But supposing . . . supposing . . ."

"Stop worrying, Mother."

I wondered what they were talking about. "Supposing what?" I asked, and received no reply.

"But something's wrong. I know it. I can feel it," Morvah cried piteously. "Oh, Adam, we must do something. . . ."

"Yes, we must," Adam said. "I'll take some men and we'll comb the island. Not that I expect it's necessary, but to set your mind at rest."

He hurried out, yelling instructions on all sides, and when he returned he was booted and looked more than ready for action of any kind. I wished I were going with him. The yen for adventure filled my soul. I had to squash it. He would not take me, even if things were well between us.

"Be careful, Adam," Morvah cried after him as he left. "If anything should happen to you . . ."

"Stop worrying. Nothing will happen to me. Nothing has happened to Robert. He'll probably come riding in as large as life before I get back and you'll wonder what all the fuss was about." He kissed her and glanced over the top of her head at me. "Take care of her," he mouthed, and I nodded wordlessly.

From his mount he called back, "Start your dinner. There's no point in waiting. And don't worry."

We waited till the galloping hooves faded away, then I took Morvah's arm and guided her toward the dining room. Not that I felt like eating, but it would give us something to do, occupy our time, which was what I was sure Adam had had in mind when he suggested it. As I turned her round I saw with astonishment an array of brown faces. Slaves seemed to have come out of the woodwork. They all stood around open-mouthed, round-eyed. I looked around for Bella. She was nowhere in sight, so I sent them about their business.

I caught sight of Meta about to go upstairs. I called to

her. "Have you seen Bella anywhere?"

"No, missie. I not see her for long time."

"Well, will you let them know in the kitchen we are ready to eat?"

"I don't want to eat," burst out Morvah, and she pulled away from me and entered the drawing room.

"I followed her anxiously. "But don't you think . . . ?"

"I'm afraid," she cried desperately. "Terribly afraid."

I went to kiss her nut-brown face. "Don't be," I begged her. "Everything will be all right. Before long Jem and Robert will come riding in like Adam said and . . ."

"But what will have happened in the meantime?" she demanded passionately.

I drew back, startled by her vehemence. "Wh-what do you mean?"

She drew in a shuddering breath, then shook her head and looked down at her hands, twisting and untwisting them in her lap.

"What could have happened?" I persisted, feeling there was much more behind all this than I was aware of. It was more than just Robert missing, Jem missing . . . Adam had tried to make light of it, but now I thought about it, there had been an underlying something—a fear—he had tried to hide.

"What could have happened, Mother?" I asked again fiercely.

Her eyes, fever-bright, focused on me. "There's unrest among the slaves. It's been brewing up for days. Haven't you felt it? Adam's tried to make light of it, but he knows . . . I know . . . that's why he went to see Jack Ransom."

Jack Ransom. That hated name. But a chill had entered my heart before Morvah had mentioned him. I recalled the frightened brown face I had spied among the bushes. The man had run away when he knew I had seen him. He might have been in fear of his life—or he might have been watching, observing, waiting for a suitable opportunity to . . . I felt my legs go weak when I thought of what might have happened, and I sat down quickly.

"It started there . . . with Billy Joe . . ." Morvah was continuing, "I told Adam . . . he wouldn't listen to me . . . you don't know the things that can happen. The slightest thing can spark off a . . ."

"Mother, please." I tried to stop her. I could see she was working herself up into a state, and though her fear had rubbed off onto me, I tried to sound cheerful. "There isn't any trouble with the slaves. There can't be. Do you think Adam would have gone off and left us alone if he thought we were in danger?"

"But it's not us I'm worried about. It's Robert," she cried wildly. "Don't you understand? Afraid of what he might do . . . what he might have done."

Fear gripped my throat. My voice was thick as I cried, "What could he have done? Why are you so afraid? He's harmless . . . isn't he?"

I had caught hold of her hands and was clinging to them tightly as if my life depended on it. Morvah stared at me wildly a few seconds more, then she seemed to come to her senses.

"Yes, yes, of course. Forgive me for frightening you, my dear. I don't know what got into me. You're right. Adam's right. There's no point in worrying—yet. We must wait and see. Wait and see." Then, surprisingly, she said, "Let's go and eat."

We sat down at the long table and soon the food was set before us. Bella had reappeared and had everything in hand. The food looked and smelled delicious, but we only pecked at it. I was chasing elusive thoughts that frightened me, and Morvah—it soon became apparent she was still thinking about Robert.

"You understand why I worry about Robert?" she said. "He's a child. He's never grown up. He may look like a man . . . but he's a child. It's so sad." Her voice broke on a sob.

"Yes, I know," I said quietly. "It is very sad. But for you, not for Robert. Robert is perfectly happy, perfectly content."

"Do you really believe so? I believe so, but sometimes I'm not so sure. He was a normal baby. At least, he seemed so. His head seemed to be a bit large, but we paid no more than a passing thought to it. A baby's head often appears large in comparison with its body. It was only later that we realized something was wrong and . . . oh, it wasn't fair. It wasn't fair. He was such a dear, friendly little thing . . . always smiling. It nearly broke my heart when . . ."

I put my hand on hers. "Please don't upset yourself, Mother. It can't be helped. We must be grateful for the fact that he does not know anything is wrong with him and that he has such a happy nature."

"Happy. Yes, he is happy, isn't he?" She looked at me eagerly. "We tried to make him happy. We forbore to place on him anything we felt he couldn't cope with. We guarded him. We watched him. We did our best by him."

She turned her hand in mine and I held it. We looked at each other in silent and mutual affection for a moment. Then we heard the sound of horses' hooves, distant, but real, then men's voices, the clatter of running feet.

"They're back," I cried and jumped up to look out where in the dim light of lanterns I made out shadowy shapes darting hither and thither. "Let's go and meet them."

"No. Wait," Morvah cried out in alarm. She remained rooted to her seat.

"Why not? They're back."

"Don't go. Wait here. It may not . . ."

Her alarm found an echo in me now. She was afraid it might not be any of our men, but slaves in revolt come to murder us. But the men were on horseback. Slaves would not ride up to the house. They had no horses. But they would have. They would steal them. Infected by her fear, I remained where I was, my heart thumping, waiting for the dining room door to be thrown open and an army of revengeful slaves to descend on us.

It was Adam who entered, and I sat down with a thud on the nearest chair. I whispered his name through bloodless lips and then noticed that his jacket was ripped and muddied. His boots and trousers were also in a sorry state. His eyes held mine, and for a moment I thought he would come across to me, but then he turned to look at his mother, still sitting stiffly upright in her chair, her face a tight mask.

He went up to her and took her in his arms. "Robert's safe," he said.

She seemed to deflate. "Thank God!" she breathed and slumped against his chest. He held her silently, and then she raised her head. "What happened?" she asked.

"Nothing much. His horse shed a shoe over on the far side of Black Ridge. They'd just got down into the gully and couldn't get back up again. He's all right. There's the stream nearby and . . ."

"Where is he now?"

"In bed. Bella's taking him some food. He wanted to come in and see you, but I thought it best for him to go and bathe . . . he's all right, don't worry. He's as merry as a cricket and thinks it all a great adventure."

"I'll go up and see him."

"Not now. Later. When he's rested," he urged her.

"Very well," she said obediently, like a child herself.

The foregoing exchange intrigued me. It occurred to me that Adam did not want his mother to see Robert at present, though on the face of it there appeared to be no valid reason why she should not. And his explanation about Black Satin's losing his shoe did not ring quite true. In fact, I thought I detected a decidedly false note in his voice. Perhaps Robert was in worse shape than Adam was prepared to admit to his mother: in which case, I applauded his wish not to distress her further this evening. She would have to be allowed to see him tomorrow, of course, but, possibly, he would be better by then.

Morvah kissed us both. "I'm going to bed," she said. "I'm tired."

My instinct was to leave with her. The last thing I wanted was to be alone with Adam, but something made me want to ask, "Where's Jem? Did you find him?"

"Yes. He was playing cards at the Crossleys'. You may remember them—you were introduced to them at Minty's party."

"Oh, yes." I had not liked them. *He* had reminded me of Thomas Green, the horrid little man I had met on board ship. He appeared to have the same bellicose nature, and he drank too much wine. *She* had an unpleasant manner and delighted in recounting unfavorable stories about her friends. I had got away from them as soon as I could. "But about Jem—he couldn't have been playing cards all day."

"No. He had gone into Seatown to keep an appointment made some time ago. When I asked him if he had thought to look for Robert after I had been to see him, he said he hadn't thought it necessary, as he believed Robert perfectly capable of taking care of himself, but when I told him Robert was still missing and my mother was greatly worried, he came at once to join us in our search."

"Where is he now?"

"Changing." Adam's eyes flashed with sudden annoyance. "And if you'll excuse me, I'll go and do the same. Oh, by the way," he announced from the doorway, "we will be receiving an invitation to dinner from the Crossleys. They asked after you and said they both looked forward to meeting you again."

I said nothing to this. I could not have cared less, in truth. With the slightest bit of luck I should be aboard ship and on my way home before the invitation arrived.

Before Adam finally departed, I called, "How did you get in such a mess? Rescuing Robert and Black Satin from the gulley, I suppose?"

"Yes," he said shortly, and was gone.

He had explained everything well, yet I was not really satisfied. In some strange way I felt he had not told me all. For one thing, I could not see Black Satin throwing Robert, even if he had lost a shoe. Robert was too expert a horseman. I could not see him trapped in a gulley, either. He was as agile as a monkey and as adept at clambering over rocks and hacking and trekking his way through the jungle. Nature may have halted the development of his brain—though I was not a hundred percent convinced of this—but there was no getting away from the fact that he had many gifts to compensate. So, I felt, unless he had been injured, he would have had no difficulty in getting himself and his horse out of that gulley.

No, I felt, there was more to this than met the eye.

However, it was only a feeling. Things could have happened the way Adam had said, and really, I had no reason to disbelieve him, yet . . . that elusive wisp of thought entered my mind again—and this time I caught it.

I looked out on the starry night in dismay. I believed I knew who the Gray Phantom was.

It was Robert.

I believed Morvah feared this. It explained why she had been afraid of what he might do . . . of what he might have done. I had not understood her words when she had spoken them. Now they seemed perfectly clear.

I believed Adam knew. Possibly Jem, too. And they were combining their efforts to keep the truth from Morvah and others, and I did not care to judge the morality of this, but I could see the naturalness of it. It was natural to protect a loved one—in this case, two loved ones. But if one of those loved ones was no better than a beast? I had not heard of anyone's being murdered by the Gray Phantom as of yet, but who could tell that it would not happen one day?

And now I was in possession of the awful truth. Could I keep quiet about it? Should I keep quiet about it?

The sooner I returned to England, the better it would be all round.

Chapter Fourteen

I was up early, matching action to plan, joyful at the thought of seeing England again, Martha's Cottage, the peacocks on the lawn. English sunshine, English clouds and rain. How I had missed the English rain softly falling out of dove-gray skies. I edged out of my mind any thought of what I might miss here once I was back in England.

Daniel saddled Lady for me. "Where you go, missie?" he asked, a trifle apprehensively. He knew; he was canny; Adam had forbidden me to ride into Seatown alone. "You want me come with you?"

I smiled cheerfully. "There's no need. I'm only going for a canter before breakfast."

His face brightened and my heart smote me, he was so easy to deceive.

"You not go far from de house den, missie. Some bad men roamin' loose," he cautioned me.

A twinge of fear made me pause, but then I spurred my horse lightly. "I'll be all right," I cried.

I reached the ramshackle hospital without meeting a

soul. The way I had discovered of avoiding riding through the town was beautiful and quiet. Once the cane fields and their disturbing sights had been passed—for the black workers were out even earlier than I—there were only the sea and the lush verdure for the eye to revel in, the multicolored birds and the swiftly darting insects.

I alighted and tied Lady to a post. Sarah was tending a patient when I entered. She looked up and a dozen different expressions flashed across her face, delight, joy, worry, fear . . . this last remained fixed.

"Barbara! What are you doing here? Does Adam know? I thought . . ."

"I must speak to Philip, Sarah," I professed urgently, concentrating on my purpose in coming there. I dare not stay long. I glanced around. "Is he here?"

Philip came out from behind the curtain he had created in a makeshift way in order to have some privacy while he operated. As Sarah had done, he exclaimed in astonishment, "Barbara! What . . . ?"

"Oh, Philip, I'm sorry to disturb you, but I must speak to you on a matter of some urgency, but I can wait if you are busy for a little while."

"I'm always busy, you know that, but you shouldn't have come here. If Adam . . ."

"Please don't scold me Philip. I had to see you. I have a very important favor to ask of you. I won't stay long. Adam will never know I have been here."

Philip glared at me angrily, then glanced across at his wife. "It won't do any harm to listen," she said.

Philip nodded. "Very well, come over here." He led us back behind the curtain. "Now, what is it? And make it quick. You must get out of here."

I plunged in at once. "You must book passage for me

on the earliest possible ship sailing for England."

"Book passage for you? I don't understand. Surely Adam . . ."

"Adam doesn't know. He mustn't know. I'm—leaving Adam."

"Leaving Adam?" Sarah's eyes almost popped out of her head. "But why?"

"Things have happened," I said, "which . . . I can't explain, just please, please believe me when I tell you it's a matter of the utmost urgency. I can't stay in Almada any longer. I must get away. You must help me. I've no one else to turn to. Please . . . please . . . help me."

I was clutching hold of Philip's arm in an anxiety to impress my need upon him. It must have got through to him. He said, "Well, of course I'll help you, but . . ."

It was enough. I swiftly outlined my plan to him.

"You want it to appear as if Sarah and I are returning to England?" Phillip said, appearing slightly dazed by my rush of words.

"Yes. I will give you the purchase money . . . enough for two . . . I have it here in this bag. One thing Adam is not mean about is money."

I tried to push the little bag into his hand, but he drew back. "No, I can't do it. I'm sorry, but everyone knows I have no money. If I am seen to be suddenly flashing money about . . ."

"But, Philip . . ."

"Besides, everyone knows I will never leave Almada. I have made it plain I am here to stay."

"But, Philip," I cried out again in anguish as all my bright plans seemed about to come to nought, "please . . ."

"Rose! Where are you? Is my wife here?"

Adam's angry voice cut mine off and set my heart

careering madly. Adam! Here! He couldn't be! He was. He tore the curtain aside. "So." Bitter resentment boiled in his eyes, searing my soul. "You are here. Are you mad to continue in this folly? I couldn't believe my eyes when I saw Lady tethered outside. As for you, Rose," he turned on Philip, "words fail me. Have I not made my wishes clear in this respect? You know I want Barbara kept outside . . . isn't it enough that you involve your own wife without involving mine?"

"Don't blame Philip," I cried out in his defense. "He didn't know I was coming. He told me to leave as soon as he saw me."

"Then you should have taken good advice when it was given to you," he snapped. "Come, let us leave at once."

"I'll go when I'm ready to go," I declared hotly, though not without fear as the two blue stones that were his eyes suddenly flashed fire.

"Please go now, Barbara," Philip said, and in answer to the mute question in my eyes, whispered, "I can't."

Adam and I rode away from the pitiful little hospital as we had done once before, angry with each other.

"So you disobeyed me," he scowled.

"I said I would," I retorted.

He drew in a long, hard breath then burst out, "Why do you insist on fighting me?"

"If you were reasonable, I shouldn't need to," I shot back.

"You go out of your way to cross me. Ever since we reached Almada you have behaved as if you hated me. Why? What have I done?"

"What have you done?" I looked at him with loathing. "You can ask that after . . ."

A spasm crossed his face that made me think for a

moment that he was in great pain. "About that," he said, "I'm sorry, truly sorry. I can't say it enough. I've never ceased to berate myself over it."

I sniffed. "Words come easy," I sneered, and looked ahead of me again.

"Not these," he said in an odd, strained voice. "I beg your forgiveness, Barbara. Please. I don't know what got into me. I . . ."

"I know what got into you," I flung back at him, determined not to give way to the little voice inside me that nagged at me to believe him. "You wished to impress upon me that I was your property, to do with as you pleased."

"No . . ."

"You wished to show me I had no more rights than the meanest of your slaves."

"Barbara!" His face had gone white. "That's not true. You know it's not true. I have always treated you with kindness, consideration . . ."

"You have made my life a misery."

I heard the hiss of his indrawn breath. "You can't mean that."

"I do."

"But I've tried to make your life happy."

"You did not try hard enough."

I spurred my horse with the heels of my boots and she leapt away. I kept ahead of Adam for the rest of the way home, giving him no further chance to argue. He was not going to get round me. I was leaving him. I was leaving Almada. Yet, contrarily, I wished he would catch me up, but he seemed content to leave things as they were.

* * *

My plans had come to naught, but I would not be defeated. There must be someone else who could help me. Perhaps Jem? Or I could rely on myself. Book passage in a false name. Hide my face behind thick veiling while speaking to the clerk. I was not beaten yet.

But I did not find it easy to put my new plan into action. Uneasily, I began to realize I was being watched. Wherever I went, whatever I did, there was Morvah or Adam or Jem—or Bella. If I so much as set foot in the stables there Adam would be, or Jem, ready to accompany me on my ride.

Adam treated me politely, but with an attendant coldness that was an echo of mine. I knew Meta found it strange that he had not come to my room again since that one wild night when she had burst in and caught us both stark naked and jumped to the wrong conclusion. But she did not speak of it. It was not her place to. She would have earned swift rebuke if she had. But she was the same Meta she had always been, caring for me with the same devotion she had always shown.

With Bella it was different. The polite reserve with the underlying antagonism with which she had always treated me had undergone a subtle change, and in the swift glances she directed toward me, which I would sometimes intercept before she could mask her unguarded feelings, I read hatred. I could not understand such hatred. It stemmed from the night Adam had come to my room. The very next morning I had felt it. She knew Adam had come to my room. She could not have known what had happened there. Yet I felt she did know and—somehow—blamed me for it.

Why, when I was the victim?

Oh, if only I could get away! I had to get away!

Everything was made worse when Morvah approached me one morning. "What has gone wrong between you and Adam now?" she inquired.

"Nothing," I prevaricated.

"Nonsense," she snapped. "Something's happened to spoil things between you. Just when I thought everything was going to be all right. But the way things are between the two of you now, stone-cold politeness, not an ounce of warmth from either side . . . what's the matter with you, don't you *want* your marriage to survive?"

I stared at her unhappily. It was unfair that she should blame me. Adam was the one at fault.

Her attitude softened. "Oh, my dear, what went wrong? I know he came to you, stayed the night with you . . ."

I shook my head and turned away from her, trying to suppress a sudden threatening sob.

"You mean he didn't come to you?" she asked wonderingly.

I shook my head.

"He did come to you?"

I nodded.

"And he made love to you!"

I swung round with a long, drawn-out cry of pain. "No-o-o-o! He raped me!"

Morvah stared at me in shock, horror, disbelief.

"Adam? I don't believe it!"

"He raped me! He raped me!" I flung in her face.

She drew in her breath sharply and her next words stunned me.

"Well, if he did, it was no more than you deserved. A man can only take so much. If you set a man on fire, you must expect to get burned. If you had behaved like a true wife to him, it would not have come to such a pass."

"But he doesn't want me as a wife, you know that. I've explained to you. He doesn't care for me. He only came to my room to assert his rights over me."

"Bah! You can't see beyond the end of your nose," she said. "You need a good whipping, girl, to bring you to your senses."

I almost wept. Morvah, usually so kind, so thoughtful, so understanding, saying such awful things to me. I could not bear it.

"You're not being fair. You don't understand. You don't know."

"That's where you're wrong. I do know. Adam's in love with you, you fool, and you're breaking his heart."

"No. You're wrong. I . . ."

"You've never given him a chance," Morvah interrupted coldly. "Only goaded him, led him on with your meek ways, lifting him up and letting him down, till he hardly knew whether he was coming or going. There's a name for women like you. You're no better than the Belmont girl. Worse. At least she . . ."

"Stop it! Stop it! You don't know what you're saying. None of those things is true about me. And you don't know your son at all if you think . . ."

I could not go on. I rushed from the room—and collided with Jem in the hall.

"Here, steady on," he laughed, but as he looked down into my tear-stained face, his smile vanished. "My dear, what's wrong? Can I be of any help? Oh, don't cry so."

I collapsed against his chest. "Take me away, Jem. Take me out of this house. Far away. It's suffocating me."

He held me close for a few brief moments of safety, which I wished could last forever, then without a word he turned me around and directed me out into the garden.

We walked in silence down to the silver-sanded beach. We walked by the edge of the ocean and the tears dried on my cheeks.

"Would you like to talk about it?" Jem asked at last.

I wanted to. It would have been a great help to unburden my soul to him, but his eyes, looking down into mine, were so full of sympathy . . . and more . . . I could not.

I lowered my eyes and kicked at the sand with my feet so that it fell about in little glinting showers. Jem put his arm about me and we continued walking till it grew dark and the moon rose.

"We had better go back, don't you think?" Jem said softly.

I drew in a deep sigh and nodded. "Yes, Jem. Thank you for being . . . for understanding."

"It was nothing," he said with a shrug of his shoulders.

But it was something. It was everything. I had not wanted to be alone, I had needed a friend, a shoulder to lean on. He had supplied that need, unstintingly.

I stood on tiptoe to kiss his cheek in gratitude. All in a moment I realized I had made a mistake. I was in his arms, his mouth pressed hard on mine. For a moment I remained passive, then I resisted, struggling to push him away.

"No, Jem. No."

He let me go. His breath was coming fast. "Forgive me," he said thickly."

"It wasn't your fault," I said. "I shouldn't have . . ."

"You know I'm in love with you, don't you?" he said.

I said nothing. I had long thought he admired me, perhaps even loved me, but I had never really believed it to be true. Now here he was spelling it out for me. I could be in doubt no longer.

"I have been from the first moment I saw you."

Still I remained silent. What could I say?

"I can't bear to see you so unhappy. I could kill Adam for what he's doing to you."

"Don't say such things." I found my voice at last.

"I must." He gripped my arms and drew me toward him again. "They're true. I love you, Barbara. I love you. I . . ."

I cut him short with a little cry of fear. "Jem, listen. Did you hear something?"

"What . . . ?" He seemed dazed.

"Listen," I hissed.

He dropped my arms and I knew he was listening as intently as I.

"There. Did you hear it?"

"A bird or an animal of some kind," he said.

"Yes, of course," I breathed out in relief. I had been imagining all sorts of things. Black faces hidden from our view. Men with axes to hack us to pieces. The Gray Phantom about to savage us. Oh, my imagination had run riot. But now Jem had relieved my fears. What else could it be, but a bird or a small nocturnal animal?

We started to walk back. I half expected Jem to take up where he had left off and I was busy forming in my mind some kindly, but blunt, words that would make it clear his attentions were unwelcome. How strange it was that I should hear words of love and not be stirred by them, except to pity. Though I might have felt a certain tenderness toward the purveyor of such sentiments, I wished for no more of them. Words of love from a man for whom one felt no deep emotion were as leaves on the wind to be blown and find no resting place.

Jem kept quiet, however, strangely quiet. It was not the friendly silence he had maintained on our outward walk, but a watchful silence—a quiet listening that sent soft fingers of fear coursing up and down my spine, and I knew he was not as sanguine about the origins of those earlier noises as he had at first appeared.

His pace increased so that I had to run in little spurts to keep up with him, and I panted at last, "Please, Jem, don't walk so fast."

He slowed and turned. "Sorry, Barbara, but . . . God! I was afraid of that."

The loud report of a pistol had shattered the night's calm.

"What . . . ? Who's shooting?" I cried in alarm.

Jem did not answer. How could he know who it was? He caught hold of my arm and began to run, pulling me with him. Another shot splintered the night. A barking and snarling of dogs. A scream—high pitched and agonized.

"Someone's been hit," I shrieked.

Jem dragged me along. "Hurry! Hurry!" And we reached High Place to find a great deal of bustle and activity going on. Slaves, dogs, horses, all adding their bits to the noise and confusion. Men were mounted, ready to ride. Adam was one of them. He jumped down when he saw us and drew me into his arms.

"Barbara! Darling, thank God you're safe. I was afraid you'd been caught up in . . ." He was mumbling into my hair, raining kisses on my head. My heart leapt. Had Morvah been right? Did he care? He had called me his darling. . . . "Where did you find her, Jem, I've been half out of my mind."

"He didn't find me. I wasn't missing." My heart thudded and thumped against my breast as I gazed adoringly up at him. It was true. He loved me. He had been half out of his mind. . . .

"We went for a walk together along the shore," Jem said, and even I recognized the implication inherent in his voice that made Adam react in the way he did. His whole body stiffened, and suddenly, I was standing alone, pushed aside.

"I see," he said; then, "Did you hear that shot?"

"Yes. It came from North End," Jem replied.

"I thought so. Get your horse, Jem. Let's go."

I was forgotten. The horses galloped away. The slaves dispersed. I stood, lost and bewildered, at the bottom of the marble steps.

Someone touched my arm. It was Morvah. "Come inside," she said, and I obeyed without demur.

Once indoors, in the drawing room, she put her arms about me. "Forgive me, Barbara. I shouldn't have spoken to you the way I did. Forgive an old woman who should keep her nose out of other people's concerns, but I thought I was doing it for your own good. I was shocked when you ran out and couldn't be found."

"You hurt me. I wanted to get away," I said.

"I know. I deliberately tried to hurt you, hoping it would make you see the harm you were doing to your marriage. Adam does loves you, Barbara. I am sure of it."

"I wish I could be," I said. "I thought . . . outside . . . but now . . . I don't know. I'm not sure about anything any more."

"Adam was furious at first when you could not be

found. He had told us all to keep an eye on you . . . in view of the situation on the island. Then his fury turned to fear. He was almost beside himself when those shots were heard. He was afraid you might have got caught up in . . . oh, my dear, you might have been . . . thank God you're safe."

"What were those shots?" I asked. "Jem said—and you said—there has been unrest among the slaves. Have they broken out? Has there been a revolt?"

"I don't know. I hardly dare think about it. But it's more than likely. And it's all due to people like your friend Philip Rose. Things were relatively quiet here till he came on the scene, till he started making his inflammatory speeches."

"It's not Philip's fault." I sprang quickly to his defense. "If he had been allowed to set up his hospital as he had first intended . . ."

"He should have stayed in England," Morvah cried passionately. "If he'd stayed in England Adam wouldn't have . . ."

"Wouldn't have what?"

"There are two factions on the island now. Those for slavery and those against. It always has been so to some extent, but we all managed to live together harmoniously, but now open warfare has broken out between them. And it's all because of Dr. Philip Rose."

"Which faction does Adam belong to?" I asked with a tightening of my stomach muscles.

"Oh, Barbara," Morvah exclaimed bitterly. "Do you need to ask?"

A silence descended on us. It was an eerie silence. In the usual way of things, the slaves would be singing around their campfires now before going to their beds.

But tonight the only melody came from the cicadas, whose chant never ceased. There was the occasional squawk of a bird, the far-off whinny of a horse, the bark of a dog. The house slaves went about their business in a hushed kind of way. Even Tommyboy had sidled away from his usual place in the hall. Everything seemed strange and abnormal. And not the least strange thing was Adam's arms tight about me, his kisses on my hair. Had it really happened? I hardly knew how to believe it.

Tommyboy appeared bearing a tray of food and steaming coffee. "You eat, missie," he said. "You not have any dinner."

Morvah said, "It comes to something when a slave remembers what I should have. I should have seen that you had something to eat."

"You're overwrought," I excused her, pouring coffee.

As we waited for the return of our menfolk, I remembered I had not seen Robert. I asked Morvah where he was.

She replied, rather too quickly, I thought, "He's in his room."

"But didn't he come down when he heard the shooting? He must have wondered what was going on."

"He's all right. Bella's with him. She knows how to deal with him when . . ." She broke off, realizing what she was saying.

I looked at her sternly. "There's something about Robert I don't know, isn't there?"

"No, it's just . . . well . . . you know he's not like other men. He may have the appearance of a man, but he's a child, and has to be looked after like a child. Sometimes he can be . . . awkward. Bella is his nurse."

"I thought she was the housekeeper," I said with quiet significance.

"She is, but . . . she also has the responsibility of looking after Robert when . . ."

"When what?"

I probed mercilessly, believing I was on the verge of learning something I had long sought the answer to. I could see Morvah wished she had not got herself into this position, but I did not intend to let her wriggle out of it.

"When what?" I asked again.

"There are times when—he has to be restrained."

She looked so miserable I almost let the matter drop there—but I did not.

"Restrained?"

"He's very strong, you see. Very strong. He doesn't realize his own strength. He's not violent in the ordinary way, but . . . it's so difficult to . . . when he gets upset he can do . . . great damage."

"And he's upset now?"

"He knows something's going on. He's curious . . . in a childlike way. He . . . doesn't like to be left out of things. He . . ." She looked silently at me for a moment as if considering what to say next, then she continued. "I shouldn't tell you this; Adam told me not to, but I feel it's something you ought to know about. It might serve to illustrate to you how fleeting life is, that love should be freely given and not withheld for whatever reason from the loved one—or it may be too late.

"Adam and Jem went to a meeting in town last night. Your doctor friend was giving one of his speeches. Exchanges were made. Things got heated. Men began throwing stones at Philip. Adam tried to get him away, but the foolish man resisted all his efforts. Soon they were surrounded by Jack Ransom and some of his henchmen. Jack was yelling, 'Hang 'em. Hang 'em. They're in it together.' And men we've known all our lives were swayed and carried away by him. They grabbed hold of Adam and Philip and began dragging them along. Jack began hitting and swearing at Adam while he was being held. Then, suddenly, he was thrust aside and two strong hands were around his throat. Robert, unknown to Adam, had followed him and had been watching from his horse on the edge of the crowd. I've told you how strong he is . . . no one could stop him. If Jem and some others had not managed to pull him away, Jack would have been dead by now.

"But he got away, and as he rode off he was heard to cry out that Robert was a maniac and ought to be locked away. He's been trying to convince people of it for years. Now he'll seize this chance to appeal to the governor to have him shut away. Oh, Barbara, if he succeeds, what a punishment it will be on me."

"Punishment on you?" I cried, taking her hands in mine, trying to give her comfort in her distress. "How can that be?"

"Jack Ransom was in love with me once, many years ago. I was young. I was flattered. I flirted with him." Morvah's eyes looked back into the past. She spoke as if she were talking to herself. I knelt with her hands in mine and kept quiet, feeling her need to unburden herself of some long-held secret. "But I never meant to fool him into believing it was anything more than that. I swear I never gave him any hint that I cared for him. Joe was the only man who ever meant anything to me. But Jack thought . . . When I began to realize what I . . . He . . . begged me to leave Joe and go and live with him. 'You care nothing for convention, neither do I. We must live for ourselves,' he said to me. I was astonished. I hadn't really thought . . . I had to tell him it had all been a game with me, just a game. I'll never forget the look that came over his face. I saw his love turn to hate in the space of a few moments.

"'I'll make you pay for this, Morvah,' he said. 'You've made a fool out of me and I won't forget it. I'll make you pay, no matter how long I have to wait—and it will be a high price, you may believe me.'"

Morvah shuddered. "Since then I've lived in fear of him. Each time Robert is away from home more than a few hours I get worried in case Jack has harmed him. He's a ruthless man, Jack Ransom. He led Joe deeply into debt, letting him think he was his true friend, leading him to believe any money owed on either side would be discounted in the end—but all the time he was plotting to take High Place away from him.

"He's my sworn enemy, Adam's enemy, and yours, too, now. Because of you he was thwarted in his attempt to gain High Place and so be able to throw me and my family out onto the streets to feed his revenge."

Morvah looked me straight in the eye. "You know why I'm telling you all this, don't you? Never play with a man's emotions, Barbara. It can prove too dangerous."

I knew what she was saying. I knew what she meant. But mine was not a like case. I had not led Adam on and Adam . . .

I refused to look further along that road. "What happened to Philip?" I asked. "Did he get away?"

"Yes. He was cut and bruised, but nothing serious. Adam said they got him home as quickly as they could. Oh, I wish he would go home, really home, back to England. He's caused nothing but trouble since he came here."

"If it hadn't been Philip, it would have been somebody else," I said. "It was bound to happen. Change must come to Almada."

"Why?" she demanded, "if it means setting men against man? If it means that Robert . . . ?"

She started to weep. I put my arms around her to comfort her in what little way I could. Robert was her son. She was afraid for his safety. She had kept him safe thus far. How much longer would she be able to do so? How much longer would there be peace in Almada? It appeared to be fast slipping away, with Jack Ransom leading the faction against the abolitionists. He couldn't win, of course, but—supposing he did. He would have great power in Almada. He might even take over from the governor. That would be revolution—but I did not think that beyond him. What a position he would be in then. He hated Adam. He hated all the Pengarths. But Adam was clever; he would be able to outwit Ransom, whereas Robert . . . With power in his hands, would Ransom condemn Robert to death—or incarceration for life?

But this would never happen. Adam would get Robert away. He would get us all away. How? I did not know, but he would.

Looking into the future, fueled by my imagination, I began to ask myself if Philip was right to carry his beliefs, his ideals to the extent he had. He was no politician. He would have done better to leave speechmaking alone and concentrate on medicine. That in itself caused him enough problems. If standing aside and letting things take their course meant slavery would exist for a few more years, would it matter, if, when it was finally routed, it would be without hatred and bloodshed?

So I crossed over from Philip's side to Adam's, or so I thought.

It was late when the men returned. Adam and Jem had joined up with other planters while they were out. Some had come back with them. Refreshments were ordered for all. Morvah and I looked at Adam for reassurance.

"It's all right," he said. "It's all over."

"Rebellion quashed," said a man who had heard. "Some slaves broke loose from Ransom's place and murdered one of his overseers."

"He shot a couple and hanged half a dozen others," said someone else.

"It was all over by the time we got there, the hanging."

"But surely," I turned on the man who had said this, "he can't hang men without a trial."

"Men, Mrs. Pengarth? Slaves, ma'am. Slaves. Slaves have no rights. Certainly, most of us here would prefer it if Ransom were less sadistic—he's not the best of masters—but the slaves who escaped were his. They belong to him. He paid good money for them. He has a right to do what he likes with them. And they did murder his overseer."

"I can't believe my ears," I cried. "You are condoning . . ."

Adam touched my arm and propelled me toward the door. He whispered in my ear, "Don't say any more, Barbara, please, I beg you."

I faced him angrily, back on Philip's side again. "I will not be silenced. It's savage. It's inhuman. A man is a man whether he's black or white, and as such he is entitled to . . ."

Adam's fingers bit deeper into my arm as he hustled me out of the room. "Go to bed. Don't ask any questions. Don't say anything more. Tommyboy, go and tell Meta missie wants to get ready for bed."

He shut the door on me. Fuming, I raced up the stairs, waving Tommyboy away. How dare he treat me so? How dare he? But I dared not disobey him.

As I reached my room I saw Bella leave Robert's. She hesitated when she saw me and I thought she would turn and go back into Robert's room, but she closed the door quietly and came on.

"How is Master Robert?" I asked.

For a moment her eyes held mine, then they shifted slightly.

"He's sleeping," she said. "He will sleep till morning."

Something made me ask pugnaciously, "How can you be so sure? Is he drugged?"

Her eyes flickered toward me again as she made a slight start. I could see I had caught her unawares. Before she could recover herself completely, she had informed me, "He has been given an herbal drink."

An herbal drink. I gazed out of my bedroom window at the flat sea, calm tonight as a mill pond. What kind of herbal drink? A tisane, to induce gentle sleep, or laudanum—to deaden his mind. How often was he given them? Those times I had missed seeing him around—was it because he had been given an herbal drink?

I had never seen any signs of violence in Robert. On the contrary, I had always thought him a gentle, diffident man—boy—I hardly knew how to refer to him. Of course, he had a childish mind, he behaved childishly, and yet, I wondered. I often thought he seemed to know more of what was going on around High Place than anyone gave him credit for.

I did not think him violent. There had been occasions when I had felt a little afraid of him, but that was because

I had never met anyone like him before. Now that I was growing used to him my fear had lessened, even if it had not disappeared altogether. But violent? I did not think so.

But, surely, they would not drug him into insensibility if it were not necessary. They did know him better than I. They had known him a lifetime, I, but a few months; though, strangely, sometimes I felt I had known him all my life.

Violent? I tried to see it. I had no evidence of it other than what had been related to me by Morvah. Morvah was his mother, and she believed he was violent. Therefore, I should believe it, too. But I could not help feeling his action was one any man would have taken seeing his brother under attack. Morvah had said Robert would have killed Jack Ransom if left to himself. If he had not been restrained, would he, even now, be a murderer?

I thought it a pity he had not strangled Jack Ransom. I would not have called it murder. I would have called it justice. Then, shocked at myself, but unrepentant, I went to lie on my bed.

The planters left. I heard them ride away. It was a hot night and I could not sleep. I tossed about restlessly, thinking about Robert and Jack Ransom, Adam, Philip and Sarah, the slaves who had been hanged. . . . The sweat rolled off me. I attempted to lie still, could not, rose, padded to the open window and went out into the veranda. It was not noticeably cooler; my nightshift clung to my skin, my hair was a long, damp cape about my shoulders, but it was better than lying in what was virtually a Turkish bath.

I rested my back against the louvred doors and closed

my eyes, then opened them again quickly at the sound of footsteps below, stealthy footfalls on the hard-baked earth.

I leaned forward, peering into the darkness. There was a half-moon, and it was light enough to make out the form hurrying away. It was Adam. I only had time to wonder where he could be going at this time of night when I heard more footsteps, saw another form following the first. It was Robert. *Robert!* But Robert was asleep in his room—drugged. No. Robert was out there, following Adam. It was a mystery I could not make head or tail of.

I stood wondering about it for a long time before I went back to bed not expecting to sleep, but at least to rest. I fell asleep at once.

I woke to bright blue skies and Meta with my breakfast tray.

"Good morning, Missie Barbry."

"Good morning, Meta. What have you brought me?"

"Grapefruit, missie, and . . ."

I had forgotten momentarily the events of the previous night, but as Meta started cataloguing the food on my tray, they came flooding back to me.

"Where is Master Adam?" I interrupted curtly.

"Why, in his office, sure, Missie Barbry."

"What time did he go there?"

"Why, usual time, missie. Eight o'clock." She looked at me slyly. I knew what she was thinking, but could not prevent myself from continuing with my questioning.

"Is he . . . does he look tired?"

It must have been about half-past three that I saw him leave the house. Had he been gone all that time, returning to go straight to his office? Or had he been back, gone to bed and . . . ?

"Massa Adam never tired, Missie Barbry." Meta grinned hugely. "He some man." Again her eyes slanted slyly at me.

"Where's Mr. Harding?" I asked. I had to make it appear I was interested in everybody, to foil conjecture.

"In de fields. Usual."

"And—Master Robert?"

Was there an infinitesimal pause before she replied to this question?

"He in his room, Missie Barbry. Sleeping."

Sleeping? For how long?

Dressed in palest green voile, my hair plaited in thick coils at the back of my head, with little ringlets escaping roguishly, I went downstairs. I had taken trouble with my appearance, had allowed Meta to spend as long as she liked on my hair. I wanted to look my best when I saw Adam. Remembering his arms about me, his whispered words, kisses on my hair—I wanted it all again.

Tommy was sitting in his usual chair in the hall. He rose when he saw me descending and bowed many times in quick succession.

"'Mornin', Missie Barbry," he said with each bow, and when I reached the bottom step, "Missie like somethin'? Tommyboy bring."

"No thank you, Tommy." I said and went to look in the drawing room. No one was in there, so I walked along the veranda to the music room. I hesitated before going in. If I walked a bit further I would be outside Adam's office.

But I went into the music room. I sat down at the piano and ran my fingers lightly up and down the keyboard, but I could not settle down to play anything. I got up and went out onto the veranda again. I wanted to see Adam—

and I wanted to know where he had gone last night, or rather this morning, at half-past three.

I walked along the veranda, my kid slippers making no sound on the floorboards. I saw Adam seated at his desk in his book-lined office, a ledger as thick as a man's arm in front of him. I had intended to go in, but took fright and turned to go back to the music room. He was busy. He wouldn't want me intruding.

But he must have heard me, or seen me, for he came after me, reaching me before I reached the music room. "Barbara," he called, and my heart began to race.

I turned to look at him. "Good morning, Adam."

"Good morning, Barbara. I'm glad I've seen you."

He looked so handsome in his white silk shirt, open at the neck. He had been working with his sleeves rolled up, and now he was busy rolling them down over his hard-muscled forearms preparatory to donning the jacket he had picked up on his way out to me.

"I . . . about last night," he said hesitantly. "You must have wondered why I hurried you out of the room like that."

I gave a slight shrug and looked down, overcome by the intensity of his gaze.

"I had to do it," he carried on earnestly. "Some of those men were cronies of Ransom's. They would have torn you to pieces if I had allowed you to say what I knew you were about to say."

"And you would have stood there and let them, I suppose." I raised my eyes quickly.

"You know I would not," he said quietly, though his eyes flashed with exasperation. "But it is better to avoid trouble if one can."

"And you are expert at doing that."

I could have bitten off my tongue at the look he gave me.

"Oh, I'm sorry. I didn't mean that. Please forgive me. I know how you stayed to help Philip when he was in trouble. You were attacked yourself, your mother told me, by Ransom and his henchmen."

His face hardened. "My mother told you?"

"Why shouldn't she? I have a right to know where you go and what you do. I am your wife." I declared.

"I'm very glad to hear you admit it at last," he said, his eyes narrowing. "I had begun to think I never would."

"Why do you have men like that in your house?" I went on. "Why have anything to do with them at all? You are not of their persuasion. I used to think you were. Now I know different. You agree with Philip, don't you? You believe he is right."

"Up to a point," he said, and I thought his hand came out toward me. His eyes were suddenly warm, and I thought: He's going to take me in his arms! But then Tommy came between us. He had brought us fruit juices and sugar and little sweet cakes. He smiled and bowed and placed the tray on a wickerwork table and departed.

Adam and I sat down. I smiled at Adam. "I don't know how he does it. I left him sitting in the hall while I went into the drawing room. I don't know how he knew I had come out here and that you were with me." I nodded toward the two glasses on the tray. "It's like magic."

"Or witchcraft," he said.

"Witchcraft?" I startled.

"Tommy's father was a witch doctor. He died when I was quite small, but I remember him well. He was a big fellow. Everyone treated him with great respect. They were afraid of him. He handed his powers down to his son, Tommyboy. But as far as I know Tommyboy never practiced the art. When he dies, his powers will descend to his son."

"Billy Joe?" I asked, wide-eyed, and when Adam nodded I added, "Will he practice it?"

"I don't know. I don't think so. They say the power can grow thin. But there are others who have not let their powers lapse, though we've tried to stamp it out."

"I don't know much about witchcraft," I murmured, touched by a sense of foreboding. "Except that—it's supposed to be evil."

"It is. It can be. It all depends. We've tried to stamp it out, as I say, but things still happen, strange things, unexplainable things."

"Such as?"

I wanted to know and I did not want to know, but I waited for his reply with a fascinated eagerness.

"Well . . . someone might suddenly die . . . for no apparent reason. He or she will just go into a decline and die. But sometimes a man will suffer agonies, from no discernible cause. Voodoo, they call it. Those who practice it make little dolls, effigies of certain people, enemies, people who have offended them. Then they stick pins into them and . . . the people fall sick and die, unless the doll is found and the pins removed."

"It's unbelievable," I gulped.

"Unbelievable, yes. And yet . . ." He drew in a deep breath. "I've seen the strangest things, inexplicable things. . . ."

"You believe in it?"

"I don't know." He shook his head and tossed the subject away. "How did we get onto this. Let's have a drink and eat some of those delicious-looking little cakes."

I poured obligingly and handed him a glass of orange juice. I knew he preferred it to grapefruit juice.

"Where did you go last night?" I asked suddenly.

"Last night? You know where I went. To investigate those pistol shots."

"No. After that. In the middle of the night."

He looked puzzled and laughed. "Nowhere. Where would I go in the middle of the night?"

"That's what I'm asking you."

Adam started frowning.

"I saw you leave the house at about half-past three," I said.

"Is this a joke?" he asked, not angry yet, but appearing ready to be so.

But I was certain I had seen him. "I saw you disappear into the darkness."

"Disappear into the darkness?" He gave a snort of laughter. "My dear girl you're letting your imagination run away with you again."

"No."

"What would I be doing out at that time of the morning? Where could I possibly go?"

"I saw you," I said stubbornly.

"And what were you doing, spying at half-past three in the morning?" His tone was smug, sarcastic.

"I wasn't spying. I couldn't sleep. I went out onto the veranda. You may make a joke of it, but I saw you leave the house—and Robert follow you."

"Robert?"

Adam's whole attitude changed. A look of fear crossed his face. He looked as if he believed me now. Why? Unless he thought, suspected, as I had done, perhaps still did, that Robert was the Gray Phantom and had been going out to do some dastardly thing. Oh, no. Now *I* was being imaginative.

Adam said, "You couldn't have seen Robert, Barbara, he was . . ." He broke off.

"Drugged?"

He appeared to be about to deny it, but then he shrugged and said, "Yes. So you see you could not have seen him leave the house, following somebody or not. He was insensible in his bed."

"No, he wasn't. He was out following you, or if not you, then, somebody else."

"Yes," he said almost to himself. "Somebody else."

"Who?" I asked.

"Who, indeed?" he said.

Who indeed? I echoed inside. If it had not been Adam, who could it have been? Adam was looking at me speculatively.

"You still don't believe I saw somebody, do you?" I said accusingly.

"Somebody? Does that mean you no longer suspect it was I?"

"No. Yes. Oh, I don't know what to think. I'm all mixed up."

Adam smiled then. A warm, widely spreading smile, that lit up his whole face and made me smile in return.

"Come." He rose and came to take hold of my hands. "Let's go for a walk."

"But your work . . ." I began, in a flurry of emotion.

"I can finish that later." His eyes burned into mine. "Wouldn't you like to go for a walk?"

"Oh, yes." I gazed helplessly—hopefully—up at him.

He drew me to my feet. I swayed toward him. He swayed toward me. In a moment he . . .

"Kiss her. Go on, kiss her."

We sprang apart as a lolloping head, a grinning face came into view over the veranda rail.

"Robert!" Adam cried brusquely. "Don't creep up on people. How many times do I have to tell you, it's a bad habit you must learn to control."

Robert hung his head shamefacedly, and though I was annoyed with him for interrupting such a warm, precious moment, one I felt instinctively might have been a turning point in my life, I felt sorry for him. He was, after all, only a child.

Adam seemed to take himself in hand, and he apologized to his brother. "I'm sorry, Robert. I shouldn't have spoken to you like that. Did you wish to speak about something?"

Robert looked up. "I wanted to speak to you," he said seriously.

"What about? Couldn't it wait?"

Robert shook his head. Adam waited to hear what he had to say, but it became obvious he wished to speak to Adam alone. I said I would go and leave them together.

"Go toward the white gazebo. I'll join you as soon as I can," Adam said softly.

I provided myself with a parasol to match my dress. My heart was singing. Adam was going to join me in the summerhouse. Tommyboy prepared to follow me as I left the house. He had got over his fear of going outside and had become my constant shadow. I was about to tell him to stay where he was today, but he always kept at a discreet distance, so I thought better of it.

A few minutes later I was glad I had.

I tripped over what I thought was a stone hidden in shade cast by the large, fleshy leaves of a gigantic succulent, and went sprawling. At least, I thought it was a stone till I started to rise and saw it was a body. The dead body of a white man who had been brutally beaten and hacked to death, his head almost completely severed from his shoulders.

I screamed, high and loud and long. I tried to get up. A searing pain shot through my foot and up my leg, bringing tears to my eyes. I tried to drag myself away from the horrifying sight. I was still screaming. I could not stop. Then kindly brown hands were helping me. Tommyboy's voice was saying, "Hold on to Tommyboy, Missie Barbry. Hold on. Tommyboy get you in de house. Missie no be afraid. Tommyboy got you."

I leaned on him, averting my eyes from the sickening sight of the mutilated body on the ground, but the grim sight, imprinted on my mind, would not leave me, and I continued screaming.

There came the sound of running feet, voices raised in alarm, and Tommyboy crying, "It's Missie Barbry. She hurt. She hurt bad."

Then I was swept into strong arms. Adam's arms. I buried my face in his coat. "Oh, Adam, he's dead. He's dead. He's dead."

"No, Tommyboy's not dead. He's . . ."

"Not Tommyboy," I moaned. "Sam. On the ground. It's terrible, terrible."

Adam's head turned sharply. "Oh, my God! Jem! Jem! Get hold of Atkinson, quick. Tell him Barbara's sprained her ankle and tell him—tell him we've a body on our hands."

Chapter Fifteen

The discovery of Sam Macpherson's body was a shock that reverberated round the island. His wife, jolly, mirth-giving Mollie, was desolate with grief. When she came for her husband's body, she kept repeating over and over again, as if in a trance, "Why Sam? Why Sam?"

Sam Macpherson had been a kindly man who never had a bad word to say about anybody. He ran a merchant shipping company, owned no slaves, and employed only free men. He had been well liked and thought not to have an enemy in the world.

Yet he had been brutally murdered.

Jem blamed the murder on a runaway slave. Adam said he was not so sure. Jem said Adam refused to face facts. The murder had all the hallmarks of the savagery of which only a heathen was capable. Others who called round to discuss the event agreed with him.

"The culprit must be found and an example made of him, before we're all murdered in our beds," said one, vengefully.

"An example will be made," vowed Jem. "More than

one. We'll let them know who's master here."

"We don't know if it was the work of a runaway slave," Adam said, striving to cool the atmosphere. "Let's wait for the inquiry before we do something we might regret."

"There's not going to be an inquiry!" Jem rounded on Adam. "Hasn't Mollie been through enough without having to suffer that? We all know who's responsible—a runaway. Ransom's still losing his slaves in spite of the examples he's made. And Bodney's light a dozen or more. So is Weston. And we all know who's behind it—Billy Joe. He's never been found—though the condition he was in when he escaped . . ."

"He could be dead," someone murmured.

"No." Jem sounded sure. "He had help from someone. He's not dead."

Jem's eyes rested on Adam, shrewd and sharp. My mouth went dry. Had he guessed? Did he know of Adam's involvement? He probably suspected. Adam slipped away from the confrontation.

"Ransom's examples clearly have not had the desired effect. His hangings were intended to stop further attempts at escape. If they haven't worked, what good would further examples be?"

"But this is different," said Jem. "This is the murder of a white man." His eyes narrowed further. "And you can't overlook the fact that it happened in your own garden. You can't rule out the fact it could have been one of your own slaves."

"Impossible!" Adam clipped back.

"You mean you don't want to believe it. But I warn you, Adam, you can't close your eyes to it much longer."

My ankle was improving and I was getting about with the aid of a stick, though I rested most of the time on a day bed on the veranda, and it was there the foregoing conversation took place. Some of the men had brought their wives, and they, growing tired of such talk, endeavored to engage me in lighter topics, but my ears were still tuned in to what the men were saying.

"Atkinson says Sam was probably killed sometime during the night, or in the early hours of the morning, judging by the degree of rigor mortis. . . ."

I felt my spine tingle. I had seen Adam leave the house in the early hours of that morning. He had denied it and succeeded in making me believe him. But now I was unsure again. Then I was sure. I relived in my mind the events of that hot, sultry night. I had seen Adam leave the house from my position on the veranda. I *had*. Why had he left the house at such an hour? Where had he gone? I knew he had moved Billy Joe from the house. He could have been going to see him. Or he could have been going to keep an assignation with Sam Macpherson. Why? Had they quarreled? Had Adam killed Sam?

No, I did not believe that. I could not believe that.

My eyes slewed round to him. He was standing, coldly rigid, arguing with Jem. Jem had his back to me. My heart turned over. He was the same height as Adam—not so dark, but from the back, at night, he could be mistaken for Adam. Had I mistaken him for Adam? I believed I had. Robert had followed the man I had seen. Robert always followed Jem about. He was greatly attached to him. So had it been Jem going out to keep an appointment with Sam Macpherson? Was Jem the murderer?

No, I did not believe that, either. Jem might be rough and tough, not flinch at punishing slaves—but murder somebody? No.

So if Adam had not done it, and Jem had not done it, it

must have been somebody else. Who else had gone out that night? Robert!

I had hit upon it. Sam's murder had been brought about by the Gray Phantom, the elusive man thought to be responsible for many unexplained brutal attacks that took place. Many thought he was a myth and blamed and punished the slaves for such offenses. But I knew better. I knew he existed.

What should I do? Should I tell?

Morvah had confided in me that Robert was a violent man who had to be drugged when he showed any sign of—strangeness, she had said. And she believed he slept the strangeness away. But what if he had learned to fake a drugged sleep? When it was thought he was safely asleep in his room, what if he were out somewhere doing . . . what? Riding his gray horse? My thoughts jerked to a halt. Robert's horse wasn't gray, it was black.

My mind took a quick journey back to the day I had seen the Gray Phantom astride his horse up on Jutting Rock. By no stretch of the imagination could his horse have been termed black. It had been gray—pale gray.

I had posed myself a problem. I was unsure again.

We all went to Sam's funeral. The service was held in the Anglican church of St. Michael and All Angels, which stood on one of the hills overlooking Seatown bay, not far from the Governor's House, and Sam was laid to rest afterward in the quiet graveyard shaded by palms and multitudinous flowers.

Philip Rose and Sarah turned up to pay their respects. Philip had always had a high regard for Sam, often saying he was one of the most enlightened men on the island. There was a slight altercation provoked by a few men, Jack Ransom among them, who protested at their coming. But Adam, backed up by Jem, with Robert grinning in his usual fashion behind them, calmed the situation and provided Philip and Sarah with their protection, even so far as seeing them back to their home.

Then we all joined the rest of the mourners in a meal with Mollie and her bereaved family, offering sympathetic support. We were among the last to leave.

On our way home Morvah told us Mollie had told her she was going back home to Scotland. She felt she was unable to go on living in Almada after what had happened to Sam.

"But she's got married daughters here, and grandchildren," I said.

"Yes, and they've each offered her a home, but she's turned them down. She's taking Agnes with her."

"Agnes won't want to go. She'll be most unhappy," I said.

"I know," Morvah returned. "She's head over heels in love with young Captain Mills. But she'll get over it. She'll find someone else. Better a little unhappiness and safety than . . ."

"Than what?" I swallowed anxiously. "Brief happiness and death?"

"Well, we all know what's going to happen, don't we?"

"Things have simmered down lately, Mrs. Pengarth," Jem said, entering the conversation.

"For how long, I wonder," Morvah mused. "It might not be a bad thing if we all left."

"We'll ride it out," declared Adam.

A knock came at my door. "Come in," I called breathlessly. I thought it might be Adam.

We had not had a chance to talk on our own since that dreadful day when Sam had been found murdered, and we had to talk sometime. I knew that. He knew that. We had to clarify that something that had sprung up between us that day. Our future depended on it.

"Can I talk to you, Barbara?"

My heart sank. It was Robert. He entered diffidently, looking at me out of eyes as solemn as any I had ever seen. There was no inane grin on his face. He seemed perfectly sane—yet I watched him close the door with a considerable degree of concern.

"Is your ankle getting better?" he asked.

He came up to my bed. He carried a bundle under his arm.

"Yes, thank you. It is much improved. I—I still get an occasional twinge, but if I rest it as I am doing now, it soon goes."

He grinned then and dumped his bundle on my bed.

"I've brought you something to look at."

"Why, thank you. What . . . ?"

"You'll see—when I've gone."

I thought—I hoped—he would go straight away, but he hovered. Perhaps he wanted me to open the bundle before he went, but as I started to undo the string, he placed his hand on mine. "No, later," he said, and I drew back quickly, afraid of his touch.

"Don't be afraid, Barbara," he said. "I'll look after you. I'll see no harm comes to you. I love you, Barbara. You're kind. You don't turn away from me."

I hardly knew how to look at him. If he only knew. I was like all the rest. Worse. I believed he was capable of murder. He went to look out of the window.

"There's going to be trouble," he said suddenly.

"What . . . what kind of trouble? Do you mean . . . the slaves . . . ? Don't worry," I had to set his mind at rest, "they . . ."

"It's not their fault," he flashed back. "Philip says it's not their fault. They're led by bad men. Bad, bad, men." He rocked on his heels for a moment, then he hugged his arms about himself. "Can you keep a secret, sister?"

"Yes," I squeaked. I wished Meta would come in.

"I know what's going to happen."

"Oh . . . good . . ." I wished anybody would come in—just so that I was not alone with Robert.

"I *know* what's going to happen, but you needn't worry. I won't let anything happen to you." He started to jerk about from side to side in an excited manner. "They don't know what I know, you see. But I do. I know everything. I heard them making plans. Jem and Araminta."

He began sidling out of the room. I was trembling. He had seemed so sane at first—then gradually, subtly, he had changed, till now his eyes were filled with a feverish light.

He closed my door quietly. I tried to puzzle out what he had said, and could not. But one phrase stood out above all others. *Jem and Araminta.* He must have meant Adam and Araminta. Was Adam seeing her again? He had told me he was going up to Welbeck's Way to see how the clearance was progressing. But could I believe him? Could he be with Araminta?

I began fiddling with the string on the bundle Robert had left on my bed. The knot was soon undone and a pile of papers fell out. As they spread over my counterpane I saw they were drawings, writings. Things he had done? I knew he sketched. Often he could be seen with a pencil in his hand scribbling away. He was not so backward that he could not read or write. And Morvah had informed me he could draw very well. But I felt I could not be bothered to look at the drawings now and began gathering them up to put back in a bundle again.

As I did so, they came into focus, registered on my mind. I slowed down and looked at them more closely. I realized they were good. Very good. They were drawings of birds and animals, particularly horses. I stared in astonished delight at a drawing of Lady, my own chestnut mare, with me astride her in the trousers I had taken to wearing when out riding—if Araminta could get away with such an outrageous procedure, I did not see why I should not. I had not sought Adam's permission and though he had scowled when he had first seen me in them, he had made no comment and I had continued to wear them.

I gazed at the drawing for a long time. I knew it was me sitting Lady—the clothes were mine, the hair, flying in long, loose strands from beneath a straw hat I had bought on one of my shopping expeditions was mine, but the heart-shaped face, animated, glowing, I hardly recognized. But it was me. I laid it to one side, reaching the conclusion that Robert was not as skillful with people as with animals.

Then I picked up a sketch of Morvah, his mother, and was astonished. It was very, very good. It must have been done quite recently, because she was as I knew her, with her gentle yet shrewd eyes alive in a brown silk skin and the smile that was all too rare just lurking at the corners of her mouth.

I was just changing my opinion when a drawing of Jem came to hand. As I had not recognized myself, so I did not recognize Jem at first. But it was he, yet looking so stern and hard he could have been a stranger.

Then my heart turned over. I held a picture of Adam in a velvet jacket, smiling, an impish light in his blue eyes, a humorous quirk to his mouth. It was good, so good it could have been alive.

There were many other sketches, mostly of slaves at their work; of Bella, of Meta, of Tommyboy. Had they been aware of him sketching them? I doubted it. They were all so natural—and so acutely observed. And—the realization made me shudder a little—I had been completely oblivious of the fact that he had been sketching me.

I shuffled through the pile thoughtfully. There was no getting away from it, Robert was an extremely gifted artist. Did his family know how gifted? Were they aware of these drawings? Probably not, though Morvah had told me he drew very well; "nicely" had been her word, but that did not cover what lay before me now. It struck me that I might be the only one who had seen these. Robert was very secretive by nature. But why should I be singled out for the honor? Because of the little gifts I had brought him occasionally? Because he truly liked me—loved me, he had said—and wanted to prove it?

Whatever the reason, I did not know it.

Meta came bustling in. "Quick, missie. Mus' tidy you. Massa Adam home. He come upstairs. See you."

She began smoothing my gown and the counterpane, all creased beneath me, dislodging in her zeal some of the papers from the bed. She bent to pick them up, tut-tutting.

"Wha's all this? Wha's all this?"

"Give them to me." I grabbed them from her perhaps a shade too sharply, but I did not think she had seen what they were.

A tap came at the door. My heart beat quicker, as it always did at the prospect of seeing Adam. A moment later he stepped inside the room and Meta left, giggling, with one of her sly, knowing looks.

Silence wrapped us both around. Neither of us could speak. The time had come for talking and all either of us could do was stare at the other. But at last, after what seemed an eternity, Adam came toward me. "How is your ankle?" he asked solicitously, just as Robert had done earlier.

"Much better, thank you. Just the odd twinge now and again."

He nodded. "It will take time for it to heal completely."

We looked at each other in silence again, then his eye fell to the drawings. He picked up a few. "Did you do these?" he asked in amazement.

I laughed. "No. I'm no artist. They're Robert's."

"Robert's? You mean, *he* drew them?" He flicked them over. "Astonishing! I can't believe it. I always knew he sketched a bit and liked coloring pictures, but I never . . . good lord! This is you!"

"Not a very good likeness, I'm afraid," I grimaced, blushing at the light that appeared in his eye, one of complete surprise and—admiration?

"It's a perfect likeness," he contradicted me, surprising me ever more. He tucked the sketch into his pocket. "He won't mind," he said, thinking he was answering an unspoken question of mine.

He sat down beside me on the bed as if it were the most natural thing in the world for him to do and my heart thudded and twisted with joy and pain at the closeness of him. I watched his strong brown hand move over the pile of drawings at my side, listened to his comments, laughed at something he said. It was like the old days, when Adam—Richard, as I'd called him then—in spite of regretting his marriage to me, had shown a certain tenderness toward me on the sea voyage from England to Almada. A harmony had grown up between us from which I had thought love might develop. It had not. There was harmony between us now. Would something develop from it this time? Would it be enough to sustain a marriage? It might be enough for Adam—would it be enough for me? I thought not. I wanted love, Adam's love. I wanted his passion—and that, I believed, was reserved for Araminta Belmont.

We ruffled through the sketches together, my joy evaporating little by little till the pain took over as I realized just how much—how little—I could look forward to receiving from Adam in our marriage. Perhaps it might be better to revert to my original plan and leave him. But would my life be better without him? Should I take what he was prepared to offer and be grateful?

I picked up another sketch of Adam, colored, lifelike. I held it out toward him. "Here's another one of you," I said dully, then drew it back quickly. "No, it's not. This man's hair is white. And yet—it looks like you." I turned it over in my hands, puzzled. There was some writing on the back. It read: "Father, on his birthday."

My eyes sought Adam, my heart starting to pound. I looked back at the sketch. I looked at Adam again. If it had not been for the white hair, both he and Adam could have been the same man. There was the same firm jaw, the deeply curved lips, the high-bridged nose, the piercing blue eyes. There was no doubt about it. The white-haired man was Adam's father.

"This is Joe Pengarth, and he is your father," I said.

Adam was staring at me, looking shocked, saying nothing.

"It's true, isn't it?"

"There's something I must tell you," he said then.

But I shook my head. "There's no need. I can see it for myself. Your father was Aunt Martha's lover."

"You don't understand, Barbara. . . ."

"You're right, I don't. Why make a secret out of it. What difference would it have made?"

"None—if that's what you believe. If that's the way it was."

I snorted with sarcasm. "You're not trying to tell me Joe Pengarth was not your father, I don't believe it. You have only to look at this picture to see it."

"No. What I'm trying to tell you is—your Aunt Martha was not my mother."

The world seemed to fall in on me.

Adam caught hold of my hands. They stayed in his, lifeless.

"I've wanted to tell you for a long time," he said. "I didn't think I'd ever be able to . . . but I have . . . and it was easier than I expected. I'm glad it's out at last."

"You mean it was all a lie, that long rigmarole you brought with you to Martha's Cottage? But you had papers. Mr. Parkes was convinced they were authentic."

"They were. No, I didn't steal them. They were given to me by my father. They were his by right. He adopted Martha Goodall's illegitimate son."

"But you said you were not . . ." I broke off as the truth began to dawn on me.

It was hardly necessary for Adam to say, "I'm not.

Robert is."

I sat very still. Robert—Martha's son. Robert—my cousin. It was not the shock it should have been. Perhaps because I had always known it, deep down, without realizing it. I had felt from the start an odd sort of kinship with him, the feeling I had known him all my life. I could see now why he had always looked so familiar to me. I had recognized Aunt Martha in him. How, I did not know, for, in actual fact, he bore no resemblance to my aunt at all, but whatever it was, some fleeting glance or expression, it had registered with me and been locked away in my brain awaiting release by Adam.

"We never knew, either of us," Adam was continuing, "that we were not truly brothers. Robert still does not know, and there's no reason why he should. I should have remained in ignorance, too, if that letter hadn't come. It was addressed to R. Goodall, Esquire. Robert had been christened Richard, though he has never been known by it, and the use of the initial gave no rise to speculation on the island. My father opened it, naturally. He was very ill at the time and deeply in debt. What he read in the letter was the means to solve all our problems, and that was when he told me the truth."

I dragged my hands away, coming back to life at last.

"You mean you both saw the chance of a fortune and jumped at it."

"Believe that, if you like," he said heavily. "The truth is that if my father died before his debts to Jack Ransom were paid—Ransom had acquired every debt my father had on the island—we would have lost High Place. We would have been homeless and penniless. 'You, on your own, might make out,' he said to me, 'but there's your mother and Robert to consider.' So I agreed to go to

England and pretend to be Martha's son. She would never be any the wiser and the people here needed to be told no more than that I was visiting a rich old aunt in England. Robert was best kept in ignorance, he wouldn't suffer from it. Nobody would suffer—or so we believed. I didn't know about you then, and when I did, and after that vile will was read out . . . if Martha Goodall had not been already beyond my reach I could cheerfully have killed her."

"You must have been devastated," I said bitterly, "when you learned you couldn't have the money without me. No wonder you reacted the way you did on our wedding night."

His eyes did not leave my face. "I intended to make you a good husband," he began, when I cut in on him as another appalling truth hit me full force. "You . . . married me under false pretenses . . . under a false name. We . . . we're not married."

"You believe I would do that? What a poor opinion you have of me." He regarded me steadily. "You have our marriage lines, I believe. Take a look at them. You'll see I married you in the name of Adam Richard Goodall Pengarth. The middle names are not my own, but the first and the last are the ones that count. I can assure you we are legally married. I'm sorry to disappoint you." His voice sounded bitter now. "But you'll still need a divorce before you can get away from me."

"Will you give it to me now?" I cried.

He rose with a sudden irritated movement, stared down at me with cold disdain, and turned to go.

"Why not?" I called after him. "You don't care for me. You never did."

He came to a full stop. His shoulders stiffened. "Oh, I

did, Barbara," he said with a stony resentment. "I cared very much. I'm only sorry you were not able to . . ."

"If you gave me a divorce you could marry Araminta," I cried wildly.

He turned back to me then. "And why," he asked, "should I want to do that?"

"Because you're in love with her," I cried defiantly. "I've always known it."

Something flickered behind his eyes. The coldness receded from them.

"I am not in love with her. I've never been in love with her," he said.

"You're always with her."

"I am not."

"You are. You are."

With a puzzled frown, he said, "I don't understand you. I see Minty occasionally—why not? She's an old friend. I've known her all my life. Why are you so concerned, anyway?" The ice returned to his glance. "What does it matter to you whose company I keep? You do not wish to give me yours. You've made it glaringly plain to me that you prefer the company of others to mine."

"No, you're wrong." I formed the words, but they did not come out of my lips. I tried again, but he had turned from me, saying, "Let's put a stop to this conversation. It serves no useful purpose." Then he was gone.

I jumped out of bed, flew to open the door. "Adam! Adam!"

I cared nothing for Tommyboy's startled brown face looking up at me from the hall, nothing for Meta's curious face emerging from around a corner, nothing for anybody who might appear, my only concern was for

Adam and the sound of pain in his voice as he left me.

He was nowhere in sight. I raced down the stairs. "Adam!"

Bella came in off the veranda. The shiny black eyes in the coffee-colored face were disapproving. "I heard you call, Mistress Barbara. Is anything wrong? Can I be of help?"

"My husband, Master Adam, where is he?" I begged urgently.

"Master Adam has just ridden away," she said, and with her usual barely perceptible bow made to continue on her way.

"Where has he gone?" I demanded, irritated by her superior manner, and certain that she knew. She seemed to be cognizant of everything that went on at High Place.

"What you want him for?" she countered, her perfect English deserting her for a moment.

"That's my business," I snapped angrily.

With a disparaging look she drew herself up to her full height, many inches above me, and said slowly and distinctly, "You one stupid lady."

Aghast at her complete disregard for my position as mistress of High Place, I was only just able to stand my ground. My instinct was to turn and run from the black-eyed giantess. "You forget yourself," I said, less forcefully than I wished.

An expression of utter loathing settled on her face. I took an involuntary step backward. I had never before been confronted by such open hatred. It was an unpalatable experience.

"Master Adam rode out to get away from you and your long face," she rasped, her voice matching her expression. "Serve you right. You treat him bad. Master Adam is a good man, best that ever lived. He lay the world at your feet and all you do is make him miserable. I would not be like you. I would treat him well. But it's you . . . you . . ." She broke off, a look of pain and fear dislodging the hate in her eyes.

I whispered her name softly, "Bella," understanding at last the reason behind her antagonism toward me. She was in love with Adam herself.

She threw my compassion back in my face. "I don't want your pity. Save it for yourself; you need it." And with her head held as high as any proud patrician, she walked away from me to disappear among the back regions of the house.

Poor Bella. I could sympathize with her now. Her love stood no chance of being reciprocated, whereas mine—mine could be, might be, if . . .

I went back to my room. I had much to think about. I had to investigate the whole of my relationship with Adam, so that when he returned I should know what to do.

Life is never simple. After much heart searching and minute investigation of events and conversations, I reached the conclusion that I was as much to blame as Adam for our present situation. Concerned about my own feelings, I had not considered his. Fearful of further rejection after the catastrophe that had been our wedding night, I had erected a facade to hide behind, topping it up whenever it showed signs of crumbling, adding a brick here, a dash of mortar there. Adam had accepted me at face value. I could not blame him.

But that time was past. That girl was not the woman

she now was; the husband was not the same. Time and experience had wrought a change. I had not noticed it happening. I saw it clearly now. Life was not simple. Life was not a romantic dream. Life was real, and one had to adjust to circumstances. If I had adjusted earlier, would Adam and I be working now to make a success of our marriage? Would an elementary affection have started to grow into a more sustaining passion? Was it too late to start now?

Adam returned home late when we were sitting down to a meal delayed because of him. He took his place opposite me, brushing aside apologies for not waiting for him, receiving my shy smile of welcome with a blank stare.

Deflated, but not deflected from my decision to regain his regard—I had all my life ahead of me in which to do it—I asked, "Did you have a good ride?"

To my surprise he frowned deeply—did he find it so hard to be civil to me? Morvah put the next question.

"Where have you been?"

"With the governor . . . for the past hour."

My heart leapt painfully. The governor! Araminta's father! Had he seen her? And if he had, what did it matter? He had said he was not in love with her and I believed him. I would not allow suspicion to sour my resolve.

"He's mustered the army. They're on alert. There's been so much sporadic violence lately, he's fearful that revolution is imminent."

"Revolution!" I gasped.

"Revolution." Robert latched on to the word, rolled it

about on his tongue. "Rev-o-lu-tion."

It sent a shiver coursing up my spine, but apart from giving him a brief glance, the others paid no attention to it.

"He wants all the women and children off the island. There's a ship in the harbor due to sail tonight, but he's ordered it to remain in port for another day so that those who wish to leave will have time to prepare."

"He thinks it's as near as that," Jem murmured, his face set in grim lines.

Adam nodded. "He's already booked Minty aboard."

"Minty's leaving?" Jem sounded surprised.

"Certainly." Adam's reply was crisp. "And you must go too, Mother . . . and you, Barbara . . . till this blows over."

Adam's glance rested on me again and this time it was not blank, but full of concern, and unspoken questions poured from his eyes. I read them all. Will you come back? Will I ever see you again? Once back in Martha's Cottage, will you stay there?

But he had said, "'Till this blows over." That meant he wanted me back. My heart flew across the table to him. If he thought I would leave him now, he did not know me at all.

"We must all go," Morvah said, breaking the small silence that had occurred. "I've always wanted to go back to Cornwall. I thought I never would. But now we've got the chance, we must take it."

"We can't all go, Mother. The men must stay here if we're not to see everything we've all worked so hard for over the years vanish overnight. Jem and I must guard High Place from possible attack. If the slaves run riot . . ."

"You'll all be killed." Morvah's voice was sharp and high with anxiety. "Every one of you. Killed."

"No, Mother. You mustn't think like that. It won't come to that. It's still not too late to stop the pot boiling over. Sending the womenfolk away is only a precaution. You will all be back before you know it, and everything will be as it was before. . . ."

Adam's voice trailed away. I could see he did not really believe what he was saying. Morvah could see it, too.

"You don't believe that, Adam," she cried, "any more than I do. Time has run out for us here. We always knew it would—and we must leave. There's nothing left for us here now."

"Nothing?" Adam's brows drew together making a deep, angry cleft in his forehead. "Is High Place nothing? Am I expected to toss High Place—our home—aside, as being of no consequence?"

"Yes, if our lives depend upon it," his mother shrilled, caught up in a violent emotional conflict. "It's only bricks and mortar. We can build another house, create another home, in Cornwall—in England, where it's safe."

"Only bricks and mortar? I don't understand you, Mother. You know it's more than that. It's all our lives—Father's life. You can't mean . . ."

"Oh-h-h-h!" Morvah moaned, "I don't know. I'm so afraid." I went to put my arms around her. She was trembling. She clutched at me with her hands, the brown paper-thin texture of her skin stretched to tearing point across her sharp knuckles. "You don't know what they can do. If you'd seen the terrible things I've seen . . ."

"You mustn't dwell on the worst that can happen. In all probability it will never occur. Parliament is bound to pass the abolition bill soon. If we can just hold on a little longer the slaves will get their freedom. And that's all they want, freedom, and to be treated like human beings, paid a fair wage for their work. . . ."

Adam's attempt to soothe his mother with calming words was shattered by a harsh interruption from Jem.

"You sound like your friend, Philip Rose. You make it all sound so simple. But you know, as well as anybody, nothing short of a bloodbath will cool the passions that have been aroused here in the last few months."

"I know nothing of the sort." Adam turned on him angrily. "There's still time to . . ."

"There's no time," Jem flashed back. "Mac's death marked the beginning of a tide of savagery nothing will stem. You're not doing your mother any favors by . . ."

"Shut up, Jem," Adam hissed, but Morvah had already begun a loud agonized wailing. "Satisfied?" he ground out through clenched teeth.

Jem, regretting immediately words he could not retract, drew in a deep, apologetic sigh and with a shrug and a sorrowful shake of his head, withdrew from the room.

Chapter Sixteen

A feeling of unease pervaded the house. Bella and Meta were upstairs packing. Morvah and I were drinking coffee with Adam in the drawing room. Robert had not joined us and Jem had not returned. Morvah was still trying to persuade her son to leave for England with us. Adam was trying to hold on to his patience, but I could see it was wearing extremely thin. He was anxious and the strain was beginning to show.

"I've tried to explain. . . ."

"I know. Oh, I know. But I can't follow your reasoning. Surely nothing is worth getting yourself killed for."

I did so agree with her, but Adam's exasperation was very evident. He drew in a long breath and went to pour himself a sustaining brandy.

Morvah turned to me. "I'm frightened, Barbara."

I covered her hand with mine. "Don't be. This time tomorrow you'll be on board the *Emily Rose* bound for England." I wished I was as calm as I sounded. "You'll have nothing more to fear. All this will be behind you."

"And you."

Adam swung round, glass in hand, his eyes piercing my soul.

I returned his gaze steadily. "I'm not going," I said.

"What?"

Only Morvah voiced surprise. Adam's eyes were locked onto mine.

"But you must. You must make her, Adam."

"I shall," he said, but he looked completely nonplussed. "You will leave with my mother. You *must* go with her. If anything happened to you, I'd never forgive myself. Don't argue. Just—go."

"I'm not going." My eyes told him why. "I never had any intention of going."

I had risen, and without our knowing how it happened we had moved toward each other. Vaguely, I heard Morvah's voice say, "Well, I'll leave you to sort it out between yourselves, but you'd better make her see sense, Adam." Then I was swept into an embrace so fierce, so possessive, I could scarcely breathe. Not that there was any thought of complaint in my mind. I would gladly have died in that embrace.

"Is it true?" Adam asked incredulously, moments later. "You love me?"

"I love you, Adam. I've always loved you. I thought you did not love me."

"Oh, my darling." He drew me close again. "I've been in love with you for months."

"Then why didn't you tell me?" It was a cry from the heart.

"I wanted to. I tried to. But you were so cold and stiff with me, and I thought it was Jem you cared for."

"Jem?"

"You always seemed to want to be with him. I knew he

had fallen for you. I thought you . . ."

"I never cared for Jem. Not in that way. It was you, always you. I thought you and Araminta . . . oh, Adam, what fools we've been, misunderstanding each other. . . ."

"Not anymore." Adam kissed me, long and deep, in a most satisfying way. "Oh, my love," he went on, "the time we've wasted, the months of anguish and despair when we could have been together. And now . . . it's too late."

"No, it's not too late," I declared passionately. "It's only just beginning."

We clung together. There would be no more wasted months. We had found each other at last. We would never be separated again. But what was he saying? Was I hearing aright?

"You must leave with Mother, tomorrow. You can't stay here. I won't let you. I wish to heaven you were already on your way safely to England. Jem was right, Barbara. I tried to make light of it for Mother's sake, but time's on a fuse here, it only needs a spark. . . ."

I put my finger on his lips. "Don't say any more. I won't listen to you. I shall stay here and face whatever there is to face with you. I can't lose you now. I won't."

He argued, but to no effect, and at last he gave up. Close in his arms, I asked him, "When did you fall in love with me, Adam?"

"I don't know, really," he said. "It may have been on board the *Indies Pride* coming over. It may have been later, it may have been sooner, I can't believe now there was ever a time when I wasn't in love with you."

"But you didn't fall in love with me at first sight as I did with you."

"No. I think at first it was only pity I felt. I saw how

your mother and sister treated you—as if you were of no account, how pliant and uncomplaining you were in the face of it, and, momentarily, I was swamped with an irresistible urge to protect you, to—take care of you. But what could I do? I stifled the feeling. Then that will was read out, and all I could feel was hate, hate for the woman who could dream up such a diabolical scheme. I saw from your face you were as disgusted as I at the idea of marriage to a total stranger. I left Martha's Cottage intending to return home immediately. But I couldn't—not without the money. I *needed* the money. So I worked out a plan. You needed affection. I could give it to you. If I could persuade you to marry me . . . it was easier than I thought it would be. No, I didn't fall in love with you then . . . I was touched by your ingenuousness. I thought, it won't be difficult to be a husband to her. . . .

"Then why did you have to get drunk before you could come to me on our wedding night?" I was stung to cry out.

"Because I was ashamed. I had not been honest with you. I had married you under false pretenses, just as you accused me of doing this morning, and I couldn't adjust my conscience to it. I wanted to admit everything to you, explain—you were so open and honest yourself. But I couldn't. There was too much at stake. I drank to try to put it out of my mind, and I drank too much. In the morning I was horrified at what I had done. I could see I had hurt you and that was the last thing in the world I wanted to do. I tried to apologize, to put things right, but you, naturally, wanted nothing to do with me. So we made a bargain. Our marriage would be in name only. I thought that was what you wanted. I thought it was what I wanted. I didn't count on falling in love with you."

"Oh, Adam, if only I'd known. If only you'd told me, made me listen."

"I've made grievous mistakes," Adam said, kissing me.

"No more than I." I kissed him back.

"I'll make it up to you, I swear."

"Me, too."

We kissed each other.

We were losing ourselves in each other when the door burst open and Morvah came in.

"Robert's not in his room," she cried. "I can't find him. Nobody seems to know where he is."

"He's probably gone for his evening swim. You know he doesn't like to miss it," Adam said.

"Oh, yes." Morvah calmed down a little. "I didn't think of that. That's where he will have gone. But will you go and tell him to come home, Adam? I'd rather he wasn't out alone—not at a time like this, when there's no knowing what might happen."

"Of course." Adam agreed and rose at once.

"Have you persuaded Barbara to leave with us?" she asked then.

"No." I answered for him. "And he won't be able to. I'm staying."

She shook her head sadly. "I think you're making a grave mistake, my dear, but I understand. I'd stay, too, if Joe . . . do go and look for Robert, Adam. I'll go and make a start on his packing."

Adam's voice rose sharply. "Robert's not going with you to England."

"But of course he is." Morvah looked puzzled. "You don't think I'd go and leave him behind?"

"But you must." A desperate note crept into Adam's voice. "Think what would happen to him in England. He wouldn't be allowed to roam about freely as he does here. They'd want to lock him up, shut him away in an asylum. That would be worse than death for him."

"But if I could get him to Cornwall, I could buy a house, land where he could . . ."

"You'd never even get him on board ship." He was being brutally frank now. "Ship's crews are notoriously superstitious. One look at Robert would be sufficient to convince them he was the devil's creature, if not the devil himself. And if you did manage to get him aboard think of the abuse that would be hurled at him. We're used to him here, yet he's laughed at and sneered at; think how much worse it would be among strangers. He would become the target for every bully. They wouldn't know till too late the strength of him. But that apart, everything that went wrong on board, he would be blamed for. If a storm blows up, he will be responsible for it. If . . ."

"All right, all right, don't go on." Morvah was almost in tears. "Very well, if Robert must stay here, then I must, too."

"No, Mother, you and Bella must leave tomorrow."

"I'm not going without Robert."

It was final. Adam let her go. He turned to me, the picture of dejection. "What could I do? I had to make her see . . ."

"Of course you had to, Adam. Don't blame yourself. I'll talk to her, if you like, try to persuade her."

"You won't be able to. I know that tone. Nothing will make her change her mind now." He gave a deep sigh, then drew himself up. "Well, I must get the barricades up, see to the distribution of arms. Perhaps you'll instruct Bella to see that all the slave women and children are housed indoors. Better get them all in tonight, just in case."

Barricades. Arms. The danger we were all in was brought home to me. "Do you think something might happen tonight?" I asked.

"I hope not." He looked steadily into my eyes. He did not want to answer in the affirmative, but he was not going to pretend to me. "But it's as well to be prepared."

He was about to kiss me once more when the door flew open, and Jem hurled himself into the room. "Adam! It's Philip! He was crawling about in the garden."

"What . . . what are you talking about? You're not making sense."

"He must have been on his way to see us when he was attacked. . . ."

"Attacked?" I heard a strange, hoarse voice. It was my own. "But who . . . how . . . ?"

"Where is he now?" Adam demanded briskly.

"They're bringing him in now. Shall I have him taken to one of the guest rooms?"

"Yes, and send for Atkinson."

"I've already done that."

"Right." Adam swung round on one of the round-eyed slave women gaping in the hall. "Go and find Bella; tell her I want to see her, at once. I think you'll find her in my mother's room."

The woman sped away; she was fat, but she was light-footed and swift as a panther. Bella was at the top of the stairs before Philip had been carried halfway up. She took in the situation at once and did not need to be told to prepare a room. Philip began murmuring incoherently.

"He's delirious," Adam said.

"He's been struck on the head, I think," said Jem. "I'll go and see if there is anything I can do to help."

"I'll come with you," said Adam.

"Sarah ought to be told," I said, tailing after them. "We must let her know." I knew I would wish to know if I were in her place.

Adam stopped and looked at me thoughtfully. "Yes, she must be told. She'd better be brought here, anyway. She'll be safer here than . . . you go on up, Jem. I'll go and fetch Sarah."

"May I come with you?" I asked, running down after him. So many times I had wanted to be with him and could not be, and now I could not bear to let him out of my sight.

"No. Stay here," he said sternly. "Tommy!"

"Massa?"

"Look after your mistress till I return."

"But Adam . . ."

Tommy's gnarled brown hand clamped onto my arm with a python's strength. I tried to shake it off. Adam had already gone out of the front door. Soon he would be swallowed up in the darkness.

"Let me go. Let me go," I ordered, but Tommyboy held on.

"No, Missie Barbry. Massa Adam say you stay here. He say Tommyboy look after you."

I glared angrily into his grizzled face. His grin did not falter. "Come, missie. You not worry. Massa Adam know what he 'bout. He come back safe and sound."

I allowed the old man to lead me back to the drawing room, aware that no matter how great his devotion to me, it paled beside his obedience to his master.

"I'd like some coffee," I said. "Bring three cups and go and ask Mr. Harding to join me. I'll go and ask Mistress Pengarth."

With a nod and a smile and a bow the old man said, "It here when you come back, missie."

Morvah was lying on her back staring up at the ceiling.

"Are you all right, Mother?" I asked worriedly.

"Of course, I am. Why shouldn't I be?"

"I thought, maybe . . . downstairs you . . ."

"Downstairs I made a fool of myself," she snapped.

"No, you didn't," I contradicted her, relieved to hear her sound more like her old self. "It was a natural reaction to want to get away to safety and take Robert with you."

"The natural reaction was yours," she returned. "To stay with the man you love. It would have been mine if Joe had been alive. It should have been where Adam is concerned. Yet it was concern for someone else's son that changed my mind." She sat upright, her eyes dark and troubled. "Can you understand it, Barbara? I can't." She did not wait for an answer, but carried straight on. "I couldn't leave Robert. He's so dependent on me. Sometimes I think I care for him more than for my own son . . . oh!"

Morvah's hand flew to her mouth as she realized what she had said. I told her I knew that Adam was her son and that Robert was my cousin.

"I'm so glad you know," she sighed. "It's been such a worry to us both. Adam's wanted to tell you for a long time, but he didn't know how. So what happened downstairs just now? Am I right in thinking . . . ? Did he . . . ? Are you . . . ?"

I laughed out loud at her hesitancy. "All is well between us," I assured her. "Adam loves me. I love him. Nothing will ever separate us now."

She placed a wizened hand on mine. "Let us hope it has

not come too late," she said.

I felt my flesh creep at her words. I knew she was referring to the present dangerous situation. Forcing brightness, I said, "I've ordered coffee to be served in the drawing room. Will you join me?"

She lay back against her pillows. "Later, perhaps." And she closed her eyes.

The coffee was waiting for me. Tommyboy poured me a cup.

"Is Mr. Harding coming?" I asked. I wanted to hear how Philip was, whether it was all right for me to go up and see him.

"Massa Harding not home, missie." Tommyboy handed me my cup. "He gone when I go look." His eyes shifted.

"Gone? Where?"

Tommyboy shrugged and lowered his eyes, quickly backed away, and resumed his position in the hall.

I sipped my coffee, not a little puzzled. Tommyboy seemed to be hiding something. What? Something concerning Jem? I never followed through my line of questioning, for I heard Dr. Atkinson arrive and went to meet him in the hall.

"Good evening, Mrs. Pengarth." He held my hand briefly. "A bad business. A bad business."

I showed him up to Philip's room. I left him shaking his head and murmuring. "Where will it all end?"

I left the drawing room door open so I could see him when he came down. He was down much more quickly than I expected. "How is he, doctor?" I said, hurrying toward him.

"Fine. Fine. That Bella would make an excellent doctor. She left me nothing to do. She's bound up the man's ribs as well as I could have done myself. A treasure. A treasure. Pity she's a half-caste. She's clever and beautiful, but no white man would wed her and she wouldn't take a black. Ah, well, that's the way of it."

I offered him coffee, which he refused, and brandy, which he accepted. Then he left to make another call.

"Take care," I warned as he mounted his horse. He was an elderly man, and I did not like to think of him out alone at a time like this when danger lurked everywhere.

But he laughed and cried, "Don't worry about me, Mrs. Pengarth. Nobody will harm me. I'm the only doctor on the island."

"Apart from Philip," I could not help declaring.

"And he's out of action," the doctor responded as he rode off into the night.

They were probably the last words he uttered in this life. Within the hour he was back, carried into the house in the arms of Jem Harding, his head half severed from his body.

"The bastards! The black bastards!" Jem growled when he saw me. I had hurried into the hall at the sound of raised voices, and when I saw the body of the man I had been talking to so recently, mangled and bloody, I turned away, retching from the pit of my stomach.

Jem sucked in his breath. "How thoughtless of me. Forgive me, Barbara, I shouldn't have brought him inside. I didn't stop to think. I'll take him out on to the veranda. He's dead, after all."

Some weird, irresistible fascination made me follow him, despite the churning in my stomach. "Who . . . who . . . who could have done such a thing? Sl-slaves? Or . . ."

But I did not want to say the Gray Phantom. I did not

want it to be the Gray Phantom. The Gray Phantom might be my cousin.

"Who else?" Jem snarled. "The murdering swine. They're all over the island . . . a rabble army . . . led by Billy Joe."

"Billy Joe!" I mouthed in silent echo, my heart thudding against my ribs.

Jem glanced around him. "Why aren't the shutters up? The shutters should be up. Where's Adam? What's he thinking about?" He started yelling instructions, and there was an immediate scurrying to do his bidding. He turned to me again. "Isn't Adam back yet?"

My eyes were on Dr. Atkinson's body on the floor of the veranda, seeing Adam there in his place. With a moan, I covered my face with my hands.

Jem took hold of me and steered me indoors. "You shouldn't be subjected to sights such as this," he said.

"Adam," I whispered. "He may be out there somewhere . . . lying . . . like that. . . ."

"Don't say such things," he chastised me. "Don't even think them." But he did not declare it impossible. "Where's Mrs. Pengarth? Where's Robert?" he asked, his voice suddenly sharp when he noticed they were not in the drawing room.

"Mrs. Pengarth's in her room," I replied. "I don't know where Robert is. Nobody does. We thought he had gone swimming, but that was a long time ago."

He clicked his tongue angrily and strode to the door. "Tommy."

"Yes, massa?" Tommy rose at once, conditioned by years of quick response to the white man's arrogance.

"Get a couple of men to the beach to look for Master Robert and bring him back."

"Massa Robert not there, massa. Massa Adam, he already tell men look."

"Then where the bloody hell is he? He should have been kept to his room. Bella should have . . ." He broke off, aware I was beside him, listening to his every word. "Forgive my language, Barbara, but I'm so worried." He turned his attention to Tommyboy again. "Where is he?"

Tommyboy shrugged. "I not know, massa. He gone, jus' gone."

With a smothered oath, Jem took hold of the old man and lifted him bodily off the floor. "Don't give me that. You know damn well where he is. Tell me, or . . . he's with that son of yours, isn't he? Don't deny it. They were always together as children. They both used to disappear for hours on end together. What did they get up to, eh? We both know, don't we? Plotting. And they're still at it, aren't they?"

He started to shake Tommyboy violently. I dragged at his arm. "Jem, stop it. What do you think you are doing? Tommy's an old man. Put him down."

Jem did not even look at me. "He knows where Robert is, and by God, he's going to tell me."

Jem was angry. His hand was half raised as if in readiness to smash across Tommyboy's face. I glimpsed the expression Robert had captured in one of his sketches and with dismay realized there was a streak of cruelty in Jem that in anger was hard to repress.

"Jem!" I screamed. "Let him go."

I thought at first he would take no notice of me, but then he let go of the old man, who nearly overbalanced, he was so frail.

"Tommyboy," I said gently, sitting him down in his

chair, "if you know where Master Robert is, please tell us."

"If he knows," Jem sneered. "Of course, he knows. He's always covering up for him. Like Bella. Where is he, you damned nigger? You'd better tell me before it's too late."

"What do you mean?" I swung round on him.

"What do you think I mean?" he clipped back. "If I don't find Adam before he does . . ."

"But he wouldn't harm Adam, his own brother."

Something in the look he gave me sent a shudder through me. He knew! He knew Adam and Robert were not brothers. What else did he know? That Robert was the Gray Phantom? Was that what made him behave the way he did? Was he afraid for Adam's life?

I turned back to Tommyboy. "Please, if you know where Master Robert is, tell me. Has he gone looking for Master Adam? If he has, and he finds him, he may harm him. Do you understand, Tommy?" I could have shaken him myself in my desperation.

"No, missie, Massa Robert not harm Massa Adam. Massa Jem on wrong track."

His brown eyes, full on my face, gave weight to his words. If only I could believe him. But I knew Robert's secret.

"What's all the screaming and shouting about?" Morvah appeared at the top of the stairs closely followed by Bella. "Has something happened? Are we being . . . ?"

Jem cut in on her. "Bella, where's Master Robert?"

"I do not know," Bella replied with her usual dignity, not according him his title of master.

"I told you to dose him with laudanum," he shouted.

"I take my orders from Master Adam," she retorted.

"Why, what's wrong?" Morvah cried anxiously. She started down the stairs, almost tumbling in her haste, and concern.

"I'll find him," Jem growled. "And when I do," he glared balefully at Tommyboy, who cringed visibly, "I'll deal with you."

"Jem!" Morvah ran after him.

I forestalled her. "Don't go out there, Mother."

"Why not? Let me go. Jem!" She tried to shake off my restraining hand, but I held on tight.

"Please, Mother. Dr. Atkinson's out there. He's . . . dead. Murdered."

"Murdered!" Her eyes filled with fear. "Who did it?"

She thought it was Robert, the Gray Phantom, as I did.

"Slaves," I said vehemently. They've broken loose. They're all over the island. They attacked Philip. . . ."

"Philip? Dr. Rose?" Her voice almost failed her.

"He's not dead," I said quickly. "He's upstairs. It was him Dr. Atkinson came to see."

Morvah's eyes swiveled away from me. "They're putting the shutters up. Yes, that's right. We must barricade ourselves in. Everyone must come indoors."

"Yes." I remembered Adam's parting instruction to me. Bella was still on the stairs. "See to it," I ordered.

"Yes, mistress," she said at once.

"Come and have some coffee," I said to Morvah, surprised at how steady my voice was in the circumstances.

The coffee would be lukewarm, but I could send for some more. Meta was standing halfway down the staircase, her eyes large and scared in her round, anxious face, watching the busy to and fro-ing of the other slaves boarding up doors, fastening shutters. It occurred to me it might be wise to give her something to do.

She caught me looking at her and bounded down toward me like a gazelle suddenly being chased by a ravenous lion. "Oh, Missie Barbry, Missie Barbry, dis am one terrible bad night."

"Go to the kitchen and make us some fresh coffee," I said. She was shivering with fright and I tried to sound stern to make her pull herself together, but when she just stood there in front of me still mumbling, "Missie Barbry, Missie Barbry," in the same scared tone, I spoke to her more gently. "Go and make coffee, Meta. Don't be afraid. There's nothing to be afraid of yet. But when you come back you may stay in the drawing room with us, if you wish."

"Oh, thank you, missie." Her face creased into the semblance of a smile and she hurried away.

The outdoor slaves started coming into the house. Tommyboy and the footmen shepherded them to the back of the house. Bella came in and with a slight bow in my direction hurried upstairs to her patient. I joined Morvah on the sofa in the drawing room, closing the door on the noise and activity in the hall.

"What happened to Dr. Rose?" Morvah asked, stirring out of the lethargy that had overtaken her.

I told her.

"And Robert's still missing," she wailed. "Where can he be? Suppose something has happened to him, Barbara."

"Nothing will have happened to him. Jem will find him and bring him back safe."

I sounded sure. I wished I felt the same way.

"Adam should be here. He should not have gone off and left us alone."

"He had to go for Sarah. He'll be back soon. He's been gone a long time."

I held my breath. He had been gone a very long time. And so had Robert. Supposing . . . ? No. I would not even think it. Adam would be back soon. He had to be.

Meta returned with the coffee and a plate full of tarts and cakes.

"Miss Bella say you need them for sustenance," she said.

"Bella?" I queried.

"She come down to kitchen for drink for Dr. Philip. She say he mighty thirsty and hungry."

I poured coffee for Morvah and said, "I think I'll just go and see how he is. If he's well enough to eat and drink, he should be well enough to talk. I'd like to know exactly what happened."

Philip was sitting up. He would have been naked to the waist if it had not been for the thick wad of bandages that bound his ribs, encasing him in a sleeveless garment. He had a bandage around his head, but he was managing to feed himself. He gave me a wan smile as I entered.

"I'm so glad to see you sitting up," I said. "I was so afraid after seeing you earlier. . . ."

"I'm a touch nut," he grinned. "Not easily cracked."

"Oh, Philip," I sighed sympathetically. "Are you well enough to talk? Can you tell me what happened?"

Bella, who had been looking on at the end of the bed, moved away. "I'll leave you together," she said, "but don't tire him too much, Mistress Barbara."

As she inclined her head, her eyes met mine warningly.

"I won't," I said meekly. She could have been the mistress of the house and I the one to take orders. But I knew she had only Philip's interests at heart and excused her peremptory manner. "I think I have misjudged Bella," I said when she had gone.

"Oh?" Philip waited for me to elaborate.

"I've never completely trusted her, but now . . ."

"You're not so sure?"

"No. I used to think she hated me. Perhaps she still does, but I think I understand her now. I even thought at one time she was a spy."

"A spy?"

"For Jack Ransom."

"Oh, Barbara. That can't be so. She was brought up at High Place. Adam told me."

"I know. There are many things I used to think that have been completely overturned lately. I know now Bella would do nothing to hurt the Pengarth family. I know she . . . but why are we talking about her? It's you I want to know about. Who attacked you? Runaway slaves? Jem said . . ."

"No, Barbara. I was not attacked by slaves. I was attacked by one man, and he was as white as myself."

"Philip!" My voice caught in my throat. "Did—did you see who it was?"

"No, not clearly. All I know is that he was tall, very tall, over six feet I should think, and he was riding a gray stallion. I think he had been waiting for me. He rode out of the bushes and caught me round the throat with a whip and slewed me to the ground. See." He raised his head and I could see a long red weal round his neck. "I remember seeing him looking down at me from the back of his horse, then . . ."

"The Gray Phantom, Philip. It was the Gray Phantom," I breathed.

"He was no phantom, I can tell you. As he came closer

I thought his horse would trample me. I tried to roll out of its way, but the rope was still round my neck. Then he jumped down and started kicking me, and all the time he was laughing . . . laughing . . . I don't think I'll ever forget that laughter. It was wild, insane."

"Insane? O-h-h-h . . ."

"Oh, I'm sorry, Barbara, I shouldn't . . ."

"No, no, it's all right. It's just that . . . go on, what happened then?"

"Well, I'm not sure. I think he must have heard something, because he looked around in a startled sort of way, then he drew the whip from round my neck and booted me off the road. I hit my head on a rock. It knocked me out. When I came round it was getting dark; my horse had gone, and I was miles away from anywhere. I tried to get up, found I couldn't, so I crawled till I found myself near High Place and, well, you know the rest. I believe Jem found me in the garden. I don't remember that part of it. I suppose I must have passed out again."

We looked at each other in silence for a few seconds. My stomach was heaving. I knew who had done this to Philip. And I could have prevented it, and all the other attacks on innocent people, if I had spoken up sooner. I wanted to speak up now. I wanted to tell him Robert had done this to him, but no words would come.

"Bella tells me Adam has gone to fetch Sarah," Philip said.

"Yes." I could hardly get it out. "They should be here soon." Then, unheeding of how rude it might appear to Philip, I hurried out of the room without another glance.

Bella was standing just outside. She gave me a sharp look. I swayed dizzily. She caught me. "Are you all right? Are you . . . ?"

"Bella," I rasped hoarsely, grabbing her arm. "Where is Master Robert? Tell me. You must tell me."

"I do not know, mistress," she replied.

"You do. You do." I grabbed her arm. "You must tell me before it's too late. He's mad, Bella. Mad."

"No, mistress." She pulled her arm away with an angry jerk. "Master Robert's not mad. There are those who would like to prove him so, but I did not think you one of them."

She spun away from me and returned to her patient. I gazed after her in exasperation. Of course she would not admit it. She was his nurse. She was responsible for him. It was she who restrained him when . . . "Adam!"

His name burst from me in anguish, and I turned and flew down the stairs. The shutters were up, but the door was still wide open. I ran through it, impelled by an urge stronger than myself to find Adam, to warn him of his danger.

Chapter Seventeen

I ran down the steps and across the hard-baked ground to the road, away from High Place, away from the light that shone from door and window, into the enveloping darkness of the tropic night, till I came to a halt at last with a stitch in my side, a thudding heart, and a heaving breast.

A half-moon danced in and out of the branches of the trees high above me. In its dim light, black shapes loomed toward me, heightening my fear. A strange sound made me whirl around, and a night bird flapping through the air almost brushed my cheeks, so that I reeled back in fright, screaming as I fell against something soft that did not resist my weight. But it was only vegetation, and after wallowing helplessly for a few moments, I managed to disentangle myself.

I looked back toward High Place, hoping to glean comfort and courage from it, but it was not there. Had I left it so far behind? How far had I run before coming to my senses?

I listened to the thudding of my heart, the song of

crickets, the croak of frogs, and the calls of other more worrisome creatures of the night, and beneath it all I was conscious of a deep, watchful silence that lay still and menacing.

My terror grew. I twisted around, eyes darting, hardly daring to breathe; I knew that apart from Adam and myself—and Robert—others were abroad this night; black slaves bent on revenge for past outrages.

I imagined soft-footed men stalking through the thick, tropical plant life all around, eyes peering at me from behind tall, fat leaves. My tongue clove to the roof of my mouth. What should I do? Should I go back? Should I go on? I had to go on. Adam was out there. Vulnerable. I had to warn him—put him on his guard against Robert.

I started off again along the road that led to Seatown. Adam was bound to return this way. I would run into him soon. But he should have been back long ago. What had delayed him? Robert? Was I too late? Was Adam lying somewhere in the inky blackness ahead, maimed, unconscious—dead?

"Oh, God, don't let him be dead!" I prayed, increasing my speed, the stitch in my side recurring, my breath coming in stunted, painful gasps. *"Don't let him be dead!"* And Sarah! would she be dead, too? Would I stumble across two bodies on the road?

I drew to a halt, afraid to go on, afraid of what I might find if I did, and while I stood there I became aware that it was getting light—dawn was breaking. Then a pungent smell assailed my nostrils, and I spun around to confront columns of black smoke spiked by tongues of flame billowing into a red glowing sky from the direction of High Place.

High Place! High Place was on fire! "No-o-o-o!" I

started running toward it—and stopped, torn in two. High Place was on fire. Morvah, Philip, and Jem were there. But there were plenty to fight the fire, to rescue any who might be in need of rescue. Adam was out in the night facing an unknown danger, and he had only me to help him. Adam, my husband, was my first priority.

I turned again, but I had not gone more than a few steps when the sound of hooves behind me made me swing round in unthinking belief.

"Adam!"

"Barbara! Thank God I've found you! They told me you'd gone out."

My heart sank. It was not Adam. It was Jem, both he and his horse blood red against the flame-lit sky. Hardly slowing down, he swept me off my feet to sit me in front of him on his horse. The thought came to me that he should have been at High Place fighting the fire, but I was glad he had ridden out to look for me. Now, together, we could find Adam. But then I realized we had left the road and were galloping toward the mountains.

"Jem," I cried. "Where are we going? We must stick to the road. We'll never find Adam if we don't stick to the road."

"Adam's dead. I saw him die."

The cold finality of truth lay in his words, silencing the denial that sprang to my lips. It was true. Adam was dead. If he had not been he would have reached home long, long ago. He was dead. My husband was dead. My cousin had killed him.

I did not weep. I did not wail. I simply stopped living. It was a cold, empty shell Jem cradled in his arms, slumped across his chest, atop the big, strong horse that carried us swiftly and easily higher and higher into the mountain forests till we came to a halt at the foot of a high rock overlooking the sea.

I could not have been completely lifeless, however. A fleeting recognition made me gasp. "Where are we?"

"The caves at Jutting Rock."

Jem pinpointed a moment in my life I would never forget as he jumped down, swinging me down after him, and as I looked up into his face, blurred though it was in the darkness, I knew; as I looked from him to his pale-colored horse, I knew, and every crime I had attributed to Robert was transferred to Jem.

"It was you. You killed Adam. You are the Gray Phantom."

"Now how do you make that out?"

Jem's voice, so calm and gentle, almost had me believing I had got it wrong.

"Your—your horse," I said.

"Diabolo?" He smiled and stroked the long, silky neck. "He's a beauty, isn't he?"

"I've never seen you ride him before. I've never seen him at High Place."

"That's because I don't keep him at High Place. His home's up here, in the mountains, where I found him three years ago—a wild young stallion. He took quite a bit of conquering, I can tell you, but I did it. He knows who's master now."

His tone had changed, grown hard and cruel.

"You *are* the Gray Phantom," I accused him again, backing away.

"Yes, I am," he said harshly. "What of it?"

"What of it?" I thought of all the people he had assaulted, murdered. "*What of it?*"

"It was a guise that paid off. A ploy to incite slaves to

rebellion." Suddenly he laughed, and, scooping me up into his arms as if I were a doll, carried me into the cave. His laughter echoed around the walls of the cave as it must have echoed around the island as Philip lay on the ground, torn and bleeding, at Jem's mercy. "They believed the Gray Phantom was their Messiah."

He placed a smacking kiss on my cheek and set me down. I cringed away from him, wiping my cheek with the back of my hand, looking about me, searching for a way of escape. But he stood squarely in front of me, blocking my only means of exit.

"It was a form of amusement at first. It was fun seeing others punished for crimes I had committed. But it palled. Then when Philip started preaching his idealistic claptrap, I saw how it could be used to my advantage."

"Advantage?" Keep him talking. Keep him talking. Look for your chance to escape.

"I had to get rid of Adam." The hate in Jem's voice was like the lash of a whip across my body. "What better way than that he should be murdered by one of the black savages he liked to mollycoddle? Only it would be the Gray Phantom who would have the honor of sending him out of this world. But first there had to be an uprising, a rebellion, so that suspicion would fall upon the slaves, for there were others I wished to rid Almada of. A rebellion would be of great help. In the past people never really believed in the Gray Phantom. That was why they called him the Gray Phantom. But lately they have been thinking differently. Those who claimed to have seen him were strongly of the opinion that he was a white man. I had to become more—circumspect."

His laughter hit the walls again, echoing around us. He was mad. I saw it now. Why had I not seen it before? But he had always seemed so sane before. One of the sanest men alive.

"But why kill Adam? He'd never harmed you."

"He was master of High Place, when I should have been. High Place was mine by rights."

"But—how could that be?"

"I was his brother. His elder brother."

He was mad. Mad people had to be placated, soothed. I tried not to sound afraid and spoke to him gently.

"No, Jem. Adam's father found you when you were no more than nine or ten, an abandoned orphan. He took you in and raised you like his own, but . . ."

I broke off, suddenly feeling this was not the right thing to say at all. Perhaps I should be agreeing with him, pretending I believed him.

"That's what we were all led to believe, don't you see?" he said. "Only I knew different. I knew why Joe Pengarth took me in, gave me a home, raised me like his own son. Why should he do those things if he were not my father? And if he were my father, I should inherit High Place. I was the elder—by two years.

"So I faced him with it—and he denied me. He'd taken me into his home, he told me, accepted me into his family, out of the goodness of his heart, but I was foolish to think I was his son. He had only two sons. Adam and Robert. I hated him after that and vowed I would be revenged."

"I joined forces with Ransom. He had cause to hate the Pengarths, too. Between us we swindled Joe Pengarth out of everything he owned. Ransom thought he was being clever, using me. He thought he would own High Place one day and have Morvah Pengarth on her knees begging for mercy. I encouraged him to think that way, but I was biding my time, strengthening a hold over him he never even dimly perceived. I was not his tool. He was mine. He would never be master of High Place. I would."

If Jem was mad, it was a clever madness. He had worked everything out so painstakingly. He knew what he wanted and had carved his way through to it with ruthless assurance.

"And then Joe died. But before he died that letter came and Adam went to England and brought you back with him. And money. Money. All my dreams and plans dwindled away to nothing. You were young, healthy, you would bear lots of children: little Pengarths to inherit what should rightfully be mine; and I would go on managing the plantation as I had always done, accepted into the family circle, but never belonging, never in my rightful place."

He drew in a long, deep breath, and though his face was only the faintest blur in the dark interior of the cave, I could see he had turned slightly, moved a little. A little more and I could run past him out of the cave. My desire for escape let my thoughts go no further than that, so that what I should do once outside, where I should go, whether he would catch me before I had got very far, or not, had no place in my mind.

"So what did you do then?" I asked, hoping that in the telling he would move further away.

"I started to plan and scheme afresh. I instructed Minty to . . ."

"Minty?" I cried out in astonishment, forgetting to keep my mind on escape. "What has she got to do with it?"

"Oh, didn't I tell you? She was helping me. I know your secret, you see. Yours and Adam's, and I wanted it brought out into the open. When it became known that Adam wasn't Joe's son after all, that would only leave Robert—and I could control Robert."

"But how did you know? We told no one."

"Robert isn't the only one who listens at doors and windows. I told Minty to trick you into admitting the truth." She would do anything to get Adam back." He laughed, making my blood run cold. "She thought I was helping her. She thought she could turn to me for amusement after Adam had left for England. But no one makes use of me. I make use of them. I soon showed her I was no man to play with. What use were a few paltry kisses to me? I took what I wanted and soon erased all thought of Adam from her mind. But when he came back she wanted him again. I had tired of her so I let her think I didn't mind, knowing I could get her back soon enough if I wanted her. She thought I was helping her when I put the suspicion in her mind about you and Adam. Little did she know it wouldn't do any good if the truth became known."

"But Adam was Joe Pengarth's son. It's Robert who isn't."

There was a moment's silence after my outburst, prompted by a longing to demolish Jem's smug confidence in himself. Then Jem laughed again.

"Adam is dead, so it doesn't signify. With him out of the way and Robert having no claim, Morvah dead . . ."

I gasped. "Morvah dead?"

"Burnt to a cinder by now, locked in her room."

I could not believe it. I did not believe it. All this could not be happening. I must have fallen on the road, knocked my head against a stone and drifted into some kind of nightmare from which I would, must, soon emerge.

But then he reached out for me and pulled me to him. "But you and I are alive. I saved you, because I love you. You've got courage. You'll be a fitting wife for me. I shall rebuild High Place and together we can . . ."

He was breathing heavily. His arms were like a vice. His lips sought mine. I felt sick.

"Ever since the day you threw yourself into my arms and begged me to take you away I've wanted to hold you like this. I knew you wanted it, too, but Adam stood in our way. Now you're free. Free to love me as you've always wanted to. And I'll love you as you've never been loved before. With me, you'll taste the glories of life."

We were on the ground now, his weight pinning me down. His mouth was fastened to mine. His hands were inside my bodice, raising my skirts, touching, feeling, exploring, filling me with revulsion, then, suddenly, he was yanked off me, and as I struggled to my feet I saw him go crashing headfirst against the jagged rock wall, sink to the ground, and lie there, still.

A shape loomed toward me. A great hand reached out to grasp mine. A voice I thought I would never be so glad to hear said, "Come, little sister. Come."

"Robert!"

I fell into his arms and he held me to him. "There, there," he said. "It's all over. Don't be afraid. Jem won't harm you anymore. There, there. There, there," just as if I were the child and he the adult.

I clung to Robert's hand as he led me out of the cave. Robert's hand? Richard's hand. Dear God, he was my cousin. Aunt Martha's son. He owned everything under her will.

No. He owned nothing. Aunt Martha's fortune went to Richard Goodall only on the condition that he marry me, and he had not married me, Adam Pengarth had, and

Adam was dead. What good had Aunt Martha's money done either of us? Adam was dead, and I might just as well be.

But life went on. Robert helped me mount Black Satin and swung himself up behind me. It was getting light. In the distance I could see the massive gray stallion that had brought me here stamping the ground, waiting for the man who would never ride him again.

I expected Robert to take me back to High Place. The fire must be out by now. High Place could not have been completely destroyed. Morvah and the others would have been saved. Surely Jem had only been giving voice to wishful thinking. But as the sun rose higher into a sky so blue it mocked my memory of black smoke plumes, tongues of flame and angry red glare, I realized we had bypassed High Place and were heading toward Seatown.

"Where are we going?" I cried, suddenly panicking. "Where are you taking me?" To where Adam's body lay, mangled, up ahead? "Why aren't we going to High Place?"

"High Place is burnt down," he said, almost without emotion. "I'm taking you to the ship, like Adam told me to."

High Place is burnt down. My heart reacted painfully at each word. But—Adam? *Adam told me to.* I gazed questioningly into my cousin's face, tentative hope rising within my breast.

"He said if anything happened to him I was to take care of you, put you on the ship bound for England."

Hope died. Let Robert take me where he would. What did it matter? Nothing mattered. Adam was dead. Dead, dead, dead.

I started to cry, hopelessly, helplessly, tears pouring

down my face in a flood. It had been too much to expect the numbness of shock that had sustained me hitherto to continue. The empty shell of me became a hive of torment as pain took hold of every nerve and turned it inside out, shredding it unmercifully. There was no relief from the torture, even in the sobs heaved into Robert's chest as he crooned above my head. "There, there, little sister. There, there."

He brought Black Satin to a halt and wrapped his arms comfortingly around me till my sobs ceased from sheer exhaustion, and only a long, shuddering sigh occasionally interrupted the rhythm of my breathing.

We rode on. We had almost reached Seatown when I clutched at Robert in fear. On the road ahead of us a group of Negroes gathered, brandishing sticks, swords, pistols, sythes. Robert slowed down, showing no sign of fear. One of the Negroes, wearing a strange headdress of feathers and carrying a stick from which more feathers and streamers trailed, came forward. He grinned up at me. "Good morning, Missie Barbry."

"Billy Joe!"

I could not believe it, and while I stared at him in wonderment, he spoke to Robert.

"When you take Missie Barbry to ship, you take Missie Rose."

"Missie Rose?" My heart started racing. "Sarah?"

"She wait in hiding place, Massa Robert. She . . ."

"Sarah's alive?" I whispered.

"She alive, but she asleep. She been shot."

"You mean she's unconscious?"

Billy Joe nodded. "We fin' her on road. At first we think she dead, then we see her breathe. We take her to hiding place."

"And Adam?" If they had found Sarah, they must have found Adam.

"We take Massa Adam away. He not go on ship." He looked at Robert. "You take Missie Rose?"

Robert nodded, and Billy Joe and the rest melted away into the surrounding countryside as if they had never been.

The quay at Seatown was a seething mass of frightened, angry people. A few soldiers were endeavoring to keep some sort of order, but the press of people and baggage was so great, they achieved little success. Robert tethered his horse and entered the melee with gusto, clearing a way for me through the throng with consummate ease. But I fought against him, hampering him, "Sarah! We haven't got Sarah."

It was useless to fight against his strength. He soon had me aboard. "Now I'll fetch Sarah," he said.

I stayed by the side of the ship and watched Robert out of sight, praying he would return with Sarah before the ship sailed. The tide was in and it was evident the ship was getting ready to set sail. The captain was not waiting for the evening tide as Governor Belmont had ordered and the people below could see this. Their anger erupted into fights and arguments. Civilized behavior gave way to primitive instincts as every man fought for himself.

Among the white faces upturned to where the lucky ones among us had reached the safety of the deck were black faces. House slaves, I guessed, who were being taken by their masters to England to serve them there. So not all the slaves had rioted, though most had, as I deduced from overheard comment, anguished conversation. Plantation owners and their families had been murdered, their houses burnt, their crops ruined, in a wave of crazed terror. Even the merchants and shopkeepers living in Seatown had not escaped some injury, large or small. The army was in tatters. Only small pockets of soldiers still remained to fight on.

And it had all been brought about by arrogance, intolerance and stupidity.

I searched the quayside with my eyes for Robert. Where was he? Why didn't he hurry? Oh, Sarah, Sarah, has he found you? My thoughts turned to Philip. Was he dead? Meta, Bella—what of them? High Place was burnt down, Robert had said. It had hardly sunk in at the time. I had simply accepted it. Now I wondered what it meant. What had happened to the people there? Were they dead? Was everybody dead? Morvah and Philip must be. If they had been alive Robert would not have left them behind. He would have brought them, with me, to board the ship for England. Oh, Sarah, Sarah, must I be the one to tell you Philip is dead? I felt the tears start to my eyes again.

"Barbara! Barbara Pengarth!"

A high, sweet voice, penetrating above the babble, made me turn swiftly. Araminta Belmont hurried toward me, looking as lovely as ever, but drawn, and as she drew nearer I saw her eyes were shadowed, the aquamarine darkened to indigo.

"Oh, I'm so glad you're safe. When we were told High Place had been fired, I . . . where's Adam? Mrs. Pengarth?"

"They're dead." I said dully.

"What? Both of them? Oh, no!"

"Jem's dead, too," I added.

Her eyes lit up. "Thank God!" she breathed. "The times I've wished him dead. He was an evil man, Barbara.

He forced me to do dreadful things. I can't tell you the things he made me do. I had hoped when Adam got back I should be able to get free of him, but . . ." Her eyes dropped before mine. "How did they die? In the fire?"

"Morvah, yes. Adam was murdered—by Jem."

"Oh, no! Oh, Barbara! My heart grieves for you."

Tears started to roll down my cheeks again at her unexpected show of sympathy. "Oh, Barbara," she said again and put her arms around me. A few moments later, she said, "We are both bereaved. My father . . ."

Tears trembled now in her own voice and I raised my face to hers. "Your father? Is he dead, too?"

"He was run through with a sword and hacked to pieces with an axe . . . in our own drawing room. Oh, Barbara, it was terrible, terrible."

We clung together in mutual grief, trying to achieve mutual comfort, Araminta Belmont and I.

Then Robert reached our side. Sarah was in his arms. She looked dead, but she was only unconscious. We took her to Araminta's cabin, the biggest and best, because it had been booked early, which she insisted we share with her, and together, on the journey back to England, we nursed Sarah back to health, under the watchful eye of the ship's doctor.

Chapter Eighteen

I sat in the big drawing room of Martha's Cottage. The first time I had sat there I had been a child of ten, overwhelmed by it and Aunt Martha and the beautiful creatures of gold and blue and green that strutted in the sun-splashed garden on lawns of velvet green amid flower gardens such as I had never seen.

I had beheld the glorious creatures in amazement and my heart had been moved almost to bursting point out of sheer delight at seeing one of them, his long-eyed tail feathers sweeping the ground, cross the threshold with disdainful step.

The full-length windows had been open then to let in the warmth of the summer sun. Now, although it was nearing the end of June, the wind was chill and the windows were closed. But I could see the vain and beautiful peacocks still strutting about beyond the mullioned glass, proud owners of all they surveyed.

I watched them and was not stirred by their beauty. It was their cries that stirred me—to remembrance of a scene I longed to forget, but would never forget.

When Robert had seen us safely installed in Araminta's cabin, with the doctor in attendance, he had slipped quietly away. I had been vaguely aware of it at the time, but had not paid particular attention to it. I thought he had just gone up on deck. I thought he would remain on board and accompany us back to England. There was nothing to keep him in Almada. Childlike, he might have been, but he was big and strong, unafraid, capable of overcoming obstacles; I looked upon him as our protector.

Later, when I asked for him, I was astounded to be told he had gone ashore. I jumped up and in great agitation ran to the ship's side to call him back. I knew he would not leave the quay till the ship had sailed and he was satisfied we were on our way to safety. Sure enough, he was standing on the quayside, head and shoulders above the rest, gazing up at the ship that was already pulling out of harbor.

I screamed at him at the top of my voice to come aboard—but how could he have, even if he had heard me above the din? He could not jump the widening gap between ship and shore. He saw me, though, and grinned and waved, and I wept hysterically as the distance between us broadened.

And then it happened. A man leapt out of the crowd wielding a long-bladed knife that reflected the rays of the sun like a mirror. As he plunged the weapon into Robert's back, I recognized him. It was Jack Ransom, his face contorted with an ugly expression—blood ran down his cheek from a wound at the temple. Robert had no chance against the vicious, cowardly assault. He slumped to the ground and did not rise again.

Whether or not a silence did actually settle on the

crowd I will never know, but I heard nothing till the evil deed was over and a high-pitched shriek rent the air. Was it mine? Someone else? It did not matter. It was taken up soon enough by others.

Then chaos reigned, with screams of terror as people scattered, pushing and trampling each other in their efforts to evade a gang of Negroes who had made their appearance, slashing to right and left with axe and scythe, clearing an uncaring way for one of their number to descend on Ransom. Billy Joe! There was no mistaking the witchdoctor headdress, the feathered stick.

Ransom just had time to see who his attacker was before crashing to the ground with a blow from the stick that must have housed in its feathered head the blade of an axe. Ransom fell, with one side of his face cleaved clean away, and then the others were upon him, exacting their revenge upon the man most hated and feared in all Almada.

I shivered and drew my shawl round me. They were all gone now. Adam, Robert, Morvah, Philip, Jem . . . only Sarah and I remained, and the child in my womb.

It stirred and I gave a little cry. The child within me was Adam's child—a part of Adam that no one could take away from me. I wanted the child, ached to hold it in my arms, but oh! oh! I wanted Adam. I would gladly have exchanged the unborn child inside me for Adam alive and well.

I ought to have been ashamed of myself; and I was. How could I even have contemplated giving up the child in my womb? Yet I had done so, out of intense longing for the man who had fathered it. Would God ever forgive me? I vowed to dedicate my life to my child. I would always love Adam, never forget him, but from now on I would live for my child.

A sudden searing pain, stronger than any I had ever known or envisioned, consumed me, blotting everything from sight and mind. Then it was gone as suddenly as it had come, leaving me perspiring, panting and afraid. I waited anxiously for it to occur again, but it did not, and I settled my huge bulk in my chair again, breathing quickly, resting my head against its embroidered back.

I had first realized I might be expecting a child when things had not been as usual with me at my time of the month. A feeling of excitement had raced through my veins at the possibility, but I knew better than to place too much credence on this one miss. It would be necessary to wait another month before I could be sure.

That second month was on board the *Emily Rose*, our ship back to England. I had been nauseated for days and blamed the motion of the ship, although the sea had been calm since we had left Almada. However, as my time came round again and nothing happened, and I continued to be sick when everyone else was perfectly well, the certainty grew in me that I was with child.

I had wept and been joyful. I had wept and been anguished. I was carrying Adam's child, and he should have been here to share my joy with me. But he was gone. I had lost him beyond recall.

Eventually my sickness eased, and I felt extraordinarily well for the rest of the voyage; even the storm we ran into did not disturb my equilibrium. I grew large and round and developed a tranquil outlook on life as I planned for the birth of my son.

I never doubted I would have a son. A boy like Adam, with dark hair and piercing blue eyes. He would be brought up at Martha's Cottage and would learn to love it as I did. He would inherit Martha's Cottage after me and all Aunt Martha's wealth. Adam might not have been legally entitled to it, but I was. I had never married her son, Richard Goodall, and so, in accordance with the codicil to her will contained in an envelope to be opened after a month if I had not married Richard Goodall, everything she died possessed of came to me, and through me, to my son.

The *Emily Rose* docked in the early hours of a mid-April morning. Almost a year to the day since I had sailed away from England, I had returned. Tears rushed to my eyes. I dashed them away. There was no point in dwelling on the past. I had to look forward to the future, for my son's sake.

So I told myself, but the moment I was alone, away from prying eyes, despair engulfed me, and I forsook my own advice.

Sarah, who had made a complete recovery during the voyage, though her eyes still held the lost expression that had entered them upon learning of Philip's death, insisted on journeying with me to Martha's Cottage to stay with me till after my baby was born. I was grateful to her. Seven months pregnant, and beginning to slow down with the extra weight I was carrying, I had begun to find my earlier equanimity deserting me and an irritation I could not account for pestering me. Sarah said it was quite usual for such little changes in one's temperament to occur at such a time. Once the baby was born, I should soon regain my equilibrium.

We sent messages of our arrival to our relations, then went to refresh ourselves at a nearby inn before setting out on the last stage of our journey. Araminta joined us, expressing her great joy at being once more on English soil.

"I shall never wish to leave it again," she said fervently, wriggling her toes inside the white stockings she held out toward the fire in our private room at the inn. "I shall find some nice country gentleman, marry him, and settle down to a quiet family life."

"I can't see you doing that, somehow," I smiled at her. "It's much more likely that you'll become the toast of London, marry a duke and become a famous hostess giving the most marvelous soirees and balls. Do you not agree, Sarah?"

Sarah agreed, and Araminta's laughter peeled through the warm, comfortable room as she rose to prance about, dancing with an imaginary partner, in her stockinged feet.

"And you must come to them," she declared. "I will introduce you to all the eligible men—for you must marry again. Oh, I know the pain of losing your husbands is still fresh in your minds," she added, seeing our smiles fade, "but life goes on and time passes . . . it's foolish to live in the past. When you lose the man you love the only sensible thing to do is find someone else to take his place. You *must* marry again, Barbara. Especially with a baby on the way."

Araminta's insensitivity appalled me. Sarah's face was ashen and a tight ache was in my throat. But with her shallow nature she would never be able to understand how deeply our losses had affected us. We were both women who loved deeply. No other man could ever take my husband's place, and I felt it was the same with Sarah.

We said good-bye to Araminta soon after that and went our separate ways, reaching Martha's Cottage late at night. My friend was enchanted with the house, as I knew she would be. Only as I gazed at it, peacefully serene in the bright moonlight, did I remember my injunction to

Mr. Parkes to let it, and my heart skipped a beat. Was it let now? Would I be barred from entering? Perhaps I should have informed Mr. Parkes of our arrival, called on him before coming here.

In agitation I lifted the door knocker and held my breath. All was well. Wilkins, the butler, greeted me emotionally and welcomed me in. The house had been let during the past year, he informed me once over the initial shock of seeing me suddenly on the doorstep, but had been empty for the past two months.

"If only you had let me know you were coming, madam," he moaned, gesturing toward the furniture covered in dustsheets, "I would have had everything in readiness for you. As it is . . ."

"All we wish for at present," I said, "are beds to sleep in and a little food. We are starving."

He beamed. "Cook will be delighted to prepare something for you. She will be overcome with joy when she knows you are here. We've all missed you, Miss Barbara—madam."

It was good to be back in Martha's Cottage. It did not make up for the loss of Adam, but it gave balm to my soul. Sarah's too. She felt the blessing of its peace.

Mr. Parkes called on me. Not the kind old man I remembered, but a younger man, Timothy, his grandson, whom I had met once or twice in the past. I was sad to learn the old man had died just over a month ago. His son was now head of the firm. Unfortunately, he was suffering from a putrid sore throat and had instructed Timothy to pay this courtesy call.

"If I can be of any service to you until your husband

joins you . . . why, what is it, Mrs. Pengarth? You've gone quite pale."

"My husband will not be joining me, Mr. Parkes," I said huskily. "He's dead. Murdered."

The poor man looked quite distraught and hardly knew what to say. He stuttered and stammered his condolences. "Please accept my deepest sympathies . . . I am sorry . . . I had heard of the uprising . . . I suppose the slaves were responsible . . . if there is anything I can do for you, anything . . ."

"Thank you. If you will be good enough to look after my affairs, you and your father, I shall be most obliged. My aunt was very well satisfied with the service your grandfather gave. I am sure I shall be equally satisfied with yours."

"Yes. Certainly. Leave everything in my hands. Did your late husband leave a will? It is necessary to ask, you understand."

"Yes, of course. I'm afraid I do not know."

"No matter. I shall look into it. I shall contact the authorities in Almada immediately. I shall not distress you with further questioning. Leave everything to me. I will . . ."

Sarah interrupted us. "Oh, please excuse me," she cried. "I did not know you had a visitor. I will come back later."

"No, don't go," I said, "I would like you to meet my solicitor, Mr. Timothy Parkes." I was unaware of what the outcome of the introduction would be.

It had been my duty to inform my mother of my return. I had not expected her to visit me. Yet before the week was out she arrived, with a new husband in tow, and my sister, Beth.

She swept in like a queen trailing furs and French perfume. "My poor widowed daughter," she exclaimed, offering no kiss, only a narrow-eyed observation of my rotund form. "And pregnant too. You didn't tell me that in your message. Only about your bereavement."

The interceding twelve months might never have been. In my mother's presence I was a little girl again, noticed only for chastisement.

"I would have told you," I began apologetically, but, as in the past, she was not interested in what I had to say. Her affairs and Beth's were of much more importance.

"This is your new stepfather." She indicated with a languid gesture the rather tall, angular man with a receding chin and expression of complete boredom standing just behind her. "A very wealthy man, as you can see." She showed off her furs. "But the best news is of Beth. She . . ."

Beth, unable to retain her decorous stance beside our mother any longer, launched herself into my arms with the cry, "Oh, Babs, I am to marry a lord!"

"Lord Erimond, heir to the Earl of Lingate." My mother made her proud statement with an air of supreme satisfaction. "Look at her. Does she not glow with happiness? Does she not shine? We are on our way now to Castle Lingate to meet the earl and stay for a few days. But it is a long way and we would like to rest here tonight and be on our way early in the morning."

So they had visited me for the convenience of a night's lodging. I might have known it was not for the pleasure of seeing me. The old feeling of rejection soured my inside.

"Will you come to my wedding, Babs?" Beth was demanding.

"When is it to be?" I asked.

"The first week in July."

"Ah, then I am afraid I shall not be able to. My baby is due around then."

I smiled. The thought of my baby filled me with joy, banished the sourness inside me, healed the wounds of rejection. My baby was my salvation.

"How provoking," my mother frowned. "You must hire a wetnurse."

"Oh, no, I could not do that."

She clicked her tongue. "What a pity the child will have no father." Her tone implied it was my fault. "You must marry again—if possible. I know what it is like to be left to bring up a child alone." She gazed fondly at Beth. "Not that the dear little thing was ever any trouble."

The fact that I, a child of four, had been around at the time went unacknowledged. At one time I would have been heartbroken at the exclusion. Now I did not care. Now I felt nothing.

"Do you think we might have something to eat, Barbara? We have come a long way and are extremely hungry. And then we must discuss what is to be done about you."

"About me?" I hesitated on my way to see to her wishes. "What do you mean, Mama?"

"Well, you are a very wealthy woman now. You will want to sell Martha's Cottage and find something more—grand."

I was stung to retort. "I seem to remember you thought Martha's Cottage quite grand in the past."

Mother pinched her lips together. "In the past, maybe. But times change. Values change. I can assure you, I have grown used to living in far grander places than this. Why, compared with my house in Essex, this is but a mere hovel."

I rose, quivering with anger. I would allow no one, not even my mother, to malign Martha's Cottage. "Then I will not detain you in it any longer. I will call for your carriage and you can leave at once."

"Tut, tut, girl, sit down. I do declare, you are as touchy as ever. Of course I didn't mean . . ."

"Oh, yes you did, Mama. You meant every belittling word."

"Really, child, you are being most disagreeable. . . ."

"I am not a child. I am a grown woman, in charge of my own life. I need no advice from you. I am perfectly capable of managing for myself."

"What do you know about it," she snapped, her voice rising shrilly in the way I remembered. "I think . . ."

"I do not care what you think," I whipped back.

"Well, really . . ." I had never seen my mother so taken aback before. "How dare you speak to me like that? I am your mother. I always have your welfare at heart."

"Was it for my welfare that you sold me to Aunt Martha for a paltry sum of money, or for yours?"

All the hurt, despair, anger, frustration of my early years found expression in those words. They silenced my mother completely.

"I don't need any help from you," I continued. "I need nothing from you. I might have once, but not now, not anymore."

She scowled at me. "You've changed, Barbara, and not for the better. You used to be such a shy, timid little thing, easily . . ."

"Put down and cast aside. I know. But as you say, I have changed. I have been married. I have been loved. I am soon to become a mother. I am rich and answerable to no one. What I do with my life is my own affair. If I choose to remain here in Martha's Cottage, that is my business, not yours. If it displeases you, I do not care. I have ceased to be afraid of displeasing you. As a matter of fact, I am thinking of turning the place into a home for waifs and strays."

My pronouncement shocked her to the core. "You can't!" she shrilled. "Think of Lord Erimond! Think of the earl!"

"You think of them, Mama. I have better things to do with my time," I said tartly.

My mother stared at me for a long time, her breath coming out of her mouth in angry gasps. Then she rose, her face hard and closed against me. "Come Beth. Come William. Let us leave this place at once. I shall not set foot in it again till I receive an abject apology."

"That will be never, then," I said, unmoved.

I never thought I should live to see the day when I would be glad to see the back of my mother. But we had grown so far apart, if indeed we had ever been close. I should not worry if I never saw her again.

I discussed my sudden idea of turning Martha's Cottage into a home for parentless, loveless children with Sarah. She showed great enthusiasm for it, as did Timothy Parkes, with whom we shared our plans. He had taken to visiting us, or rather Sarah, almost every day, and at last I chaffed her, "I think you have a suitor there, Sarah."

She reddened, the first color to touch her cheeks for a long long time, and pooh-poohed the suggestion with far too much vehemence, so that I looked at her sharply and wondered.

"Sarah . . ." I began, then clutched at her with a little

shriek as a sudden pain seemed to tear me apart.

It was my first warning that my child was preparing to come into the world.

It was a long labor and a difficult birth. I did not recover my strength as quickly as I should have, and for a time it was feared I should lose my life. But Sarah would not let me die and nursed me devotedly. On the borders of my conscious mind I heard her voice admonishing me. "You must not die, Barbara. You must live. Think of your newborn son. He needs you. I need you. You must make the effort. You must live."

But I did not want to live. I wanted to join Adam.

I lay for over a fortnight in a twilight condition, neither dead nor alive. But gradually I improved. I saw and held my son for the first time, and the feel of him, the softness of him, the warm smell of him, the sight of his somewhat pugnacious little face with the already determined jaw, his vivid blue eyes, so like Adam's, made my heart swell with love and pride. I *had* to rise from my bed for his sake. And Adam's. Adam would not want me to leave our child to face life without either of us to guide him.

I started to cry, silent, hopeless tears, for my lost love, then bitterly, noisily, heavy droplets falling upon my son's face. Not unnaturally, he started to bawl in competition with me, and Sarah hurried to take him from me and return him to his cradle where, as she rocked, he grew quiet once more.

My tears were not so easily quenched. I wept for days, for no apparent reason. I could not understand it. My health was improving. I was eating well. And I had my son. Why, then, was I so lethargic and downcast all the time?

It was Dr. Bright, my physician, who came up with the suggestion that I set down the story of my life in writing. He was a man with very advanced ideas, which had been Aunt Martha's reason for engaging him in the first place. He was well known in medical circles for expouding the theory that the health of the body was interwoven with the health of the mind.

"Set everything down on paper," he said, "just as it happened to you. There is nothing physically wrong with you. The sickness must be in your mind. I think something is locked away there that needs to be loosened."

"What, doctor?" I frowned in puzzlement.

"I don't know, my dear, but I fancy it may be that you have not yet faced squarely the loss of your husband."

"But I have. I have. I face it morning, noon, and night."

"You kept calling for him in your delirium. That to my mind indicates a reluctance to come to terms with your bereavement, and the fact that, as you say, your loss is before you morning, noon, and night confirms my belief. Try it my dear; you have nothing to lose. The mere act of setting everything down, your thoughts, your joys, your fears, will prove a most beneficial exercise, I am certain."

So I followed his advice, and the foregoing is the result. It has not worked a complete cure, there is still an empty ache in my heart—I fear there always will be—but it has strengthened me and determined me to concentrate on the future, to bring up my son in the way Adam would wish.

Chapter Nineteen

It is mid-September. Dahlias and chrysanthemums are ablaze in the garden and as I look out of the window I can see Sarah and Timothy walking side by side. They see me and wave. I pick up my pen to write an ending to my story. An ending and a beginning.

I had long suspected Sarah and Timothy were falling in love and was therefore not surprised when they told me they had become engaged and were looking forward to a Christmas wedding. I congratulated them heartily. Sarah deserves happiness, and Timothy is a fine, upright young man steadfast and sincere. I have no doubt he will be a true and good husband to her.

Sarah confided in me. "I will never forget Philip. I loved him dearly. I never thought I should ever fall in love again, but I have, and I'm so happy. Timothy is such a kind, thoughtful man—I am lucky to have found him. I pray that you will be as lucky, Barbara, and find happiness again, as I have done."

It was a blessing to both of us that she would not be going far away after her wedding. We would be able to visit each other often. But it was a blow to me that I should not have her beside me when I eventually opened the Martha Home for Waifs and Strays. It was still in my mind to do this. Sarah said she would always be on hand to help and Timothy's advice would always be available. But it would not be the same. It would mean adjusting to another change in my life.

On a day of brilliant sunshine, sitting beneath a shady tree, with notes and plans strewn on my lap and on the grass, I contemplated the daunting enterprise I envisioned. I looked across at the house, my peaceful house, so serene and blessed, and wondered if I had the courage to carry out my plans, institute the necessary changes that would have to be made. I looked at Benjamin Adam asleep in his pram. Martha's Cottage was his birthright. Was it fair of me to consider changing it? Oh, I was suddenly in a quandary. If only Adam were here to advise me.

Adam . . . Adam . . . why are you not here? I raged in sudden anger at the fate that had snatched him from me at the very moment of my happiness.

My son—Adam's son—gave a little gurgling sound and I became aware of his vivid blue stare lingering on my face. My heart somersaulted. Adam was still here with me in my son.

I bent to kiss him and pick him up when a slight movement caught my eye and I straightened up. Timothy was coming toward me. I was expecting him; we had business to discuss. I turned my full gaze in his direction and thought I was going mad. Adam was walking toward me.

My head threatened to burst. My heart lodged in my throat. Adam? No, it couldn't be. I had been thinking of

Adam and now I thought I saw him. It was really Timothy, a trick of the light making him appear to be Adam. If I closed my eyes, when I opened them again it would be Timothy.

I closed my eyes, then dared not open them. I was afraid. Afraid I would see Timothy. Afraid I would see Adam. Afraid I would not see Adam.

"Barbara."

It was his voice speaking my name. But I had heard his voice so often in my dreams, waking and sleeping. This was just another dream. I kept my eyes tight shut.

"Barbara, open your eyes. It's me, Adam."

I opened them slowly.

It *was* Adam. Tall, impeccably dressed, as always. Thick black eyebrows, dark hair, piercing blue eyes, strong jaw—there was no mistaking him, even with the long jagged scar down one cheek.

It *was* Adam. But was he real? Or a ghost, a figment of my imagination? My fingers strayed upward to touch the scar on his cheek. His flesh was warm, pulsating, alive.

"Adam!" I shrieked.

Then I was in his arms, crushed against his chest in a hold so tight I could hardly breathe. I did not care. He could crush the life out of me and I would not care, just as long as he did not let me go. He was alive. He was here. Adam, my beloved.

"It's a miracle," I breathed. "A miracle."

"My love, my love," he murmured against my lips, my cheeks, my eyes. "How I've longed for this moment, dreamed of holding you in my arms, kissing you, loving you. . . ."

We clung together passionately, kissing and speaking all at once.

"I've longed for it, too . . . never dreamed it would happen. I thought you were dead. Jem told me you were dead. What happened? How . . . ?"

"Hush. It's a long story. I'll tell you about it later. Now, I just want to hold you, feel you near me."

That was all I wanted too, but my son, our son, had other ideas. He started bawling his head off to attract our attention. I picked him up and introduced him to his father.

It was Billy Joe and his gang of runaway slaves who had found Adam and Sarah lying in the road after Jem had attacked them and left them for dead. Sarah was already unconscious, but Adam was able to name their attacker before he slid into the same state.

The runaway slaves knew Adam to be their friend and Sarah the wife of their champion, Philip Rose, and they scarcely needed to be asked to lift them up and carry them back to High Place. (So were theirs the soft footfalls I thought I had imagined treading the lush vegetation as I searched the road for Adam? Had I passed so close to him and not known it?) But just as they reached the driveway up to the house the first flames shot up into the sky. High Place had been set on fire.

Adam fell silent when he reached this part of the story, and I took the opportunity to tell him what had happened to me and how Robert had rescued me and got me aboard the *Emily Rose.* How he had gone back for Sarah . . . and how he had died.

Then Adam took up the tale again.

The insurrection had soon been quelled. It had not spread beyond Almada. Jack Ransom and Jem, for their own foul purposes, had been the instigators of it, and once troops had arrived from the other islands there were many men eager to point the finger of accusation in order to save their own skins. It had not saved them from imprisonment, but their punishment was mild compared to that meted out to the renegade slaves. A few slaves had managed to escape, Billy Joe among them, but what would happen to them if they were caught was easy to imagine.

"What I can't understand," I said a little later, "is why, if Sarah could be brought to the ship, you could not. You were not dead."

"There was no time. Only Robert could get us away, and he, strong as he was, could not manage the two of us at once, unconscious as we were. In any case, it seemed evident I should die."

"But you didn't," I cried out swiftly.

"No." Adam gave a sudden grin. "A Pengarth takes a lot of killing."

I shuddered and curled up more closely to him. "Don't joke about it, Adam, please."

"I'm sorry." He kissed the tip of my nose, then my lips, and we almost forgot Sarah sitting opposite us nursing Benjamin on her lap. Almost, but not quite.

She asked quietly, "Did you go back to High Place, Adam?"

"Briefly," he replied. "It was a moldering shell."

"Was—nobody saved?"

"Some. Those who were downstairs. Those who were upstairs—my mother, Philip, Bella, had no chance. The fire had been started in many places at once . . . and with so much wood . . ."

We were all silent for a few moments contemplating

what it must have been like, then Adam went on, "Meta escaped."

"Oh, I'm so glad." Meta's round face, cheerful, always smiling, rose up before my eyes. "Did you manage to see her before you left Almada?"

"Yes. It was she who filled me in with all the details. She's engaged now at the Governor's Mansion as a maid-servant."

"Is she happy there?"

"She seemed so."

And so ends the story of my life up to the present time. A new chapter is beginning, one which I shall not need to write down in order to exorcise it from my mind, for I shall be too busy living it. My life stretches before me full of promise and deep contentment. I have the man I love, the child I love, the house I love. Perhaps Aunt Martha knew what she was doing, after all, when she made her extraordinary will.